FACETS

"You a cop, buck?"

Here the new style was something called Urban Surgery. The girl bore the first example Ric had ever seen close up. The henna-red hair was in cornrows, braided with transparent plastic beads holding fast-mutating phosphorescent bacteria that constantly reformed themselves in glowing patterns.

The nose had been broadened and flattened to cover most of the cheeks. The teeth had been replaced by alloy transplants, sharp as razors. The eyebrows were gone altogether and beneath them were dark plastic implants that covered the eye sockets. Ric couldn't tell whether there were eyes in there anymore, or sophisticated scanners tagged to the optic nerve.

The effect was to flatten the face, turn it into a canvas for the tattoo artist who had covered every inch of exposed flesh. Below the black plastic eye implants were urban skyscapes, silhouettes of buildings providing a false horizon across the flattened nose. The chin appeared to be a circuit diagram.

Ric looked into the dark eye sockets and tried not to flinch. "No," he said. "I'm just passing through."

From "Video Star" — just one of the
remarkable visions you'll find in
Walter Jon Williams's FACETS

Tor books by Walter Jon Williams

WALTER JON WILLIAMS

FACETS

A TOM DOHERTY ASSOCIATES BOOK
NEW YORK

FACETS

Copyright © 1990 by Walter Jon Williams

A Tor Book
Published by Tom Doherty Associates, Inc.
49 West 24th Street
New York, N.Y. 10010

Cover art by Rodney Matthews

ISBN: 0-812-50181-0

Library of Congress Catalog Card Number: 89-25714

Printed in the United States of America

First edition: January 1990
First mass market printing: April 1991

0 9 8 7 6 5 4 3 2 1

ACKNOWLEDGMENTS

CONTENTS

INTRODUCTION

BY ROGER ZELAZNY

Walter Jon Williams is one of the brighter things to happen to science fiction in a season of brightness.

I began writing in the 1960s, when the era of 3-D stories and 2-D characters had already passed; when it had long been realized that anything was fair game for speculation; and when the last of the space opera heroes had already blasted off into the nova-set. Well . . . The periods in which such writings were prominent had gone by. I don't believe that a subgenre is ever entirely lost. But looking back to the time when I began writing, I feel that it might have been easier breaking in then than it is now. It was certainly easier to know pretty much everything that had gone before, to keep up with everything new and to see what needed doing next.

Today no one—not even a professional reviewer—can read every science fiction book that comes out. The genre has digested an additional couple-of-decades' worth of ideas, experiments, syntheses. The standards are higher. Ask any editor who remembers the slush piles of the sixties to compare them with those of the present day. They're bigger now, as there are a lot more people trying to write the stuff; and there are a lot more good things coming out of them than ever before. Even allowing for the operation of Sturgeon's Law, the Good Ten Percent is almost too much to keep up with if you want to do anything else at all.

Still, certain stories and their authors do stand out, claiming respect as well as attention. Take, for example, Walter Jon Williams. His stories strike me as uncommonly well fashioned. I do not say this simply because we are acquainted, as are some of our characters who once engaged in a knock-down-fly-away-with fight in a Wild Cards epic, nor even because we are, by New Mexico standards, almost next-door neighbors. No. Not even because he wrote a classy sequel to my tale *The Graveyard Heart*. It is his versatility which first attracted my attention and which continues to hold it.

The first story in this collection, "Surfacing," is marked in my memory because it juggles not just a couple but a variety of ideas I have never seen juxtaposed in quite this fashion. Its world is interesting, its characters engaging, its situations touched with mysteries, dilemmas. While it stands by itself, I would be one of the first to buy a copy of the novel, should Walt decide to expand it and tell the whole story.

"Side Effects" is one of that species of brief, mordant social commentary tales which makes its point and stops, appropriately.

"Witness" is a tale of a hero fit for epics, and the reason he is not remembered as such.

"Wolf Time"—one of my favorites here—is a fast-paced, high-tech adventure that goes off like a string of firecrackers, leaving the head ringing afterward.

"Flatline" is amusing both in spite of and because of its predictability; "Video Star" extremely clever, for the detailed social background as well as the story line itself. "The Bob Dylan Solution" lies somewhere in between, reminding me again how essential a sense of humor is to mental well-being.

"Dinosaurs" is a Big Canvas story set in the distant future against an immense interstellar backdrop. And "No Spot of Ground" occupies a nineteenth-century parallel worlds position with elegance and clever speculation.

A book such as this exhibits the variety and versatility of which Walter is capable, and it comes at a good time, I feel, as his career is beginning to gather momentum, to show the readers and remind the editors of the range of his abilities.

Back in 1960, in his book *New Maps of Hell*, Kingsley Amis compared science fiction to jazz, saying in effect that science fiction stood to modern literature as jazz did to other contemporary music. A generation has since passed. Jazz as well as science fiction has continued to evolve. With its twenties classicism, thirties swing, forties bop, fifties soul, and sixties expressionist periods jazz did seem to pace or be paced by the scientific romances of the twenties, the space operas of the thirties, the Campbellian hard science stories of the forties, the beginnings of social consciousness in the fifties, and the expressionism of the sixties. And in both areas the seventies seemed a period of synthesis. Now, in the eighties, looking back, I realize that what I said earlier still holds. All of the periods have their proponents; all are still with us, in both jazz and sf; and the hip modern practitioner of either may well be a kind of fusion artist. Walter is a versatile writer in a great period for versatility. The genre is still young but is possessed of sufficient traditions to present a greater range of stories than ever before. It is a bright time in which to be young and talented.

It is interesting to speculate, at this point in his career, as to just what sort of things Walter will be writing ten years from now. Interesting, but ultimately fruitless. To answer that properly one would have to have some sort of idea what sf as a whole will be like a decade down the line. While no one can say for certain what it will be, I do feel that Walt will be one of those who helps to make it that way.

SURFACING

There was an alien on the surface of the planet. A Kyklops had teleported into Overlook Station, and then flown down on the shuttle. Since, unlike humans, it could teleport without apparatus, presumably it took the shuttle just for the ride. The Kyklops wore a human body, controlled through an n-dimensional interface, and took its pleasures in the human fashion.

The Kyklops expressed an interest in Anthony's work, but Anthony avoided it: he stayed at sea and listened to aliens of another kind.

Anthony wasn't interested in meeting aliens who knew more than he did.

The boat drifted in a cold current and listened to the cries of the sea. A tall grey swell was rolling in from the southwest, crossing with a wind-driven easterly chop. The boat tossed, caught in the confusion of wave patterns.

It was a sloppy ocean, somehow unsatisfactory. Marking a sloppy day.

Anthony felt a thing twist in his mind. Something that, in its own time, would lead to anger.

The boat had been out here, both in the warm current and then in the cold, for three days. Each more unsatisfactory than the last.

The growing swell was being driven toward land by a storm that was breaking up fifty miles out to sea: the remnants of the storm itself would arrive by midnight and make things even more unpleasant. Spray feathered across the tops of the waves. The day was growing cold.

Spindrift pattered across Anthony's shoulders. He ignored it, concentrated instead on the long, grating harmonic moan picked up by the microphones his boat dangled into the chill current. The moan ended on a series of clicks and trailed off. Anthony tapped his computer deck. A resolution appeared on the screen. Anthony shaded his eyes from the pale sun and looked at it.

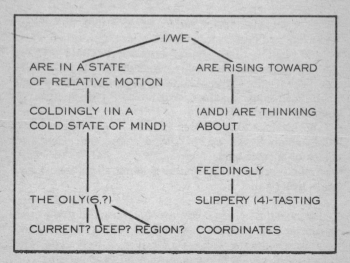

Anthony gazed stonily at the translation tree. "I am rising toward and thinking hungrily about the slippery-tasting coordinates" actually made the most objective sense, but the right-hand branch of the tree was the most literal and most of what Anthony suspected was context had been lost. "I and the oily current are in a state of motion toward one another" was perhaps more literal, but "We (the oily deep and I) are in a cold state of mind" was perhaps equally valid.

The boat gave a corkscrew lurch, dropped down the face of a swell, came to an abrupt halt at the end of its drogue. Water slapped against the stern. A mounting screw, come loose from a bracket on the bridge, fell and danced brightly across the deck.

The screw and the deck are in a state of relative motion, Anthony thought. The screw and the deck are in a motion state of mind.

Wrong, he thought, there is no Other in the Dwellers' speech.

We, I and the screw and the deck, are feeling cold.

We, I and the Dweller below, are in a state of mutual incomprehension.

A bad day, Anthony thought.

Inchoate anger burned deep inside him.

Anthony saved the translation and got up from his seat. He went to the bridge and told the boat to retrieve the drogue and head for Cabo Santa Pola at flank speed. He then went below and found a bottle of bourbon that had three good swallows left.

The trailing microphones continued to record the sonorous moans from below, the sound now mingled with the thrash of the boat's propellers.

The screw danced on the deck as the engines built up speed.

Its state of mind was not recorded.

The video news, displayed above the bar, showed the Kyklops making his tour of the planet. The Kyklops' human body, male, was tall and blue-eyed and elegant. He made witty conversation and showed off his naked chest as if he were proud of it. His name was Telamon.

His real body, Anthony knew, was a tenuous uncorporeal mass somewhere in n-dimensional space. The human body had been grown for it to wear, to move like a puppet. The nth dimension was interesting only to a mathematician: its inhabitants preferred wearing flesh.

Anthony asked the bartender to turn off the vid.

The yacht club bar was called the Leviathan, and Anthony hated the name. His creatures were too important, too much themselves, to be awarded a name that stank of human myth, of human resonance that had nothing to do with the creatures themselves. Anthony never called them Leviathans himself. They were Deep Dwellers.

There was a picture of a presumed Leviathan above the bar. Sometimes bits of matter were washed up on shore, thin tenuous membranes, long tentacles, bits of phosphorescence, all encrusted with the local equivalent of barnacles and infested with parasites. It was assumed the stuff had broken loose from the larger Dweller, or were bits of one that had died. The artist had done his best and painted something that looked like a whale covered with tentacles and seaweed.

The place had fake-nautical decor, nets, harpoons, flashing rods, and knicknacks made from driftwood, and the bar was regularly infected by tourists: that made it even worse. But the regular bartender and the divemaster and the steward were real sailors, and that made the yacht club bearable, gave him some company. His mail was delivered here as well.

Tonight the bartender was a substitute named Christopher: he was married to the owner's daughter and got his job that way. He was a fleshy, sullen man and no company.

We, thought Anthony, the world and I, are drinking alone. Anger burned in him, anger at the quality of the day and the opacity of the Dwellers and the storm that beat brainlessly at the windows.

"*Got* the bastard!" A man was pounding the bar. "Drinks

on me." He was talking loudly, and he wore gold rings on his fingers. Raindrops sparkled in his hair. He wore a flashing harness, just in case anyone missed why he was here. Hatred settled in Anthony like poison in his belly.

"Got a thirty-foot flasher," the man said. He pounded the bar again. "Me and Nick got it hung up outside. Four hours. A four-hour fight!"

"Why have a fight with something you can't eat?" Anthony said.

The man looked at him. He looked maybe twenty, but Anthony could tell he was old, centuries old maybe. Old and vain and stupid, stupid as a boy. "It's a game fish," the man said.

Anthony looked into the fisherman's eyes and saw a reflection of his own contempt. "You wanna fight," he said, "you wanna have a game, fight something *smart*. Not a dumb animal that you can outsmart, that once you catch it will only rot and stink."

That was the start.

Once it began, it didn't take long. The man's rings cut Anthony's face, and Anthony was smaller and lighter, but the man telegraphed every move and kept leading with his right. When it was over, Anthony left him on the floor and stepped out into the downpour, stood alone in the hammering rain and let the water wash the blood from his face. The whiskey and the rage were a flame that licked his nerves and made them sing.

He began walking down the street. Heading for another bar.

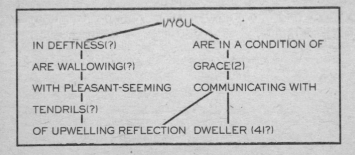

GRACE(2) meant grace in the sense of physical grace, dexterity, harmony of motion, as opposed to spiritual grace, which was GRACE(1). The Dweller that Anthony was listening to was engaged in a dialogue with another, possibly the same known to the computer as 41, who might be named "Upwelling Reflection," but Deep Dweller naming systems seemed inconsistent, depending largely on a context that was as yet opaque, and "upwelling reflection" might have to do with something else entirely.

Anthony suspected the Dweller had just said hello.

Salt water smarted on the cuts on Anthony's face. His swollen knuckles pained him as he tapped the keys of his computer deck. He never suffered from hangover, and his mind seemed filled with an exemplary clarity; he worked rapidly, with burning efficiency. His body felt energized.

He was out of the cold Kirst Current today, in a warm, calm subtropical sea on the other side of the Las Madres archipelago. The difference of forty nautical miles was astonishing.

The sun warmed his back. Sweat prickled on his scalp. The sea sparkled under a violet sky.

The other Dweller answered.

Through his bare feet, Anthony could feel the subsonic overtones vibrating through the boat. Something in the

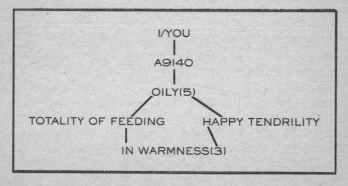

cabin rattled. The microphones recorded the sounds, raised the subsonics to an audible level, played it back. The computer made its attempt.

A9140 was a phrase that, as yet, had no translation.

The Dweller language, Anthony had discovered, had no separation of subject and object; it was a trait in common with the Earth cetaceans whose languages Anthony had first learned. "I swim toward the island" was not a grammatical possibility: "I and the island are in a condition of swimming toward one another" was the nearest possible approximation.

The Dwellers lived in darkness, and, like Earth's cetaceans, in a liquid medium. Perhaps they were psychologically unable to separate themselves from their environment, from their fluid surroundings. Never approaching the surface—it was presumed they could not survive in a nonpressurized environment—they had no idea of the upper limit of their world.

They were surrounded by a liquid three-dimensional wholeness, not an air-earth-sky environment from which they could consider themselves separate.

A high-pitched whooping came over the speakers, and Anthony smiled as he listened. The singer was one of the humpbacks that he had imported to this planet, a male called The One with Two Notches on His Starboard Fluke.

Two Notches was one of the brighter whales, and also the most playful. Anthony ordered his computer to translate the humpback speech.

Anthony, I and a place of bad smells have found one another, but this has not deterred our hunger.

The computer played back the message as it displayed the translation, and Anthony could understand more context from the sound of the original speech: that Two Notches was floating in a cold layer beneath the bad smell, and that the bad smell was methane or something like it—humans couldn't smell methane, but whales could. The overliteral

translation was an aid only, to remind Anthony of idioms he
might have forgotten.

Anthony's name in humpback was actually He Who Has
Brought Us to the Sea of Rich Strangeness, but the
computer translated it simply. Anthony tapped his reply.

What is it that stinks, Two Notches?

**Some kind of horrid jellyfish. Were they-and-I feed-
ing, they-and-I would spit one another out. I/They will
give them/me a name: they/me are the jellyfish that
smell like indigestion.**

That is a good name, Two Notches.

**I and a small boat discovered each other earlier
today. We itched, so we scratched our back on the
boat. The humans and I were startled. We had a good
laugh together in spite of our hunger.**

Meaning that Two Notches had risen under the boat,
scratched his back on it, and terrified the passengers
witless. Anthony remembered the first time this had
happened to him back on Earth, a vast female humpback
rising up without warning, one long scalloped fin breaking
the water to port, the rest of the whale to starboard,
thrashing in cetacean delight as it rubbed itself against a
boat half its length. Anthony had clung to the gunwale,
horrified by what the whale could do to his boat, but still
exhilarated, delighted at the sight of the creature and its
glorious joy.

Still, Two Notches ought not to play too many pranks on
the tourists.

*We should be careful, Two Notches. Not all humans
possess our sense of humor, especially if they are hungry.*

**We were bored, Anthony. Mating is over, feeding has
not begun. Also, it was Nick's boat that got scratched.
In our opinion Nick and I enjoyed ourselves, even
though we were hungry.**

Hunger and food seemed to be the humpback subtheme
of the day. Humpback songs, like the human, were made up
of text and chorus, the chorus repeating itself, with varia-
tions, through the message.

I and Nick will ask each other and find out, as we feed.

Anthony tried to participate in the chorus/response about food, but he found himself continually frustrated at his clumsy phrasing. Fortunately the whales were tolerant of his efforts.

Have we learned anything about the ones that swim deep and do not breathe and feed on obscure things?

Not yet, Two Notches. Something has interrupted us in our hungry quest.

A condition of misfortune exists, like unto hunger. We must learn to be quicker.

We will try, Two Notches. After we eat.

We would like to speak to the Deep Dwellers now, and feed with them, but we must breathe.

We will speak to ourselves another time, after feeding.

We are in a condition of hunger, Anthony. We must eat soon.

We will remember our hunger and make plans.

The mating and calving season for the humpbacks was over. Most of the whales were already heading north to their summer feeding grounds, where they would do little but eat for six months. Two Notches and one of the other males had remained in the vicinity of Las Madres as a favor to Anthony, who used them to assist in locating the Deep Dwellers, but soon—in a matter of days—the pair would have to head north. They hadn't eaten anything for nearly half a year; Anthony didn't want to starve them.

But when the whales left, Anthony would be alone—again—with the Deep Dwellers. He didn't want to think about that.

The system's second sun winked across the waves, rising now. It was a white dwarf and emitted dangerous amounts of X-rays. The boat's falkner generator, triggered by the computer, snapped on a field that surrounded the boat and guarded it from energetic radiation. Anthony felt the warmth on his shoulders decrease. He turned his attention back to the Deep Dwellers.

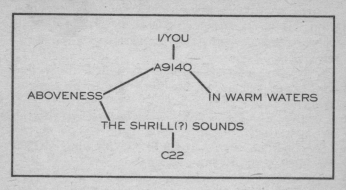

A blaze of delight rose in Anthony. The Dwellers, he realized, had overheard his conversation with Two Notches, and were commenting on it. Furthermore, he knew, A9140 probably was a verb form having to do with hearing—the Dwellers had a lot of them. "I/You hear the shrill sounds from above" might do as a working translation, and although he had no idea how to translate C22, he suspected it was a comment on the sounds. In a fever, Anthony began to work. As he bent over his keys he heard, through water and bone, the sound of Two Notches singing.

The Milky Way was a dim watercolor wash overhead. An odd twilight hung over Las Madres, a near-darkness that marked the hours when only the dwarf star was in the sky, providing little visible light but still pouring out X-rays. Cabo Santa Pola lay in a bright glowing crescent across the boat's path. Music drifted from a waterfront tavern, providing a counterpoint to the Deep Dweller speech that still rang in Anthony's head. A familiar figure waited on the dock, standing beneath the yellow lamp that marked Anthony's slip. Anthony waved and throttled the boat back.

A good day. Even after the yellow sun had set, Anthony

still felt in a sunny mood. A9140 had been codified as "listen(14)," meaning listen solely in the sense of listening to a sound that originated from far outside the Dwellers' normal sphere—from outside their entire universe, in fact, which spoke volumes for the way the Dwellers saw themselves in relation to their world. They knew something else was up there, and their speech could make careful distinction between the world they knew and could perceive directly and the one they didn't. C22 was a descriptive term involving patterning: the Dwellers realized that the cetacean speech they'd been hearing wasn't simply random. Which spoke rather well for their cognition.

Anthony turned the boat and backed into the slip. Nick Kanellopoulos, whom the humpbacks called The One Who Chases Bad-Tasting Fish, took the sternline that Anthony threw him and tied it expertly to a cleat. Anthony shut off the engines, took a bowline, and hopped to the dock. He bent over the cleat and made his knot.

"You've gotta stop beating up my customers, Anthony," Nick said.

Anthony said nothing.

"You even send your damn whales to harass me."

Anthony jumped back into the boat and stepped into the cabin for a small canvas bag that held his gear and the data cubes containing the Dwellers' conversation. When he stepped back out of the cabin, he saw Nick standing on one foot, the other poised to step into the boat. Anthony gave Nick a look and Nick pulled his foot back. Anthony smiled. He didn't like people on his boat.

"Dinner?" he asked.

Nick gazed at him. A muscle moved in the man's cheek. He was dapper, olive-skinned, about a century old, the second-youngest human on the planet. He looked in his late teens. He wore a personal falkner generator on his belt that protected him from the dwarf's X-rays.

"Dinner. Fine." His brown eyes were concerned. "You look like hell, Anthony."

Anthony rubbed the stubble on his cheeks. "I feel on top of the world," he said.

"Half the time you don't even talk to me. I don't know why I'm eating supper with you."

"Let me clean up. Then we can go to the Villa Mary."

Nick shook his head. "Okay," he said. "But you're buying. You cost me a customer last night."

Anthony slapped him on the shoulder. "Least I can do, I guess."

A good day.

Near midnight. Winds beat at the island's old volcanic cone, pushed down the crowns of trees. A shuttle, black against the darkness of the sky, rose in absolute silence from the port on the other side of the island, heading toward the bright fixed star that was Overlook Station. The alien, Telamon, was aboard, or so the newscasts reported.

Deep Dwellers still sang in Anthony's head. Mail in hand, he let himself in through the marina gate and walked toward his slip. The smell of the sea rose around him. He stretched, yawned. Belched up a bit of the tequila he'd been drinking with Nick. He intended to get an early start and head back to sea before dawn.

Anthony paused beneath a light and opened the large envelope, pulled out page proofs that had been mailed, at a high cost, from the offices of the *Xenobiology Review* on Kemps. Discontent scratched at his nerves. He frowned as he glanced through the pages. He'd written the article over a year before, at the end of the first spring he'd spent here, and just glancing through it he now found the article overtentative, overformal, and, worse, almost pleading in its attempt to justify his decision to move himself and the whales here. The palpable defensiveness made him want to squirm.

Disgust filled him. His fingers clutched at the pages, then tore the proofs across. His body spun full circle as he scaled the proofs out to the sea. The wind scattered thick chunks of paper across the dark waters of the marina.

He stalked toward his boat. Bile rose in his throat. He wished he had a bottle of tequila with him. He almost went back for one before he realized the liquor stores were closed.

"Anthony Maldalena?"

She was a little gawky, and her skin was pale. Dark hair in a single long braid, deep eyes, a bit of an overbite. She was waiting for him at the end of his slip, under the light. She had a bag over one shoulder.

Anthony stopped. Dull anger flickered in his belly. He didn't want anyone taking notice of the bruises and cuts on his face. He turned his head away as he stepped into his boat, dropped his bag on a seat.

"Mr. Maldalena. My name is Philana Telander. I came here to see you."

"How'd you get in?"

She gestured to the boat two slips down, a tall FPS-powered yacht shaped like a flat oval with a tall flybridge jutting from its center so that the pilot could see over wavetops. It would fly from place to place, but she could put it down in the water if she wanted. No doubt she'd bought a temporary membership at the yacht club.

"Nice boat," said Anthony. It would have cost her a fair bit to have it gated here. He opened the hatch to his forward cabin, tossed his bag onto the long couch inside.

"I meant," she said, "I came to this *planet* to see you."

Anthony didn't say anything, just straightened from his stoop by the hatch and looked at her. She shifted from one foot to another. Her skin was yellow in the light of the lamp. She reached into her bag and fumbled with something.

Anthony waited.

The clicks and sobs of whales sounded from the recorder in her hand.

"I wanted to show you what I've been able to do with your work. I have some articles coming up in *Cetology Journal* but they won't be out for a while."

"You've done very well," said Anthony. Tequila swirled

in his head. He was having a hard time concentrating on a subject as difficult as whale speech.

Philana had specialized in communication with female humpbacks. It was harder to talk with the females: although they were curious and playful, they weren't vocal like the bulls; their language was deeper, briefer, more personal. They made no songs. It was almost as if, solely in the realm of speech, the cows were autistic. Their psychology was different and complicated, and Anthony had had little success in establishing any lasting communication. The cows, he had realized, were speaking a second tongue: the humpbacks were essentially bilingual, and Anthony had only learned one of their languages.

Philana had succeeded where Anthony had found only frustration. She had built from his work, established a structure and basis for communication. She still wasn't as easy in her speech with the cows as Anthony was with a bull like Two Notches, but she was far closer than Anthony had ever been.

Steam rose from the coffee cup in Philana's hand as she poured from Anthony's vacuum flask. She and Anthony sat on the cushioned benches in the stern of Anthony's boat. Tequila still buzzed in Anthony's head. Conflicting urges warred in him. He didn't want anyone else here, on his boat, this close to his work; but Philana's discoveries were too interesting to shut her out entirely. He swallowed more coffee.

"Listen to this," Philana said. "It's fascinating. A cow teaching her calf about life." She touched the recorder, and muttering filled the air. Anthony had difficulty understanding: the cow's idiom was complex, and bore none of the poetic repetition that made the males' language easier to follow. Finally he shook his head.

"Go ahead and turn it off," he said. "I'm picking up only one phrase in five. I can't follow it."

Philana seemed startled. "Oh. I'm sorry. I thought—"

Anthony twisted uncomfortably in his seat. "I don't know every goddamn thing about whales," he said.

The recorder fell silent. Wind rattled the canvas awning over the flybridge. Savage discontent settled into Anthony's mind. Suddenly he needed to get rid of this woman, get her off his boat and head to sea right now, away from all the things on land that could trip him up.

He thought of his father upside down in the smokehouse. Not moving, arms dangling.

He should apologize, he realized. We are, he thought, in a condition of permanent apology.

"I'm sorry," he said. "I'm just . . . not used to dealing with people."

"Sometimes I wonder," she said. "I'm only twenty-one, and . . ."

"Yes?" Blurted suddenly, the tequila talking. Anthony felt disgust at his own awkwardness.

Philana looked at the planks. "Yes. Truly. I'm twenty-one, and sometimes people get impatient with me for reasons I don't understand."

Anthony's voice was quiet. "I'm twenty-six."

Philana was surprised. "But. I thought." She thought for a long moment. "It seems I've been reading your papers for . . ."

"I was first published at twenty," he said. "The finback article."

Philana shook her head. "I'd never have guessed. Particularly after what I saw in your new *XR* paper."

Anthony's reaction was instant. "You saw that?" Another spasm of disgust touched him. Tequila burned in his veins. His stomach turned over. For some reason his arms were trembling.

"A friend on Kemps sent me an advance copy. I thought it was brilliant. The way you were able to codify your conceptions about a race of which you could really know nothing, and have it all pan out when you began to understand them. That's an incredible achievement."

"It's a piece of crap." Anthony wanted more tequila badly. His body was shaking. He tossed the remains of his coffee over his shoulder into the sea. "I've learned so much since. I've given up even trying to publish it. The delays are too long. Even if I put it on the nets, I'd still have to take the time to write it, and I'd rather spend my time working."

"I'd like to see it."

He turned away from her. "I don't show my work till it's finished."

"I . . . didn't mean to intrude."

Apology. He could feel a knife twisting in his belly. He spoke quickly. "I'm sorry, Miss Telander. It's late, and I'm not used to company. I'm not entirely well." He stood, took her arm. Ignoring her surprise, he almost pulled her to her feet. "Maybe tomorrow. We'll talk again."

She blinked up at him. "Yes. I'd like that."

"Good night." He rushed her off the boat and stepped below to the head. He didn't want her to hear what was going to happen next. Acid rose in his throat. He clutched his middle and bent over the small toilet and let the spasms take him. The convulsions wracked him long after he was dry. After it was over he stood shakily, staggered to the sink, washed his face. His sinuses burned and brought tears to his eyes. He threw himself on the couch.

In the morning, before dawn, he cast off and motored out into the quiet sea.

The other male, The One Who Sings of Others, found a pair of Dwellers engaged in a long conversation and hovered above them. His transponder led Anthony to the place, fifty miles south into the bottomless tropical ocean. The Dwellers' conversation was dense. Anthony understood perhaps one word-phrase in ten. Sings of Others interrupted from time to time to tell Anthony how hungry he was.

The recordings would require days of work before Anthony could even begin to make sense of them. He wanted to stay on the site, but the Dwellers fell silent, neither Anthony nor Sings of Others could find another conversation, and Anthony was near out of supplies. He'd been working so intently he'd never got around to buying food.

The white dwarf had set by the time Anthony motored into harbor. Dweller mutterings did a chaotic dance in his mind. He felt a twist of annoyance at the sight of Philana Telander jumping from her big air yacht to the pier. She had obviously been waiting for him.

He threw her the bowline and she made fast. As he stepped onto the dock and fastened the sternline, he noticed sunburn reddening her cheeks. She'd spent the day on the ocean.

"Sorry I left so early," he said. "One of the humpbacks found some Dwellers, and their conversation sounded interesting."

She looked from Anthony to his boat and back. "That's all right," she said. "I shouldn't have talked to you last night. Not when you were ill."

Anger flickered in his mind. She'd heard him being sick, then.

"Too much to drink," he said. He jumped back into the boat and got his gear.

"Have you eaten?" she asked. "Somebody told me about a place called the Villa Mary."

He threw his bag over one shoulder. Dinner would be his penance. "I'll show you," he said.

"Mary was a woman who died," Anthony said. "One of the original Knight's Move people. She chose to die, refused the treatments. She didn't believe in living forever." He looked up at the arched ceiling, the moldings on walls and ceiling, the initials ML worked into the decoration. "Brian McGivern built this place in her memory," Anthony said. "He's built a lot of places like this, on different worlds."

Philana was looking at her plate. She nudged an ichthyoid exomembrane with her fork. "I know," she said. "I've been in a few of them."

Anthony reached for his glass, took a drink, then stopped

himself from taking a second swallow. He realized that he'd drunk most of a bottle of wine. He didn't want a repetition of last night.

With an effort he put the glass down.

"She's someone I think about, sometimes," Philana said. "About the choice she made."

"Yes?" Anthony shook his head. "Not me. I don't want to spend a hundred years dying. If I ever decide to die, I'll do it quick."

"That's what people say. But they never do it. They just get older and older. Stranger and stranger." She raised her hands, made a gesture that took in the room, the decorations, the entire white building on its cliff overlooking the sea. "Get old enough, you start doing things like building Villa Marys all over the galaxy. McGivern's an oldest-generation immortal, you know. Maybe the wealthiest human anywhere, and he spends his time immortalizing someone who didn't want immortality of any kind."

Anthony laughed. "Sounds like you're thinking of becoming a Diehard."

She looked at him steadily. "Yes."

Anthony's laughter froze abruptly. A cool shock passed through him. He had never spoken to a Diehard before: the only ones he'd met were people who mumbled at him on street corners and passed out incoherent religious tracts.

Philana looked at her plate. "I'm sorry," she said.

"Why sorry?"

"I shouldn't have brought it up."

Anthony reached for his wine glass, stopped himself, put his hand down. "I'm curious."

She gave a little, apologetic laugh. "I may not go through with it."

"Why even think about it?"

Philana thought a long time before answering. "I've seen how the whales accept death. So graceful about it, so matter-of-fact—and they don't even have the myth of an afterlife to comfort them. If they get sick, they just beach themselves; and their friends try to keep them company.

And when I try to give myself a reason for living beyond my natural span, I can't think of any. All I can think of is the whales."

Anthony saw the smokehouse in his mind, his father with his arms hanging, the fingers touching the dusty floor. "Death isn't nice."

Philana gave him a skeletal grin and took a quick drink of wine. "With any luck," she said, "death isn't anything at all."

Wind chilled the night, pouring upon the town through a slot in the island's volcanic cone. Anthony watched a streamlined head as it moved in the dark wind-washed water of the marina. The head belonged to a cold-blooded amphibian that lived in the warm surf of the Las Madres; the creature was known misleadingly as a Las Madres seal. They had little fear of humanity and were curious about the new arrivals. Anthony stamped a foot on the slip. Planks boomed. The seal's head disappeared with a soft splash. Ripples spread in starlight, and Anthony smiled.

Philana had stepped into her yacht for a sweater. She returned, cast a glance at the water, saw nothing.

"Can I listen to the Dwellers?" she asked. "I'd like to hear them."

Despite his resentment at her imposition, Anthony appreciated her being careful with the term: she hadn't called them Leviathans once. He thought about her request, could think of no reason to refuse save his own stubborn reluctance. The Dweller sounds were just background noise, meaningless to her. He stepped onto his boat, took a cube from his pocket, put it in the trapdoor, pressed the PLAY button. Dweller murmurings filled the cockpit. Philana stepped from the dock to the boat. She shivered in the wind. Her eyes were pools of dark wonder.

"So different."

"Are you surprised?"

"I suppose not."

"This isn't really what they sound like. What you're

hearing is a computer-generated metaphor for the real thing. Much of their communication is subsonic, and the computer raises the sound to levels we can hear, and also speeds it up. Sometimes the Dwellers take three or four minutes to speak what seems to be a simple sentence."

"We would never have noticed them except for an accident," Philana said. "That's how alien they are."

"Yes."

Humanity wouldn't know of the Dwellers' existence at all if it weren't for the subsonics confusing some automated sonar buoys, followed by an idiot computer assuming the sounds were deliberate interference and initiating an ET scan. Any human would have looked at the data, concluded it was some kind of seismic interference, and programmed the buoys to ignore it.

"They've noticed *us*," Anthony said. "The other day I heard them discussing a conversation I had with one of the humpbacks."

Philana straightened. Excitement was plain in her voice. "They can conceptualize something alien to them."

"Yes."

Her response was instant, stepping on the last sibilant of his answer. "And theorize about our existence."

Anthony smiled at her eagerness. "I . . . don't think they've got around to that yet."

"But they are intelligent."

"Yes."

"Maybe more intelligent than the whales. From what you say, they seem quicker to conceptualize."

"Intelligent in certain ways, perhaps. There's still very little I understand about them."

"Can you teach me to talk to them?"

The wind blew chill between them. "I don't," he said, "talk to them."

She seemed not to notice his change of mood, stepped closer. "You haven't tried that yet? That would seem to be reasonable, considering they've already noticed us."

He could feel his hackles rising, mental defenses sliding into place. "I'm not proficient enough," he said.

"If you could attract their attention, they could teach you." Reasonably.

"No. Not yet." Rage exploded in Anthony's mind. He wanted her off his boat, away from his work, his existence. He wanted to be alone again with his creatures, solitary witness to the lonely and wonderful interplay of alien minds.

"I never told you," Philana said, "why I'm here."

"No. You didn't."

"I want to do some work with the humpback cows."

"Why?"

Her eyes widened slightly. She had detected the hostility in his tone. "I want to chart any linguistic changes that may occur as a result of their move to another environment."

Through clouds of blinding resentment Anthony considered her plan. He couldn't stop her, he knew: anyone could talk to the whales if they knew how to do it. It might keep her away from the Dwellers. "Fine," he said. "Do it."

Her look was challenging. "I don't need your permission."

"I know that."

"You don't own them."

"I know that, too."

There was a splash far out in the marina. The Las Madres seal chasing a fish. Philana was still staring at him. He looked back.

"Why are you afraid of my getting close to the Dwellers?" she asked.

"You've been here two days. You don't know them. You're making all manner of assumptions about what they're like, and all you've read is one obsolete article."

"You're the expert. If my assumptions are wrong, you're free to tell me."

"Humans interacted with whales for centuries before they learned to speak with them, and even now the speech is limited and often confused. I've only been here two and a half years."

"Perhaps," she said, "you could use some help. Write those papers of yours. Publish the data."

He turned away. "I'm doing fine," he said.

"Glad to hear it." She took a long breath. "What did I *do*, Anthony? Tell me."

"Nothing," he said. Anthony watched the marina waters, saw the amphibian surface, its head pulled back to help slide a fish down its gullet. Philana was just standing there. We, thought Anthony, are in a condition of nonresolution.

"I work alone," he said. "I immerse myself in their speech, in their environment, for months at a time. Talking to a human breaks my concentration. I don't know *how* to talk to a person right now. After the Dwellers, you seem perfectly . . ."

"Alien?" she said. Anthony didn't answer. The amphibian slid through the water, its head leaving a short, silver wake.

The boat rocked as Philana stepped from it to the dock. "Maybe we can talk later," she said. "Exchange data or something."

"Yes," Anthony said. "We'll do that." His eyes were still on the seal.

Later, before he went to bed, he told the computer to play Dweller speech all night long.

Lying in his bunk the next morning, Anthony heard Philana cast off her yacht. He felt a compulsion to talk to her, apologize again, but in the end he stayed in his rack, tried to concentrate on Dweller sounds. I/We remain in a condition of solitude, he thought, the Dweller phrases coming easily to his mind. There was a brief shadow cast on the port beside him as the big flying boat rose into the sky, then nothing but sunlight and the slap of water on the pier supports. Anthony climbed out of his sleeping bag and went into town, provisioned the boat for a week. He had been too close to land for too long: a trip into the sea, surrounded by

nothing but whales and Dweller speech, should cure him of
his unease.

Two Notches had switched on his transponder: Anthony
followed the beacon north, the boat rising easily over deep
blue rollers. Desiring sun, Anthony climbed to the flybridge
and lowered the canvas cover. Fifty miles north of Cabo
Santa Pola there was a clear dividing line in the water, a line
as clear as a meridian on a chart, beyond which the sea was
a deeper, purer blue. The line marked the boundary of the
cold Kirst current that had journeyed, wreathed in mist from
contact with the warmer air, a full three thousand nautical
miles from the region of the South Pole. Anthony crossed
the line and rolled down his sleeves as the temperature of
the air fell.

He heard the first whale speech through his microphones
as he entered the cold current: the sound hadn't carried
across the turbulent frontier of warm water and cold. The
whales were unclear, distant and mixed with the sound of
the screws, but he could tell from the rhythm that he was
overhearing a dialogue. Apparently Sings of Others had
joined Two Notches north of Las Madres. It was a long
journey to make overnight, but not impossible.

The cooler air was invigorating. The boat plowed a
straight, efficient wake through the deep blue sea. Anthony's spirits rose. This was where he belonged, away from
the clutter and complication of humanity. Doing what he did
best.

He heard something odd in the rhythm of the whalespeech; he frowned and listened more closely. One of the
whales was Two Notches; Anthony recognized his speech
patterns easily after all this time; but the other wasn't Sings
of Others. There was a clumsiness in its pattern of chorus
and response.

The other was a human. Annoyance hummed in Anthony's nerves. Back on Earth, tourists or eager amateur
explorers sometimes bought cheap translation programs and
tried to talk to the whales, but this was no tourist program:
it was too eloquent, too knowing. Philana, of course. She'd

followed the transponder signal and was busy gathering data about the humpback females. Anthony cut his engines and let the boat drift slowly to put its bow into the wind; he deployed the microphones from their wells in the hull and listened. The song was bouncing off a colder layer below, and it echoed confusingly.

Deep Swimmer and her calf, called The One That Nudges, are possessed of one another. I and that one am the father. We hunger for one another's presence.

Apparently hunger was once again the subtheme of the day. The context told Anthony that Two Notches was swimming in cool water beneath a boat. Anthony turned the volume up:

We hunger to hear of Deep Swimmer and our calf.

That was the human response: limited in its phrasing and context, direct and to the point.

I and Deep Swimmer are shy. We will not play with humans. Instead we will pretend we are hungry and vanish into deep waters.

The boat lurched as a swell caught it at an awkward angle. Water splashed over the bow. Anthony deployed the drogue and dropped from the flybridge to the cockpit. He tapped a message into the computer and relayed it.

I and Two Notches are pleased to greet ourselves. I and Two Notches hope we are not too hungry.

The whale's reply was shaded with delight. **Hungrily I and Anthony greet ourselves. We and Anthony's friend, Air Human, have been in a condition of conversation.**

Air Human, from the flying yacht. Two Notches went on.

We had found ourselves some Deep Dwellers, but some moments ago we and they moved beneath a cold layer and our conversation is lost. I starve for its return.

The words echoed off the cold layer that stood like a wall between Anthony and the Dwellers. The humpback inflections were steeped in annoyance.

Our hunger is unabated, Anthony typed. *But we will wait for the nonbreathers' return.*

We cannot wait long. Tonight we and the north must begin the journey to our feeding time.

The voice of Air Human rumbled through the water. It sounded like a distant, throbbing engine. *Our finest greetings, Anthony. I and Two Notches will travel north together. Then we and the others will feed.*

Annoyance slammed into Anthony. Philana had abducted his whale. Clenching his teeth, he typed a civil reply:

Please give our kindest greetings to our hungry brothers and sisters in the north.

By the time he transmitted his speech his anger had faded. Two Notches' departure was inevitable in the next few days, and he'd known that. Still, a residue of jealousy burned in him. Philana would have the whale's company on its journey north; he would be stuck here by Las Madres without the keen whale ears that helped him find the Dwellers.

Two Notches' reply came simultaneously with a programmed reply from Philana. Lyrics about greetings, hunger, feeding, calves, and joy whined through the water, bounced from the cold layer. Anthony looked at the hash his computer made of the translation and laughed. He decided he might as well enjoy Two Notches' company while it lasted.

That was a strange message to hear from our friend, Two Mouths, he typed. "Notch" and "mouth" were almost the same phrase: Anthony had just made a pun.

Whale amusement bubbled through the water. **Two Mouths and I belong to the most unusual family between surface and cold water. We-All and air breathe each other, but some of us have the bad fortune to live in it.**

The sun warmed Anthony's shoulders in spite of the cool air. He decided to leave off the pursuit of the Dwellers and spend the day with his humpback.

He kicked off his shoes, then stepped down to his cooler and made himself a sandwich.

* * *

The Dwellers never came out from beneath the cold layer. Anthony spent the afternoon listening to Two Notches tell stories about his family. Now that the issue of hunger was resolved by the whale's decision to migrate, the cold layer beneath them became the new topic of conversation, and Two Notches amused himself by harmonizing with his own echo. Sings of Others arrived in late afternoon and announced he had already begun his journey: he and Two Notches decided to travel in company.

Northward homing! Cold watering! Reunion joyous! The phrases dopplered closer to Anthony's boat, and then Two Notches broke the water thirty feet off the port beam, salt water pouring like Niagara from his black jaw, his scalloped fins spread like wings eager to take the air . . . Anthony's breath went out of him in surprise. He turned in his chair and leaned away from the sight, half in fear and half in awe . . . Even though he was used to the whales, the sight never failed to stun him, thrill him, freeze him in his tracks.

Two Notches toppled over backward, one clear brown eye fixed on Anthony. Anthony raised an arm and waved, and he thought he saw amusement in Two Notches' glance, perhaps the beginning of an answering wave in the gesture of a fin. A living creature the size of a bus, the whale struck the water not with a smack, but with a roar, a sustained outpour of thunder. Anthony braced himself for what was coming. Salt water flung itself over the gunwale, struck him like a blow. The cold was shocking: his heart lurched. The boat was flung high on the wave, dropped down its face with a jarring thud. Two Notches' flukes tossed high and Anthony could see the mottled pattern, grey and white, on the underside, distinctive as a fingerprint . . . and then the flukes were gone, leaving behind a rolling boat and a boiling sea.

Anthony wiped the ocean from his face, then from his computer. The boat's auto-bailing mechanism began to throb. Two Notches surfaced a hundred yards off, spouted a round cloud of steam, submerged again. The whale's amusement stung the water. Anthony's surprise turned to joy, and he echoed the sound of laughter.

I'm going to run my boat up your backside, Anthony promised; he splashed to the controls in his bare feet, withdrew the drogue and threw his engines into gear. Props thrashed the sea into foam. Anthony drew the microphones up into their wells, heard them thud along the hull as the boat gained way. Humpbacks usually took breath in a series of three: Anthony aimed ahead for Two Notches' second rising. Two Notches rose just ahead, spouted, and dove before Anthony could catch him. A cold wind cut through Anthony's wet shirt, raised bumps on his flesh. The boat increased speed, tossing its head on the face of a wave, and Anthony raced ahead, aiming for where Two Notches would rise for the third time.

The whale knew where the boat was and was able to avoid him easily; there was no danger in the game. Anthony won the race: Two Notches surfaced just aft of the boat, and Anthony grinned as he gunned his propellers and wrenched the rudder from side to side while the boat spewed foam into the whale's face. Two Notches gave a grunt of disappointment and sounded, tossing his flukes high. Unless he chose to rise early, Two Notches would be down for five minutes or more. Anthony raced the boat in circles, waiting. Two Notches' taunts rose in the cool water. The wind was cutting Anthony to the quick. He reached into the cabin for a sweater, pulled it on, ran up to the flybridge just in time to see Two Notches leap again half a mile away, the vast dark body silhouetted for a moment against the setting sun before it fell again into the welcoming sea.

Goodbye, goodbye. I and Anthony send fragrant farewells to one another.

White foam surrounded the slick, still place where Two Notches had fallen into the water. Suddenly the flybridge was very cold. Anthony's heart sank. He cut speed and put the wheel amidships. The boat slowed reluctantly, as if it, too, had been enjoying the game. Anthony dropped down the ladder to his computer.

Through the spattered windscreen, Anthony could see Two Notches leaping again, his long wings beating air, his silhouette refracted through seawater and rainbows. Anthony tried to share the whale's exuberance, his joy, but the thought of another long summer alone on his boat, beating his head against the enigma of the Dwellers, turned his mind to ice.

He ordered an infinite repeat of Two Notches' last phrase and stepped below to change into dry clothes. The cold layer echoed his farewells. He bent almost double and began pulling the sweater over his head.

Suddenly he straightened. An idea was chattering at him. He yanked the sweater back down over his trunk, rushed to his computer, tapped another message.

Our farewells need not be said just yet. You and I can follow one another for a few days before I must return. Perhaps you and the nonbreathers can find one another for conversation.

Anthony is in a condition of migration. Welcome, welcome. Two Notches' reply was jubilant.

For a few days, Anthony qualified. Before too long he would have to return to port for supplies. Annoyed at himself, he realized he could as easily have victualed for weeks.

Another voice called through the water, sounded faintly through the speakers. *Air Human and Anthony are in a state of tastiest welcome.*

In the middle of Anthony's reply, his fingers paused at the keys. Surprise rose quietly to the surface of his mind.

After the long day of talking in humpback speech, he had forgotten that Air Human was not a humpback. That she was, in fact, another human being sitting on a boat just over the horizon.

Anthony continued his message. His fingers were clumsy now, and he had to go back twice to correct mistakes. He wondered why it was harder to talk to Philana, now that he remembered she wasn't an alien.

He asked Two Notches to turn on his transponder, and, all through the deep shadow twilight when the white dwarf was in the sky, the boat followed the whale at a half-mile's distance. The current was cooperative, but in a few days a new set of northwest trade winds would push the current off on a curve toward the equator and the whales would lose its assistance.

Anthony didn't see Philana's boat that first day: just before dawn, Sings of Others heard a distant Dweller conversation to starboard. Anthony told his boat to strike off in that direction and spent most of the day listening. When the Dwellers fell silent, he headed for the whales' transponders again. There was a lively conversation in progress between Air Human and the whales, but Anthony's mind was still on Dwellers. He put on headphones and worked far into the night.

The next morning was filled with chill mist. Anthony awoke to the whooping cries of the humpbacks. He looked at his computer to see if it had recorded any announcement of Dwellers, and there was none. The whales' interrogation by Air Human continued. Anthony's toes curled on the cold, damp planks as he stepped on deck and saw Philana's yacht two hundred yards to port, floating three feet over the tallest swells. Cables trailed from the stern, pulling hydrophones and speakers on a subaquatic sled. Anthony grinned at the sight of the elaborate store-bought rig. He suspected that he got better acoustion with his homebuilt equipment, the translation softwear he'd programmed himself, and his hopelessly old-fashioned boat that couldn't even rise out of the water, but that he'd equipped with the latest-generation silent propellers.

He turned on his hydrophones. Sure enough, he got more audio interference from Philana's sled than he received from his entire boat.

While making coffee and an omelette of mossmoon eggs

Anthony listened to the whales gurgle about their grandparents. He put on a down jacket and stepped onto the boat's stern and ate breakfast, watching the humpbacks as they occasionally broke surface, puffed out clouds of spray, sounded again with a careless, vast toss of their flukes. Their bodies were smooth and black: the barnacles that pebbled their skin on Earth had been removed before they gated to their new home.

Their song could be heard clearly even without the amplifiers. That was one change the contact with humans had brought: the males were a lot more vocal than once they had been, as if they were responding to human encouragement—or perhaps they now had more worth talking about. Their speech was also more terse than before, less overtly poetic; the humans' directness and compactness of speech, caused mainly by their lack of fluency, had influenced the whales to a degree.

The whales were adapting to communication with humans more easily than the humans were adapting to them. It was important to chart that change, be able to say how the whales had evolved, accommodated. They were on an entire new planet now, explorers, and the change was going to come fast. The whales were good at remembering, but artificial intelligences were better. Anthony was suddenly glad that Philana was here, doing her work.

As if on cue she appeared on deck, one hand pressed to her head, holding an earphone: she was listening intently to whalesong. She was bundled up against the chill, and gave a brief wave as she noticed him. Anthony waved back. She paused, beating time with one hand to the rhythm of whalespeech, then waved again and stepped back to her work.

Anthony finished breakfast and cleaned the dishes. He decided to say good morning to the whales, then work on some of the Dweller speech he'd recorded the day before. He turned on his computer, sat down at the console, typed his greetings. He waited for a pause in the conversation, then transmitted. The answer came back sounding like a distant buzzsaw.

We and Anthony wish one another a passage filled with splendid odors. We and Air Human have been scenting one another's families this morning.

We wish each other the joy of converse, Anthony typed.

We have been wondering, Two Notches said, **if we can scent whether we and Anthony and Air Human are in a condition of rut.**

Anthony gave a laugh. Humpbacks enjoyed trying to figure out human relationships: they were promiscuous themselves, and intrigued by ways different from their own.

Anthony wondered, sitting in his cockpit, if Philana was looking at him.

Air Human and I smell of aloneness, unpairness, he typed, and he transmitted the message at the same time that Philana entered the even more direct, *We are not.*

The state is not rut, apartness is the smell, Two Notches agreed readily—it was all one to him—and the lyrics echoed each other for a long moment, *aloneness, not, unpairness, not. Not.* Anthony felt a chill.

I and the Dwellers' speech are going to try to scent one another's natures, he typed hastily, and turned off the speakers. He opened his case and took out one of the cubes he'd recorded the day before.

Work went slowly.

By noon the mist had burned off the water. His head buzzing with Dweller sounds, Anthony stepped below for a sandwich. The message light was blinking on his telephone. He turned to it, pressed the play button.

"May I speak with you briefly?" Philana's voice. "I'd like to get some data, at your convenience." Her tone shifted to one of amusement. "The condition," she added, "is not that of rut."

Anthony grinned. Philana had been considerate enough not to interrupt him, just to leave the message for whenever he wanted it. He picked up the telephone, connected directory assistance in Cabo Santa Pola, and asked it to route a call to the phone on Philana's yacht. She answered.

"Message received," he said. "Would you join me for lunch?"

"In an hour or so," she said. Her voice was abstracted. "I'm in the middle of something."

"When you're ready. Bye." He rang off, decided to make a fish chowder instead of sandwiches, and drank a beer while preparing it. He began to feel buoyant, cheerful. Siren wailing sounded through the water.

Philana's yacht maneuvered over to his boat just as Anthony finished his second beer. Philana stood on the gunwale, wearing a pale sweater with brown zigzags on it. Her braid was undone, and her brown hair fell around her shoulders. She jumped easily from her gunwale to the flybridge, then came down the ladder. The yacht moved away as soon as it felt her weight leave. She smiled uncertainly as she stepped to the deck.

"I'm sorry to have to bother you," she said.

He offered a grin. "That's okay. I'm between projects right now."

She looked toward the cabin. "Lunch smells good." Perhaps, he thought, food equaled apology.

"Fish chowder. Would you like a beer? Coffee?"

"Beer. Thanks."

They stepped below and Anthony served lunch on the small foldout table. He opened another beer and put it by her place.

"Delicious. I never really learned to cook."

"Cooking was something I learned young."

Her eyes were curious. "Where was that?"

"Lees." Shortly. He put a spoonful of chowder in his mouth so that his terseness would be more understandable.

"I never heard the name."

"It's a planet." Mumbling through chowder. "Pretty obscure." He didn't want to talk about it.

"I'm from Earth."

He looked at her. "Really? Originally? Not just a habitat in the Sol system?"

"Yes. Truly. One of the few. The one and only Earth."

"Is that what got you interested in whales?"

"I've *always* been interested in whales. As far back as I can remember. Long before I ever saw one."

"It was the same with me. I grew up near an ocean, built a boat when I was a boy and went exploring. I've never felt more at home than when I'm on the ocean."

"Some people live on the sea all the time."

"In floating habitats. That's just moving a city out onto the ocean. The worst of both worlds, if you ask me."

He realized the beer was making him expansive, that he was declaiming and waving his free hand. He pulled his hand in.

"I'm sorry," he said, "about the last time we talked."

She looked away. "My fault," she said. "I shouldn't have—"

"You didn't do anything wrong." He realized he had almost shouted that, and could feel himself flushing. He lowered his voice. "Once I got out here I realized . . ." This was really hopeless. He plunged on. "I'm not used to dealing with people. There were just a few people on Lees and they were all . . . eccentric. And everyone I've met since I left seems at least five hundred years old. Their attitudes are so . . ." He shrugged.

"Alien." She was grinning.

"Yes."

"I feel the same way. Everyone's so much older, so much more . . . sophisticated, I suppose." She thought about it for a moment. "I *guess* it's sophistication."

"*They* like to think so."

"I can feel their pity sometimes." She toyed with her spoon, looked down at her bowl.

"And condescension." Bitterness striped Anthony's tongue. "The attitude of, oh, we went through that once, poor darling, but now we know better."

"Yes." Tiredly. "I know what you mean. Like we're not really people yet."

"At least my father wasn't like that. He was crazy, but he let me be a person. He—"

His tongue stumbled. He was not drunk enough to tell this story, and he didn't think he wanted to anyway.

"Go ahead," said Philana. She was collecting data, Anthony remembered, on families.

He pushed back from the table, went to the fridge for another beer. "Maybe later," he said. "It's a long story."

Philana's look was steady. "You're not the only one who knows about crazy fathers."

Then you tell me about yours, he wanted to say. Anthony opened the beer, took a deep swallow. The liquid rose again, acid in his throat, and he forced it down. Memories rose with the fire in Anthony's throat, burning him. His father's fine madness whirled in his mind like leaves in a hurricane. We are, he thought, in a condition of mutual distrust and permanent antagonism. Something therefore must be done.

"All right." He put the beer on the top of the fridge and returned to his seat. He spoke rapidly, just letting the story come. His throat burned. "My father started life with money. He became a psychologist and then a fundamentalist Catholic lay preacher, kind of an unlicensed messiah. He ended up a psychotic. Dad concluded that civilization was too stupid and corrupt to survive, and he decided to start over. He initiated an unauthorized planetary scan through a transporter gate, found a world that he liked, and moved his family there. There were just four of us at the time, dad and my mother, my little brother, and me. My mother was—is—she's not really her own person. There's a vacancy there. If you're around psychotics a lot, and you don't have a strong sense of self, you can get submerged in their delusions. My mother didn't have a chance of standing up to a full-blooded lunatic like my dad, and I doubt she tried. She just let him run things.

"I was six when we moved to Lees, and my brother was

two. We were—" Anthony waved an arm in the general direction of the invisible Milky Way overhead. "—we were half the galaxy away. Clean on the other side of the hub. We didn't take a gate with us, or even instructions and equipment for building one. My father cut us off entirely from everything he hated."

Anthony looked at Philana's shocked face and laughed. "It wasn't so bad. We had everything but a way off the planet. Cube readers, building supplies, preserved food, tools, medical gear, wind and solar generators—Dad thought falkner generators were the cause of the rot, so he didn't bring any with him. My mother pretty much stayed pregnant for the next decade, but luckily the planet was benign. We settled down in a protected bay where there was a lot of food, both on land and in the water. We had a smokehouse to preserve the meat. My father and mother educated me pretty well. I grew up an aquatic animal. Built a sailboat, learned how to navigate. By the time I was fifteen I had charted two thousand miles of coast. I spent more than half my time at sea, the last few years. Trying to get away from my dad, mostly. He kept getting stranger. He promised me in marriage to my oldest sister after my eighteenth birthday." Memory swelled in Anthony like a tide, calm green water rising over the flat, soon to whiten and boil.

"There were some whale-sized fish on Lees, but they weren't intelligent. I'd seen recordings of whales, heard the sounds they made. On my long trips I'd imagine I was seeing whales, imagine myself talking to them."

"How did you get away?"

Anthony barked a laugh. "My dad wasn't the only one who could initiate a planetary scan. Seven or eight years after we landed some resort developers found our planet and put up a hotel about two hundred miles to the south of our settlement." Anthony shook his head. "Hell of a coincidence. The odds against it must have been incredible. My father frothed at the mouth when we started seeing their flyers and boats. My father decided our little settlement was

too exposed and we moved farther inland to a place where
we could hide better. Everything was camouflaged. He'd
hold drills in which we were all supposed to grab necessary
supplies and run off into the forest."

"They never found you?"

"If they saw us, they thought we were people on
holiday."

"Did you approach them?"

Anthony shook his head. "No. I don't really know why."

"Well. Your father."

"I didn't care much about his opinions by that point. It
was so *obvious* he was cracked. I think, by then, I had all
I wanted just living on my boat. I didn't see any reason to
change it." He thought for a moment. "If he actually tried
to marry me off to my sister, maybe I would have run for
it."

"But they found you anyway."

"No. Something else happened. The water supply for the
new settlement was unreliable, so we decided to build a
viaduct from a spring nearby. We had to get our hollow-log
pipe over a little chasm, and my father got careless and had
an accident. The viaduct fell on him. Really smashed him
up, caused all sorts of internal injuries. It was very obvious
that if he didn't get help, he'd die. My mother and I took my
boat and sailed for the resort."

The words dried up. This was where things got ugly.
Anthony decided he really couldn't trust Philana with it, and
that he wanted his beer after all. He got up and took the
bottle and drank.

"Did your father live?"

"No." He'd keep this as brief as he could. "When my
mother and I got back, we found that he'd died two days
before. My brothers and sisters gutted him and hung him
upside down in the smokehouse." He stared dully into
Philana's horrified face. "It's what they did to any large
animal. My mother and I were the only ones who remembered what to do with a dead person, and we weren't there."

"My God. Anthony." Her hands clasped below her face.

"And then—" He waved his hands, taking in everything, the boat's comforts, Overlook, life over the horizon. "Civilization. I was the only one of the children who could remember anything but Lees. I got off the planet and got into marine biology. That's been my life ever since. I was amazed to discover that I and the family were rich—my dad didn't tell me he'd left tons of investments behind. The rest of the family's still on Lees, still living in the old settlement. It's all they know." He shrugged. "They're rich, too, of course, which helps. So they're all right."

He leaned back on the fridge and took another long drink. The ocean swell tilted the boat and rolled the liquid down his throat. Whale harmonics made the bottle cap dance on the smooth alloy surface of the refrigerator.

Philana stood. Her words seemed small after the long silence. "Can I have some coffee? I'll make it."

"I'll do it."

They both went for the coffee and banged heads. Reeling back, the expression on Philana's face was wide-eyed, startled, fawnlike, as if he'd caught her at something she should be ashamed of. Anthony tried to laugh out an apology, but just then the white dwarf came up above the horizon and the quality of light changed as the screens went up, and with the light her look somehow changed. Anthony gazed at her for a moment and fire began to lap at his nerves. In his head the whales seemed to urge him to make his move.

He put his beer down and grabbed her with an intensity that was made ferocious largely by Anthony's fear that this was entirely the wrong thing, that he was committing an outrage that would compel her shortly to clout him over the head with the coffee pot and drop him in his tracks. Whalesong rang frantic chimes in his head. She gave a strangled cry as he tried to kiss her and thereby confirmed his own worst suspicions about this behavior.

Philana tried to push him away. He let go of her and stepped back, standing stupidly with his hands at his sides. A raging pain in his chest prevented him from saying a word. Philana surprised him by stepping forward and putting her hands on his shoulders.

"Easy," she said. "It's all right, just take it easy."

Anthony kissed her once more, and was somehow able to restrain himself from grabbing her again out of sheer panic and desperation. By and by, as the kiss continued, his anxiety level decreased. I/You, he thought, are rising in warmness, in happy tendrils.

He and Philana began to take their clothes off. He realized this was the first time he had made love to anyone under two hundred years of age.

Dweller sounds murmured in Anthony's mind. He descended into Philana as if she were a midnight ocean, something that on first contact with his flesh shocked him into wakefulness, then relaxed around him, became a taste of brine, a sting in the eyes, a fluid vagueness. Her hair brushed against his skin like seagrass. She surrounded him, buoyed him up. Her cries came up to him as over a great distance, like the faraway moans of a lonely whale in love. He wanted to call out in answer. Eventually he did.

Grace(1), he thought hopefully. Grace(1).

Anthony had an attack of giddiness after Philana returned to her flying yacht and her work. His mad father gibbered in his memory, mocked him and offered dire warnings. He washed the dishes and cleaned the rattling bottle cap off the fridge, then he listened to recordings of Dwellers and eventually the panic went away. He had not, it seemed, lost anything.

He went to the double bed in the forepeak, which was piled high with boxes of food, a spool of cable, a couple spare microphones, and a pair of rusting Danforth anchors. He stowed the food in the hold, put the electronics in the compartment under the mattress, jammed the Danforths farther into the peak on top of the anchor chain where they belonged. He wiped the grime and rust off the mattress and realized he had neither sheets nor a second pillow. He would need to purchase supplies on the next trip to town.

The peak didn't smell good. He opened the forehatch and tried to air the place out. Slowly he became aware that the whales were trying to talk to him. **Odd scentings,** they said, **Things that stand in water.** Anthony knew what they meant. He went up on the flybridge and scanned the horizon. He saw nothing.

The taste is distant, he wrote. *But we must be careful in our movement.* After that he scanned the horizon every half hour.

He cooked supper during the white dwarf's odd half-twilight and resisted the urge to drink both the bottles of bourbon that were waiting in their rack. Philana dropped onto the flybridge with a small rucksack. She kissed him hastily, as if to get it over with.

"I'm scared," she said.

"So am I."

"I don't know why."

He kissed her again. "I do," he said. She laid her cheek against his woolen shoulder. Blind with terror, Anthony held on to her, unable to see the future.

After midnight Anthony stood unclothed on the flybridge as he scanned the horizon one more time. Seeing nothing, he nevertheless reduced speed to three knots and rejoined Philana in the forepeak. She was already asleep with his open sleeping bag thrown over her like a blanket. He raised a corner of the sleeping bag and slipped beneath it. Philana turned away from him and pillowed her cheek on her fist. Whale music echoed from a cold layer beneath. He slept.

Movement elsewhere in the boat woke him. Anthony found himself alone in the peak, frigid air drifting over him from the forward hatch. He stepped into the cabin and saw Philana's bare legs ascending the companion to the flybridge. He followed. He shivered in the cold wind.

Philana stood before the controls, looking at them with a peculiar intensity, as though she were trying to figure out which switch to throw. Her hands flexed as if to take the wheel. There was gooseflesh on her shoulders and the wind tore her hair around her face like a fluttering curtain. She looked at him. Her eyes were hard, her voice disdainful.

"Are we lovers?" she asked. "Is that what's going on here?" His skin prickled at her tone.

Her stiff-spined stance challenged him. He was afraid to touch her.

"The condition is that of rut," he said, and tried to laugh.

Her posture, one leg cocked out front, reminded him of a haughty water bird. She looked at the controls again, then looked aft, lifting up on her toes to gaze at the horizon. Her nostrils flared, tasted the wind. Clouds scudded across the sky. She looked at him again. The white dwarf gleamed off her pebble eyes.

"Very well," she said, as if this was news. "Acceptable." She took his hand and led him below. Anthony's hackles rose. On her way to the forepeak Philana saw one of the bottles of bourbon in its rack and reached for it. She raised the bottle to her lips and drank from the neck. Whiskey coursed down her throat. She lowered the bottle and wiped her mouth with the back of her hand. She looked at him as if he were something worthy of dissection.

"Let's make love," she said.

Anthony was afraid not to. He went with her to the forepeak. Her skin was cold. Lying next to him on the mattress she touched his chest as if she were unused to the feel of male bodies. "What's your name?" she asked. He told her. "Acceptable," she said again, and with a sudden taut grin raked his chest with her nails. He knocked her hands away. She laughed and came after him with the bottle. He parried the blow in time and they wrestled for possession, bourbon splashing everywhere. Anthony was surprised at her strength. She fastened teeth in his arm. He hit her in the face with a closed fist. She gave the bottle up and laughed in a cold metallic way and put her arms around him. Anthony threw the bottle through the door into the cabin. It thudded somewhere but didn't break. Philana drew him on top of her, her laugh brittle, her legs opening around him.

Her dead eyes were like stones.

In the morning Anthony found the bottle lying in the main cabin. Red clawmarks covered his body, and the reek of liquor caught at the back of his throat. The scend of the ocean had distributed the bourbon puddle evenly over the teak deck. There was still about a third of the whiskey left in the bottle. Anthony rescued it and swabbed the deck. His mind was full of cotton wool, cushioning any bruises. He was working hard at not feeling anything at all.

He put on clothes and began to work. After a while Philana unsteadily groped her way from the forepeak, the sleeping bag draped around her shoulders. There was a stunned look on her face and a livid bruise on one cheek. Anthony could feel his body tautening, ready to repel assault.

"Was I odd last night?" she asked.

He looked at her. Her face crumbled. "Oh no." She passed a hand over her eyes and turned away, leaning on the side of the hatchway. "You shouldn't let me drink," she said.

"You hadn't made that fact clear."

"I don't remember any of it," she said. "I'm sick." She pressed her stomach with her hands and bent over. Anthony narrowly watched her pale buttocks as she groped her way to the head. The door shut behind her.

Anthony decided to make coffee. As the scent of the coffee began to fill the boat, he heard the sounds of her weeping. The long keening sounds, desperate throat-tearing noises, sounded like a pinioned whale writhing helplessly on the gaff.

A vast flock of birds wheeled on the cold horizon, marking a colony of drift creatures. Anthony informed the whales of the creatures' presence, but the humpbacks already knew and were staying well clear. The drift colony was what they had been smelling for hours.

While Anthony talked with the whales, Philana left the

head and drew on her clothes. Her movements were
tentative. She approached him with a cup of coffee in her
hand. Her eyes and nostrils were rimmed with red.

"I'm sorry," she said. "Sometimes that happens."

He looked at his computer console. "Jesus, Philana."

"It's something wrong with me. I can't control it." She
raised a hand to her bruised cheek. The hand came away
wet.

"There's medication for that sort of thing," Anthony
said. He remembered she had a mad father, or thought she
did.

"Not for this. It's something different."

"I don't know what to do."

"I need your help."

Anthony recalled his father's body twisting on the end of
its rope, fingertips trailing in the dust. Words came reluctantly to his throat.

"I'll give what help I can." The words were hollow: any
real resolution had long since gone. He had no clear notion
to whom he was giving this message, the Philana of the
previous night or this Philana or his father or himself.

Philana hugged him, kissed his cheek. She was excited.

"Shall we go see the drifters?" she asked. "We can take
my boat."

Anthony envisioned himself and Philana tumbling
through space. He had jumped off a precipice, just now.
The two children of mad fathers were spinning in the
updraft, waiting for the impact.

He said yes. He ordered his boat to circle while she
summoned her yacht. She held his hand while they waited
for the flying yacht to drift toward them. Philana kept
laughing, touching him, stropping her cheek on his shoulder
like a cat. They jumped from the flybridge to her yacht and
rose smoothly into the sky. Bright sun warmed Anthony's
shoulders. He took off his sweater and felt warning pain
from the marks of her nails.

The drifters were colony creatures that looked like
miniature mountains twenty feet or so high, complete with

a white snowcap of guano. They were highly organized but unintelligent, their underwater parts sifting the ocean for nutrients or reaching out to capture prey—the longest of their gossamer stinging tentacles was up to two miles in length, and though they couldn't kill or capture a hump-back, they were hard for the whale to detect and could cause a lot of stinging wounds before the whale noticed them and made its escape. Perhaps they were unintelligent, distant relatives of the Deep Dwellers, whose tenuous character they resembled. Many different species of sea birds lived in permanent colonies atop the floating islands, thousands of them, and the drifters processed their guano and other waste. Above the water, the drifters' bodies were shaped like a convex lens set on edge, an aerodynamic shape, and they could clumsily tack into the wind if they needed to. For the most part, however, they drifted on the currents, a giant circular circumnavigation of the ocean that could take centuries.

Screaming sea birds rose in clouds as Philana's yacht moved silently toward their homes. Philana cocked her head back, laughed into the open sky, and flew closer. Birds hurtled around them in an overwhelming roar of wings. Whistlelike cries issued from peg-toothed beaks. Anthony watched in awe at the profusion of colors, the chromatic brilliance of the evolved featherlike scales.

The flying boat passed slowly through the drifter colony. Birds roared and whistled, some of them landing on the boat in apparent hopes of taking up lodging. Feathers drifted down; birdshit spattered the windscreen. Philana ran below for a camera and used up several data cubes taking pictures. A trickle of optimism began to ease into Anthony at the sight of Philana in the bright morning sun, a broad smile gracing her face as she worked the camera and took picture after picture. He put an arm around Philana's waist and kissed her ear. She smiled and took his hand in her own. In the bright daylight the personality she'd acquired the previous night seemed to gather unto itself the tenebrous, unreal quality of a nightmare. The current Philana seemed far more tangible.

Philana returned to the controls; the yacht banked and increased speed. Birds issued startled cries as they got out of the way. Wind tugged at Philana's hair. Anthony decided not to let Philana near his liquor again.

After breakfast, Anthony found both whales had set their transponders. He had to detour around the drifters—their insubstantial, featherlike tentacles could foul his state-of-the-art silent props—but when he neared the whales and slowed, he could hear the deep murmurings of Dwellers rising from beneath the cold current. There were half a dozen of them engaged in conversation, and Anthony worked the day and far into the night, transcribing, making hesitant attempts at translation. The Dweller speech was more opaque than usual, depending on a context that was unstated and elusive. Comprehension eluded Anthony; but he had the feeling that the key was within his reach.

Philana waited for the Dwellers to end their converse before she brought her yacht near him. She had heated some prepared dinners and carried them to the flybridge in an insulated pouch. Her grin was broad. She put her pouch down and embraced him. Abstracted Dweller subsonics rolled away from Anthony's mind. He was surprised at how glad he was to see her.

With dinner they drank coffee. Philana chattered bravely throughout the meal. While Anthony cleaned the dishes, she embraced him from behind. A memory of the other Philana flickered in his mind, disdainful, contemptuous, cold. Her father was crazy, he remembered again.

He buried the memory deliberately and turned to her. He kissed her and thought, I/We deny the Other. The Other, he decided, would cease to exist by a common act of will.

It seemed to work. At night his dreams filled with Dwellers crying in joy, his father warning darkly, the touch of Philana's flesh, breath, hands. He awoke hungry to get to work.

The next two days a furious blaze of concentration burned in Anthony's mind. Things fell into place. He found a word that, in its context, could mean nothing but light, as opposed to fluorescence—he was excited to find out the Dwellers knew about the sun. He also found new words for darkness, for emotions that seemed to have no human equivalents, but which he seemed nevertheless to comprehend. One afternoon a squall dumped a gallon of cold water down his collar and he looked up in surprise: he hadn't been aware of its slow approach. He moved his computer deck to the cabin and kept working. When not at the controls he moved dazedly over the boat, drinking coffee, eating what was at hand without tasting it. Philana was amused and tolerant; she buried herself in her own work.

On preparing breakfast the morning of the third day, Anthony realized he was running out of food. He was farther from the archipelago than he'd planned on going, and he had about two days' supply left; he'd have to return at flank speed, buy provisions, and then run out again. A sudden hot fury gripped him. He clenched his fists. He could have provisioned for two or three months—why hadn't he done it when he had the chance?

Philana tolerantly sipped her coffee. "Tonight I'll fly you into Cabo Santa Pola. We can buy a ton of provisions, have dinner at Villa Mary, and be back by midnight."

Anthony's anger floundered uselessly, looking for a target, then gave up. "Fine," he said.

She looked at him. "Are you ever going to talk to them? You must have built your speakers to handle it."

Now the anger had finally found a home. "Not yet," he said.

In late afternoon, Anthony set out his drogue and a homing transponder, then boarded Philana's yacht. He watched while she hauled up her aquasled and programmed the navigation computer. The world dimmed as the falkner field increased in strength. The transition to full speed was almost instantaneous. Waves blurred silently past, providing the only sensation of motion—the field cut out both wind and inertia. The green-walled volcanic islands of the Las Madres archipelago rolled over the horizon in minutes. Traffic over Cabo Santa Pola complicated the approach somewhat; it was all of six minutes before Philana could set the machine down in her slip.

A bright, hot sun brightened the white-and-turquoise waterfront. From a cold Kirst current to the tropics in less than half an hour.

Anthony felt vaguely resentful at this blinding efficiency. He could have easily equipped his own boat with flight capability, but he hadn't cared about speed when he'd set out, only the opportunity to be alone on the ocean with his whales and the Dwellers. Now the very tempo of his existence had changed. He was moving at unaccustomed velocity, and the destination was still unclear.

After giving him her spare key, Philana went to do laundry—when one lived on small boats, laundry was done whenever the opportunity arose. Anthony bought supplies. He filled the yacht's forecabin with crates of food, then changed clothes and walked to the Villa Mary.

Anthony got a table for two and ordered a drink. The first drink went quickly and he ordered a second. Philana didn't appear. Anthony didn't like the way the waiter was looking at him. He heard his father's mocking laugh as he munched the last bread stick. He waited for three hours before he paid and left.

There was no sign of Philana at the laundry or on the yacht. He left a note on the computer expressing what he considered a contained disappointment, then headed into town. A brilliant sign that featured aquatic motifs called him to a cool, dark bar filled with bright green aquaria. Native fish gaped at him blindly while he drank something tall and cool. He decided he didn't like the way the fish looked at him and left.

He found Philana in his third bar of the evening. She was with two men, one of whom Anthony knew slightly as a charter boat skipper whom he didn't much like. He had his hand on her knee; the other man's arm was around her.

Empty drinks and forsaken hors d'oeuvres lay on a table in front of them.

Anthony realized, as he approached, that his own arrival could only make things worse. Her eyes turned to him as he approached; her neck arched in a peculiar, balletic way that he had seen only once before. He recognized the quick, carnivorous smile, and a wash of fear turned his skin cold. The stranger whispered into her ear.

"What's your name again?" she asked.

Anthony wondered what to do with his hands. "We were supposed to meet."

Her eyes glittered as her head cocked, considering him. Perhaps what frightened him most of all was the fact there was no hostility in her look, nothing but calculation. There was a cigarette in her hand; he hadn't seen her smoke before.

"Do we have business?"

Anthony thought about this. He had jumped into space with this woman, and now he suspected he'd just hit the ground. "I guess not," he said, and turned.

"Qué pasó, hombre?"

"Nada."

Pablo, the Leviathan's regular bartender, was one of the planet's original Latino inhabitants, a group rapidly being submerged by newcomers. Pablo took Anthony's order for a double bourbon and also brought him his mail, which consisted of an inquiry from *Xenobiology Review* wondering what had become of their galley proofs. Anthony crumpled the note and left it in an ashtray.

A party of drunken fishermen staggered in, still in their flashing harnesses. Triumphant whoops assaulted Anthony's ears. His fingers tightened on his glass.

"Careful, Anthony," said Pablo. He poured another double bourbon. "On the house," he said.

One of the fishermen stepped to the bar, put a heavy hand on Anthony's shoulder. "Drinks on me," he said. "Caught a twelve-meter flasher today." Anthony threw the bourbon in his face.

He got in a few good licks, but in the end the pack of fishermen beat him severely and threw him through the front window. Lying breathless on broken glass, Anthony brooded on the injustice of his position and decided to rectify matters. He lurched back into the bar and knocked down the first person he saw.

Small consolation. This time they went after him with the flashing poles that were hanging on the walls, beating him senseless and once more heaving him out the window. When Anthony recovered consciousness he staggered to his feet, intending to have another go, but the pole butts had hit him in the face too many times and his eyes were swollen shut. He staggered down the street, ran face-first into a building, and sat down.

"You finished there, cowboy?" It was Nick's voice.

Anthony spat blood. "Hi, Nick," he said. "Bring them here one at a time, will you? I can't lose one-on-one."

"Jesus, Anthony. You're such an asshole."

Anthony found himself in an inexplicably cheerful mood. "You're lucky you're a sailor. Only a sailor can call me an asshole."

"Can you stand? Let's get to the marina before the cops show up."

"My boat's hundreds of miles away. I'll have to swim."

"I'll take you to my place, then."

With Nick's assistance Anthony managed to stand. He was still too drunk to feel pain, and ambled through the streets in a contented mood. "How did you happen to be at the Leviathan, Nick?"

There was weariness in Nick's voice. "They always call me, Anthony, when you fuck up."

Drunken melancholy poured into Anthony like a sudden cold squall of rain. "I'm sorry," he said.

Nick's answer was almost cheerful. "You'll be sorrier in the morning."

Anthony reflected that this was very likely true.

* * *

Nick gave him some pills that, by morning, reduced the swelling. When Anthony awoke he was able to see. Agony flared in his body as he staggered out of bed. It was still twilight. Anthony pulled on his bloody clothes and wrote an incoherent note of thanks on Nick's computer.

Fishing boats were floating out of harbor into the bright dawn. Probably Nick's was among them. The volcano above the town was a contrast in black stone and green vegetation. Pain beat at Anthony's bones like a rain of fists.

Philana's boat was still in its slip. Apprehension tautened Anthony's nerves as he put a tentative foot on the gunwale. The hatch to the cabin was still locked. Philana wasn't aboard. Anthony opened the hatch and went into the cabin just to be sure. It was empty.

He programmed the computer to pursue the transponder signal on Anthony's boat, then as the yacht rose into the sky and arrowed over the ocean, Anthony went into Philana's cabin and fell asleep on a pillow that smelled of her hair.

He awoke around noon to find the yacht patiently circling his boat. He dropped the yacht into the water, tied the two craft together, and spent half the afternoon transferring his supplies to his own boat. He programmed the yacht to return to Las Madres and orbit the volcanic spire until it was summoned by its owner or the police.

I and the sea greet one another, he tapped into his console, and as the call wailed out from his boat he hauled in the drogue and set off after the humpbacks. *Apartness is the smell*, he thought, *aloneness is the condition.* Spray shot aboard and spattered Anthony, and salt pain flickered from the cuts on his face. He climbed to the flybridge and hoped for healing from the sun and the glittering sea.

The whales left the cold current and suddenly the world was filled with tropic sunshine and bright water. Anthony made light conversation with the humpbacks and spent the rest of his time working on Dweller speech. Despite hours of concentrated endeavor he made little progress. The sensation was akin to that of smashing his head against a stone wall over and over, an act that was, on consideration, not unlike the rest of his life.

After his third day at sea his boat's computer began signaling him that he was receiving messages. He ignored this and concentrated on work.

Two days later he was cruising north with a whale on either beam when a shadow moved across his boat. Anthony looked up from his console and saw without surprise that Philana's yacht was eclipsing the sun. Philana, dark glasses over her deep eyes and a floppy hat over her hair, was peering down from the starboard bow.

"We have to talk," she said.

Joyously we greet Air Human, whooped Sings of Others.

I and Air Human are pleased to detect one another's presence, called Two Notches.

Anthony went to the controls and throttled up. Microphones slammed at the bottom of his boat. Two Notches poked one large brown eye above the waves to see what was happening, then cheerfully set off in pursuit.

Anthony and Air Human are in a state of excitement, he chattered. **I/We are pleased to join our race.**

The flying yacht hung off Anthony's stern. Philana shouted through cupped hands. "Talk to me, Anthony!"

Anthony remained silent and twisted the wheel into a fast left turn. His wake foamed over Two Notches' face and the humpback burbled a protest. The air yacht seemed to have little trouble following the turn. Anthony was beginning to have the sense of that stone wall coming up again, but he tried a few more maneuvers just in case one of them worked. Nothing succeeded. Finally he cut the throttle and let the boat slow on the long blue swells.

The trade winds had taken Philana's hat and carried it away. She ignored it and looked down at him. Her face was pale and beneath the dark glasses she looked drawn and ill.

"I'm not human, Anthony," she said. "I'm a Kyklops. That's what's really wrong with me."

Anthony looked at her. Anger danced in his veins. "You really are full of surprises."

"I'm Telamon's other body," she said. "Sometimes he inhabits me."

Whalesong rolled up from the sea. **We and Air Human send one another cheerful salutations and expressions of good will.**

"Talk to the whales first," said Anthony.

"Telamon's a scientist," Philana said. "He's impatient, that's his problem."

The boat heaved on an ocean swell. The trade wind moaned through the flybridge. "He's got a few more problems than that," Anthony said.

"He wanted me for a purpose but sometimes he forgets." A tremor of pain crossed Philana's face. She was deeply hung over. Her voice was ragged: Telamon had been smoking like a chimney and Philana wasn't used to it.

"He wanted to do an experiment on human psychology. He wanted to arrange a method of recording a person's memories, then transferring them to his own . . . sphere. He got my parents to agree to having the appropriate devices implanted, but the only apparatus that existed for the connection of human and Kyklops was the one the Kyklopes use to manipulate the human bodies that they wear when they want to enjoy the pleasures of the flesh. And Telamon is . . ." She waved a dismissive arm. "He's a decadent, the way a lot of the Kyklopes turn once they discover how much fun it is to be a human and that their real self doesn't get hurt no matter what they do to their clone bodies. Telamon likes his pleasures, and he likes to interfere. Sometimes, when he dumped my memory into the nth dimension and had a look at it, he couldn't resist the temptation to take over my body and rectify what he considered my errors. And occasionally, when he's in the middle of one of his binges, and his other body gives out on him, he takes me over and starts a party wherever I am."

"Some scientist," Anthony said.

"The Kyklopes are used to experimenting on pieces of themselves," Philana said. "Their own beings are tenuous and rather . . . detachable. Their ethics aren't against it. And he doesn't do it very often. He must be bored wherever he is—he's taken me over twice in a week." She raised her fist to her face and began to cough, a real smoker's hack. Anthony fidgeted and wondered whether to offer her a glass of water. Philana bent double and the coughs turned to cries of pain. A tear pattered on the teak.

A knot twisted in Anthony's throat. He left his chair and held Philana in his arms. "I've never told anyone," she said.

Anthony realized to his transient alarm that once again he'd jumped off a cliff without looking. He had no more idea of where he would land than last time.

Philana, Anthony was given to understand, was Greek for "lover of humanity." The Kyklopes, after being saddled with a mythological name by the first humans who had contacted them, had gone in for classical allusion in a big way. Telamon, Anthony learned, meant (among other things) "the supporter." After learning this, Anthony referred to the alien as Jockstrap.

"We should do something about him," Anthony said. It was late—the white dwarf had just set—but neither of them had any desire to sleep. He and Philana were standing on the flybridge. The falkner shield was off and above their heads the uninhibited stars seemed almost within reach of their questing fingertips. Overlook Station, fixed almost overhead, was bright as a burning brand.

Philana shook her head. "He's got access to my memory. Any plans we make, he can know in an instant." She thought for a moment. "If he bothers to look. He doesn't always."

"I'll make the plans without telling you what they are."

"It will take forever. I've thought about it. You're talking court case. He can sue me for breach of contract."

"It's your parents who signed the contract, not you. You're an adult now."

She turned away. Anthony looked at her for a long moment, a cold foreboding hand around his throat. "I hope," he said, "you're going to tell me that you signed that contract while Jockstrap was riding you."

Philana shook her head silently. Anthony looked up into the Milky Way and imagined the stone wall falling from the void, aimed right between his eyes, spinning slightly as it grew ever larger in his vision. Smashing him again.

"All we have to do is get the thing out of your head," Anthony said. "After that, let him sue you. You'll be free, whatever happens." His tone reflected a resolve that was absent entirely from his heart.

"He'll sue you, too, if you have any part of this." She turned to face him again. Her face pale and taut in the starlight. "All my money comes from him—how else do you think I could afford the yacht? I owe everything to him."

Bitterness sped through Anthony's veins. He could feel his voice turning harsh. "Do you want to get rid of him or not? Yes or no."

"He's not entirely evil."

"Yes or no, Philana."

"It'll take years before he's done with you. And he could kill you. Just transport you to deep space somewhere and let you drift. Or he could simply teleport me away from you."

The bright stars poured down rage. Anthony knew himself seconds away from violence. There were two people on this boat and one of them was about to get hurt. *"Yes or no!"* he shouted.

Philana's face contorted. She put her hands over her ears. Hair fell across her face. "Don't shout," she said.

Anthony turned and smashed his forehead against the control panel of the flybridge. Philana gave a cry of surprise and fear. Anthony drove himself against the panel again. Philana's fingers clutched at his shoulders. Anthony could feel blood running from his scalp. The pain drained his anger, brought a cold, brilliant clarity to his mind. He smashed himself a third time. Philana cried out. He turned to her. He felt a savage, exemplary satisfaction. If one were going to drive oneself against stone walls, one should at least take a choice of the walls available.

"Ask me," Anthony panted, "if I care what happens to me."

Philana's face was a mask of terror. She said his name.

"I need to know where you stand," said Anthony. Blood drooled from his scalp, and he suppressed the unwelcome thought that he had just made himself look ridiculous.

Her look of fear broadened.

"Am I going to jump off this cliff by myself, or what?" Anthony demanded.

"I want to get rid of him," she said.

Anthony wished her voice had contained more determination, even if it were patently false. He spat salt and went in search of his first aid kit. We are in a condition of slow movement through deep currents, he thought.

In the morning he got the keys to Philana's yacht and changed the passwords on the falkner controls and navigation comp. He threw all his liquor overboard. He figured that if Jockstrap appeared and discovered that he couldn't leave the middle of the ocean, and he couldn't have a party where he was, he'd get bored and wouldn't hang around for long.

From Philana's cabin he called an attorney who informed him that the case was complex but not impossible, and furthermore that it would take a small fortune to resolve. Anthony told him to get to work on it. In the meantime he told the lawyer to start calling neurosurgeons. Unfortunately there were few neurosurgeons capable of implanting, let alone removing, the rider device. The operation wasn't performed that often.

Days passed. A discouraging list of neurosurgeons either turned him down flat or wanted the legal situation clarified first. Anthony told the lawyer to start calling *rich* neuro-surgeons who might be able to ride out a lawsuit.

Philana transferred most of her data to Anthony's computer and worked with the whales from the smaller boat. Anthony used her yacht and aquasled and cursed the bad sound quality. At least the yacht's flight capability allowed him to find the Dwellers faster.

As far as the Dwellers went, he had run all at once into a dozen blind alleys. Progress seemed measured in microns.

"What's B1971?" Philana asked once, looking over his shoulder as he typed in data.

"A taste. Perhaps a taste associated with a particular temperature striation. Perhaps an emotion." He shrugged. "Maybe just a metaphor."

"You could ask them."

His soul hardened. "Not yet." Which ended the conversation.

Anthony wasn't sure whether or not he wanted to touch her. He and Jockstrap were at war and Philana seemed not to have entirely made up her mind which side she was on. Anthony slept with Philana on the double mattress in the peak, but they avoided sex. He didn't know whether he was helping her out of love or something else, and while he figured things out, desire was on hold, waiting.

Anthony's time with Philana was occupied mainly by his attempt to teach her to cook. Anything else waited for the situation to grow less opaque. Anthony figured Jockstrap would clarify matters fairly soon.

Anthony's heart lurched as he looked up from lunch to see the taut, challenging grin on Philana's face. Anthony realized he'd been foolish to expect Telamon to show up only at night, as he always had before.

Anthony drew his lips into an answering grin. He was ready, no matter what the hour.

"Do I know you?" Anthony mocked. "Do we have business?"

Philana's appraisal was cold. "I've been called Jockstrap before," Telamon said.

"With good reason, I'm sure."

Telamon lurched to his feet and walked aft. He seemed not to have his sea legs yet. Anthony followed, his nerves dancing. Telamon looked out at the sea and curled Philana's lip as if to say that the water held nothing of interest.

"I want to talk about Philana," Telamon said. "You're keeping her prisoner here."

"She can leave me anytime she wants. Which is more than she can say about you."

"I want the codes to the yacht."

Anthony stepped up to Telamon, held Philana's cold gaze. "You're hurting her," he said.

Telamon stared at him with eyes like obsidian chips. He pushed Philana's long hair out of his face with an unaccustomed gesture. "I'm not the only one, Maldalena. I've got access to her mind, remember."

"Then look in her mind and see what she thinks of you."

A contemptuous smile played about Philana's lips. "I know very well what she thinks of me, and it's probably not what she's told you. Philana is a very sad and complex person, and she is not always truthful."

"She's what you made her."

"Precisely my next point." He waved his arm stiffly, unnaturally. The gesture brought him off balance, and Philana's body swayed for a moment as Telamon adjusted to the tossing of the boat. "I gave her money, education, knowledge of the world. I have corrected her errors, taught her much. She is, in many ways, my creation. Her feelings toward me are ambiguous, as any child's feelings would be toward her father."

"Daddy Jockstrap." Anthony laughed. "Do we have business, Daddy? Or are you going to take your daughter's body to a party first?"

Anthony jumped backward, arms flailing, as Philana disappeared, her place taken by a young man with curly dark hair and bright blue eyes. The stranger was dressed in a white cotton shirt unbuttoned to the navel and a pair of navy blue swimming trunks. He had seen the man before on vid, showing off his chest hairs. The grin stayed the same from one body to the next.

"She's gone, Maldalena. I teleported her to someplace safe." He laughed. "I'll buy her a new boat. Do what you like with the old one."

Anthony's heart hammered. He had forgotten the Kyklopcs could do that, just teleport without the apparatus required by humans. And teleport other things as well.

He wondered how many centuries old the Kyklops' body was. He knew the mind's age was measured in eons.

"This doesn't end it," Anthony said.

Telamon's tone was mild. "Perhaps I'll find a nice planet for you somewhere, Maldalena. Let you play Robinson Crusoe, just as you did when you were young."

"That will only get you in trouble. Too many people know about this situation by now. And it won't be much fun holding Philana wherever you've got her."

Telamon stepped toward the stern, sat on the taffrail. His movements were fluid, far more confident than they had been when he was wearing the other, unaccustomed body. For a moment Anthony considered kicking Telamon into the drink, then decided against it. The possible repercussions had a cosmic dimension that Anthony preferred not to contemplate.

"I don't dislike you, Maldalena," the alien said. "I truly don't. You're an alcoholic, violent lout, but at least you have proven intelligence, perhaps a kind of genius."

"Call the kettle black again. I liked that part."

Two Notches' smooth body rose a cable's length to starboard. He exhaled with an audible hiss, mist drifting over his back. Telamon gave the whale a disinterested look, then turned back to Anthony.

"Being the nearest thing to a parent on the planet," he said, "I must say that I disapprove of you as a partner for Philana. However—" He gave a shrug. "Parents must know when to compromise in these matters." He looked up at

Anthony with his blue eyes. "I propose we share her, Anthony. Formalize the arrangement we already seem to possess. I'll only occupy a little of her time, and for all the rest, the two of you can live out your lives with whatever sad domestic bliss you can summon. Till she gets tired of you, anyway."

Two Notches rolled under the waves. A cetacean murmur echoed off the boat's bottom. Anthony's mind flailed for an answer. He felt sweat prickling his scalp. He shook his head in feigned disbelief.

"Listen to yourself, Telamon. Is this supposed to be a scientist talking? A researcher?"

"You don't want to share?" The young man's face curled in disdain. "You want everything for yourself—the whole planet, I suppose, like your father."

"Don't be ridiculous."

"I know what Philana knows about you, and I've done some checking on my own. You brought the humpbacks here because you needed them. Away from *their* home, *their* kind. You *asked* them, I'm sure; but there's no way they could make an informed decision about this planet, about what they were doing. You needed them for your Dweller study, so you took them."

As if on cue, Two Notches rose from the water to take a breath. Telamon favored the whale with his taut smile. Anthony floundered for an answer while the alien spoke on.

"You've got data galore on the Dwellers, but do you publish? Do you share it with anybody, even with Philana? You hoard it all for yourself, all your specialized knowledge. You don't even talk to the Dwellers!" Telamon gave a scornful laugh. "You don't even want the *Dwellers* to know what Anthony knows!"

Anger poured through Anthony's veins like a scalding fire. He clenched his fists, considered launching himself at Telamon. Something held him back.

The alien stood, walked to Anthony, looked him up and down. "We're not so different," he said. "We both want what's ours. But *I'm* willing to share. Philana can be our common pool of data, if you like. Think about it."

Anthony swung, and in that instant Philana was back, horror in her eyes. Anthony's fist, aimed for the taller Telamon's chin, clipped Philana's temple and she fell back, flailing. Anthony caught her.

"It just happened, didn't it?" Her voice was woeful.

"You don't remember?"

Philana's face crumpled. She swayed and touched her temple. "I never do. The times when he's running me are just blank spots."

Anthony seated her on the port bench. He was feeling queasy at having hit her. She put her face in her hands. "I hate when that happens in front of people I know," she said.

"He's using you to hide behind. He was here in person, the son of a bitch." He took her hands in his own and kissed her. Purest desire flamed through him. He wanted to commit an act of defiance, make a statement of the nature of things. He put his arms around her and kissed her nape. She smelled faintly of pine, and there were needles in her hair. Telamon had put her on Earth, then, in a forest somewhere.

She strained against his tight embrace. "I don't know if this is a good idea," she said.

"I want to send a message to Telamon," Anthony said.

They made love under the sun, lying on the deck in Anthony's cockpit. Clear as a bell, Anthony heard Dweller sounds rumbling up the boat. Somewhere in the boat a metal mounting bracket rang to the subsonics. Philana clutched at him. There was desperation in her look, a search for affirmation, despair at finding none. The teak punished Anthony's palms. He wondered if Telamon had ever possessed her thus, took over her mind so that he could fuck her in his own body, commit incest with himself. He found the idea exciting.

His orgasm poured out, stunning him with its intensity. He kissed the moist juncture of Philana's neck and shoulder, and rose on his hands to stare down into Telamon's brittle grin and cold, knowing eyes.

"Message received, Anthony." Philana's throat convulsed in laughter. "You're taking possession. Showing everyone who's boss."

Horror galvanized Anthony. He jumped to his feet and backed away, heart pounding. He took a deep breath and mastered himself, strove for words of denial and could not find them. "You're sad, Telamon," he said.

Telamon threw Philana's arms over her head, parted her legs. "Let's do it again, Anthony." Taunting. "You're so masterful."

Anthony turned away. "Piss off, Telamon, you sick fuck." Bile rose in his throat.

"What happened?" Anthony knew Philana was back. He turned and saw her face crumple. "We were making love!" she wailed.

"A cheap trick. He's getting desperate." He squatted by her and tried to take her in his arms. She turned away from him.

"Let me alone for a while," she said. Bright tears filled her eyes.

Misplaced adrenaline ran charges through Anthony's body—no one to fight, no place to run. He picked up his clothes and went below to the main cabin. He drew on his clothing and sat on one of the berths, hands helpless on the seat beside him. He wanted to get blind drunk.

Half an hour later Philana entered the cabin. She'd braided her hair, drawn it back so tight from her temples it must have been painful. Her movements were slow, as if suddenly she'd lost her sea legs. She sat down at the little kitchen table, pushed away her half-eaten lunch.

"We can't win," she said.

"There's got to be some way," Anthony said tonelessly. He was clean out of ideas.

Philana looked at Anthony from reddened eyes. "We can give him what he wants," she said.

"No."

Her voice turned to a shout. "It's not *you* he does this to! It's not you who winks out of existence in the middle of doing laundry or making love, and wakes up somewhere else." Her knuckles were white as they gripped the table edge. "I don't know how long I can take this."

"All your life," said Anthony, "if you give him what he wants."

"At least then he wouldn't use it as a *weapon*!" Her voice was a shout. She turned away.

Anthony looked at her, wondered if he should go to her. He decided not to. He was out of comfort for the present.

"You see," Philana said, her head still turned away, "why I don't want to live forever."

"Don't let him beat you."

"It's not that. I'm afraid . . ." Her voice trembled. "I'm afraid that if I got old I'd *become* him. The Kyklopes are the oldest living things ever discovered. And a lot of the oldest immortals are a lot like them. Getting crazier, getting . . ." She shook her head. "Getting less human all the time."

Anthony saw a body swaying in the smokehouse. Philana's body, her fingernails trailing in the dust. Pain throbbed in his chest. He stood up, swayed as he was caught by a slow wave of vertigo. Somewhere his father was laughing, telling him he should have stayed on Lees for a life of pastoral incest.

"I want to think," he said. He stepped past her on the way to his computer. He didn't reach out to touch her as he passed. She didn't reach for him, either.

He put on the headphones and listened to the Dwellers. Their speech rolled up from the deep. Anthony sat unable to comprehend, his mind frozen. He was helpless as Philana. Whose was the next move? he wondered. His? Philana's?

Whoever made the next move, Anthony knew, the game was Telamon's.

At dinnertime Philana made a pair of sandwiches for Anthony, then returned to the cabin and ate nothing herself.

Anthony ate one sandwich without tasting it, gave the second to the fish. The Dweller speech had faded out. He left his computer and stepped into the cabin. Philana was stretched out on one of the side berths, her eyes closed. One arm was thrown over her forehead.

Her body, Anthony decided, was too tense for this to be sleep. He sat on the berth opposite.

"He said you haven't told the truth," Anthony said.

Anthony could see Philana's eyes moving under translucent lids as she evaluated this statement, scanning for meaning. "About what," she said.

"About your relationship to him."

Her lips drew back, revealing teeth. Perhaps it was a smile.

"I've known him all my life. I gave you the condensed version."

"Is there more I should know?"

There was another pause. "He saved my life."

"Good for him."

"I got involved with this man. Three or four hundred years old, one of my professors in school. He was going through a crisis—he was a mess, really. I thought I could do him some good. Telamon disagreed, said the relationship was sick." Philana licked her lips. "He was right," she said.

Anthony didn't know if he really wanted to hear about this.

"The guy started making demands. Wanted to get married, leave Earth, start over again."

"What did you want?"

Philana shrugged. "I don't know. I hadn't made up my mind. But Telamon went into my head and confronted the guy and told him to get lost. Then he just took me out of there. My body was half the galaxy away, all alone on an undeveloped world. There were supplies, but no gates out."

Anthony gnawed his lip. This was how Telamon operated.

"Telamon kept me there for a couple weeks till I calmed down. He took me back to Earth. The professor had taken up with someone else, another one of his students. He married her, and six weeks later she walked out on him. He killed her, then killed himself."

Philana sighed, drew her hand over her forehead. She opened her eyes and sat up, swinging her legs off the berth. "So," she said. "That's one Telamon story. I've got more."

"When did this happen?"

"I'd just turned eighteen." She shook her head. "That's when I signed the contract that keeps him in my head. I decided that I couldn't trust my judgment about people. And Telamon's judgment of people is, well, quite good."

Resentment flamed in Anthony at this notion. Telamon had made his judgment of Anthony clear, and Anthony didn't want it to become a subject for debate. "You're older now," he said. "He can't have a veto on your life forever."

Philana drew up her legs and circled her knees with her arms. "You're violent, Anthony."

Anthony looked at her for a long moment of cold anger. "I hit you by accident. I was aiming at *him*, damn it."

Philana's jaw worked as she returned his stare. "How long before you aim at *me*?"

"I wouldn't."

"That's what my old professor said."

Anthony turned away, fury running through him like chill fire. Philana looked at him levelly for a moment, then dropped her forehead to her knees. She sighed. "I don't know, Anthony. I don't know anymore. If I ever did."

Anthony stared fixedly at the distant white dwarf, just arrived above the horizon and visible through the hatch. We are, he thought, in a condition of permanent bafflement. "What do you want, Philana?" he asked.

Her head came up, looked at him. "I want not to be a tennis ball in your game with Telamon, Anthony. I want to know I'm not just the prize given the winner."

"I wanted you before I ever met Telamon, Philana."

"Telamon changed a few things." Her voice was cold. "Before you met him, you didn't use my body to send messages to people."

Anthony's fists clenched. He forced them to relax.

Philana's voice was bitter. "Seems to me, Anthony, that's one of Telamon's habits you're all too eager to adopt."

Anthony's chest ached. He didn't seem able to breathe in enough air. He took a long breath and hoped his tension would ease. It didn't. "I'm sorry," he said. "It's not . . . a normal situation."

"For you, maybe."

Silence hung in the room, broken only by the whale clicks and mutters rising through the boat. Anthony shook his head. "What do we do, then?" he asked. "Surrender?"

"If we have to." She looked at him. "I'm willing to fight Telamon, but not to the point where one of us is destroyed." She leaned toward him, her expression intent. "And if Telamon wins, could you live with it?" she asked. "With surrender? If we had to give him what he wanted?"

"I don't know."

"I *have* to live with it. You don't. That's the difference."

"That's *one* difference." He took a breath, then rose from his place. "I have to think," he said.

He climbed into the cockpit. Red sunset was splattered like blood across the windscreen. He tried to breathe the sea air, clear the heaviness he felt in his chest, but it didn't work. Anthony went up onto the flybridge and stared forward. His eyes burned as the sun went down in flames.

The white dwarf was high overhead when Anthony came down. Philana was lying in the forepeak, covered with a sheet, her eyes staring sightlessly out the open hatch. Anthony took his clothes off and crawled in beside her.

"I'll surrender," he said. "If I have to, I'll surrender." She turned to him and put her arms around him. Hopeless desire burned in his belly.

He made love to Philana, his nerves numb to the possibility that Telamon might reappear. Her hungry mouth drank in his pain. He didn't know whether this was affirmation or not, whether this meant anything other than the fact there was nothing left to do at this point than stagger blindly into one another's embrace.

A Dweller soloed from below, the clearest Anthony had ever heard one. **We call to ourselves,** the Dweller said, **We speak of things as they are.** Anthony rose from bed and set his computer to record. Sings of Others, rising alongside to breathe, called a hello. Anthony tapped his keys, hit TRANSMIT.

Air Human and I are in a condition of rut, he said.

We congratulate Anthony and Air Human on our condition of rut, Sings of Others responded. The whooping whale cries layered atop the thundering Dweller noises. **We wish ourselves many happy copulations.**

Happy copulations, happy copulations, echoed Two Notches.

A pointless optimism began to resonate in Anthony's mind. He sat before the computer and listened to the sounds of the Deep Dwellers as they rumbled up his spine.

Philana appeared at the hatch. She was buttoning her shirt. "You told the whales about us?" she said.

"Why not?"

She grinned faintly. "I guess there's no reason not to."

Two Notches wailed a question. **Are Anthony and Air Human copulating now?**

Not at present, Anthony replied.

We hope you will copulate often.

Philana, translating the speech on her own, laughed. "Tell them we hope so, too," she said.

And then she stiffened. Anthony's nerves poured fire. Philana turned to him and regarded him with Telamon's eyes.

"I thought you'd see reason," Telamon said. "*I'll surrender.* I like that."

Anthony looked at the possessed woman and groped for a vehicle for his message. Words seemed inadequate, he decided, but would have to do. "You haven't won yet," he said.

Philana's head cocked to one side as Telamon viewed him. "Has it occurred to you," Telamon said, "that if she's free of me, she won't need you at all?"

"You forget something. I'll be rid of *you* as well."

"You can be rid of me any time."

Anthony stared at Telamon for a moment, then suddenly he laughed. He had just realized how to send his message. Telamon looked at him curiously. Anthony turned to his computer deck and flipped to the Dweller translation file.

I/We, he typed, *live in the warm brightness above. We are new to this world, and send good wishes to the Dwellers below.*

Anthony pressed TRANSMIT. Rolling thunder boomed from the boat's speakers. The grammar was probably awful, Anthony knew, but he was fairly certain of the words, and he thought the meaning would be clear.

Telamon frowned, stepped to gaze over Anthony's shoulder.

Calls came from below. A translation tree appeared on the screen.

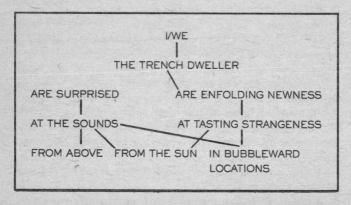

"Trench Dweller" was probably one of the Dwellers' names. "Bubbleward" was a phrase for "up," since bubbles rose to the surface. Anthony tapped the keys.

We are from far away, recently arrived. We are small and foreign to the world. We wish to brush the Dwellers with our thoughts. We regret our lack of clarity in diction.

"I wonder if you've thought this through," Telamon said.

Anthony hit TRANSMIT. Speakers boomed. The subsonics were like a punch in the gut.

"Go jump off a cliff," Anthony said.

"You're making a mistake," said Telamon.

The Dweller's answer was surprisingly direct.

```
                        WE
                        |
              ARE IN A CONDITION
                        |
            OF RISING BUBBLEWARD
                        |
         TO PERCEIVE ONE ANOTHER DIRECTLY
```

Anthony's heart crashed in astonishment. Could the Dwellers stand the lack of pressure on the surface? *I/We*, he typed, *Trench Dweller, proceed with consideration for safety. I/We recollect that we are small and weak.* He pressed TRANSMIT and flipped to the whalespeech file.

Deep Dweller rising to surface, he typed. *Run fast northward.*

The whales answered with cries of alarm. Flukes pounded the water. Anthony ran to the cabin and cranked the wheel hard to starboard. He increased speed to separate himself from the humpbacks. Behind him, Telamon stumbled in his unfamiliar body as the boat took the waves at a different angle.

Anthony returned to his computer console. *I/We are in a state of motion,* he reported. *Is living in the home of the light occasion for a condition of damage to us/Trench Dweller?*

"You're mad," said Telamon, and then Philana staggered. "He's done it *again*," she said in a stunned voice. She stepped to the starboard bench and sat down. "What's happening?" she asked.

"I'm talking to the Dwellers. One of them is rising to say hello."

"Now?"

He gave her a skeletal grin. "It's what you wanted, yes?" She stared at him.

I'm going over cliffs, he thought. One after another.

That, Anthony concluded, is the condition of existence. Subsonics rattled crockery in the kitchen.

```
BUBBLEWARD PLATEAU IS CONDITION
            FOR DAMAGE
                |
      DAMAGE IS ACCEPTABLE
```

Anthony typed, *I/We happily await greeting ourselves* and pressed TRANSMIT, then REPEAT. He would give the Dweller a sound to home in on.

"I don't understand," Philana said. He moved to join her on the bench, put his arm around her. She shrugged him off. "Tell me," she said. He took her hand.

"We're going to win."

"How?"

"I don't know yet."

She was too shaken to argue. "It's going to be a long fight," she said.

"I don't care."

Philana took a breath. "I'm scared."

"So am I," said Anthony.

The boat beat itself against the waves. The flying yacht followed, a silent shadow.

Anthony and Philana waited in silence until the Dweller

rose, a green-grey mass that looked as if a grassy reef had just calved. Foam roared from its back as it broke water, half an ocean running down its sides. Anthony's boat danced in the sudden white tide, and then the ocean stilled. Bits of the Dweller were all around, spread over the water for leagues—tentacles, filters, membranes. The Dweller's very mass had calmed the sea. The Dweller was so big, Anthony saw, it constituted an entire ecosystem. Sea creatures lived among its folds and tendrils: some had died as they rose, their swim bladders exploding in the release of pressure; others leaped and spun and shrank from the brightness above.

Sunlight shone from the Dweller's form, and the creature pulsed with life.

Terrified, elated, Philana and Anthony rose to say hello.

VIDEO STAR

I

Ric could feel the others closing in. They were circling outside the Falcon Quarter as if on midsummer thermals, watching the Cadillacs with glittering raptor eyes, occasionally swooping in to take a little nibble at Cadillac business, Cadillac turf, Cadillac sources. Testing their own strength as well as the Cadillac nerves, applying pressure just to see what would happen, find out if the Cadillacs still had it in them to respond . . .

Ric knew the game well: he and the other Cadillacs had played it five years before, up and down the streets and datancts of the Albaicín, half-grown kids testing their strength against the gangs entrenched in power, the Cruceros, the Jerusalem Rangers, the Piedras Blancas. The older gangs seemed slow, tentative, uncertain, and when the war came the Cadillacs won in a matter of days: the others were too entrenched, too visible, caught in a network of old connections, old associations, old manners . . . the young Cadillacs, coming up out of nowhere, found their own sources, their own products and connections, and in the end they and their allies gutted the old boys' organization, absorbing what was still useful and letting the rest die along with the remnants of the Cruceros, Rangers, and Blancas, the bewildered survivors who were still looking for a remaining piece of turf on which to make their last stand.

At the time Ric had given the Cadillacs three years before the same thing started happening to them, before their profile grew too high and the next generation of snipers rose in confidence and ability. The Cadillacs had in the end lasted five years, and that wasn't bad. But, Ric thought, it was over.

The other Cadillacs weren't ready to surrender. The heat was mounting, but they thought they could survive this challenge, hold out another year or two. They were dreaming, Ric thought.

During the hot dog days of summer, people began to die. Gunfire echoed from the pink walls of the Alhambra. Networks disintegrated. Allies disappeared. Ric made a proposition to the Cadillacs for a bank to be shared with their allies, a fund to keep the war going. The Cadillacs in their desperation agreed.

Ric knew then it was time to end it, that the Cadillacs had lost whatever they once had. If they agreed to a proposition like this, their nerve and their smarts were gone.

So there was a last meeting, Ric of the Cadillacs, Mares of the Squires, Jacob of the Last Men. Ric walked into the meeting with a radar-aimed dart gun built into the bottom of his briefcase, each dart filled with a toxin that would stop the heart in a matter of seconds. When he walked out it was with a money spike in his pocket, a stainless steel needle tipped with liquid crystal. In the heart of the crystal was data representing over eighty thousand Seven Moons dollars, ready for deposit into any electric account into which he could plug the needle.

West, Ric thought. He'd buy into an American condecology somewhere in California and enjoy retirement. He was twenty-two years old.

He began to feel sick in the Tangier to Houston suborbital shuttle, a crawling across his nerves, pinpricks in the flesh. By the time he crossed the Houston port to take his domestic flight to L.A. there were stabbing pains in his joints and behind his eyes. He asked a flight attendant for aspirin and chased the pills with American whiskey.

As the plane jetted west across Texas, Ric dropped his whiskey glass and screamed in sudden pain. The attendants gave him morphine analogue but the agony only increased, an acid boiling under his skin, a flame that gutted his body. His vision had gone and so had the rest of his senses except for the burning knowledge of his own pain. Ric tried to tear his arms open with his fingernails, pull the tortured nerves clean out of his body, and the attendants piled on him, holding him down, pinning him to the floor of the plane like a butterfly to a bed of cork.

As they strapped him into a stretcher at the unscheduled stop in Flagstaff, Ric was still screaming, unable to stop himself. Jacob had poisoned him, using a neurotoxin that stripped away the myelin sheathing on his nerves, leaving them raw cords of agonized fiber. Ric had been in a hurry to finish his business and had only taken a single sip of his wine: that was the only thing that had saved him.

2

He was months in the hospital in Flagstaff, staring out of a glass wall at a maze of other glass walls—office buildings and condecologies stacked halfway to Phoenix, flanking the silver alloy ribbon of an expressway. The snows fell heavily that winter, then in the spring melted away except for patches of white in the shadows. For the first three months he was completely immobile, his brain chemically isolated from his body to keep the pain away while he took an endless series of nerve grafts, drugs to encourage nerve replication and healing. Finally there was physical therapy that had him screaming in agony at the searing pain in his reawakened limbs.

At the end there was a new treatment, a new drug. It dripped into his arm slowly via an IV and he could feel a lightness in his nerves, a humming in his mind. Even the air seemed to taste better. The pain was no worse than usual and he felt better than he had since walking out of the meeting back in Granada with the money spike in his pocket.

"What's in the IV?" he asked, next time he saw the nurse.

The nurse smiled. "Everyone asks that," he said. "Genesios Three. We're one of the few hospitals that has the security to distribute the stuff."

"You don't say."

He'd heard of the drug while watching the news. Genesios Three was a new neurohormone, developed by the orbital Pink Blossom policorp, that could repair almost any amount of nerve damage. As a side effect it built additional neural connections in the brain, raising the IQ, and made people high. The hormone was rare because it was very complex and expensive to synthesize, though the gangs were trying. On the west coast lots of people had died in a war for control of the new black labs. On the street it was called Black Thunder.

"Not bad," said Ric.

The treatment and the humming in Ric's brain went on for a week. When it was over he missed it. He was also more or less healed.

3

The week of Genesios therapy took fifteen thousand dollars out of Ric's spike. The previous months of treatment had accounted for another sixty-two thousand. What Ric didn't know was that Genesios therapy could have been started at once and saved him most of his funds, but that the artificial intelligences working for the hospital had tagged him as a suspect character, an alien of no particular standing, with no work history, no policorporate citizenship, and a large amount of cash in his breast pocket. The AIs concluded that Ric was in no position to complain, and they were right.

Computers can't be sued for malpractice. The doctors followed their advice.

All that remained of Ric's money was three thousand SM dollars. Ric could live off of that for a few years, but it wasn't much of a retirement.

The hospital was nice enough to schedule an appointment for him with a career counselor, a woman who would find him a job. She worked in the basement of the vast glass hospital building, and her name was Marlene.

4

Marlene worked behind a desk littered with the artifacts of other people's lives. There were no windows in the office, two ashtrays, both full, and on the walls there were travel posters that showed long stretches of emptiness, white beaches, blue ocean, faraway clouds. Nothing alive.

Her green eyes had an opaque quality, as if she was watching a private video screen somewhere in her mind. She wore a lot of silver jewelry on her fingers and forearms and a grey rollneck sweater with cigarette burn marks. Her eyes bore elaborate makeup that looked like the wings of a Red Admirable. Her hair was almost blond. The only job she could find him was for a legal firm, something called assistant data evaluator.

Before Ric left Marlene's office he asked her to dinner. She turned him down without even changing expression. Ric had the feeling he wasn't quite real to her.

The job of assistant data evaluator consisted of spending the day walking up and down a four-story spiral staircase in the suite of a law firm, moving files from one office to another. The files were supposedly sensitive and not committed to the firm's computer lest someone attempt to steal them. The salary was insulting. Ric told the law firm that the job was just what he was looking for. They told him to start in two days.

Ric stopped into Marlene's office to tell her he got the job and to ask her to dinner again. She laughed, for what reason he couldn't tell, and said yes.

A slow spring snowfall dropped onto the streets while they ate dinner. With her food Marlene took two red capsules and a yellow pill, grew lively, drank a lot of wine. He walked her home through the snow to her apartment on the seventh floor of an old fourth-rate condeco, a place with water stains on the ceiling and bare bulbs hanging in the halls, the only home she could afford. In the hallway Ric brushed snow from her shoulders and hair and kissed her. He took Marlene to bed and tried to prove to her that he was real.

The next day he checked out of the hospital and moved in.

5

Ric hadn't bothered to show up on his first day as an assistant data evaluator. Instead he'd spent the day in Marlene's condeco, asking her home comp to search library files and print out everything relating to what the scansheets in their willful ignorance called "Juvecrime." Before Marlene came home Ric called the most expensive restaurant he could find and told them to deliver a five-course meal to the apartment.

The remains of the meal were stacked in the kitchen. Ric paced back and forth across the small space, his mind humming with the information he'd absorbed. Marlene sat on an adobe-colored couch and watched, a wine glass in one hand and a cigarette in the other, silhouetted by the glass self-polarizing wall that showed the bright aluminum-alloy expressway cutting south across melting piles of snow. Plans were vibrating in Ric's mind, nothing firm yet, just neurons stirring on the edge of his awareness, forming fast-mutating combinations. He could feel the tingle, the high, the half-formed ideas as they flickered across neural circuits.

Marlene reached into a dispenser and took out a red pill and a green capsule with orange stripes. Ric looked at her. "How much of that stuff do you take, anyway? Is it medication, or what?"

"I've got anxieties." She put the pills into her mouth, and with a shake of her head dry-swallowed them.

"How big a dose?"

"It's not the dose that matters. It's the proper *combination* of doses. Get it right and the world feels like a lovely warm swimming pool. It's like floating underwater and still being able to breathe. It's wonderful."

"If you say so." He resumed his pacing. Fabric scratched his bare feet. His mind hummed, a blur of ideas that hadn't yet taken shape, flickering, assembling, dissolving without his conscious thought.

"You didn't show up for work," Marlene said. "They gave me a call about that."

"Sorry."

"How are you gonna afford this taste you have for expensive food?" Marlene asked. "Without working, I mean."

"Do something illegal," Ric said. "Most likely."

"That's what I thought." She looked up at him, sideways. "You gonna let me play?"

"If you want."

Marlene swallowed half her wine, looked at the littered apartment, shrugged.

"Only if you really want," Ric said. "It has to be a thing you decide."

"What else have I got to do?" she said.

"I'm going to have to do some research, first," he said. "Spend a few days accessing the library."

Marlene was looking at him again. "Boredom," she said. "In your experience, is that why most people turn to crime?"

"In my experience," he said, "most people turn to crime because of stupidity."

She grinned. "That's cool," she said. "That's sort of what I figured." She lit a cigarette. "You have a plan?"

"Something I can only do once. Then every freak in Western America is going to be looking for me with a machine gun."

Marlene grinned. "Sounds exciting."

He looked at her. "Remember what I said about stupidity."

She laughed. "I've been smart all my life. What's it ever got me?"

Ric, looking down at her, felt a warning resonate through him, like an unmistakable taste drawn across his tongue. "You've got a lot to lose, Marlene," he said. "A lot more than I do."

"Shit. Motherfucker." The cigarette had burned her fingers. She squashed it in the ashtray, too fast, spilling ashes on the couch. Ric watched her for a moment, then went back to his thinking.

People were dying all over California in a war over the neurohormone Genesios Three. There had to be a way to take advantage of it.

6

"You a cop, buck?"

The style was different from the people Ric knew in

Iberia. In Granada, Ric had worn a gaucho mode straight from Argentina, tight pants with silver dollars sewn down the seams, sashes wound around nipped-in waists, embroidered vests.

He didn't know what was worn by the people who had broken up the Cadillacs. He'd never seen any of them.

Here the new style was something called Urban Surgery. The girl bore the first example Ric had ever seen close up. The henna-red hair was in cornrows, braided with transparent plastic beads holding fast-mutating phosphorescent bacteria that constantly re-formed themselves in glowing patterns. The nose had been broadened and flattened to cover most of the cheeks, turning the nostrils into a pair of lateral slits, the base of the nose wider than the mouth. The teeth had been replaced by alloy transplants sharp as razors that clacked together in a precise, unpleasant way when she closed her mouth. The eyebrows were gone altogether and beneath them were dark plastic implants that covered the eye sockets. Ric couldn't tell, and probably wasn't supposed to know, whether there were eyes in there anymore, or sophisticated scanners tagged to the optic nerve.

The effect was to flatten the face, turn it into a canvas for the tattoo artist who had covered every inch of exposed flesh. Complex mathematical statements ran over the forehead. Below the black plastic eye implants were urban skyscapes, silhouettes of buildings providing a false horizon across the flattened nose. The chin appeared to be a circuit diagram.

Ric looked into the dark eye sockets and tried not to flinch. "No," he said. "I'm just passing through."

One of her hands was on the table in front of him. It was tattooed as completely as the face and the fingernails had been replaced by alloy razors, covered with transparent plastic safety caps.

"I saw you in here yesterday," she said. "And again today. I was wondering if you want something."

He shrugged. It occurred to him that, repellent as Urban

Surgery was, it was fine camouflage. Who was going to be able to tell one of these people from another?

"You're a little old for this place, buck," the girl said. He figured her age as about fourteen. She was small-waisted and had narrow hips and large breasts. Ric did not find her attractive.

This was his second trip to Phoenix. The bar didn't have a name, unless it was simply BAR, that being all that was said on the sign outside. It was below street level, in the storage cellar of an old building. Concrete walls were painted black. Dark plastic tables and chairs had been added, and bare fluorescent tubes decorated the walls. Speaker amps flanked the bar, playing cold electronic music devoid of noticeable rhythm or melody.

He looked at the girl and leaned closer to her. "I need your permission to drink here, or what?" he said.

"No," she said. "Just to deal here."

"I'm not dealing," he said. "I'm just observing the passing urban scene, okay?" He was wearing a lightweight summer jacket of a cream color over a black T-shirt with Cyrillic lettering, black jeans, white sneakers. Nondescript street apparel.

"You got credit?" the girl asked.

"Enough."

"Buy me a drink then?"

He grinned. "I need your permission to deal, and you don't have any credit? What kind of outlaw are you?"

"A thirsty outlaw."

Ric signaled the bartender. Whatever it was that he brought her looked as if it was made principally out of cherry soda.

"Seriously," she said. "I can pay you back later. Someone I know is supposed to meet me here. He owes me money."

"My name's Marat," said Ric. "With a silent *t*."

"I'm Super Virgin. You from Canada or something? You talk a little funny."

"I'm from Switzerland."

Super Virgin nodded and sipped her drink. Ric glanced around the bar. Most of the patrons wore Urban Surgery or at least made an effort in the direction of its style. Super Virgin frowned at him.

"You're supposed to ask if I'm really cherry," she said. "If you're wondering, the drink should give you a clue."

"I don't care," Ric said.

She grinned at him with her metal teeth. "You don't wanna ball me?"

Ric watched his dual reflection, in her black eye sockets, slowly shake its head. She laughed. "I like a guy who knows what he likes," she said. "That's the kind we have in Cartoon Messiah. Can I have another drink?"

There was an ecology in kid gangs, Ric knew. They had different reasons for existing and filled different functions. Some wanted turf, some trade, some the chance to prove their ideology. Some moved information, and Ric's research indicated that that seemed to be Cartoon Messiah's function.

But even if Cartoon Messiah were smart, they hadn't been around very long. A perpetual problem with groups of young kids involving themselves in gang activities was that they had very short institutional memories. There were a few things they wouldn't recognize or know to prepare for, not unless they'd been through them at least once. They made up for it by being faster than the opposition, by being more invisible.

Ric was hoping Cartoon Messiah was full of young, fresh minds.

He signaled the bartender again. Super Virgin grinned at him.

"You sure you don't wanna ball me?"

"Positive."

"I'm gonna be cherry till I die. I'm just not interested. None of the guys seem like anybody I'd want to fuck." Ric didn't say anything. She sipped the last of her drink. "You think I'm repulsive-looking, right?"

"That seems to be your intention."

She laughed. "You're okay, Marat. What's it like in Switzerland?"

"Hot."

"So hot you had to leave, maybe?"

"Maybe."

"You looking for work?"

"Not yet. Just looking around."

She leaned closer to him. "You find out anything interesting while you're looking, I'll pay you for it. Just leave a message here, at the Bar."

"You deal in information?"

She licked her lips. "That and other things. This Bar, see, it's in a kind of interface. North of here is Lounge Lizard turf, south and east are the Cold Wires, west is the Silicon Romantics. The Romantics are on their way out." She gave a little sneer. "They're brocade commandos, right?—their turf's being cut up. But here, it's no-gang's-land. Where things get moved from one buyer to another."

"Cartoon Messiah—they got turf?"

She shook her head. "Just places where we can be found. Territory is not what we're after. Two-Fisted Jesus—he's our sort-of chairman—he says only stupid people like brocade boys want turf, when the real money's in data."

Ric smiled. "That's smart. Property values are down, anyway."

He could see his reflection in her metal teeth, a pale smear. "You got anything you wanna deal in, I can set it up," she said. "Software? Biologicals? Pharmaceuticals? Wetware?"

"I have nothing. Right now."

She turned to look at a group of people coming in the door. "Cold Wires," she said. "These are the people I'm supposed to meet." She tipped her head back and swallowed the rest of her drink. "They're so goddam bourgeois," she said. "Look—their surgery's fake, it's just good makeup. And the tattoos—they spray 'em on through a stencil. I hate people who don't have the courage of their convictions, don't you?"

"They can be useful, though." Smiling, thin-lipped.

She grinned at him. "Yeah. They can. Stop by tomorrow and I'll pay you back, okay? See ya." She pushed her chair back, scraping alloy on the concrete floor, a small metal scream.

Ric sipped his drink, watching the room. Letting its rhythm seep through his skin. Things were firming in his mind.

7

"Hi."

The security guard looked up at him from under the plastic brim of his baseball cap. He frowned. "Hi. You need something? I seen you around before."

"I'm Warren Whitmore," Ric said. "I'm recovering from an accident, going to finish the course of treatment soon. Go out into the real world." Whitmore was one of Ric's former neighbors, a man who'd had his head split in half by a falling beam. He hadn't left any instructions about radical life preservation measures and the artificial intelligences who ran the hospital were going to keep him alive till they burned up the insurance and then the family's money.

"Yeah?" the guard said. "Congratulations." There was a plastic tape sewed on over the guard's breast pocket that said LYSAGHT.

"The thing is, I don't have a job waiting. Cigar?"

Ric had seen Lysaght smoking big stogies outside the hospital doors. They wouldn't let him light up inside. Ric had bought him the most expensive Havanas available at the hospital gift shop.

Lysaght took the cigar, rolled it between his fingers while he looked left and right down the corridor, trying to decide whether to light it or not. Ric reached for his lighter.

"I had some military training in my former life," Ric said. "I thought I might look into the idea of getting into the security business, once I get into the world. Could I buy you a drink, maybe, after you get off shift? Talk about what you do."

Lysaght drew on the cigar, still looking left and right, seeing only patients. He was a big fleshy man, about forty, dressed in a black uniform with body armor sewn into pockets on his chest and back. His long dark hair was slicked back behind his ears, falling over his shoulders in greased ringlets. His sideburns came to points. A brushed-alloy gun with a hardwood custom grip and a laser sight hung conspicuously on one hip, next to the gas grenades, next to the plastic handwrap restraints, next to the combat staff, next to the portable gas mask.

"Sure," Lysaght said. "Why not?" He blew smoke in the general direction of an elderly female patient walking purposefully down the corridor in flowery pajamas. The patient blinked but kept walking.

"Hey, Mrs. Calderone, how you doin'?" Lysaght said. Mrs. Calderone ignored him. "Fuckin' head case," said Lysaght.

"I want to work for a sharp outfit though," Ric said. He looked at Lysaght's belt. "With good equipment and stuff, you know?"

"That's Folger Security," Lysaght said. "If we weren't good, we wouldn't be working for a hospital this size."

During his time in the Cadillacs and elsewhere, Ric had been continually surprised by how little it actually took to bribe someone. A few drinks, a few cigars, and Lysaght was working for him. And Lysaght didn't even know it yet. Or, with luck, ever.

"Listen," Lysaght was saying. "I gotta go smoke this in the toilet. But I'll see you at the guard station around five, okay?"

"Sounds good."

8

That night, his temples throbbing with pain, Ric entered
Marlene's condeco and walked straight to the kitchen for
something to ease the long raw ache that coated the insides
of his throat. He could hear the sounds of *Alien Inquisitor*
on the vid. He was carrying a two-liter plastic bottle of
industrial-strength soap he'd just stolen from the custodian's
storeroom here in Marlene's condeco. He put down the
bottle of soap, rubbed his sore shoulder muscle, took some
whiskey from the shelf, and poured it into a tall glass. He
took a slow, deliberate drink and winced as he felt the fire
in his throat. He added water to the glass. *Alien Inquisitor*
diminished in volume, then he heard the sound of Marlene's
flipflops slapping against her heels.

Her eyes bore the heavy eye makeup she wore to work.
"Jesus," Marlene said. She screwed up her face. "You
smell like someone's been putting out cigarettes in your
pockets. Where the hell have you been?"

"Smoking cigars with a rentacop. He wears so much
equipment and armor he has to wear a truss, you know that?
He got drunk and told me."

"Which rentacop?"

"One who works for the hospital."

"The hospital? We're going to take off the hospital?"
Marlene shook her head. "That's pretty serious, Ric."

Ric was wondering if she'd heard *take off* used that way
on the vid. "Yes." He eased the whiskey down his throat
again. Better.

"Isn't that dangerous? Taking off the same hospital where
you were a patient?"

"We're not going to be doing it in person. We're going to
have someone else do the work."

"Who?"

"Cartoon Messiah, I think. They're young and promising."

"What's the stuff in the plastic bottle for?"

He looked at her, swirling the whiskey absently in the glass. "This cleaner's mostly potassium hydroxide," he said. "That's wood lye. You can use it to make plastic explosive."

Marlene shrugged, then reached in her pocket for a cigarette. Ric frowned. "You seem not to be reacting to that, Marlene," he said. "Robbing a hospital is serious, plastic explosive isn't?"

She blew smoke at him. "Let me show you something." She went back into the living room and then returned with her pouch belt. She fished in it for a second, then threw him a small aerosol bottle.

Ric caught it and looked at the label. "Holy fuck," he said. He blinked and looked at the bottle again. "Jesus Christ."

"Ten-ounce aerosol bottle of mustard gas," Marlene said. "Sixteen dollars in Starbright scrip at your local boutique. For personal protection, you know? The platinum designer bottle costs more."

Ric was blinking furiously. "Holy fuck," he said again.

"Some sixteen-year-old asshole tried to rape me once," Marlene said. "I hit him with the gas and now he's reading braille. You know?"

Ric took another sip of the whiskey and then wordlessly placed the mustard gas in Marlene's waiting palm. "You're in America now, Ric," Marlene said. "You keep forgetting that, singing your old Spanish marching songs."

He rubbed his chin. "Right," he said. "I've got to make adjustments."

"Better do it soon," Marlene said, "if you're going to start busting into hospitals."

9

The next day Ric went to the drugstore, where he purchased a large amount of petroleum jelly, some nasal mist that came in squeeze bottles, liquid bleach, a bottle of toilet cleaner, a small amount of alcohol-based lamp fuel, and a bottle of glycerin. Then he drove to a chemical supply store, where he brought some distilling equipment and some litmus paper.

On his way back he stopped by an expensive liquor store and bought some champagne. He didn't want the plastic bottles the domestic stuff came in; instead he bought the champagne imported from France, in glass bottles with the little hollow cone in the bottom. It was the biggest expense of the day.

Back in Marlene's apartment he opened the tops of the nasal inhalers and drained the contents into the sink. He cleaned each and set them out to dry. He set up his distilling equipment, mixing the toilet-bowl cleaner with the liquid bleach, then bubbled the resulting chlorine gas through the wood lye until the litmus paper showed it had been neutralized. He emptied the stuff into a pan and brought it to a simmer on the stove. When crystals began forming he took it off the burner and let the pan cool. He repeated the process two more times and, in the end, he had almost pure potassium chlorate. Ric then mixed the potassium chlorate with petroleum jelly to make plastic explosive. He put it in an old coffee can in the refrigerator.

Feeling pleased with his handiwork, he opened a bottle of champagne to celebrate. He drank a glass and then set up his distilling equipment again.

He put glycerine and some of the toilet bowl cleaner in a flask, mixed it, then put it over a flame. He distilled out a couple ounces of acrolein and then put the chemical in the empty nasal spray containers. He capped them. He drank another glass of champagne, put away all his materials, and turned on the vid. Something called *Video Vixens* was just starting. Ric settled into his chair. He hadn't seen that one.

10

"I made plastic explosive today," Ric said. "It's in the icebox."

"Great." Marlene had just come home from work and was tired. She was drinking champagne and waiting for the night's pills to kick in.

"I'll show you a trick," Ric said. He got some twine from the cupboard, cut it into strips, and soaked it in the lamp fuel. While it was soaking he got a large mixing bowl and filled it with water and ice. Then he tied the string around the empty champagne bottles, about three inches above the topmost point of the little hollow cone on the bottom. He got his lighter and set fire to the thread. It burned slowly, with a cool blue flame, for a couple minutes. Then he took the bottle and plunged it into the ice water. It split neatly in half with a crystalline snapping sound.

Ric took some of the plastic explosive and packed it into the bottom of the champagne bottle. He pushed a pencil into the middle of it, making a narrow hole for the detonator.

"There," he said. "That's a shaped charge. I'll make the detonators tomorrow, out of peroxide, acetone, and sulphuric acid. It's easy."

"What's a shaped charge, Ricardo?"

"It's used for blowing a hole through armor. Steel doors, cars. Tanks. Things like that."

Marlene looked at him appraisingly. "You're adjusting yourself to America, all right," she said.

Ric took a bus to Phoenix and rented a motel room with a kitchenette, paying five days in advance and using a false name. In the motel he changed clothes and took a cab to the Bar. Super Virgin waved as he came in. She was with her friend, Captain Islam. He was a long, gawky boy, about sixteen, with his head shaved and covered with the tattoos of Urban Surgery. He hadn't had any alterations yet, or the eye implants this group favored—instead he wore compli- cated mirrorshades with twin minicameras mounted above the bridge of the nose. They registered radiation in UV and infrared as well as the normal spectrum and featured liquid-crystal video displays on the backs of the eyepieces that received input from the minicameras or from any vid program he felt like seeing. Ric wondered if things weren't real to him, not unless he saw them on the vid. Captain Islam didn't talk much, just sat quietly behind his drink and his shades and watched whatever it was that he watched. The effect was unsettling and was probably meant to be. Ric could be talking to him and would never know whether the man was looking at him or at *Video Vixens*. Ric had first pegged him for a user, but Super Virgin said not.

Ric got a whiskey at the bar and joined the two at their table. "Slow night?" he asked.

"We're waiting for the jai alai to come on," Super Virgin said. "Live from Bilbao. We've got some money down."

"Sounds slow to me."

She gave a brittle laugh. "Guess so, Marat. You got any ideas for accelerating our motion?"

Ric frowned. "I have something to sell. Some informa- tion. But I don't know if it's something you'd really want to deal with."

"Too hot?" The words were Captain Islam's. Ric looked at his own distorted face in the Captain's spectacles.

"Depends on your concept of *hot*. The adjective I had in mind was *big*."

"Big." The word came with a pause before and after, as if Captain Islam had never heard the word before and was wondering what it meant.

Ric took a bottle of nasal mist out of his pocket and squeezed it once up each nostril.

"Got a virus?" Virgin asked.

"I'm allergic to Arizona."

Captain Islam was frowning. "So what's this action of yours, buck?" he asked.

"Several kilos of Thunder."

Captain Islam continued to stare into the interior of his mirrors. Super Virgin burst into laughter.

"I knew you weren't a fucking tourist, Marat!" she cackled. " 'Several kilos'! *One* kilo is weight! What the hell is 'several'?"

"I don't know if you people can move that much," Ric said. "Also, I'd like an agreement. I want twenty percent of the take, and I want you to move my twenty percent for me, free of charge. If you think you can move that kind of weight at all, that is." He sipped his whiskey. "Maybe I should talk to some people in California."

"You talk to them, you end up dead," Virgin said. "They're not friendly to anyone these days, not when Thunder's involved."

Ric smiled. "Maybe you're right."

"Where is it? Who do we have to steal it from?"

"Another thing," Ric said. "I want certain agreements. I don't want any excessive force used, here. Nobody shot."

"Sometimes things happen," Captain Islam said. Ric had the feeling that the Captain was definitely looking at him this time. "Sometimes things can't be avoided."

"This stuff is guarded by an organization who won't forget it if any of their people get hurt," Ric explained. "If you try to move this kind of weight, word's going to get out that it's you that has the Thunder, and that means these characters are going to find out sooner or later. You might be tempted to give me to them as a way of getting the heat off you. Which would be a mistake, because I intend on establishing an alibi. That would mean that they're going to be extremely upset with you misleading them." Ric sipped his whiskey and smiled. "I'm just looking out for all our interests."

"A hospital," Captain Islam said. He shook his head. "You want us to take off a hospital. The one up in Flag, right? You stupid shit."

"I have a plan," Ric said. "I know their defenses, to a certain point. I know how they're organized. I know how they *think*."

"That's Folger Security, for chrissake," Captain Islam said. "They're tough. They don't forget when someone makes idiots out of them."

"That's why it's got to be my rules," Ric said. "But I should probably mention something, here." He grinned, seeing the smile reflected in the Captain's quicksilver eyes. "It's an inside job," Ric said. "I'm friends with someone on their force."

Virgin whooped and banged him on the shoulder with her left hand, the one with the sheathed claws. "Why didn't you say so?" she said.

"You people," Ric said. "You've got to learn to be patient."

12

Treble whimpered against a throbbing bass line. Shafts of red sunset sliced into the violet depths of the Grand Canyon. Marlene backed, spun, turned back to Ric, touched palms. She was wearing Indian war paint. Colors zigzagged across her face. Her eyes and smile were bright.

The band was dressed like hussars, lights glittering off brocade, the lead singer sweating under her dolman, threatening to split her tight breeches with each of her leaps. Her eye makeup dazzled like butterfly wings. Her lyrics were all heroism, thunder, revolution. The romantic wave against which Cartoon Messiah and Urban Surgery were a cool reaction.

Marlene stepped forward, pressing herself against him. He circled her with his arms, felt her sacral dimples as they leaned back and spun against each other. At the end of the five-bar chorus she gave a grind of her hips against him, then winked.

He laughed. While he was establishing his alibi, Cartoon Messiah were working for him back in Flagstaff. And they didn't even know it.

13

Readiness crackled from Ric's nerves as he approached the hotel door. They could try to kill him, he knew. Now would be the best time. Black Thunder tended to generate that kind of behavior. He'd been telling them he had ideas for other jobs, that he'd be valuable to them alive, but he couldn't be sure if they believed him.

The door opened and Super Virgin grinned at him with her metal teeth. "Piece of cake, Marat," she said. "Your cut's on the table."

The hotel room was dark, the walls draped in blueblack plastic. More plastic sheets covered the floors, the ceiling, some of the furniture. Coldness touched Ric's spine. There could be a lot of blood spilled in here, and the plastic would keep it from getting on anything. Computer consoles and vid sets gave off quiet hums. Cables snaked over the floor, held down with duct tape. On a table was a half-kilo white paper packet. Captain Islam and Two-Fisted Jesus sat beside it, tapping into a console. Jesus looked up.

"Just in time," he said, "for the movies."

He was a skinny boy, about eighteen, his identity obscured by the obsessive mutilations of Urban Surgery. He wore a T-shirt featuring a picture of a muscular, bearded man in tights, with cape and halo. Here in this place, the hotel room he had hung with plastic and filled with electronics, he moved and spoke with an assurance the others hadn't absorbed, the kind of malevolent grace displayed by those who gave law and style to others, unfettered by conscience. Ric could appreciate Jesus' moves. He'd had them once himself.

Rick walked to the paper packet and hefted it. He tore open a corner, saw a row of little white envelopes, each labeled Genesios Three with the pharmaceutical company sigil in the corner. He didn't know a test for B-44 so he just stuffed the envelope in his pocket.

"This is gonna be great," Super Virgin said. She came up behind him and handed him a highball glass half-filled with whiskey. "You got time to watch the flick? We went in packing cameras. We're gonna cut a documentary of the whole thing and sell it to a station in Nogales. They'll write some scenes around it and use it on an episode of *VidWar*." She giggled. "The Mexicans don't care how many gringo hospitals get taken off. They'll put some kind of plot around it. A dumb love story or something. But it's the highest-rated program, 'cause people know it's real. Except for *Australian Rules Firefight Football*, and that's real, too."

Ric looked around and found a chair. It seemed as if these people planned to let him live. He reached into his pocket and fired a round of nasal mist up each nostril. "Sure. I'll watch," he sniffed. "I got time."

"This is a rough cut only, okay?" Captain Islam's voice. "So bear with us."

There was a giant-sized liquid-crystal vid display set up on the black plastic on the wall. A picture sizzled into existence. The hospital, a vast concrete fortress set in an aureole of halogen light. Ric felt his tongue go dry. He swallowed with difficulty.

The image moved, jolting. Whoever was carrying the camera was walking, fast, across the parking lot. Two-Fisted Jesus tapped the keys of his computer. The image grew smooth. "We're using a lot of computer enhancement on the vid, see?" Super Virgin said. "We can smooth out the jitters from the moving camera. Except for select bits to enhance the ver—the versi—"

"Verisimilitude," said Captain Islam.

"Right. Just to let everyone know this is the real thing. And we're gonna change everyone's appearance electronically, so no one can recognize us."

Cut to someone moving into the hospital's front door, moving right past the metal detectors. Ric saw a tall girl, blond, dressed in pink shorts and a tube top. White sandal straps coiled about her ankles.

"A mercenary," Virgin said. "We hired her for this. The slut."

Captain Islam laughed. "She's an actress," he explained. "Trying for a career south of the border. Wants the publicity."

The girl stepped up to a guard. Ric recognized Lysaght. She was asking directions, pointing. Lysaght was gazing at her breasts as he replied. She smiled and nodded and walked past. He looked after her, chewed his cigar, hiked up his gunbelt. Ric grinned. As long as guards like Lysaght were around, nothing was safe.

The point of view changed abruptly, a subjective shot, someone moving down a hospital corridor. Patients in ordinary clothes moving past, smiling.

"We had a camera in this necklace she was wearing. A gold owl, about an inch long, with 3D vidcams behind the eyes. Antenna in the chain, receiver in her bag. We pasted it to her chest so it would always be looking straight forward and wouldn't get turned around or anything. Easy stuff."

"We gotta do some pickups, here," Jesus said. "Get a picture of the girl moving down a corridor. Then we tell the computer to put all the stripes on the walls. It'll be worth more when we sell it."

Subjective shot of someone moving into a woman's toilet, stepping into a stall, reaching into handbag for a pair of coveralls.

"Another pickup shot," Jesus muttered. "Gotta get her putting on her coveralls." He made a note on a pad.

The point of view lurched upward, around, out of the stall. Centered on a small ventilator intake high on a wall. Hands came into the picture, holding a screwdriver.

"Methanethiol," Super Virgin said. "That stuff's gonna be real useful from now on. How'd you know how to make it?"

"Elementary chemistry," Ric said. He'd used it to clear out political meetings of which the Cadillacs didn't approve.

The screen was off the ventilator. Hands were reaching into the bag, taking out a small glass bottle. Carefully loosening the screw top. The hands placed the bottle upright in the ventilator. Then the point of view dipped, a hand reached down to pick up the ventilator screen. Then the ventilator screen was shoved violently into the hole, knocking the bottle over.

Airborne methanethiol gave off a horrible, nauseating smell at one-fiftieth of a part per billion. The psychology wing of the hospital was going to get a dose considerably in excess of that.

The subjective camera was moving with great rapidity down hospital corridors. To a stairwell, then down.

Cut to Super Virgin in a phone booth. She had a small voice recorder in her hand, and was punching buttons.

"Freeze that," said Two-Fisted Jesus. Virgin's image turned to ice. Jesus began tapping keys.

The tattooing shifted, dissolved to a different pattern. Super Virgin laughed. Her hair shortened, turned darker. The black insets over her eyes vanished. Brown eyes appeared, then they turned a startling pale blue.

"Leave the teeth," she said.

"Nah. I have an idea." Two-Fisted Jesus sat tapping keys for about thirty seconds. He pressed the Enter button and the metal teeth disappeared completely. He moved the picture forward a second, then back. Virgin's tongue moved readily behind her tattooed lips. The interior of the mouth was pink, a lot of gum, no teeth at all. She clapped her hands.

"That's strange, man," she said. "I like that."

"The Mexicans will probably replace her image with some vidstar, anyway," Captain Islam said. "Urban Surgery is too much for them, right now."

"Okay. I want to see this in three dimensions," Jesus said. Super Virgin's image detached itself from the background and began rotating. He stopped it every so often and made small adjustments.

"Make me taller," Super Virgin said. "And skinnier. And give me smaller tits. I hate my tits."

"We do that every time," Jesus said. "People are gonna start to twig."

"Chrome tits. Leather tits. Anything."

Captain Islam laughed. Two-Fisted Jesus made minor adjustments and ignored Super Virgin's complaints.

"Here we go. Say your line."

The image began moving. Virgin's new green eyes sparkled as she held the recorder up to the mouthpiece of the telephone.

"This is Royal Flag." It was the name of one of Arizona's more ideological kid gangs. The voice had been electronically altered and sounded flat. "We've just planted a poison gas bomb in your psychology wing. All the head cases are gonna see Jesus. The world's gene pool will be much healthier from now on. Have yourself a pleasant day."

Super Virgin was laughing. "Wait'll you see the crowd scenes. Stellar stuff, believe me."

"I believe," said Ric.

14

The video was full of drifting smoke. Vague figures moved through it. Jesus froze the picture and tried to enhance the images, without any success. "Shit," he said. "More pickups."

Ric had watched the action as members of Cartoon Messiah in Folger Security uniforms had hammered their way into a hospital back door. They had moved faultlessly through the corridors to the vault and blasted their way in with champagne-bottle–shaped charges. The blasts had set off tremblor alarms in the vault and the Folger people realized they were being hit. Now the raiders were in the corridor before the vault, retracing their steps at a run.

"Okay," Super Virgin said. "The moment of truth, coming up."

The corridor was full of billowing tear gas. Crouched figures moved through it. Commands were yammering down the monitored Folger channels. Then, coming through the smoke, another figure. A tall woman in a helmet, her hand pressed to her ear, trying to hear the radio. There was a gun in her hand. She raised the gun.

Thuds on the sound track. Tear-gas canisters, fired at short range. One of them struck the woman in her armored chest and bounced off. It hadn't flown far enough to arm itself and it just rolled down the corridor. The woman fell flat.

"Just knocked the wind out of her." Captain Islam was grinning. "How about that for keeping our deal, huh?" Somebody ran forward and kicked the gun out of her hand. The camera caught a glimpse of her lying on the floor, her mouth open, trying to breathe. There were dots of sweat on her nose. Her eye makeup looked like butterfly wings.

"Now that's what I call poignant," Jesus said. "Human interest stuff. You know?"

The kids ran away across the parking lot, onto their fuelcell tricycles, and away, bouncing across the parking lot and the railroad tracks beyond.

"We're gonna spice this up a bit," Jesus said. "Cut in some shots of guards shooting at us, that kind of thing. Steal some suspenseful music. Make the whole thing more exciting. What do you think?"

"I like it," said Ric. He put down his untasted whiskey. Jacob and his neurotoxin had made him cautious. "Do I get any royalties? Being scriptwriter and all?"

"The next deal you set up for us. Maybe."

Ric shrugged. "How are you gonna move the Thunder?"

"Small pieces, probably."

"Let me give you some advice," Ric said. "The longer you hang on to it, the bigger the chance Folger will find out you have it and start cramping your action. I have an idea. Can you handle a large increase of capital?"

15

"Is this the stuff? Great." Marlene swept in the motel room door, grinning, with her overnight bag. She gave Ric a brief hug, then went to the table of the kitchenette. She picked up the white packet, hefted it in her hand.

"Light," she said.

"Yeah."

"I can't believe people kill each other over this."

"They could kill *us*," Ric said. "Don't forget that."

Marlene licked her lips and peeled the packet. She took one of the small white envelopes and tore it open, spilling dark powder into her cupped palm. She cocked her head.

"Doesn't look like much. How do you take it?"

Ric remembered the flood of well-being in his body, the way the world had suddenly tasted better. No, he thought. He wasn't going to get hung up on Thunder. "Intravenous, mostly," he said. "Or they could put it in capsules."

Marlene sniffed at it. "Doesn't smell like anything. What's the dose?"

"I don't know. I wasn't planning on taking any."

She began licking in her palm. Ric watched her little pink tongue lapping at the powder. He turned his eyes away.

"Take it easy," he said.

"Tastes funny. Kind of like green pepper sauce, with a touch of kerosene."

"A touch of stupidity," he said. "A touch of . . ." He moved around the room, hands in his pockets. "A touch of craziness. People who are around Black Thunder get crazy."

Marlene finished licking her palm and kicked off her shoes. "Craziness sounds good," she said. She stepped up behind him and put her arms around him. "How crazy do you think we can get tonight?"

"I don't know." He thought for a minute. "Maybe I could show you our movie."

16

Ric faced the window in the motel room, watching, his mind humming. The window had been dialed to polarize completely and he could see himself, Marlene behind him on the untidy bed, the plundered packet of Thunder on the table. It had been eight days since the hospital had been robbed. Marlene had taken the bus to Phoenix every evening.

"You should try some of our product," Marlene said. "The stuff's just . . . when I use it, I can feel my mind just start to click. Move faster, smoother. Thoughts come out of nowhere."

"Right," Ric said. "Nowhere."

Ric saw Marlene's reflection look up at his own dark plateglass ghost. "Do I detect sarcasm, here?"

"No. Preoccupation, that's all."

"Half the stuff's mine, right? I can eat it, burn it, drop it out the window. Drop it on your head, if I want to. Right?"

"That is correct," said Ric.

"Things are getting dull," Marlene said. "You're spending your evenings off drinking with Captain Islam and

Super Virgin and Krishna Commando . . . I get to stay here and watch the vid."

"Those people I'm drinking with," Ric said. "There's a good chance they could die because of what we're going to do. They're our victims. Would you like to have a few drinks with them? A few smokes?" He turned from the window and looked at her. "Knowing they may die because of you?"

Marlene frowned up at him. "Are you scared of them?" she asked. "Is that why you're talking like this?"

Ric gave a short laugh. Marlene ran her fingers through her almost-blond hair. Ric watched her in the mirror.

"You don't have to involve yourself in this part, Marlene," Ric said. "I can do it by myself, I think."

She was looking at the darkened vid screen. Her eyes were bright. A smile tugged at her lips.

"I'm ready," she said. "Let's do it."

"I've got to get some things ready first."

"Hurry up. I don't want to waste this feeling I've got."

Ric closed his eyes. He didn't want to see his reflection anymore. "What feeling is that?" he asked.

"The feeling that my time is coming. To try something new."

"Yeah," Ric said. His eyes were still closed. "That's what I thought."

17

Ric, wearing leather gardener's gloves, smoothed the earth over the plastic-wrapped explosive device he had just buried under a pyracantha bush. He was crouched in the shadow of a vacation cabin. Drizzle rattled off his collar. His knees were growing wet. He took the aerial for the radio detonator and pulled it carefully along one of the stems of the bush.

Marlene stood next to him in red plastic boots. She was

standing guard, snuffling in the cold. Ric could hear the sound of her lips as she chewed gum.

White shafts of light tracked over their heads, filtered by juniper scrub that stood between the cabins and the expressway heading north out of Flagstaff. Ric froze. His form, caught among pyracantha barbs, cast a stark moving shadow on the peeling white wall.

"Flashlight," he said, when the car had passed. Moving between the light and any onlookers, Marlene flicked it on. Ric carefully smoothed the soil, spread old leaves. He thought the thorns on the pyracantha would keep most people away, but he didn't want disturbed soil attracting anyone.

Rain danced down in the yellow light. "Thanks," he said. Marlene popped a bubble. Ric stood up, brushing muck from his knees. There were more bundles to bury, and it was going to be a long, wet night.

18

"They're going to take you off if they can," Ric said. "They're from California and they know this is a one-shot deal, so they don't care if they offend you or leave you dead. But they think it's going to happen in Phoenix, see." Ric, Super Virgin, and Two-Fisted Jesus stood in front of the juniper by the alloy road, looking down at the cluster of cabins. "They may hire people from the Cold Wires or whoever, so that they can have people who know the terrain. So the idea is, we move the meet at the last minute. Up here, north of Flag."

"We don't know the terrain, either," Jesus said. He looked uncomfortable here, his face a monochrome blotch in the unaccustomed sun.

Ric took a squeeze bottle of nasal mist from his pocket and squeezed it once up each nostril. He sniffed. "You can learn it between now and then. Rent all the cabins, put soldiers in the nearest ones. Lay in your commo gear." Ric pointed up at the ridge above where they stood. "Put some people with long guns up there, some IR goggles and scopes. Anyone comes in, you'll know about it."

"I don't know, Marat. I like Phoenix. I know the way that city thinks." Jesus shook his head in disbelief. "Fucking tourist cabins."

"They're better than hotel rooms. Tourist cabins have back doors."

"Hey." Super Virgin was grinning, metal teeth winking in the sun as she tugged on Jesus' sleeve. "Expand your horizons. This is the *great outdoors*."

Jesus shook his head. "I'll think about it."

19

Marlene was wearing war paint and dancing in the middle of her condeco living room. The furniture was pushed back to the walls, the music was loud enough to rattle the crystal on the kitchen shelves.

"You've got to decide, Marlene," Ric said. He was sitting behind the pushed-back table, and the paper packets of Thunder were laid out in front of him. "How much of this do you want to sell?"

"I'll decide later."

"Now. Now, Marlene."

"Maybe I'll keep it all."

Ric looked at her. She shook sweat out of her eyes and laughed.

"Just a joke, Ric."

He said nothing.

"It's just happiness," she said, dancing. "Happiness in paper envelopes. Better than money. You ought to use some. It'll make you less tense." Sweat was streaking her war paint. "What'll you use the money for, anyway? Move to Zanzibar and buy yourself a safe condeco and a bunch of safe investments? Sounds boring to me, Ric. Why'n't you use it to create some excitement?"

He could not, Ric thought, afford much in the way of regret. But still a sadness came over him, drifting through his body on slow opiate time. Another few days, he thought, and he wouldn't have to use people anymore. Which was good, because he was losing his taste for it.

20

A kid from California was told to be by a certain public phone at a certain time, with his bank and without his friends. The phone call told him to go to another phone booth and be there within a certain allotted time. He complained, but the phone hung up in mid-syllable.

At the second phone he was told to take the keys taped to the bottom of the shelf in the phone booth, go to such-and-such a car in the parking lot, and drive to Flagstaff to another public phone. His complaints were cut short by a slamming receiver. Once in Flagstaff, he was given another set of directions.

By now he had learned not to complain.

If there were still people with him they were very good, because they hadn't been seen at any of the turns of his course.

He was working for Ric, even though he didn't know it.

21

Marlene was practicing readiness. New patterns were constantly flickering through her mind and she loved watching her head doing its tricks.

She was wearing her war paint as she sat up on a tall ridge behind the cabins, her form encased in a plastic envelope that dispersed her body heat in patterns unrecognizable to infrared scanners. She had a radio and a powerful antenna, and she was humming "Greensleeves" to herself as she looked down at the cabins through long binoculars wrapped in a scansheet paper tube to keep the sun from winking from the lenses. Marlene also had headphones and a parabolic mike pointed down at the cabins, so that she could hear anything going on. Right now all she could hear was the wind.

She could see the cabins perfectly, as well as the two riflemen on the ridge across the road. She was far away from anything likely to happen, but if things went well she wouldn't be needed for anything but pushing buttons on cue anyway.

"Greensleeves" hummed on and on. Marlene was having a good time. Working for Ric.

22

Two-Fisted Jesus had turned the cabin into another plastic-hung cavern, lit by pale holograms and cool video monitors, filled with the hum of machinery and the brightness of liquid crystal. Right in the middle, a round coffee table full of crisp paper envelopes.

Ric had been allowed entry because he was one of the principals in the transaction. He'd undergone scanning as he entered, both for weapons and for electronics. Nothing had been found. His Thunder, and about half of Marlene's, was sitting on the table.

Only two people were in the room besides Ric. Super Virgin had the safety caps off her claws and was carrying an automatic with laser sights in a belt holster. Ric considered the sights a pure affectation in a room this small. Jesus had a sawed-off twin-barrel shotgun sitting in his lap. The pistol grip might break his wrist but the spread would cover most of the room, and Ric wondered if Jesus had considered how much electronics he'd lose if he ever used it.

23

Where three lightposts had been marked with fluorescent tape, the kid from California pulled off on the verge of the alloy road that wound ahead to leap over the Grand Canyon into Utah. Captain Islam pulled up behind him with two soldiers, and they scanned the kid right there, stripped him of a pistol and a homing sensor, and put him in the back of their own car.

"You're beginning to piss me off," the kid said.

"Just do what we tell you," Captain Islam said, pulling away, "and you'll be king of Los fucking Angeles."

24

Ric's hands were trembling so hard he had to press them against the arms of his chair in order to keep it from showing. He could feel sweat oozing from his armpits. He really wasn't good at this kind of thing.

The kid from California was pushed in the door by Captain Islam, who stepped out and closed the door behind him. The kid was black and had clear plastic eye implants, with the electronics gleaming inside the transparent eyeball. He had patterned scarring instead of the tattoos, and was about sixteen. He wore a silver jacket, carried a duffel to put the Thunder in, and seemed annoyed.

"Once you step inside," Jesus said, "you have five minutes to complete our transaction. Go ahead and test any of the packets at random."

"Yeah," the kid said. "I'll do that." He crouched by the table, pulled vials from his pockets, and made a series of tests while Jesus counted off at fifteen-second intervals. He managed to do four tests in three minutes, then stood up. Ric could see he was salivating for the stuff.

"It's good," he said.

"Let's see your key." The kid took a credit spike from his pocket and handed it to Jesus, who put it in the computer in front of him. Jesus transferred two hundred fifteen thousand in Starbright policorporate scrip from the spike to his own spike that was jacked into slot two.

"Take your stuff," Jesus said, settling back in his seat. "Captain Islam will take you back to your car. Nice doing business."

The kid gave a sniff, took his spike back, and began to stuff white packets into his duffel. He left the cabin without saying a word. Adrenaline was wailing along Ric's nerves. He stood and took his own spike from his left-hand jacket pocket. His other hand went to the squeeze bottle of nasal mist in his right. Stray novae were exploding at the peripherals of his vision.

"Look at this, Virgin," Ric said. "Look at all the money sitting in this machine." He laughed. Laughter wasn't hard, but stopping the laughter was.

"Twenty percent is yours, Marat," Jesus said. "Give me your spike."

As Super Virgin stepped up to look at the monitor, Ric brought the squeeze bottle out of his pocket and fired acrolein into her face. His spin toward Jesus was so fast that Virgin's scream had barely begun before he fired another burst of the chemical at Jesus, slamming one hand down on the shotgun to keep him from bringing it up. He'd planned on just holding it there till the boy's grip loosened, but nerves took over and he wrenched it effortlessly from Jesus' hands and barely stopped himself from smashing Jesus in the head with it.

Virgin was on her hands and knees, mucus hanging from her nose and lips. She was trying to draw the pistol. Ric kicked it away. It fell on muffled plastic.

Ric turned and pulled the spikes from the machine. Jesus

had fallen out of his chair, was clawing at his face. "Dead man," Jesus said, gasping the words.

"Don't threaten me, asshole," Ric said. "It could have been mustard gas."

And then Marlene, on the ridge far above, watched the sweep hand touch five minutes, thirty seconds, and she pressed her radio button. All the buried charges went off, blasting bits of the other cabins into the sky and doubtless convincing the soldiers in the other buildings that they were under fire by rocket or mortar, that the kid from California had brought an army with him. Simultaneous with the explosive, other buried packages began to gush concealing white smoke into the air. The wind was strong but there was a lot of smoke.

Ric opened the back door and took off, the shotgun hanging in his hand. Random fire burst out but none of it came near. The smoke provided cover from both optical scanners and infrared, and it concealed him all the way across the yard behind the cabin and down into the arroyo behind it. Sixty yards down the arroyo was a culvert that ran under the expressway. Ric dashed through it, wetting himself to the knees in cold spring snowmelt.

He was now on the other side of the expressway. He didn't think anyone would be looking for him here. He threw the shotgun away and kept running. There was a cross-country motorbike waiting a little farther up the stream.

25

"There," Ric said, pressing the Return button. "Half of it's yours."

Marlene was still wearing her war paint. She sipped cognac from a crystal glass and took her spike out of the computer. She laughed. "A hundred K of Starbright," she said, "and paper packets of happiness. What else do I need?"

"A fast armored car, maybe," Ric said. He pocketed his spike. "I'm taking off," he said. He turned to her. "There's room on the bike for two."

"To where?" She was looking at him sidelong.

"To Mexico, for starters," he said. A lie. Ric planned on heading northeast and losing himself for a while in Navajoland.

"To some safe little country. A safe little apartment."

"That's the idea."

Marlene took a hefty swig of cognac. "Not me," she said. "I'm planning on staying in this life."

Ric felt a coldness brush his spine. He reached out to take her hand. "Marlene," he said carefully. "You've got to leave this town. Now."

She pulled her hand away. "Not a chance, Ricardo. I plan on telling my boss just what I think of him. Tomorrow morning. I can't wait."

There was a pain in Ric's throat. "Okay," he said. He stood up. "See you in Mexico, maybe." He began to move for the door. Marlene put her arms around him from behind. Her chin dug into his collarbone.

"Stick around," she said. "For the party."

He shook his head, uncoiled her arms, slid out of them.

"You treat me like I don't know what I'm doing," Marlene said.

He turned and looked at her. Bright eyes looked at him from a mask of bright paint. "You don't," he said.

"I've got lots of ideas. You showed me how to put things together."

"Now I'm showing you how to run and save your life."

"Hah. I'm not going to run. I'm going to stroll out with a briefcase full of happiness and a hundred K in my pocket."

He looked at her and felt a pressure hard in his chest. He knew that none of this was real to her, that he'd never been able to penetrate that strange screen in her mind that stood between Marlene and the rest of the world. Ric had never pierced it, but soon the world would. He felt a coldness filling him, a coldness that had nothing to do with sorrow.

It was hard not to run when he turned and left the apartment.

His breathing came more freely with each step he took.

26

When Ric came off the Navajo Reservation he saw scansheet headlines about how the California gang wars had spilled over into Phoenix, how there were dead people turning up in alleys, others were missing, a club had been bombed. All those people working for him, covering his retreat.

In New Zealand he bought into a condecology in Christchurch, a big place with armored shutters and armored guards, a first-rate new artificial intelligence to handle investments, and a mostly foreign clientele who profited by the fact that a list of the condeco's inhabitants was never made public . . . this was before he found out that he could buy private property here, a big house on the South Island with a view of his own personal glacier, without a chance of anybody's war accidentally rolling over him.

It was an interesting feeling, sitting alone in his own house, knowing there wasn't anyone within five thousand miles who wanted to kill him.

Ric made friends. He played the market and the horses. And he learned to ski.

At a ski party in late September, held in the house of one of his friends, he drifted from room to room amid a murmur of conversation punctuated with brittle laughter. He had his arm around someone named Reiko, the sheltered daughter of a policorporate bigwig. The girl, nineteen and a student, had long black hair that fell like a tsunami down her shoulders, and she was fascinated with his talk of life in the real world. He walked into a back room that was bright with the white glare of video, wondering if the jai alai scores had been posted yet, and he stared into his own face as screams rose around him and his nerves turned to hot magnesium flares.

"Ugh. Mexican scum show," said Reiko, and then she saw the actor's face and her eyes widened.

Ric felt his knees trembling and he sank into an armchair in the back of the room. Ice tittering in his drink. The man on the vid was flaying alive a woman who hung by her wrists from a beam. Blood ran down his forearms. The camera cut quickly to his tiger's eyes, his thin smile. Ric's eyes. Ric's smile.

"My god," said Reiko. "It's really you, isn't it?"

"No," Ric said. Shaking his head.

"I can't believe they let this stuff even on pirate stations," someone said from the hallway. Screams rose from the vid. Ric's mind was flailing in the dark.

"I can't watch this," Reiko said, and rushed away. Ric didn't see her go. Burning sweat was running down the back of his neck.

The victim's screams rose. Blood traced artful patterns down her body. The camera cut to her face.

Marlene's face.

Nausea swept Ric and he doubled in his chair. He remembered Two-Fisted Jesus and his talent for creating video images, altering faces, voices, action. They'd found Marlene, as Ric had thought they would, and her voice and body were memorized by Jesus' computers. Maybe the torture was even real.

"It's got to be him," someone in the room said. "It's even his voice. His accent."

"He never did say," said another voice, "what he used to do for a living."

Frozen in his chair, Ric watched the show to the end. There was more torture, more bodies. The video-Ric enjoyed it all. At the end he went down before the blazing guns of the Federal Security Directorate. The credits rolled over the video-Ric's dead face. The director was listed as Jesus Carranza. The film was produced by VideoTek S.A. in collaboration with Messiah Media.

The star's name was given as Jean-Paul Marat.

"A new underground superstar," said a high voice. The voice of someone who thought of himself as an underground connoisseur. "He's been in a lot of pirate video lately. He's the center of a big controversy about how far scum shows can go."

And then the lights came on and Ric saw eyes turning to him in surprise. "It's not me," he said.

"Of course not." The voice belonged to his host. "Incredible resemblance, though. Even your mannerisms. Your accent."

"Not me."

"Hey." A quick, small man, with metal-rimmed glasses that gazed at Ric like barrels of a shotgun. "It really is you!" The high-pitched voice of the connoisseur grated on Ric's nerves like the sound of a bonesaw.

"No." A fast, sweat-soaked denial.

"Look. I've taped all your vids I could find."

"Not me."

"I'm having a party next week. With entertainment, if you know what I mean. I wonder—"

"I'm not interested," Ric said, standing carefully, "in any of your parties."

He walked out into the night, to his new car, and headed north, to his private fortress above the glacier. He took the pistol out of the glove compartment and put it on the seat next to him. It didn't make him feel any safer.

Get a new face, Ric thought. Get across the border into Uzbekistan and check into a hospital. Let them try to follow me there.

He got home at four in the morning and checked his situation with the artificial intelligence that managed his accounts. All his funds were in long-term investments and he'd take a whopping loss if he pulled out now.

He looked at the figures and couldn't understand them.

There seemed to be a long, constant scream in Ric's mind and nerves, a scream that echoed Marlene's, the sound of someone who has just discovered what is real. His body was shaking and he couldn't stop it.

Ric switched off his monitor and staggered to bed. Blood filled his dreams.

When he rose it was noon. There were people outside his gates, paparazzi with cameras. The phone had recorded a series of requests for an interview with the new, controversial vid star. Someone at the party had talked. It took Ric a long time to get a line out in order to tell the AI to sell.

The money in his pocket and a gun in his lap, he raced his car past the paparazzi, making them jump aside as he tried his best to run them down. He had to make the next suborbital shuttle out of Christchurch to Mysore, then head northwest to a hospital and to a new life. And somehow he'd have to try to cover his tracks. Possibly he'd buy some hair bleach, a false mustache. Pay only cash.

Getting away from Cartoon Messiah wouldn't be hard. Shaking the paparazzi would take a lot of fast thinking.

Sweat made his grip on the wheel slippery.

As he approached Christchurch he saw a streak across the bright northeast sky, a shuttle burning its way across the Pacific from California.

He wondered if there were people on it that he knew.

In his mind, the screams went on.

NO SPOT OF
GROUND

The dead girl came as a shock to him. He had limped into the Starker house from the firelit military camp outside, from a cacophony of wagons rattling, men driving tent pegs, provost marshals setting up the perimeter, a battalion of Ewell's Napoleon guns rolling past, their wheels lifting dust from the old farm road, dust that drifted over the camp, turning the firelight red and the scene into a pictured outpost of Hell. . . .

And here, to his surprise, was a dead girl in the parlor. She was perhaps sixteen, with dark hair, translucent skin, and cheeks with high spots of phthisis red. Her slim form was dressed in white. She lay in her coffin with candles at her head and feet, and her long-faced relatives sat in a semicircle of chairs under portraits of ancestors and Jefferson Davis.

A gangly man, probably the dead girl's father, rose awkwardly to welcome the surprised stranger, who had wandered into the parlor in hopes of asking for a glass of lemonade.

The intruder straightened in surprise. He took off his soft white hat and held it over his heart. The little gold knots on the ends of the hat cord rattled on the brim like muffled mourning drums.

"I am sorry to intrude on your grief," he said.

The father halted in what he was going to say, nodded, and dropped back into his chair. His wife, a heavy woman in dark silk, reached blindly toward him, and took his hand.

The intruder stood for a long moment out of respect, his eyes fixed on the corpse, before he turned and put on his hat and limped out of the house. Once he had thought this sight the saddest of all; once he had written poems about it.

What surprised him now was that it still happened, that people still died this way.

He had forgotten, amid all this unnatural slaughter, that a natural death was possible.

That morning he had brought his four brigades north into Richmond, marching from the Petersburg and Weldon depot south of the James break-step across the long bridge to the Virginia Central depot in the capital. Until two days ago he'd commanded only a single brigade in the defense of Petersburg; but poor George Pickett had suffered a collapse after days of nerve-wrenching warfare in his attempt to keep the city safe from Beast Butler's Army of the James; and Pickett's senior brigadier was, perforce, promoted to command of the whole division.

The new commander was fifty-five years old, and even if he was only a division commander till Pickett came back, he was still the oldest in the army.

At school he had been an athlete. Once he swam six miles down the James River, fighting against the tide the whole way, in order to outdo Byron's swim across the Hellespont. Now he was too tired and ill to ride a horse except in an emergency, so he moved through the streets of Richmond in a two-wheel buggy driven by Sextus Pompeiius, his personal darky.

He was dressed elegantly, a spotless gray uniform with

the wreathed stars of a brigadier on his collar and bright
gold braid on the arms, English riding boots, black doeskin
gloves. His new white wide-brimmed hat, a replacement for
the one shot off his head at Port Walthall Junction twenty
days ago, was tilted back atop his high forehead. Even
when he was young and couldn't afford anything but old and
mended clothes, he had always dressed well, with the taste
and style of a gentleman. Sextus had trimmed his grizzled
mustache that morning, back in camp along the Petersburg
and Weldon, and snipped at the long gray curls that hung
over the back of his collar. A fine white-socked thoroughbred gelding, the one he was too ill to ride, followed the
buggy on a lead. When he had gone south in 1861 he had
come with twelve hundred dollars in gold and silver, and
with that and his army pay he had managed to keep himself
in modest style for the last three years.

As he rode past the neat brick houses he remembered
when it was otherwise. Memories still burned in his mind:
the sneers of Virginia planters' sons when they learned of
his background, of his parents in the theater and stepfather
in commerce; his mounting debts when his stepfather Mr.
Allan had twice sent him to college, first to the University
of Virginia and then to West Point, and then not given him
the means to remain; the moment Allan had permitted the
household slaves to insult him to his face; and those
countless times he wandered the Richmond streets in black
despondent reverie, when he couldn't help gazing with
suspicion upon the young people he met, never knowing
how many of them might be living insults to his stepmother,
another of Mr. Allan's plentiful get of bastards. . . .

The brigadier looked up as the buggy rattled over rusting
iron tracks, and there it was: Ellis & Allan, General
Merchants, the new warehouse of bright red brick lying
along a Virginia Central siding, its loading dock choked
with barrels of army pork. The war that had so devastated
the Confederate nation had been kind only to two classes:
carrion crows and merchants. The prosperous Ellis & Allan
was run by his stepbrothers now, he presumed, possibly in

partnership with an assortment of Mr. Allan's bastards—in *that* family, who could say? The brute Allan, penny-pinching as a Jew with the morals of a nigger, might well have given part of the business to his illegitimate spawn, if for no other reason than to spite his foster son. Such was the behavior of the commercial classes that infected this city.

Richmond, he thought violently. Why in the name of heaven are we defending the place? Let the Yanks have it, and let them serve it as Rome served Carthage, burned to the foundations and the scorched plain sown with salt. There are other parts of the South better worth dying for.

Sextus Pompeiius pulled the mare to a halt, and the general limped out of the buggy and leaned on his stick. The Virginia Central yards were filled with trains, the cars shabby, the engines worn. Sad as they were, they would serve to get the division to where it was going, another fifteen miles up the line to the North Anna River, and save shoe leather while doing it.

The detestable Walter Whitman, the general remembered suddenly, wrote of steam engines in his poems. Whitman surely had not been thinking of engines like these, worn and ancient, leaking steam and oil as they dragged from front to front the soldiers as worn and tattered as the engines. Not trains, but ghosts of trains, carrying a ghost division, itself raised more than once from the dead.

The lead formation, the general's old Virginia brigade, was marching up behind the buggy, their colors and band to the front. The bandsmen were playing "Bonnie Blue Flag." The general winced—brass and percussion made his taut nerves shriek, and he could really tolerate only the soft song of stringed instruments. Pain crackled through his temples.

Among the stands of brigade and regimental colors was another stand, or rather a perch, with a pair of black birds sitting quizzically atop: Hugin and Munin, named after the ravens of Wotan. The brigade called themselves the Ravens, a compliment to their commander.

The general stood on the siding and watched the brigade as it came to a halt and broke ranks. A few smiling bandsmen helped the general load his horses and buggy on a flatcar, then jumped with their instruments aboard their assigned transport. The ravens were taken from their perch and put in cages in the back of the general's carriage.

A lance of pain drove through the general's thigh as he swung himself aboard. He found himself a seat among the divisional staff. Sextus Pompeiius put the general's bags in the rack over his head, then went rearward to sit in his proper place behind the car, in the open between the carriages.

A steam whistle cried like a woman in pain. The tired old train began to move.

Poe's Division, formerly Pickett's, began its journey north to fight the Yanks somewhere on the North Anna River. When, the general thought, would these young men see Richmond again?

One of the ravens croaked as it had been taught: "Nevermore!"

Men laughed. They thought it a good omen.

General Poe stepped out of the mourning Starker house, the pale dead girl still touching his mind. When had he changed? he wondered. When had his heart stopped throbbing in sad, harmonic sympathy at the thought of dead young girls? When had he last wept?

He knew when. He knew precisely when his heart had broken for the last time, when he had ceased at last to mourn Virginia Clemm, when the last ounce of poetry had poured from him like a river of dark veinous blood. . . .

When the Ravens had gone for that cemetery, the tombstones hidden in dust and smoke.

When General Edgar A. Poe, CSA, had watched them go, that brilliant summer day, while the bands played "Bonnie Blue Flag" under the trees and the tombstones waited, marking the factories of a billion happy worms . . .

Poe stood before the Starker house and watched the dark form of his fourth and last brigade, the new North Carolina outfit that had shown their mettle at Port Walthall Junction, now come rising up from the old farm road like an insubstantial battalion of mournful shades. Riding at the head came its commander, Thomas Clingman. Clingman saw Poe standing on Starker's front porch, halted his column, rode toward the house, and saluted.

"Where in hell do I put my men, General? One of your provost guards said up this way, but—"

Poe shook his head. Annoyance snapped like lightning in his mind. No one had given him any orders at all. "You're on the right of General Corse, out there." Poe waved in the general direction of Hanover Junction, the little town whose lights shone clearly just a quarter mile to the east. "You should have gone straight up the Richmond and Fredericksburg tracks from the Junction, not the Virginia Central."

Clingman's veinous face reddened. "They told me wrong, then. Ain't anybody been over the ground, Edgar?"

"No one from *this* division. Ewell pulled out soon's he heard we were coming, but that was just after dark and when we came up, we had no idea what to do. There was just some staff creature with some written orders, and he galloped away before I could ask him what they meant."

No proper instruction, Poe thought. His division was part of Anderson's corps, but he hadn't heard from Anderson and didn't know where the command post was. If he was supposed to report to Lee, he didn't know where Lee was either. He was entirely in the dark.

Contempt and anger snarled in him. Poe had been ignored again. No one had thought to consult him; no one had remembered him; but if he failed, everyone would blame him. Just like the Seven Days'.

Clingman snorted through his bushy mustache. "Confound it anyway."

Poe banged his stick into the ground in annoyance. "Turn your men around, Thomas. It's only another half mile or so. Find an empty line of entrenchments and put your people in. We'll sort everyone out come first light."

"Lord above, Edgar."

"Fitz Lee's supposed to be on your right. Don't let's have any of your people shooting at him by mistake."

Clingman spat in annoyance, then saluted and started the process of getting his brigade turned around. Poe stared after him and bit back his own anger. Orders would come. Surely his division hadn't been forgotten.

"Massa Poe?"

Poe gave a start. With all the noise of marching feet and shouted orders, he hadn't heard Sextus Pompeiius creeping up toward him. He looked at his servant and grinned.

"You gave me a scare, Sextus. Strike me if you ain't invisible in the dark."

Sextus chuckled at his master's wit. "I found that cider, Massa Poe."

Poe scowled. If his soft cider hadn't got lost, he wouldn't have had to interrupt the Starkers' wake in search of lemonade. He began limping toward his headquarters tent, his cane sinking in the soft ground.

"Where'd you find it?" he demanded.

"That cider, it was packed in the green trunk, the one that came up with the divisional train."

"I instructed you to pack it in the brown trunk."

"I know that, Massa Poe. That fact must have slipped my mind, somehow."

Poe's hand clenched the ivory handle of his cane. Renewed anger poured like fire through his veins. "Worthless nigger baboon!" he snapped.

"Yes, Massa Poe," Sextus said, nodding, "I is. I *must* be, the way you keep saying I is."

Poe sighed. One really couldn't expect any more from an African. Changing his name from Sam to Sextus hadn't given the black any more brains than God had given him in the first place.

"Well, Sextus," he said. "*Fortuna favet fatuis*, you know." He laughed.

"Massa always has his jokes in Latin. He always does."

Sextus's tone was sulky. Poe laughed and tried to jolly the slave out of his mood.

"We must improve your knowledge of the classics. Your *litterae humaniores*, you understand."

The slave was annoyed. "Enough human litter around here as it is."

Poe restrained a laugh. "True enough, Sextus." He smiled indulgently. "You are excused from your lessons."

His spirits raised by the banter with his darky, Poe limped to his headquarters tent, marked by the division flags and the two ravens on their perch, and let Sextus serve him his evening meal. The ravens gobbled to each other while Poe ate sparingly, and drank two glasses of the soft cider. Poe hadn't touched spirits in fifteen years, even though whiskey was a lot easier to find in this army than water.

Not since that last sick, unholy carouse in Baltimore.

Where were his orders? he wondered. He'd just been ordered to occupy Ewell's trenches. Where was the rest of the army? Where was Lee? No one had told him anything.

After the meal, he'd send couriers to find Lee. Somebody had to know something.

It was impossible they'd forgotten him.

Eureka, he called it. His prose poem had defined the universe, explained it all, a consummate theory of matter, energy, gravity, art, mathematics, the mind of God. The universe was expanding, he wrote, had exploded from a single particle in a spray of evolving atoms that moved outward at the speed of divine thought. The universe was still expanding, the forms of its matter growing ever more complex; but the expansion would slow, reverse; matter would coalesce, return to its primordial simplicity; the Divine Soul that resided in every atom would reunite in perfect self-knowledge.

It was the duty of art, he thought, to reunite human thought with that of the Divine, particled with unparticled matter. In his poetry he had striven for an aesthetic purity of thought and sentiment, a detachment from political, moral, and temporal affairs. . . . Nothing of Earth shone in his verse, nothing contaminated by matter—he desired harmonies, essences, a striving for Platonic perfection, for the dialogue of one abstract with another. Beyond the fact that he wrote in English, nothing connected the poems with America, the nineteenth century, its life, its movements. He disdained even standard versification—he wrote with unusual scansions, strange metrics—the harmonies of octameter catalectic, being more rarified, seemed to rise to the lofty ear of God more than could humble iambic pentameter, that endless trudge, trudge, trudge across the surface of the terrestrial globe. He wanted nothing to stand between himself and supernal beauty, nothing to prevent the connection of his own mind with that of God.

He had poured everything into *Eureka*, all his soul, his hope, his grief over Virginia, his energy. In the end there was the book, but nothing left of the man. He lectured across America, the audiences polite and appreciative, their minds perhaps touched by his own vision of the Divine— but all his own divinity had gone into the book, and in the end Earth reached up to claim him. Entire weeks were spent in delirium, reeling drunk from town to town, audience to audience, woman to woman. . . .

Ending at last in some Baltimore street, lying across a gutter, his body a dam for a river of half-frozen October sleet.

After the meal Poe stepped outside for a pipe of tobacco. He could see the soft glow of candlelight from the Starker parlor, and he thought of the girl in her coffin, laid out in her dress of virgin white. How much sadder it would have been had she lived, had she been compelled to grow old in this new, changing world, this sad and deformed Iron Age dedicated to steam and slaughter . . . better she was dead, her spirit purged of particled matter and risen to contemplation of the self-knowing eternal.

His thoughts were interrupted by the arrival of a man on horseback. Poe recognized Colonel Moxley Sorrel, a handsome Georgian, still in his twenties, who was Longstreet's chief of staff. He had been promoted recently as a result of leading a flank assault in the Wilderness that had crushed an entire Union corps, though, as always, the triumph had come too late in the day for the attack to be decisive.

"General." Sorrel saluted. "I had a devil of a time finding you. Ewell had his command post at Hackett's place, over yonder." He pointed at the lights of a plantation house just north of Hanover Junction. "I reckoned you'd be there."

"I had no notion of where Ewell was. No one's told me a thing. This place seemed as likely as any." Poe looked off toward the lights of Hanover Junction. "At least there's a good view."

Sorrel frowned. He swung out of the saddle, and Sextus came to take the reins from his hand. "Staff work has gone up entirely," Sorrel said. "There's been too much chaos at the top for everything to get quite sorted out."

"Yes." Poe looked at him. "And how is General Longstreet?"

The Georgian's eyes were serious. "He will recover, praise God. But it will be many months before he can return to duty."

Poe looked up at the ravens, half expecting one of them to croak out "Nevermore." But they'd stuck their heads under their wings and gone to sleep.

He will recover, Poe thought. That's what they'd said of Stonewall; and then the crazed Presbyterian had died suddenly.

Just like old Stonewall to do the unexpected.

The army had been hit hard the last few weeks. First Longstreet wounded in the Wilderness, then Jeb Stuart killed at Yellow Tavern, just a few days ago. They were the two best corps commanders left to Lee, in Poe's opinion. Longstreet had been replaced by Richard Anderson; but Lee had yet to appoint a new cavalry commander—both, in Poe's mind, bad decisions. Anderson was too mentally lazy to command a corps—he was barely fit to command his old division—and the cavalry needed a firm hand now, with their guiding genius gone.

"Will you come inside, Colonel?" Poe gestured toward the tent flap with his stick.

"Thank you, sir."

"Share some cider with me? That and some biscuits are all the *rafraîchissements* I can manage."

"You're very kind." Sorrel looked at the uncleared table. "I've brought your orders from General Anderson."

Poe pushed aside his gold-rimmed dinner plate and moved a lantern onto the table. Sorrel pulled a folded map out of his coat and spread it on the pale blue tablecloth. Poe reached for his spectacles and put them on his nose. The map gave him, for the first time, an accurate look at his position.

This part of the Southern line stretched roughly northwest to southeast, a chord on the arc of the North Anna. The line was more or less straight, though it was cut in half by a swampy tributary of the North Anna, with steep banks on either side, and at that point Poe's entrenchments bent back a bit. The division occupied the part of the line south of the tributary. In front of him was dense hardwood forest, not very useful for maneuver or attack.

"We're going on the offensive tomorrow," Sorrel said, "thank the lord." He gave a thin smile. "Grant's got himself on the horns of a dilemma, sir, and General Lee intends to see he's gored."

Poe's temper crackled. "No one's going to get gored if division commanders don't get their instructions!" he snapped.

Sorrel gave him a wary smile. "That's why I'm here, sir."

Poe glared at him, then deliberately reined in his anger. "So you are." He took a breath. "Pardon my . . . display."

"Staff work, as I say, sir, has been a mite precarious of late. General Lee is ill, and so is General Hill."

Poe's anxiety rose again. "Lee?" he demanded. "Ill?"

"An intestinal complaint. We would have made this attack yesterday had the general been feeling better."

Poe felt his nervousness increase. He was not a member of the Cult of Lee, but he did not trust an army without a capable hand at the top. Too many high-ranking officers were out of action or incompetent. Stuart was dead, Longstreet was wounded, Lee was sick—great heavens, he'd already had a heart attack—Ewell hadn't been the same since he lost his leg, Powell Hill was ill half the time. . . . And the young ones, the healthy ones, were as always dying of bullets and shells.

"Your task, General," Sorrel said, "is simply to hold. Perhaps to demonstrate against the Yanks, if you feel it possible."

"How am I to know if it's possible?" He was still angry. "I don't know the ground. I don't know where the enemy is."

Sorrel cocked an eyebrow at him, said, "Ewell didn't show you anything?" But he didn't wait for an answer before beginning his exposition.

The Army of Northern Virginia, he explained, had been continually engaged with Grant's army for three weeks— first in the Wilderness, then at Spotsylvania, now on the North Anna; there hadn't been a single day without fighting. Every time one of Grant's offensives bogged down, he'd slide his whole army to his left and try again. Two days before, on May 24, Grant had gone to the offensive again, crossing the North Anna both upstream and down of Lee's position.

Grant had obviously intended to overlap Lee on both flanks and crush him between his two wings; but Lee had anticipated his enemy by drawing his army back into a V shape, with the center on the river, and entrenching heavily. When the Yanks saw the entrenchments they'd come to a stumbling halt, their offensive stopped in its tracks without more than a skirmish on either flank.

"You're facing a Hancock's Second Corps, here on our far right flank," Sorrel said. His manicured finger jabbed at the map. Hancock appeared to be entirely north of the swampy tributary. "Warren and Wright are on our left, facing Powell Hill. Burnside's Ninth Corps is in the center—he tried to get across Ox Ford on the twenty-fourth, but General Anderson's guns overlook the ford and Old Burn called off the fight before it got properly started. Too bad—" Grinning. "Could've been another Fredericksburg."

"We can't hope for more than one Fredericksburg, alas," Poe said. "Not even from Burnside." He looked at the map. "Looks as if the Federals have broken their army into pieces for us."

"Yes, sir. We can attack either wing, and Grant can't reinforce one wing without moving his people across the North Anna twice."

General Lee had planned to take advantage of that with an offensive against half Grant's army. He intended to pull Ewell's corps off the far right, most of Anderson's out of the center, and combine them with Hill's for a strike at Warren and Wright. The attack would have been made the day before if Lee hadn't fallen ill. In the end he'd postponed the assault by one day.

The delay, Poe thought, had given the Yanks another twenty-four hours to prepare. Confederates aren't the only ones who know how to entrench.

Plans already laid, he thought. Nothing he could do about it.

Poe looked at the map. Now that Ewell and most of Anderson's people had pulled out, he was holding half the Confederate line with his single division.

"It'll probably work to the good," Sorrel said. "Your division came up to hold the right for us, and that will allow us to put more soldiers into the attack. With your division and Bushrod Johnson's, which came up a few days ago, we've managed to replace all the men we've lost in this campaign so far."

Had the Yankees? Poe wondered.

"When you hear the battle start," Sorrel said, "you might consider making a demonstration against Hancock. Keep him interested in what's happening on his front."

Poe looked up sharply. "One division," he said, "against the Yankee Second Corps? Didn't we have enough of that at Gettysburg?"

"A demonstration, General, not a battle." Politely. "General Anderson has also put under your command the two brigades that are holding the center, should you require them."

"Whose?"

"Gregg's Brigade, and Law's Alabamans."

Poe's mind worked through this. "Are Gregg and Law aware they are under my orders?"

"I presume so."

"Presume," Poe echoed. There was too much *presuming* in this war. He took off his spectacles and put them in his pocket. "Colonel Sorrel," he said, "would you do me the inestimable favor of riding to Gregg and Law tonight and telling them of this? I fear the staff work may not have caught up with General Anderson's good intent."

Sorrel paused, then gave a resigned shrug. "Very well, General. If you desire it."

"Thank you, Colonel." His small triumph made Poe genial. "I believe I have been remiss. I remember promising you cider."

"Yes. A glass would be delightful, thank you."

They sat at the folding table, and Poe called for Sextus to serve. He opened a tin box and offered it to Sorrel. "I have some of Dr. Graham's dietary biscuits, if you desire."

"Thank you, sir. If I may put some in my pockets for later . . . ?"

"Make free of them, sir."

Sorrel, possessing by now an old soldier's reflexes, loaded his pockets with biscuits and then took a hearty swallow of the cider. Sextus refilled his glass.

"General Pickett's campaign south of the James," Sorrel said, "has been much appreciated here."

"The form of appreciation preferable to us would have been reinforcements from General Lee."

"We were, ah, tangled up with Grant at the time, sir."

"Still, for several days we had two brigades against two entire corps. Two *corps*, sir!" Indignation flared in Poe. His fists knotted in his lap.

"The glory of your victory was all the greater." The Georgian's tone was cautious, his eyes alert.

Condescending, Poe thought. A black anger settled on him like a shroud. These southern gentlemen were always condescending. Poe knew what Sorrel was thinking. It's just Poe, hysterical Code-breaker Poe. *Poe* always thinks he's fighting the whole Yankee army by himself. *Poe* is always sending off messages screaming for help and telling other people what to do. What? Another message from Poe? It's just the fellow's nerves again. Ignore it.

"I've always been proved right!" Poe snapped. "I was *right* during the Seven Days when I said Porter was dug in behind Boatswain Swamp! I was *right* about the Yankee signal codes, I was right about the charge at Gettysburg, and I was right again when I said Butler had come ashore at Bermuda Hundred with two whole Yankee corps! If my superiors would have given me a little credit—"

"Your advice has always been appreciated," said Sorrel.

"My God!" Poe said. "Poor General Pickett is broken down because of this! It may be months before his nerves recover! Pickett—if he could stand what Lee did to the Division at Gettysburg, one might think he could stand anything! But *this*—*this* broke him! Great heavens, if Butler had committed more than a fraction of the forces available to him, he would have lost Petersburg, and with Petersburg, Richmond!"

"I do not think this is the place—" Sorrel began.

Too late. Poe's mind filled with the memory of the Yankees coming at the Ravens at Port Walthall Junction, four brigades against Pickett's two, and those four only the advance of Butler's entire army. He remembered the horror of it, the regimental flags of the Federals breaking out of the cover of the trees, brass and bayonets shining in the wind; shellfire bursting like obscene overripe blossoms; the whistling noise made by the tumbling bullet that had carried

away Poe's hat; the sight of George Pickett with his face
streaked by powder smoke, his long hair wild in the wind,
as he realized his flanks were caving in and he was facing
another military disaster . . .

"Screaming for reinforcements!" Poe shouted. "We were
screaming for reinforcements! And what does Richmond
send? *Harvey Hill!* Hah! Major General interfering Harvey
Hill!"

Sorrel looked at him stonily. The old fight between Poe
and Hill was ancient history.

"Hill is a madman, sir!" Poe knew he was talking too
much, gushing like a chain pump, but he couldn't stop
himself. Let at least one person know what he thought. "He
is a fighter, I will grant him that, but he is quarrelsome,
tempestuous—impossible to reason with. He is not a
rational man, Colonel. He hasn't an ounce of rationality or
system in him. No more brains than a nigger."

Sorrel finished his cider, and raised a hand to let Sextus
know not to pour him more. "We may thank God that the
movement was made by Butler," he said.

Poe looked at him. "The Yankees will not forever give
their armies to men like Butler," he said.

Sorrel gazed resentfully at the lantern for a long moment.
"Grant is no Butler, that is certain. But we will do a
Chancellorsville on him nonetheless."

"We may hope so," said Poe. He had no confidence in
this offensive. Lee no longer had the subordinates to carry
things out properly, could no longer do anything in the
attack but throw his men headlong at Federal entrenchments.

The young colonel rose. "Thank you for the cider,
General. I will visit Generals Law and Gregg on my return
journey."

Poe rose with him, memory still surging through his mind
like the endless waves of Yankee regiments at Port Walthall
Junction. He knew he had not made a good impression, that
he had confirmed in Sorrel's mind, and through him the

minds of the corps staff, the stories of his instability, his hysteria, and his egotism.

Harvey Hill, he thought, seething. Send Harvey Hill to tell *me* what to do.

Sextus brought Colonel Sorrel his horse and helped the young man mount. "Thank you for speaking to Gregg and Law," Poe said.

"Use their forces as you see fit," Sorrel said.

"This division has had hard fighting," Poe said. "I will be sparing in my use of them."

"We've all had hard fighting, sir," Sorrel said. A gentle reproach. "But with God's help we will save Richmond again this next day."

Poe gave a swift, reflexive glance to the ravens, anticipating another "Nevermore," but now they were still asleep. No more omens tonight.

Sorrel saluted, Poe returned it, and the Georgian trotted off into the night.

Poe looked out at the Yankee campfires burning low off on his left. How many times, he wondered, would this army have to save Richmond? McDowell had come for Richmond, and McClellan, and Pope, Burnside, Hooker, Meade, and Butler. Now there was Grant, who had seized hold of Lee's army in the Wilderness and declined to let it go, even though he'd probably lost more men than the others put together.

Maybe Lee would turn tomorrow into another Chancellorsville.

But even if he did, Poe knew, one day this or another Yank general would come, and Richmond would not be saved. Even Lee could only fight history for so long.

The politicians were counting on the Northern elections to save them, but Poe had no more confidence in George McClellan as a candidate than as a general—Lincoln could outmaneuver him at the polls as handily as Lee had in the Seven Days' Battle.

No, the South was doomed, its Cause lost. That was obvious to anyone with any ratiocinative faculty whatever.

But there was nothing else to do but fight on, and hope the North kept giving armies to the likes of Ben Butler.

"Massa Poe?" Sextus was at his elbow. "Will we be sleeping outside tonight?"

Poe cocked an eye at the sky. There was a heavy dew on the ground, but the few clouds in sight were high and moving fast. There should be no rain.

"Yes," Poe said. "Set up the beds."

"Whatever you say, massa."

Sextus was used to it, poor fellow. Poe hadn't been able to sleep alone since Virginia died, and he had always disliked confined spaces. Sleeping out of doors, under a heavy buffalo cloak, with Sextus wrapped in another robe nearby, was the ideal solution. Poe loved to look up at the sweep of brilliant stars, each an eye of God, to feel his soul rising beyond the atmosphere, through the luminiferous ether to merge with the Eternal, the Sublime. . . .

How he came to the gutter in Baltimore he would never know. He had apparently given a lecture there a few nights before, but he couldn't remember it. Perhaps he would have died there, had not a passing widow recognized him, drunk and incapable, and brought him into her carriage. She had talked with him after his lecture, she told him, and found his conversation brilliant. He couldn't remember her either.

Her name was Mrs. Forster. Her late husband had been addicted to alcohol, and she had cured him; she would apply her cure as well to Mr. Poe.

Her plantation, within a half day's journey of Baltimore, was called Shepherd's Rest; she owned close to two thousand slaves and the better part of a county. She loved poetry and philosophy, read French and German, and had a passing knowledge of Latin.

She had a daughter named Evania, a green-eyed girl of fourteen. When Poe first saw her, sitting in the east parlor with the French wallpaper only a shade darker than her eyes, Evania was playing the guitar, her long fingers caressing the strings as if they were a lover's hair. Her long tresses, falling down her neck, seemed to possess the mutable spectrum of a summer sunrise.

Once before Poe, at the end of his wits and with the black hand of self-slaughter clutching at his throat, had been rescued by a widow with a daughter. In Mrs. Forster Poe could almost see Mrs. Clemm—but Mrs. Clemm idealized, perfected, somehow rarified, her poverty replaced by abundance, her sadness by energy, inspiration, and hope. How could he help but see Virginia in her sparkling daughter? How could he help but give her his love, his troth, his ring—He was not being faithless to Virginia, he thought; his second marriage was a fulfillment of the first. Did Evania and Virginia not possess, through some miracle of transubstantiation, the same soul, the same perfection of spirit? Were they not earthly shades of the same pure, angelic lady, differing only in color, one dark, one bright?

Were they not blessings bestowed by Providence, a just compensation for poor Poe, who had been driven nearly mad by soaring, like Icarus, too near the divine spark?

For a moment, after Poe opened his eyes, he saw her floating above him—a woman, dark-tressed, pale-featured, crowned with stars. He could hear her voice, though distantly; he could not make sense of her speech, hearing only a murmur of long vowel sounds. . . .

And then she was gone, faded away, and Poe felt a knife of sorrow enter his heart. He realized he was weeping. He threw off his buffalo robe and rolled upright.

The Starker house loomed above him, black against the Milky Way. The candles' glow still softly illuminated the parlor window.

Poe bent over, touching his forehead to his knees until he could master himself. He had seen the woman often in his dreams, sometimes in waking moments. He remembered her vividly, the female form rising over the streets of Richmond, during some barely-sane moments after Virginia's death, the prelude to that last spree in Baltimore. Always he had felt comforted by her presence, confirmed in his dreams, his visions. When she appeared it was to confer a blessing.

He did not remember seeing her since his war service started. But then, his war service was not blessed.

Poe straightened, and looked at the soft candlelight in the Starker windows. He looked at the foot of his cot, and saw Sextus wrapped in blankets, asleep and oblivious to his master's movements. Sometimes Poe thought he would give half his worth for a single night of sleep as deep and dreamless as that of his body-servant.

He put his stockinged feet in the carpet slippers that waited where Sextus had put them, then rose and stepped out into the camp in his dressing gown. The slippers were wet with dew inside and out. Poe didn't care. A gentle, warm wind was flitting up from the south. With this heavy dew, Poe thought, the wind would raise a mist before dawn. Maybe it would postpone Lee's offensive.

He remembered hiking in New York with Virginia, spending days wandering down hilly lanes, spending their nights in country inns or, when the weather was fine and Virginia's health permitted, wrapped in blankets beneath the open sky. His friends had thought his interest in nature morbid. Buried in the life of the city and the life of the mind, they could not understand how his soul was drawn skyward by the experience of the outdoors, how close he felt to the Creator when he and Virginia shared a soft bank of moist timothy and kissed and caressed one another beneath the infinite range of fiery stars. . . .

Poe realized he was weeping again. He looked about and saw he had wandered far from his tent, amid his soldiers' dying campfires.

Nothing like this had happened to him in years. The sight of that dead girl had brought back things he thought he'd forgotten.

He mastered himself once more and walked on. The rising southern wind stirred the gray ashes of campfires, brought little sparks winking across his path. He followed them, heading north.

Eventually he struck his entrenchments, a deep line of the kind of prepared works this army could now throw up in a few hours, complete with head log, communications trenches, firing step, and parapet. Soldiers huddled like potato sacks in the trenches, or on the grass just behind the line. An officer's mare dozed over its picket. Beyond, Poe could hear the footsteps of the sentries patrolling.

Once, just after the war had first started, Robert Lee had tried to get this army to dig trenches—and the soldiers had mocked him, called him "The King of Spades," and refused to do the work. Digging was not fit work for a white man, they insisted, and besides, only a coward would fight from entrenchments.

Now the army entrenched at every halt. Three years' killing had made them lose their stupid pride.

Poe stepped onto the firing step, and peered out beneath the head log as he tried to scan his front. Beyond the vague impression of gentle rolling hills, he could see little. Then he lifted his head as he heard the challenging scream of a stallion. The sound came from away north, well past the entrenchments.

The mare picketed behind the entrenchments raised its head at the sound. The stallion challenged again. Then another horse screamed, off to the right, and another. The mare flicked its ears and gave an answer.

The mare was in heat, Poe realized. And she was flirting with Yankee horses. None of his men could be out that far.

The wind had carried the mare's scent north, to the nose of one northern stallion. Other stallions that hadn't scented the mare nevertheless answered the first horse's challenge.

Poe's head moved left to right as one horse after another screamed into the night. Sorrel's map hadn't shown the Yankee line stretching that far, well south of the tributary, beyond Clingman's brigade to where Fitz Lee's cavalry was supposed to be, out on his right flank.

He listened as the horses called to one another like bugles before a battle, and he thought: *The Yankees are moving, and they're moving along my front.*

Suddenly the warm south wind turned chill.

How many? he thought.

Sobbing in the mist like men in the extremes of agony, the crying horses offered no answer.

He became a child again, living with Evania in her perfect kingdom, that winding blue river valley west of Baltimore. Never before had he known rest; but there he found it, a cease from the despairing, agonized wanderings that had driven him, like a leaf before a black autumn storm, from Richmond to Boston and every city between.

At last he knew what it was to be a gentleman. He had *thought* he had achieved that title before, through education and natural dignity and inclination—but now he knew that before he had only aspired to the name. Mr. Allan fancied himself a gentleman; but his money was tainted with trade, with commerce and usury. Now Poe understood that the highest type of gentleman was produced only through ease and leisure—not laziness, but rather the freedom from material cares that allowed a man to cultivate himself endlessly, to refine his thought and intellect through study and application of the highest forms of human aspiration.

He was not lazy. He occupied himself in many ways. He moved Mrs. Clemm to Baltimore, bought her a house, arranged for her an annuity. He added to the mansion, creating a new façade of Italian marble that reflected the colors of the westering sun; he employed the servants to move tons of earth in order to create a landscape garden of fully forty acres that featured, in the midst of a wide artificial lake, an arabesque castle, a lacy wedding-cake gift to his bride.

He had always thought landscape gardening fully an equal of poetry in its ability to invoke the sublime and reveal the face of the deity. In this he was a disciple of de Carbonnieres, Piranesi, and Shenstone: The garden was nature perfected, as it had been in the mind of God, a human attempt to restore the divine, Edenic sublimity. He crafted his effects carefully—the long, winding streams through which one approached Poe's demiparadise in swan-shaped boats, the low banks crowded with moss imported from Japan, natural-seeming outcroppings of uniquely colored and textured rock. At the end was a deep, black chasm through which the water rushed alarmingly, as if to Hades—but then the boat was swept into the dazzling wide lake, the sun sparkling on the white sand banks, the blue waters—and then, as the visitor's eyes adjusted from blackness to brightness, one perceived in the midst of a blue-green island the white castle with its lofty, eyelike windows, the symbol of purest Mind in the midst of Nature.

Nothing was suffered to spoil the effects that had taken a full six years to create. Not a stray leaf, not a twig, not a cattail was permitted to sully the ground or taint the water—fully thirty Africans were constantly employed to make certain that Poe's domain was swept clean.

It cost money—but money Poe had, and if not there was always more to be obtained at three and one half percent. His days of penny-counting were over, and he spent with a lavish hand.

He fulfilled another ambition: he started a literary magazine, the *Southern Gentleman*, with its offices in Baltimore. For it he wrote essays, criticism, occasional stories, once or twice a poem.

Only once or twice.

Somehow, he discovered, the poetry had fled his soul.

And he began to feel, to his growing horror, that his loss of poetry was nothing but a just punishment. True poetry, he knew, could not reside in the breast of a man as faithless as he.

The Starker house on its small eminence stood hard-edged and black against a background of shifting mist, like an isolated tor rising above the clouds. It was a little after four. The sun had not yet risen, but already the eastern horizon was beginning to turn gray. The ravens, coming awake, crackled and muttered to one another as they shook dew from their feathers.

Poe leaned on his stick before a half-circle of his brigadiers and their mingled staffs. Hugin and Munin sat on their perch behind him. Poe was in his uniform of somber gray, a new paper collar, a black cravat, the black doeskin gloves. Over his shoulders he wore a red-lined black cloak with a high collar, an old gift from Jeb Stuart who had said it made him look like a proper raven.

Most of his life Poe had dressed all in black. The uniform was a concession to his new profession, but for sake of consistency with his earlier mode of dress he had chosen the darkest possible gray fabric, so dark it was almost blue.

There was the sound of galloping; riders rose out of the mist. Poe recognized the man in the lead; Fitzhugh Lee, Robert Lee's nephew and the commander of the cavalry division on his right. He was a short man, about Poe's height, a bandy-legged cavalryman with a huge spade-shaped beard and bright, twinkling eyes. Poe was surprised to see him—he had asked only that Lee send him a staff officer.

He and Poe exchanged salutes. "Decided to come myself, General." He dropped from his horse. "Your messenger made it seem mighty important."

"I thank you, sir." Fitz Lee, Poe realized, outranked him. He could take command here if he so desired.

He would not *dare*, Poe thought. A cold anger burned through him for a moment before he recollected that Fitz Lee had as yet done nothing to make him angry.

Still, Poe was uneasy. He could be superseded so easily.

"I think the Yankees are moving across my front," he said. He straightened his stiff leg, felt a twinge of pain. "I think Grant is moving to his left again."

The cavalryman considered this. "If he wants Richmond," he said, "he'll go to his right. The distance is shorter."

"I would like to submit, *apropos*, that Grant may not want Richmond so much as to defeat us in the field."

Fitz Lee puzzled his way through this. "He's been

fighting us nonstop, that's the truth. Hasn't broken off so much as a day."

"Nevermore," said one of the ravens. Fitz Lee looked startled. Poe's men, used to it, shared grins. Poe's train of thought continued uninterrupted.

"Moreover, if Grant takes Hanover Junction, he will be astride both the Virginia Central and the Richmond and Fredericksburg. That will cut us off from the capital and our sources of supply. We'll have to either attack him there or fall back on Richmond."

"Mebbe that's so."

"All that, of course, is speculation—a mere exercise of the intuition, if you like. Nevertheless, whatever his intent, it is still an *observed* fact that Grant is moving across my front. *Quod erat demonstrandum.*"

Lee's eyes twinkled. "*Quod libet*, I think, rather." Not quite convinced.

"I have heard their horses. They are well south of where they are supposed to be."

Lee smiled through his big beard and dug a heel into the turf. "If he's moving past you, he'll run into my two brigades. I'm planted right in his path."

There was a saying in the army, *Who ever saw a dead cavalryman?* Poe thought of it as he looked at Lee. "Can you hold him?" he asked.

"Nevermore," said a raven.

Lee's smile turned to steel. "With all respect to your pets, General, I held Grant at Spotsylvania."

Gravely, Poe gave the cavalryman an elaborate, complimentary bow, and Lee returned it. Poe straightened and hobbled to face his brigade commanders.

Perhaps he had Fitz Lee convinced, perhaps not. But he knew—and the knowledge grated on his bones—that Robert Lee would not be convinced. Not with Poe's reputation for hysteria, for seeing Yankees everywhere he looked. The army commander would just assume his high-strung imagination created illusory armies behind every swirl of mist. As much as Poe hated it, he had to acknowledge this.

"General Lee has made his plans for today," he said. "He will attack to the west, where he conceives General Grant to be. He may not choose to believe any message from his other wing that the Yanks are moving."

Poe waited for a moment for a reply from the cavalryman. Fitz Lee was the commanding general's nephew; perhaps he could trade on the family connection somehow. But the bearded man remained silent.

"They are going to strike us, that is obvious," Poe said. "Grant has his back to the bend of the river, and he'll have to fight his way into the clear. But his men will have to struggle through the woods, and get across that swamp and the little creek, and they're doing it at night, with a heavy mist. They will not be in position to attack at first light. I suggest, therefore, that we attack him as soon as the mist clears, if not before. It may throw him off balance and provide the evidence we need to convince the high command that Mr. Grant has stolen a march upon us."

"Nevermore," said the ravens. "Nevermore."

Poe looked at Sextus, who was standing respectfully behind the half-circle of officers. "Feed the birds," he said. "It may keep them quiet."

"Yes, massa."

"General Poe." Fitz Lee was speaking. "There are two bridges across that creek—small, but they'll take the Yankees across. The water won't hold up the Yanks as long as you might think."

Poe looked at him. "The bridges were not burned after Hancock crossed the North Anna?"

Lee was uneasy. "General Ewell may have done it without my knowledge."

"If the bridges exist, that's all the more reason to attack as soon as we can."

"General." Clingman raised a hand. "Our brigades marched up in the dark. We ain't aligned, and we'll need to sort out our men before we can go forward."

"First light, General," said Poe. "Arrange your men, then go forward. We'll be going through forest, so give each man about two feet of front. Send out one combined company per regiment to act as skirmishers—we'll want to overwhelm their pickets and get a look at what lies in there before your main body strikes them."

Another brigadier piped up. "What do we align on, sir?"

"The rightmost brigade of the division—that's Barton's?" Heads nodded. Poe continued, gesturing into the mist with his stick, sketching out alignments. "Barton will align on the creek, and everyone will guide on him. When Barton moves forward, the others will move with him." He turned to Gregg and Law, both of whom were looking dubious. "I cannot suggest to Generals Gregg and Law how to order their forces. I have not been over the ground."

Law folded his arms. "General. You're asking us to attack a Yankee corps that's had two days to entrench."

"And not just any corps," Gregg added. "This is *Hancock*."

"We'll be outnumbered eight to one," Law said. "And we don't have any woods to approach through, the way y'all do. We'll have to cross a good quarter mile of open ground before we can reach them."

Poe looked at him blackly. Frustration keened in his heart. He took a long breath and fought down his growing rage.

Winfield Scott Hancock, he thought, known to the Yanks as Hancock the Superb. The finest of the Yankee commanders. He thought about the Ravens going up that little green slope toward the cemetery, with Hancock and his corps waiting on top, and nodded.

"Do as best as you can, gentlemen," he said. "I leave it entirely to you. I wish only that you show some activity. Drive in his pickets. Let him see some regimental flags, think he is going to be attacked."

Law and Gregg looked at one another. "Very well, sir," Law said.

Anger stabbed Poe again. They'd do nothing. He knew it; and if he ordered them into a fight they'd just appeal over his head to Anderson.

Nothing he could do about it. Keep calm.

Poe turned toward Fitz Lee. "I hope I may have your support."

The small man nodded. "I'll move some people forward." He gave a smile. "My men won't like being in the woods. They're used to clear country."

"Any additional questions?"

There were none. Poe sent his generals back to their commands and thanked Fitzhugh Lee for his cooperation.

"This may be the Wilderness all over again," Lee said. "Woods so heavy no one could see a thing. Just one big ambush with a hundred thousand men flailing around in the thickets."

"Perhaps the Yankees will not see our true numbers, and take us for a greater force," Poe said.

"We may hope, sir." Lee saluted, mounted, and spurred away.

Poe found himself staring at the black Starker house, that one softly lit eye of a window. Thinking of the dead girl inside, doomed to be buried on a battlefield.

Virginia Poe had been beautiful, so beautiful that sometimes Poe's heart would break just to look at her. Her skin was translucent as bone china, her long hair fine and black as midnight, her violet eyes unnaturally large, like those of a bird of Faerie. Her voice was delicate, as fragile and evanescent as the tunes she plucked from her harp. Virginia's aspect was unearthly, refined, ethereal, like an angel descended from some Mussulman paradise, and as soon as Poe saw his cousin he knew he could never rest unless he had that beauty for him always.

When he married her she was not quite fourteen. When she died, after five years of advancing consumption, she was not yet twenty-five. Poe was a pauper. After Virginia's death came *Eureka*, dissipation, madness. He had thought he could not live without her, had no real intention of doing so.

But now he knew he had found Virginia again, this time

in Evania. With Evania, as with Virginia, he could throw off his melancholy and become playful, gentle, joyful. With her he could sit in the parlor with its French wallpaper, play duets on the guitar, and sing until he could see the glow of his happiness reflected in Evania's eyes.

But in time a shadow seemed to fall between them. When Poe looked at his young bride, he seemed to feel an oppression on his heart, a catch in the melody of his love. Virginia had not asked for anything in life but to love her cousin. Evania was proud; she was willful; she grew in body and intellect. She developed tastes, and these tastes were not those of Poe. Virginia had been shy, otherworldly, a presence so ethereal it seemed as if the matter had been refined from her, leaving only the essence of perfected beauty and melancholy; Evania was a forthright presence, bold, a tigress in human form. She was a material presence; her delights were entirely those of Earth.

Poe found himself withdrawing before Evania's growing clarity. He moved their sleeping chamber to the topmost floor of the mansion, beneath a roof of glass skylights. The glass ceiling was swathed in heavy Oriental draperies to keep out the heat of the day; the windows were likewise covered. Persian rugs four deep covered the floor. Chinese bronzes were arranged to pour gentle incense into the room from the heads of dragons and lions.

With the draperies blocking all sources of the light, in the near-absolute, graveyard darkness, Poe found he could approach his wife. The fantastic decor, seen only by such light as slipped in under the door or through cracks in the draperies, heightened Poe's imagination to a soaring intensity. He could imagine that the hair he caressed was dark as a raven's wing; that the cheek he softly kissed was porcelain-pale; he could fancy, under the influence of the incense, that the earthy scent of Evania had been transformed to a scent far more heavenly; and he could almost perceive, as ecstasy flooded him, that the eyes that looked up into his were the large, luminous, angelic eyes of his lost love, the lady Virginia.

* * *

Poe sat in his tent and tried to eat an omelette made of eggs scavenged from Starker chickens. Fried ham sat untouched on the plate. Around him, the reserve divisional artillery creaked and rattled as the guns were set up on the Starkers' slight eminence. The ravens gobbled and cawed.

Poe put down his fork. He was too agitated to eat.

A drink, he thought. A soothing glass of sherry. The Starkers must have some; it would be easy to obtain.

He took a gulp of boiled coffee, took his stick, and hobbled out of the tent. The sky had lightened, and the mist had receded from the Starker plantation; Poe could see parts of his own line, a flag here and there, the crowns of trees. His men were moving forward out of their trenches, forming up on the far side of the abatis beyond. Officers' shouts carried faintly to his ear. The alignment was proceeding with difficulty. The battalions had become too confused as they marched to their places in the dark.

He remembered the Ravens in the cemetery, shrouded by gray gunsmoke as they were now hidden by gray mist.

Sherry, he thought again. The thought seemed to fill his mind with a fine, clear light. He could almost feel the welcome fire burning along his veins. A drink would steady him.

A color sergeant came running up from the Ravens, saluted, and took the two birds away to march with their brigade. Limbers rattled as horses pulled them out of harm's way down the reverse slope of the hill. Artillerymen lounged by their Napoleons and Whitworths, waiting for a target.

My god, Poe thought, why am I doing this? Suddenly it seemed the most pointless thing in the world. An offensive would only make things worse.

A horse trotted toward him from the Starker driveway. Poe recognized Moses, another of Anderson's aides, an eagle-nosed miniature sheeny that Longstreet had unaccountably raised to the rank of major. One of Longstreet's little lapses in taste, Poe thought; but unfortunately, as someone with pretensions to the title himself, he was honor-bound to treat the Hebrew as if his claim to the title of gentleman were genuine.

Sextus took Major Moses's horse, and Moses and Poe exchanged salutes. There weren't many men shorter than Poe, but Moses was one of them—he was almost tiny, with hands and feet smaller than a woman's. "General Anderson's compliments, sir," Moses said. "He wants to emphasize his desire for a diversionary attack."

"Look about you, Major," Poe said. "What do you see?"

Moses looked at the grayback soldiers rolling out of their entrenchments and shuffling into line, the artillerists waiting on the hilltop for a target, officers calling up and down the ranks.

"I see that General Anderson has been anticipated, sir," Moses said. "My mission has obviously been in vain."

"I would be obliged if you'd wait for a moment, Major," Poe said. "I may have a message for General Anderson by and by."

"With permission, sir, I should withdraw. The general may need me." Moses smiled. Dew dripped from his shoulder-length hair onto his blue riding cape. "Today promises to be busy, sir."

"I need you *here*, sir!" Poe snapped. "I want you to witness something."

Moses seemed startled. He recovered, a sly look entering his eyes, then he nodded. "Very well, sir."

In a motionless instant of perfect clarity, Poe understood the conspiracy of this calculating Jew. Moses would hang back, wait for confirmation of Poe's madness, Poe's error, then ride back to Anderson to try to have Poe removed from command. Moxley Sorrel might already have filled the staff tent with tales of Poe's nerves about to crack. Perhaps, Poe thought furiously, the sheeny intended to replace Poe *himself!*

Cold triumph rolled through Poe. Conspire though Moses might, Poe would be too crafty for him.

"When will the attack begin, Major?" Poe asked.

"It has already begun, sir. The mist cleared early to the west of us. The men were moving out just as I left General Anderson's headquarters."

Poe cocked his head. "I hear no guns, Major Moses."

"Perhaps there has been a delay. Perhaps—" Moses shrugged. "Perhaps the wet ground is absorbing the sound. Or there is a trick of the wind—"

"Nevertheless," Poe said, "I hear no guns."

"Yes, sir." Moses cleared his throat. "It is not unknown, sir."

"Still, Major Moses," said Poe. "I hear no guns."

Moses fell silent at this self-evident fact. Poe whirled around, his black cape flying out behind him, and stalked toward his tent. He could hear Moses's soft footsteps following behind.

Men on horseback came, reporting one brigade after another ready to move forward. Poe told them to wait here for the word to advance, then return to their commanders. Soon he had heard from every brigade but those of Gregg and Law—a messenger even came from Fitz Lee, reporting the cavalryman's readiness to move forward at Poe's signal. After ten minutes of agitated waiting, while the sky grew ever paler and the mist retreated to lurk among the trees, Poe sent an aide to inquire.

Poe gave an irritated look at his division waiting in their ranks for the signal. If the enemy had scouts out this way, they'd see the Confederates ready for the attack and warn the enemy.

Go forward with the four brigades he had? he wondered. Yes. No.

He decided to wait till his aide came back. He looked at his watch, then cast a glance over his shoulder at Major Moses.

"I hear no guns, Major," he said.

"You are correct, sir." Moses smiled thinly. "I take it you intend to enlighten me as to the significance of this?"

Poe nodded benignly. "In time, Major."

Moses swept off his hat in an elaborate bow. "You are

known as the master of suspense, sir. I take my hat off to
you, sir, I positively do."

Poe smiled. The Jew was amusing. He tipped his own
hat. "Thank you, Major."

Moses put on his hat. "I am an enthusiast of your work,
sir. I have a first edition of the *Complete Tales*. Had I
known I would encounter you, I would have had my wife
send it to me and begged you to inscribe it."

"I should be glad to sign it," Poe said, surprised. The
Complete and Corrected Tales and Poems of Edgar A. Poe
had been published at his own expense six years ago and
had sold precisely two hundred and forty-nine copies
throughout the United States—he knew precisely, because
the rest of the ten-thousand-copy edition was sitting in a
lumber room back home at Shepherd's Rest.

"Before the war," Moses said, "I used to read your work
aloud to my wife. The poems were particularly lovely, I
thought—so delicate. And there was nothing that would
bring a blush to her lovely cheek—I *particularly* appreciate
that, sir." Moses grew indignant. "There are too many
passages from poets that one cannot in decency read to a
lady, sir. Even in Shakespeare—" Moses shook his head.

"Fortunately," said Poe, "one has Bowdler."

"I thank that gentleman from my heart," said Moses. "As
I thank Tennyson, and Mr. Dickens, and Keats."

"Keats." Poe's heart warmed at the mention of the name.
"One scarcely could anticipate encountering his name here,
on a battlefield."

"True, sir. He is the most rarified and sublime of
poets—along, I may say, with yourself, sir."

Poe was surprised. "You flatter me, Major."

"I regret only that you are not more appreciated, sir." His
tiny hands gestured whitely in the air. "Some of my
correspondents have informed me, however, that you are
better known in Europe."

"Yes," Poe said. A dark memory touched him. "A
London publisher has brought out an edition of the *Complete Tales*. Unauthorized, of course. It has achieved some

success, but I never received so much as a farthing from it."

"I am surprised that such a thing can happen, sir."

Poe gave a bitter laugh. "It isn't the money—it is the brazen provocation of it that offended me. I hired a London solicitor and had the publisher prosecuted."

"I hope he was thrown in jail, sir."

Poe gave a smile. "Not quite. But there will be no more editions of my work in London, one hopes."

"I trust there won't be."

"Or in France, either. I was being translated there by some overheated poet named Charles Baudelaire—no money from that source, either, by the way—and the fellow had the effrontery to write me that many of my subjects, indeed entire texts, were exactly the same as those he had himself composed—except mine, of course, had been written earlier."

"Curious." Moses seemed unclear as to what he should make of this.

"This *gueux* wrote that he considered himself my *alter ego*." A smile twisted across Poe's face at the thought of his triumph. "I wrote that what *he* considered miraculous, *I* considered plagiarism, and demanded that he cease any association with my works on penalty of prosecution. He persisted in writing to me, so I had a French lawyer send him a stiff letter, and have not heard from him since."

"Very proper." Moses nodded stoutly. "I have always been dismayed at the thought of so many of these disreputable people in the literary world. Their antics can only distract the public from the true artists."

Poe gazed in benevolent surprise at Major Moses. Perhaps he had misjudged the man.

A horseman was riding toward him. Poe recognized the spreading mustachios of the aide he'd sent to Gregg and Law. The young man rode up and saluted breathlessly.

"I spoke to General Law, sir," he said. "His men were still eating breakfast. He and General Gregg have done *nothing*, sir, *nothing!*"

Poe stiffened in electric fury. "You will order Generals Gregg and Law to attack *at once!*" he barked.

The aide smiled. "Sir!" he barked, saluted, and turned his horse. Dirt clods flew from the horse's hooves as he pelted back down the line.

Poe hobbled toward the four messengers his brigadiers had sent to him. Anger smoked through his veins. "General Barton will advance at once," he said. "The other brigades will advance as soon as they perceive his movement has begun. Tell your commanders that I desire any prisoners to be sent to me." He pointed at Fitzhugh Lee's aide with his stick. "Ride to General Lee. Give him my compliments, inform him that we are advancing, and request his support."

Men scattered at his words, like shrapnel from his explosion of temper. He watched them with cold satisfaction.

"There is nothing more beautiful, sir," said Major Moses in his ear, "than the sight of this army on the attack."

Poe looked with surprise at Moses; in his burst of temper he had forgotten the man was here. He turned to gaze at the formed men a few hundred yards below him on the gentle slope. They had been in garrison for almost a year, and their uniforms and equipment were in better condition than most of this scarecrow army. They were not beautiful in any sense that Poe knew of the word, but he understood what the major meant. There was a beauty in warfare that existed in a realm entirely distinct from the killing.

"I know you served in Greece, sir," Moses said. "Did the Greek fighters for liberty compare in spirit with our own?"

Poe's heart gave a lurch, and he wondered in alarm if his ears were burning. "They were—indifferent," he said. "Variable." He cleared his throat. "Mercenary, if the truth be told."

"Ah." Moses nodded. "Byron found that also."

"I believe he did." Poe stared at the ground and wondered how to extricate himself. His Greek service was a lie he had encouraged to be published about himself. He had never fought in Greece when young, or served, as he had also claimed, in the Russian army. Instead—penniless, an outcast, thrown on his own resources by his Shylock of a stepfather—he had enlisted in the American army out of desperation, and served three years as a volunteer.

It had been his dread, these years he'd served the Confederacy, that he would encounter some old soldier who remembered serving alongside the eighteen-year-old Private Edgar A. Perry. His fears had never been realized, fortunately, but he had read everything he could on Byron and the Greek War of Independence in hopes he would not be tripped up by the curious.

"Ah," Poe said. He pointed with his stick. "The men are moving."

"A brilliant sight, sir." Moses's eyes shone.

Calls were rolling up the line, one after another, from Barton on the left to the Ravens next in line, then to Corse—all Virginia brigades—and then to Clingman's North Carolinians on the right. Poe could hear the voices distinctly.

"Attention, battalion of direction! Forward, guide cen-terrrr—*march*!"

The regiments moved forward, left to right, clumps of skirmishers spreading out ahead. Flags hung listlessly in the damp. Once the order to advance had been given, the soldiers moved in utter silence, in perfect parade-ground formation.

Just as they had gone for that cemetery, Poe thought. He remembered his great swell of pride at the way the whole division had done a left oblique under enemy fire that day, taking little half-steps to swing the entire line forty-five degrees, and then paused to dress the line before marching onward.

Sweeping through tendrils of mist that clung to the soldiers' legs, the division crossed the few hundred yards of ground between the entrenchments and the forest, and disappeared into the darkness and mist.

Poe wondered desperately if he was doing the right thing.

"Did you know Byron, sir?" Moses again.

Poe realized he'd been holding his breath, anticipating the sound of disaster as soon as his men began their attack. He let his breath go, felt relief spreading outward, like rot, from his chest.

"Byron died," he said, "some years before I went abroad."

Byron had been feeding worms for forty years, Poe thought, but there were Byrons still, hundreds of them, in this army. Once he had been a Byron himself—an American Childe Harold dressed in dramatic black, ready with the power of his mind and talent to defeat the cosmos. Byron had intended to conquer the Mussulman; Poe would do him better, with *Eureka*, by conquering God.

Byron had died at Missolonghi, bled to death by his personal physician as endless gray rain fell outside his tent and drowned his little army in the Peloponnesian mud. And nothing had come of Byron in the end, nothing but an example that inspired thousands of other young fools to die in similar pointless ways throughout the world.

For Poe the war had come at a welcome moment. His literary career had come to a standstill, with nine thousand seven hundred fifty-one copies of the *Complete Tales* sitting in his lumber room; his mother-in-law had bestirred herself to suggest, in kind but firm fashion, that his literary and landscaping projects were running up too fantastic a debt; and his relations with Evania—on Poe's part at least—were at best tentative.

When Virginia seceded and Maryland seemed poised to follow, Poe headed south with Sextus, a pair of fine horses, equipage, a curved Wilkinson light cavalry sword, Hardee's *Tactics*, a brace of massive nine-shot Le Mat revolvers, and of course the twelve hundred in gold. He kissed Evania and his beloved Mrs. Forster farewell—within a few months he would return with an army and liberate Shepherd's Rest and the rest of Maryland. He, as well as Byron, could be martial when the cause of liberty required it. He rode away with a singing heart.

Before him, as he woke in his bed his first night in

Richmond, he saw his vision, the benevolent madonna giving him her benediction. In going south he was being, he thought, faithful to Virginia; and he hoped to find the spirit, as well as the name, of his lost love embodied in the state to which he swore allegiance.

Jefferson Davis was pleased to give a colonel's commission to a veteran of the wars of Greek liberation, not to mention a fellow West Pointer—the West Point story, at least, being true, though Poe did not remind the President that, because the horrid Allan refused to support him, Poe had got himself expelled from the academy after six months.

There was no regiment available for the new colonel, so Poe began his military career on the staff of General Joseph E. Johnston, commanding in the Shenandoah Valley. He occupied himself by creating a cypher for army communications which, so far as he knew, had survived three years unbroken.

Johnston's army moved east on the railroad to unite with Beauregard's at First Manassas, and there Poe saw war for the first time. He had expected violence and death, and steeled himself against it. It gave him no trouble, but what shocked him was the *noise*. The continual roll of musketry, buzzing bullets, shouted orders, the blast of cannon, and the shriek of shells—all were calculated to unstring the nerves of a man who couldn't abide even a loud orchestra. Fortunately he was called upon mainly to rally broken troops—it had shocked him that Southern men could run like that—but in the end, after he'd got used to the racket, he had ridden, bullets singing over his head, in the final screaming, exhilarating charge that swept the Yankee army from the field, and he could picture himself riding that way forever, the fulfillment of the Byronic ideal, sunset glowing red on the sword in his hand as he galloped north to Maryland and the liberation of his home. . . .

Maryland never managed to secede, somehow, and Poe's Byronic liberation of his home state had to be postponed. Via blockade-runner, Poe exchanged passionate letters with his wife while remaining, in his heart, faithful to Virginia.

At the horrible, bungled battle of Seven Pines the next year, Major General Daniel Harvey Hill made a properly Byronic, if unsupported, attack against McClellan's left and lost half his men, as well as one of his brigadiers. Poe was promoted and given the shattered brigade. Joe Johnston, during the same battle, had been severely wounded, and the Army of Northern Virginia now had a new commander, one Robert E. Lee.

It did not take Poe long to discover that the ferocious, dyspeptic Harvey Hill was both an ignoramus and a lunatic. Before more than a few days had passed, neither spoke to the other: they communicated only in writing. Poe broke the Yanks' wigwag signal code, which didn't mean much at the time but was of help later, at Second Manassas.

But by then Poe was not with the army. Only a few days after taking command, Lee went on the offensive, and Poe, supported by exemplary reasoning and logic, refused point-blank Harvey Hill's order to take his brigade into Boatswain Swamp.

Now, after three years of war, almost all the American Byrons were dying or had been shot to pieces. Jeb Stuart, Jackson, Albert Sidney Johnston, Dick Garnett, Ewell, Hood, now Longstreet—all dead or maimed.

And Edgar A. Poe, leaning on his stick, a sick ache throbbing in his thigh, knew in his heart that Byron's death had been more merciful than anyone had known.

He had written the eulogy himself, never knowing it at the time. *But he grew old— /This knight so bold— /And o'er his heart a shadow /Fell as he found /No spot of ground /That looked like Eldorado.*

Byron's eulogy. Poe's, too. Stuart's, everyone's.

"Forty years dead," he said. "We have other poets now."

"Yourself, of course," said Major Moses, "and Tennyson."

"Walter Whitman," said Poe. The name left a savage, evil taste in his mouth.

"Obscene." Moses shivered. "Filth."

"I agree."

"You have denounced him yourself."

"Repeatedly."

Poe stared at the dark trees that had swallowed up his entire division. How many, he wondered, would come out of those woods nevermore? Sickness welled up inside him. In another minute he might weep. He turned and shouted for Sextus to bring him a chair.

The first edition of *Leaves of Grass* had happily escaped his notice. The second edition, with the preface by Emerson, had been sent to him for review at the *Southern Gentleman*. He had denounced it. Whitman and Emerson replied; Poe printed their replies and returned fire, and the fight went on for years, a war that prefigured the more deadly one begun in 1861.

A showdown, he had thought triumphantly. He had long distrusted the New England clique and feared their grip on the *North American Review*—the fact that they regarded the pedestrian and bourgeois Longfellow as a genius was reason enough for distrust. But now the South had its own literary magazine; Poe was no longer dependent on the approval of New England literary society for employment and regard.

Whitman, he wrote, knew nothing of versification. Whitman thought prostitutes and steam engines and common laborers fit subject for verse. Whitman knew nothing of the higher truths, of the sublime. Whitman filled his verses with the commonplace, with references so mundane and contemporary that in a hundred years no one would know what he was talking about. Whitman did not even *look* like a literary man. In the ambrotype used as a frontispiece, Whitman was dressed only in his shirt, looking like a farmer just come in from the fields, not an elevated, rarified, idealized creature—a poet—who spoke the language of the gods.

And Whitman was obscene. Grossly so. Clearly he was a degenerate of the worst description. Poe preferred not to imagine what Whitman did with those young men he wrote about in such evocative terms. Emerson might have used every rhetorical trick he knew to disguise the filth, or talk around it, but he never denied it—and this from someone who affected to worship the transcendental, meaning the refined and pure. It was then that Poe knew how bankrupt the North was, how desperate, as compared with his refined, elegant southland.

"Whitman is the perfect Yankee poet," Poe said. He drove his stick into the soil as if the earth hid Walter Whitman's heart. "No sublimity, no beauty, just stacks of prose disguised as poetry—sometimes not even prose, only lists. Lists of ordinary things. Produced so much stanzas an hour, like yards of cloth in a shoddyworks." He drove the stick again. "Like Yankee soldiers. Not inspired, just numerous."

Moses gave a laugh. "I must remember that, sir. For when General Longstreet returns. It will amuse him."

Poe stared at the woods, grinding his teeth. He hadn't meant to be witty; he was trying to make a point.

There was sudden musketry from the hardwoods, a succession of popping sounds turned hollow by multiple echoes. Then there was silence. Poe listened intently for a moment.

"Pickets," Moses said.

How many Yankees? Poe wondered. He turned back in the direction of his tent. Sextus was nowhere to be seen. "Bring a chair, you blasted orangutan!" he shouted. He had no idea whether or not Sextus heard him.

More popping sounds came from the woods—individual shots this time. From a different part of the line, Poe thought.

"Byrons can only die," he said. Moses looked at him in surprise. "We real poets, we're all too in love with death. Whitman writes about life, even the obscene parts of it, and that's why he will win. Why," he took a breath, trying to make himself clearer, "why the North will win."

Moses seemed to be struggling to understand this. "Sir," he said. "Sir, I don't understand."

More crackling from the woods. Poe's head moved left

and right, trying to find where it was coming from. A savage exultation beat a long tattoo in his heart. He was right, he was right, he was right *again*. He stepped up to Moses, stared into his eyes at a few inches' range.

"Do you hear guns from the west, Major?" he demanded. "Do you hear anything at all from Lee's offensive?"

"Why—" Major Moses stopped dead, licked his lips. There was pure bewilderment in his eyes. "Why are you doing this? Why are you fighting for the Cause?"

"I *hate* Whitman!" Poe shrieked. "I hate him, and I hate steam engines, I hate ironclad ships and repeating rifles and rifled artillery!"

"Your chair, Massa Poe," said Sextus.

A cacophony of sound was coming from the woods now, regular platoon volleys, one after another. The sound battered Poe's ears.

"I fight for the South because we are *right*, Major Moses!" Poe shouted. "I believe it—I have proved it rationally—we are *superior*, sir! The South fights for the right of one man to be superior to another, because he *is* superior, because he *knows* he is superior."

"Here's your chair, Massa Poe," said Sextus.

"Superior in mind, superior in cognitive faculty, superior in erudition! Superior in knowledge, in training, in sagacity! In appreciation of beauty, of form, of moral sense!" Poe pointed his stick at the woods. "Those Yankees—they are democracy, sir! Dragging even *poetry* into the muck! Walter Whitman addresses his verses to *women of the street—that* is democracy for you! Those Yankee soldiers, they are Whitmans with bayonets! I fight them because I must, because *someone* must fight for what is noble and eternal, even if only to die, like Byron, in some pointless—pointless—"

Pain seized his heart and he doubled over, coughing. He swung toward where Sextus stood with his camp chair, the cane still outstretched, and though he didn't mean to strike the African he did anyway, a whiplike crack on the upper arm. Sextus dropped the chair and stepped back, surprise on his face. Anger crackled in Poe, fury at the African's stupidity and inability to get out of the way.

"Take that, damn you, worthless nigger!" Poe spat. He spun and fell heavily into his chair.

The battle in the woods had progressed. Now Poe heard only what Great Frederick called *bataillenfeuer*, battle fire, no longer volleys but simply a continuous din of musketry as the platoon sergeants lost tactical control of their men and the battle dissolved into hundreds of little skirmishes fought simultaneously. Poe heard no guns—no way to get artillery through those woods.

Moses was looking at Poe with wide, staring eyes. He reached into a pocket and mopped Poe's spittle from his face. Poe gave him an evil look.

"Where is Lee's offensive, sir?" he demanded. "Where is the sound of *his* fight?"

Moses seemed confused. "I should get back to General Anderson, sir," he said. "I—"

"Stay by me, Major," Poe said. His voice was calm. An absolute lucidity had descended upon him; perhaps he was the only man within fifty miles who knew precisely what was happening here. "I have not yet shown you what I wish to show you."

He listened to the fight roll on. Sometimes it nearly died away, but then there would be another outburst, a furious racket. Lines of gunsmoke rose above the trees. It would be pointless for Poe to venture into the woods himself—he could not control an entire division if he could not see twenty feet beyond his own position.

A horseman galloped up. "General Gregg's compliments, sir. He and General Law are ready to advance."

Poe felt perfectly sunny. "My compliments to General Gregg. Tell him that Poe's division is a little ahead of him. I would be obliged if he'd catch up."

The man rode away. People were leaking back out of the woods now: wounded men, some crawling; skulkers, stragglers; bandsmen carrying people on stretchers. Here and there were officers running, bearing messages, guards marching back with blue prisoners.

"Lots of Yankees, sir!" The first messenger, a staff lieutenant of perhaps nineteen, was winded and staggering with the effort it had taken him to run here. "We've hit them in flank. They were in column of march, sir. Colonel Terry wishes you to know he's driving them, but he expects they'll stiffen."

"Good job, boy." Terry was the man who commanded the Ravens in Poe's absence. "Give Colonel Terry my thanks."

"Sir!" Another messenger. "General Clingman's compliments. We've driven them in and captured a battery of guns."

Guns, Poe thought. Useless in the woods. We can't get them away, and the Yankees'll have them back ere long.

The sound of musketry staggered higher, doubled and tripled in fury. The messengers looked at each other, breathing hard, appalled at the noise. The Yanks, Poe concluded, had rallied and were starting to fight back.

"Tell Colonel Terry and General Clingman to press them as hard as possible. Try to hold them in the woods. When the Yanks press too hard, retire to the trenches."

"Yes, sir."

"Prisoners, sir." Another voice. "General Barton sends them as requested."

Stunned-looking Yanks in dew-drenched caped overcoats, all captured in the first rush. None of them looked over twenty. Poe rose from his chair and hobbled toward them. He snatched the cap from the first prisoner and swung toward Major Moses.

"Major Moses," he said in triumph, "do you know the motto of the Yankee Second Corps?"

Moses blinked at him. "No, sir."

"'Clubs are Trumps'!" Poe told him. "Do you know why, sir?"

Moses shook his head.

"Because Hancock's Corps wears a trefoil badge on their

forage caps, like a club on a playing card." He threw the prisoner's cap down before Moses's feet. "What do you see on *that* forage cap, sir?" he asked.

"A cross," said Moses.

"A *saltire*, sir!" Poe laughed.

He had to be thorough. The upper echelons were never easily convinced. Two years before, during the Seven Days, he had demonstrated, with complete and irrefutable logic, that it was suicidal for Harvey Hill's division to plunge forward into Boatswain Swamp in hopes of contacting Yankees on the other side. When the ignorant madman Hill repeated his order, Poe had stood on his logic and refused— and been removed from command and placed under arrest. He had not been comforted when he had been proven right. His cherished new brigade, along with the rest of D.H. Hill's division, had been shattered by three lines of Union infantry dug into a hill just behind the swamp, with artillery lined hub-to-hub on the crest. And when, red-faced with anger, he had challenged Hill to a duel, the lunatic had only laughed at him to his face.

"Specifically," Poe said pedantically, pointing at the Yankee forage cap, "a *white* saltire on a blue background! That means these men come from the Second Division of the Sixth Corps—*Wright's* Corps, Major, not Hancock's! The same Sixth Corps that Lee was supposed to attack this morning, on the other end of the line! *I am facing at least two Yankee corps with one division, and Lee is marching into empty air! Grant has moved his army left again while we slept!*"

Moses's eyes widened. "My God," he said.

"Take that cap to General Anderson with my compliments! Tell him I will need his support!"

Moses picked up the cap. "Yes, sir."

Poe lunged among the prisoners, snatching off caps, throwing them to his aides. "Take *that* to General Lee! And *that* to Ewell! And *that* to A.P. Hill! Say I must have their support! Say that *Wright* is here!"

As Moses and Poe's aides galloped away, the firing died

down to almost nothing. One side or another had given way.

Poe returned to his seat and waited to see which side it had been.

It was Poe's division that had given way in the woods, but not by much. Messengers panting back from his brigades reported that they'd pushed the Yanks as far as possible, then fallen back when they could push no more. The various units were trying to reestablish contact with one another in the woods and form a line. They knew the Yankee assault was coming.

Pull them back? Poe wondered. He'd made his case to his superiors—maybe he'd better get his men back into their trenches before the Yanks got organized and smashed them.

Action, he thought, and reaction. The two fundamental principles of the operating Universe, as he had demonstrated in *Eureka*. His attack had been an action; the Yankee reaction had yet to come.

He tapped gloved fingers on the arm of his chair while he made careful calculations. The Yankees had been struck in the right flank as they were marching south along narrow forest roads. Due to surprise and their tactical disadvantage, they had been driven in, then, as the rebel attack dissipated its force, turned and fought. This reaction, then, had been instinctive—they had not fought as units, which must have been shattered, but as uncoordinated masses of individuals. The heavy forest had broken up the rebel formation in much the same manner, contributing to their loss of momentum.

The Yankees would react, but in order to do so in any coordinated way they would have to reassemble their units, get them in line of battle, and push them forward through trees that would tend to disperse their cohesion. Wright had three divisions; normally it would take a division about an hour, maybe more, to deploy to the right front from a column of march. The woods would delay any action. The bluecoats' own confusion would worsen things even more. Say two hours, then.

Any attack made before then would be uncoordinated,

just local commanders pushing people forward to the point of contact. Poe's men could handle that. But in two hours a coordinated attack would come, and Poe's division would be swamped by odds of at least three to one, probably more.

Poe looked at his watch. He would keep his men in the woods another ninety minutes, then draw them back. Their presence in the woods might serve to make the Yanks cautious, when what Grant really wanted to do was drive straight forward with everything he had.

His thoughts were interrupted by a message from Evander Law on his left flank. He and Gregg had about completed their preparations to advance, the messenger reported, when they discovered that Hancock's men across the woods were leaving their trenches and preparing to attack them. Gregg and Law had therefore returned to their trenches to ready themselves for the attack.

Poe bit back on his temper. It *might* be true. He would have to see in person. He told one of his aides to remain there and direct any messages to the left of the line, then told Sextus to ready his buggy.

Sextus looked at him in a sullen, provoking way. He was cradling the arm Poe had struck with his cane. "You'll have to drive yourself, massa," he said. "You broke my arm with that stick."

Annoyance warmed Poe's nerves. "Don't be ridiculous! I did not hit you with sufficient force. Any schoolboy—"

"I'm sorry, massa. It's broke. I broke an arm before, I know what it's like."

Poe was tempted to hit Sextus again and break the arm for certain; but instead he lurched for his buggy, hopped inside, and took the reins. He didn't have the time to reason with the darky now. Sextus heaved himself up into the seat beside Poe, and Poe snapped the reins. His staff, on horseback, followed.

The battle broke on the left as he drove, a searing, ripping sound bounding up from the damp, dead ground. Poe seized the whip and labored his horse; the light buggy bounded over the turf, threatened to turn over, righted itself.

The first attack was over by the time Poe's buggy rolled behind Law's entrenchments, and the wall of sound had died down to the lively crackle of sharpshooters' rifles and the continual boom of smoothbore artillery. It took Poe a while to find Law—he was in the first line of works—and by the time Poe found him, the second Yankee attack was beginning, a constant hammering roar spreading across the field.

Law stood in the trench, gnawing his lip, his field glasses in his hand. There was a streak of powder residue across his forehead and great patches of sweat under the arms of his fine gray jacket. Law jumped up on the firing step, jostling his riflemen who were constantly popping up with newly loaded muskets, and pointed. "Gibbon's men, sir! The Black Hats! Look!"

Poe swung himself up behind the brigadier, peered out beneath the head log, and saw, through rolling walls of gunsmoke and the tangle of abatis, lines of blue figures rolling toward him. He heard the low moaning sound made by Northern men in attack, like a choir of advancing bears. . . . The ones coming for him were wearing black felt hats instead of their usual forage caps, which marked them as the Iron Brigade of Gibbon's division, the most hard-hitting unit of the hardest-hitting corps in the Yankee army. *We've got two brigades here,* Poe thought frantically, *and we've got an entire corps coming at us.*

A Yankee Minié whacked solidly into the head log above him. Poe jerked his head back and turned to Law. The smell of powder was sharp in his nostrils. The air filled with the whistling sound of cannon firing canister at close range.

"You must hold, sir! No going back!"

Law grinned. "Do you think the Yankees'll *let* us go back?"

"Hold to the last! I will bring up support!"

Law only looked at him as if he were mad. And then the Yankees were there, their presence at first marked by a swarm of gray soldiers surging back from the firing step, almost knocking Poe from his feet as he was carried to the

muddy back of the trench, the soldiers pointing their
muskets upward, groping in their belts for bayonets . . .

Poe reached automatically for one of his Le Mat revolvers and then realized he'd left them in his headquarters
tent—they were just too heavy to carry all the time. His
only weapon was his stick. He stiffened and took a firmer
grip on the ivory handle. His mind reeled at the suddenness
of it all.

The sky darkened as bluecoats swarmed up on the head
log, rifles trained on the packed Confederates. The Stars
and Stripes, heavy with battle honors, rose above the
parapet, waved by an energetic sergeant with a bushy red
beard and a tattered black hat. Musketry crackled along the
trench as men fired into one another's faces. "Look at 'em
all!" Law screamed. "Look at 'em all!" He shoved a big
Joslyn revolver toward the Yankees and pulled the trigger
repeatedly. People were falling all over. Screams and roars
of defiance and outrage echoed in Poe's ears.

He stood, the sound battering at his nerves. All he could
do here, he thought bitterly, was get shot. He was amazed
at his own perfect objectivity and calm.

And then the Union standard-bearer was alone, and
grayback infantry were pointing their rifles at him. "Come
to the side of the Lord!" Evander Law shouted; and the red
beard looked around him in some surprise, then shrugged,
jumped into the ditch, and handed over the flag of the
Twenty-fourth Michigan.

The soldiers declined to shoot him, Poe thought, as a
compliment to his bravery. *Never let it be said we are not
gallant.*

Poe jumped for the firing step, and saw the blue lines in
retreat. Dead men were sprawled over the abatis, their black
hats tumbled on the ground. The ground was carpeted with
wounded Yanks trying to find little defilades where they
would be sheltered from the bullets that whimpered above
their heads. They looked like blue maggots fallen from the
torn belly of something dead, Poe thought, and then

shuddered. Where was the poetry in this? Here even death was unhallowed.

Soldiers jostled Poe off the firing step and chased off the bluecoats with Minié balls. Confederate officers were using swords and knives to cut up the Yankee flag for souvenirs. Poe stepped up to Law.

"They'll be back," Law said, mumbling around a silver powder flask in his teeth. He was working the lever of his Joslyn revolver, tamping a bullet down on top of the black powder charge.

"I will bring men to your relief."

"Bring them soon, sir."

"I will find them somewhere."

Law rotated the cylinder and poured another measured round of fine black powder. "Soon, sir. I beg you."

Poe turned to one of his aides. "Find General Gregg on the left. Give him my compliments, and tell him what I have told General Law. He must hold till relieved. After that, ride to General Anderson and persuade him to release the rest of Field's division to come to the aid of their comrades."

Wounded men groaned in the trenches and on the firing step, cursing, trying to stop their bleeding. Yankee blood dripped down the clay trench wall. Cannon still thundered, flailing at the bluecoats. Southern sharpshooters banged away with Armstrong rifles equipped with telescopic sights almost as long as the gun, aiming at any officers. Poe found himself astounded that he could have an intelligible conversation in this raucous, unending hell.

He limped away down a communications trench and found Sextus in the rear, holding his buggy amid a group of waiting artillery limbers. Poe got into the buggy without a word and whipped up the horses.

Behind him, as he rode, the thunder of war rose in volume as Hancock pitched into another attack. This time the sound didn't die down.

On the way back to his tent Poe encountered a courier from Fitz Lee. His men had moved forward dismounted, run into some startled bluecoats from Burnside's Ninth Corps, and after a short scrap had pulled back into their entrenchments.

Burnside. That meant three Yankee corps were facing two southern divisions, one of them cavalry.

Burnside was supposed to be slow, and everyone knew he was not the most intelligent of Yankees—anyone who conducted a battle like Fredericksburg had to be criminally stupid. Poe could only hope he would be stupid today.

Back at his tent, he discovered Walter Taylor, one of Robert Lee's aides, a young, arrogant man Poe had never liked. Poe found himself growing angry just looking at him.

"Burnside, sir!" he snapped, pulling the buggy to a halt. "Burnside, Wright, *and* Hancock, and they're all on my front!"

Taylor knit his brows. "Are you certain about Burnside, sir?" he asked.

"Fitzhugh Lee confirms it! That's three-fourths of Grant's army!"

Taylor managed to absorb this with perfect composure. "General Lee would like to know if you have any indication of the location of Warren's Fifth Corps."

Poe's vitals burned with anger. "I don't!" he roared. "But I have no doubt they'll soon be heading this way!"

Poe lurched out of his buggy and headed for his tent and the Le Mat revolvers waiting in his trunk. Judging by the sound, Gregg and Law were putting up a furious fight behind him. There was more fighting going on, though much less intense, on his own front.

Poe flung open the green trunk, found the revolvers, and buckled on the holsters. He hesitated for a moment when he saw the saber, then decided against it and dropped the trunk lid. Chances were he'd just trip on the thing. Lord knew the revolvers were heavy enough.

Taylor waited outside the tent, bent over to brush road dirt from his fine gray trousers. He straightened as Poe hobbled out. "I will inform General Lee you are engaged," he said.

Poe opened his mouth to scream at the imbecile, but took a breath instead, tried to calm his rage. With the high command, he thought, always patience. "My left needs help," Poe said. "Hancock's attacking two brigades with his entire corps. I'm facing Wright on my front with four brigades, and Fitz Lee's facing Burnside with two on the right."

"I will inform General Lee."

"Tell him we are in direst extremity. Tell him that we cannot hold onto Hanover Junction unless substantially reinforced. Tell him my exact words."

"I will, sir." Taylor nodded, saluted, mounted his horse, rode away. Poe stared after him and wondered if the message was going to get through it all, or if the legend of Poe's alarmism and hysteria were going to filter it—alter it—make it as nothing.

More fighting burst out to his front. Poe cupped his ears and swiveled his head, trying to discover direction. The war on his left seemed to have died away. Poe returned to his chair and sat heavily. His pistols were already weighing him down.

Through messengers he discovered what had happened. On his third attack, Hancock had succeeded in getting a lodgment in the Confederate trenches between Gregg and Law. They had been ejected only by the hardest, by an attack at bayonet point. Evander Law had been killed in the fighting; his place had been taken by Colonel Bowles of the 4th Alabama. Bowles requested orders. Poe had no hope to give him.

"Tell Colonel Bowles he must hold until relieved."

There was still firing to his front. His brigadiers in the woods were being pressed, but the Yankees as yet had made no concerted assault. Poe told them to hold on for the present. It would be another forty-five minutes, he calculated, before the Yanks could launch a coordinated assault.

Comparative silence fell on the battlefield. Poe felt his nerves gnawing at him, the suspense spreading through him like poison. After forty-five minutes, he gave his brigades in the woods permission to fall back to their entrenchments.

As he saw clumps of men in scarecrow gray emerging from the woods, he knew he could not tell them what he feared, that Robert Lee was going to destroy their division. Again.

After the Seven Days' Battles, Lee had chosen to lose the paperwork of Poe's impending court-martial. Poe, his brigade lost, his duel unfought, was assigned to help construct the military defenses of Wilmington.

Later, Poe would be proven right about Harvey Hill. Lee eventually shuffled him west to Bragg's army, but Bragg couldn't get along with him either and soon Hill found himself unemployed.

Poe took small comfort in Hill's peregrinations as he languished on the Carolina coast while Lee's army thrashed one Yankee commander after another. He wrote long letters to any officials likely to get him meaningful employment, and short, petulant articles for Confederate newspapers: Why wasn't the South building submarine rams? Why did they not take advantage, like the North, of observation from balloons? Why not unite the forces of Bragg and Johnston, make a dash for the Ohio, and reclaim Kentucky?

There were also, in Wilmington, women. Widows, many of them, or wives whose men were at war. Their very existence unstrung his nerves, made him frantic; he wrote them tempestuous letters and demanded their love in terms alternately peremptory and desperate. Sometimes, possibly because it seemed to mean so much to him, they surrendered. None of them seemed to mind that he snuffed all the candles, drew all the drapes. He told them he was concerned for their reputation, but he wanted darkness for his own purposes.

He was remaining faithful to Virginia.

Perhaps the letter-writing campaign did some good; perhaps it was just the constant attrition of experienced officers that mandated his reemployment. His hopes, at any rate, were justified. A brigade was free under George

Pickett, and furthermore it was a lucky brigade, one that all three Confederate corps commanders had led at one time or another. Perhaps, Poe thought, that was an omen.

Poe was exultant. Lee was going north after whipping Hooker at Chancellorsville. Poe thought again of liberating Maryland, of riding on his thoroughbred charger to Shepherd's Rest, galloping to the heart of the place, to the white arabesque castle that gazed in perfect isolate splendor over the fabulous creation of his soul, his own water paradise. Once he fought for it, Shepherd's Rest would be *his*; he could dispossess the restless spirits that had made him so uneasy the last few years.

Determination entered his soul. He would be the perfect soldier. He would never complain, he would moderate his temper, he would offer his advice with diffidence. He had a reputation to disprove. The army, to his relief, welcomed him with open arms. Hugin and Munin appeared, delivered by grinning staff men who wore black feathers in their hats and chanted "Nevermore." His immediate superior, the perfumed cavalier George Pickett, was not a genius; but unlike many such he knew it, and happily accepted counsel from wiser heads. Longstreet, Poe's corps commander, was absolutely solid, completely reliable, the most un-Byronic officer imaginable but one that excited Poe's admiration. Poe enjoyed the society of his fellow brigadiers, white-haired Lo Armistead and melancholy Dick Garnett. The Southern officer corps was young, bright, and very well educated—riding north they traded Latin epigrams, quotations from *Lady of the Lake* or *The Corsair*, and made new rhymes based on those of their own literary celebrity, whose works had been read to many in childhood. *Of the rapture that runs*, quoth Lo Armistead, *To the banging and the clanging of the guns, guns, guns. Of the guns, guns, guns, guns, guns, guns, guns—To the roaring and the soaring of the guns!*

It was perfect. During the long summer marches into the heart of the North, Poe daydreamed of battle, of the wise gray father Lee hurling his stalwarts against the Yankees, breaking them forever, routing them from Washington, Baltimore, Shepherd's Rest. Lee was inspired, and so was his army. Invincible.

Poe could feel History looking over his shoulder. The world was holding its breath. This could be the last fight of the war. If he could participate in this, he thought, all the frustrating months in North Carolina, all the battles missed, would be as nothing.

Pickett's division, the army's rear guard, missed the first two days of the battle centered around the small crossroads town in Pennsylvania. Arriving that night, they made camp behind a sheltering ridge and were told that they would attack the next day in the assault that would shatter the Yankees for good and all. Pickett, who had been assigned elsewhere during Lee's last two victories, was delighted. At last he would have his opportunity for glory.

The next morning the officers of Pickett's division and the other two divisions that would make the attack were taken forward over the sheltering ridge to see the enemy positions. The attack would go *there*, said Lee, pointing with a gloved hand. Aiming for those umbrella-shaped trees on the enemy-held ridge, beneath which there was said to be a cemetery.

Standing in the stirrups of his white-socked thoroughbred, craning at the enemy ridge, Poe felt a darkness touching his heart. Across a half-mile of open ground, he thought, in plain sight of the enemy, an enemy who has had two days in which to dig in . . .

Was Lee serious? he thought. Was Lee mad?

No. It was not to be thought of. Lee hadn't lost a major battle in his entire career, Sharpsburg, of course, being a draw. There was method in this, he thought, and he could discern it through ratiocination. Perhaps the Yanks were weary, perhaps they were ready to give way. In any case, he had resolved not to complain.

Pickett left the ridge whistling, riding toward the Yanks to scout out the ground. Poe and the other brigadiers followed.

Longstreet remained behind. Poe discovered later that he had seen the same things that Poe had seen, and wanted a last chance to change Lee's mind. When time came to order the advance, Longstreet could not give the order. He just nodded, and then turned his head away.

Later that day Poe brought his men forward, marching with drawn sword at the head of the Ravens, Hugin and Munin crackling and fluffing their feathers on their perch just behind. He remembered with vivid intensity the wild-flowers in the long grass, the hum of bees, the chaff rising from the marching feet, the absolute, uncharacteristic silence of the soldiers, seeing for the first time what was expected of them.

And then came the guns. There were two hundred cannon in the Northern lines, or so the Yankee papers boasted afterward, and there was not a one of them without an unobstructed target. In the last year Poe had forgotten what shell-fire was like, the nerve-shattering shriek like the fabric of the universe being torn apart, the way the shells seemed to hover in air forever, as if deliberately picking their targets, before plunging into the Confederate ranks to blossom yellow and black amid the sounds of buzzing steel and crying men.

The sound was staggering, the banging and the clanging of the guns, guns, guns, but fortunately Poe had nothing to do but keep his feet moving forward, one after another. The officers had been ordered to stay dismounted, and all had obeyed but one: Dick Garnett, commanding the brigade on Poe's left, was too ill to walk all that way, and had received special permission to ride.

Garnett, Poe knew, would die. The only mounted man in a group of twelve thousand, he was doomed and knew it.

Somehow there was an air of beauty about Garnett's sacrifice, something fragile and lovely. Like something in a poem.

The cemetery, their target, was way off on the division's left, and Pickett ordered a left oblique, the entire line of five thousand swinging like a gate toward the target. As the

Ravens performed the operation, Poe felt a slowly mounting horror. To his amazement he saw that his brigade was on the absolute right of the army, nothing beyond him, and he realized that the oblique exposed his flank entirely to the Union batteries planted on a little rocky hill on the Yankee left.

Plans floated through his mind. Take the endmost regiment and face it toward Yankees? But that would take it out of the attack. Probably it was impossible anyway. But who could guard his flank?

In the meantime Pickett wanted everyone to hit at once, in a compact mass, and so he had the entire division dress its ranks. Five thousand men marked time in the long grass, each with his hand on the shoulder of the man next to him, a maneuver that normally took only a few seconds but that now seemed to take forever. The guns on the rocky hill were plowing their shot right along the length of the rebel line, each shell knocking down men like tenpins. Poe watched, his nerves wailing, as his men dropped by the score. The men couldn't finish dressing their ranks, Poe thought, because they were taking so many casualties they could never close the ranks fast enough, all from the roaring and the soaring of the guns, guns, guns. . . . He wanted to scream in protest: *Forward! Guide center!* but the evolution went on, men groping to their left and closing up as the shells knocked them down faster than they could close ranks.

Finally Pickett had enough and ordered the division onward. Poe nearly shrieked in relief. At least now the Yankees had a moving target.

But now they were closer, and the men on the Yankee ridge opened on Poe's flank with muskets. Poe felt his nerves cry at every volley. Men seemed to drop by the platoon. How many had already gone? Did he even have half the brigade left?

The target was directly ahead, the little stand of trees on the gentle ridge, and between them was a little white Pennsylvania farmhouse, picture-book pretty. Somewhere around the house Poe and his men seemed to lose their sense of direction. They were still heading for the cemetery, but somehow Garnett had gotten in front of them. Poe could see Garnett's lonely figure, erect and defiant on his horse, still riding, floating really, like a poem above the battle.

The cemetery was closer, though, and he could see men crouched behind a stone wall, men in black hats. The Iron Brigade of Hancock's Corps, their muskets leveled on the stone wall, waiting for Garnett to approach . . .

And then suddenly the battle went silent, absolutely silent, and Poe was sitting upright on the ground and wondering how he got there. Some of his aides were mouthing at him, but he snatched off his hat and waved it, peremptory, pointing at the cemetery, ordering everyone forward. As he looked up he saw in that instant the Federal front blossom with smoke, and Dick Garnett pitch off his horse with perhaps a dozen bullets in him; and it struck Poe like a blow to the heart that there was no poetry in this, none whatever. . . .

His men were plowing on, following Garnett's. Poe tried to stand, but a bolt of pain flashed through him, and all he could do was follow the silent combat from his seated position. A shell had burst just over his head, deafening him and shattering his right thigh with a piece of shrapnel that hadn't even broken his skin.

Another line of men rushed past Poe, Armistead's, bayonets leveled. Poe could see Armistead in the lead, his black hat raised on saber-tip as a guide for his men, his mouth open in a silent cheer, his white mane flying. . . . And then the last of Pickett's division was past, into the smoke and dust that covered the ridge, charging for the enemy trees and the cemetery that claimed them, leaving Poe nothing to do but sit in the soft blossoming clover and watch the bees travel in silence from one flower to another. . . .

The first sound he heard, even over the tear of battle, was a voice saying "Nevermore." Hugin and Munin were croaking from the clover behind him, their standard-bearer having been killed by the same shell that had dropped Poe.

The sounds of battle gradually worked their way back into his head. Some of his men came back, and a few of them picked him up and carried him rearward, carried him along with the ravens back to the shelter of the ridge that marked the Confederate line. Poe insisted on facing the Yanks the entire way, so that if he died his wounds would be in the front. A pointless gesture, but it took away some of the pain. The agony from the shattered bone was only a foretaste of the soul-sickness that was to come during the long, bouncing, agonizing ambulance ride to the South as the army deserted Pennsylvania and the North and the hope of victory that had died forever there with Armistead. He had died on Cemetery Ridge, shot dead carrying his plumed hat aloft on the tip of his sword, his other hand placed triumphantly on the barrel of a Yankee gun.

"Law is dead, General Gregg is wounded," Poe reported. "Their men have given way entirely. Colonel Bowles reports he's lost half his men, half at least, and the remainder will not fight. They have also lost some guns, perhaps a dozen."

Robert Lee looked a hundred years dead. His intestinal complaint having struck him again, Lee was seated in the back of a closed ambulance that had been parked by the Starker house. He wore only a dressing gown, and his white hair fell over his forehead. Pain had drawn claws down his face, gouging deep tracks in his flesh.

"I have recalled the army," Lee said. "Rodes's division will soon be up." He gave a look to the man who had drawn his horse up beside the wagon. "Is that not correct, General Ewell?"

"I have told them to come quickly, General." Ewell was a bald man with pop eyes. He was strapped in the saddle, having lost a leg at Second Manassas during a fight with those damned Black Hats. Now that Poe thought about it, perhaps the Black Hats were becoming a *Leitmotiv* in all this shambles. Ewell's horse was enormous, a huge shambling creature, and the sight of it loping along with Ewell bobbing atop was considered by the soldiers to be a sight of pure high comedy.

Poe thought it pathetic. All that stands between Grant and Richmond, he thought, is a bunch of sick old men who cannot properly sit a horse. The thought made him angry.

"We must assemble," Lee said. His voice was faint. "We must assemble and strike those people."

Perhaps, Poe thought, Lee was a great man. Poe could not bring himself, any longer, to believe it. The others here had memories of Lee's greatness. Poe could only remember George Pickett, tears streaming down his face, screaming at Lee when the old man asked him to rally his command: *"General Lee, I have no division!"*

Poe looked from Ewell to Lee. "Gentlemen," he said, "I would suggest that Rodes be sent north to contain Hancock."

Lee nodded.

"The next division needs to be sent to Hanover Junction. If we lose the railroad, we will have to fall back to Richmond or attack Grant where he stands."

Lee nodded again. "Let it be so." A spasm passed across his face. His hands clutched at his abdomen and he bent over.

We may lose the war, Poe thought, because our commander has lost control of his bowels. And a case of the sniffles killed Byron, because his physician was a cretin.

The world will always destroy you, he thought. *And the world will make you ridiculous while it does so.*

General Lee's spasms passed. He looked up, his face hollow. Beads of sweat dotted his nose. "I will send an urgent message to General W.H.F. Lee," he said. "His cavalry division can reinforce that of General Fitzhugh Lee."

Bitter amusement passed through Poe at Lee's careful correctness. He would not call his son "Rooney," the way everyone else did; he referred to him formally, so there would be no hint of favoritism. Flattened by dysentery the man might be, and the Yankees might have stolen a day's march on him; but he would not drop his Southern courtesy.

Another spasm struck Lee. He bent over double. "Pardon me, gentlemen," he gasped. "I must retire for a moment."

His aides carefully drew the little rear doors of the ambulance to allow the commander-in-chief a little privacy. Ewell turned his head and spat.

Poe hobbled a few paces away and looked down at his own lines. Gregg and Law's brigades had given way an hour ago, on the fourth assault, but of the Yanks in the woods there had been no sign except for a few scouts peering at the Confederate trenches from the cover of the trees. Poe knew that the longer the Yankees took to prepare their attack, the harder it would be.

A four-wheel open carriage came up, drawn by a limping plow horse, probably the only horse the armies had spared the soberly dressed civilians who rode inside.

They were going to the funeral of the Starker girl. Battle or no, the funeral would go on. There was humor in this, somewhere; Poe wondered if the funeral was mocking the battle or the other way around.

He tipped his new hat to the ladies dismounting from the carriage and turned to study the woods with his field glasses.

Hancock had broken through to the north of the swampy stream, but hadn't moved much since then—victory had disorganized his formations as much as defeat had disorganized the losers. Hancock, when he moved, could either plunge straight ahead into the rear of Anderson's corps or pivot his whole command, like a barn door, to his left and into Poe's rear. In the latter case Poe would worry about him, but not till then. If Hancock chose to make that lumbering turn, a path which would take him through dense woods that would make the turn difficult to execute in any case, Poe would have plenty of warning from the remnants of Gregg and Law's wrecked brigades.

The immediate danger was to his front. What were Burnside and Wright waiting for? Perhaps they had got so

badly confused by Poe's attack that they were taking forever
to sort themselves out.

Perhaps they were just being thorough.

Poe limped to where his camp chair waited and was
surprised that the short walk had taken his breath away. The
Le Mats were just too heavy. He unbuckled his holsters, sat,
and waited.

To the west, Rodes's division was a long cloud of dust.
To the south, Rooney Lee's cavalry division was another.

Another long hour went by. A train moved tiredly east on
the Virginia Central. Rooney Lee's men arrived and went
into position on the right. Amid the clatter of reserve
artillery battalions galloping up were more people arriving
for the funeral: old men, women, children. The young men
were either in the army or hiding from conscription. Soon
Poe heard the singing of hymns.

Then the Yankees were there, quite suddenly and without
preamble, the trees full of blue and silver, coming to the old
Presbyterian melody rising from the Starker house. The
bluecoats made no more noise on the approach than
Pickett's men had on the march to Cemetery Ridge. Poe
blinked in amazement. Where had they all come from?

Then suddenly the world was battle, filled with the
tearing noise of musketry from the trenches, the boom of
Napoleon guns, the eerie banshee wail of the hexagonal-
shaped shells from the Whitworth rifled artillery fired over
the heads of Poe's men into the enemy struggling through
the abatis, then finally the scream and moan and animal
sounds of men fighting hand to hand. . . .

Poe watched through his field glasses, mouth dry, nerves
leaping with every cannon shot. There was nothing he could
do, no reserves he could lead into the fight like a Walter
Scott cavalier on horseback, no orders he could give that his
own people in the trenches wouldn't know to give on their
own. He was useless.

He watched flags stagger forward and back, the bluecoats
breaking into his trenches at several points, being flung
again into the abatis. He felt a presence over his shoulder

and turned to see Lee, hobbling forward in his dressing gown and slippers, an expression of helplessness on his face. Even army commanders were useless in these situations.

The fighting died down after Wright's first assault failed, and for the first time Poe could hear another fight off on his right, where the Lee cousins were holding off Burnside. The battle sounded sharp over there. Poe received reports from his commanders. Three of his colonels were wounded, one was dead, and Clingman had been trampled by both sides during a squabble over a trench but rose from the mud full of fight.

The Yankees came on again, still with that grim do-or-die silence, and this time they gained a lodgement between the Ravens and Corse, and the Confederates tried to fling them out but failed. "Tell them they must try again," Poe told his messengers. He had to shout over the sound of Whitworths firing point-blank into the Yankee salient. He looked at the sad figure of Lee standing there, motionless in his carpet slippers, his soft brown eyes gazing over the battlefield. "Tell the men," Poe said, "the eyes of General Lee are upon them."

Maybe it was Lee's name that did it. Poe could no longer believe in great men but the men of this army believed at least in Lee. The second counterattack drove the shattered Yankees from the works.

The Yankees paused again, but there was no lack of sound. The Confederate artillery kept firing blind into the trees, hoping to smash as many of the reassembling formations as they could.

What did a man mean in all this? Poe wondered. Goethe and Schiller and Shelley and Byron thought a man was all, that inspiration was everything, that divine intuition should overthrow dull reason—but what was inspiration against a Whitworth shell? The Whitworth shell would blow to shreds any inspiration it came up against.

Poe looked at Lee again.

A messenger came from Fitz Lee to tell the commanding

general that the cavalry, being hard-pressed, had been obliged by the enemy to retire. A fancy way, Poe assumed, for saying they were riding like hell for the rear. Now both Poe's flanks were gone.

Lee gave a series of quiet orders to his aides. Poe couldn't hear them. And then Lee bent over as another spasm took him, and his young men carried him away to his ambulance.

There was no more fighting for another hour. Eventually the rebel artillery fell silent as they ran short of ammunition. Reserve ammunition was brought up. Messages came to Poe: Hancock was moving, and Burnside was beginning a turning movement, rolling up onto Poe's right flank. Poe ordered his right flank bent back, Clingman's men moving into Hanover Junction itself, making a fort of every house. His division now held a U-shaped front.

What did a man mean in all this? Poe wondered again. Nothing. Byron and Shelley were ego-struck madmen. All a man could do in this was die, die along with everything that gave his life meaning. And it was high time he did.

Poe rose from the chair, strapped on his pistols, and began to walk the quarter mile to his trenches. He'd give Walter Whitman a run for his money.

The fight exploded before Poe could quite walk half the distance. Wright's men poured out of the woods; Burnside, moving fast for once in his life, struck at Hanover Junction on the right; and unknown to anyone Hancock had hidden a few brigades in the swampy tributary of the North Anna, and these came screaming up out of the defile onto Poe's undermanned left flank.

The battle exploded. Poe began limping faster.

The battle ended before Poe could reach it. His men gave way everywhere, the Yankees firing massed volley into their backs, then going after them with bayonets. Poe wanted to scream in rage. The world would not let him make even a futile gesture.

The shattered graybacks carried him back almost bodily, back to the Starker house where civilians were solemnly loading a coffin into a wagon, and there Poe collapsed on the lovely green lawn while the batteries opened up, trying to slow down the advance of Wright's triumphant men. Limbers were coming up, ready to drag the guns away. Lee's ambulance was already gone.

Poe found himself looking at the coffin. A dead girl was a poem, he thought as his head rang with gunfire, but no one had asked the girl if she wanted to be a poem. She would probably have chosen to live and become prose, healthy bouncing American prose, like his Evania. That was why he couldn't love her, he thought sadly; he couldn't love prose. And the world was becoming prose, and he couldn't love that either.

The artillery began pulling out. Poe could hear Yankee cheers. Poe's staff had vanished, lost in the whirlwind of the retreat, but there was Sextus, standing by the buggy, looking at the advancing Yankee line with a strange, intent expression. Poe dragged himself upright and walked toward the buggy.

"Come along, Sextus," he said. "We must go."

Sextus gave him a look. There was wildness in it.

Poe scowled. This was no time for the African to take fright. Bullets fluttered overhead. "Take the reins, Sextus. I'm too tired. We must leave this *champ du Mars*."

At the sound of the French, Poe saw a strange comprehension in Sextus's eyes. Then Sextus was running, clutching his supposedly injured arm, running down the gentle hill as fast as his legs could carry him, toward the advancing Northern army. Poe looked after him in amusement.

"Sextus!" he called. "You fool! That's the wrong way!" The fighting had obviously turned the darky's wits.

Sextus gave no indication he had heard. "The wrong way! We're running *away* from the Yankees, not *toward* them!" Poe limped after him. "*Madman!*" he shrieked. "*Baboon! Animal!*" His nerves turned to blazing fire, and he clawed for one of his Le Mat revolvers. Holding the heavy thing two-handed, Poe drew the hammer back and sighted carefully. A few Yankee bullets whistled over his head.

Sextus kept running. The dark masses of Union men were just beyond him. The pistol's front sight wavered in Poe's vision.

Stupid, Poe thought.

He cocked his arm back and threw the revolver spinning after Sextus. There was a bang as the Le Mat went off on impact, but Poe didn't bother to look. He turned to the buggy and stepped into it; he whipped up the mare and followed the guns and the funeral procession through a cornfield toward the Confederate rear. Behind him he heard Yankee cheers as they swarmed up onto the deserted Starker lawn.

The corn was just sprouting. The buggy bounded over furrows. The field was covered with wounded Confederates staggering out of the way of the retreating guns. There was a cloud of dust on the border of the field.

Oh, no, Poe thought.

Men moved out of the dust, became two divisions of A.P. Hill's corps, moving in perfect battle formation. Marching to the rescue, like something out of Walter Scott.

Poe halted, examined the advancing Confederates through his field glasses, and then whipped up again once he found the man he wanted to see.

Little Powell Hill was riding in another buggy—another officer too sick to ride—but he was wearing the red flannel he called his "battle shirt," and his heavy beard, a contrasting shade of red, was veritably bristling with eagerness for battle.

Poe passed through Hill's lines, turned his buggy in a wide circle, and brought it on a parallel course to Hill. He and Hill exchanged salutes.

"I hope you've left some Yankees for us, General." Hill's voice was cheerful.

Poe looked at him. "Plenty of Yankees, sir," he said. "None of *my* men left, but plenty of Yankees."

Powell Hill grinned. "I'll reduce 'em for you."

"I hope you will."

"You should rally your men. I need your support."

Where were you when I needed your support! Poe wanted to say it, but he couldn't. Instead he just saluted, and brought the buggy to a halt.

His broken men gathered around him. Hill's marched on, into the swelling battle.

The battle died down at sunset. The blows and counter-blows weren't clear to Poe, but Hanover Junction, after having changed hands several times, ended up back with the Confederacy, and Grant's army was safely penned in the bend of the North Anna. The burning Starker house was a bright glow on the horizon, a pillar of fire. Someone's shellfire had set it alight.

Among all the other dead was Hugin, shot by a Yankee bullet. The raven lay wrapped in a handkerchief at the foot of his tall perch. Munin moved from side to side on the perch, his head bobbing, mourning the loss of his mate.

Poe stood under the perch in the light of a campfire, listening to reports from his subordinates. Torn and dying men were lying around him in neat rows. The living, some distance off, were cooking meat; Poe could smell salt pork in the air. From the reports he gathered that he had lost about sixty percent of his men, killed, wounded, or missing. He had lost eighty percent of his officers the rank of captain or above. The figures were almost as bad as the attack at Gettysburg, last July.

A buggy moved carefully through the darkness and came to a halt. Walter Taylor helped Robert Lee out. Lee had apparently recovered somewhat; he was dressed carefully in a well-brushed uniform. Poe hobbled to him and saluted.

"General Lee."

Lee nodded. "This army owes you its thanks," he said. "You have saved Richmond."

"I have lost my division."

Lee was silent a moment. "That is hard," he said. "But you must tell your men how well they fought, how they have saved the capital. Perhaps it will make their sorrows easier to bear."

Poe nodded. "I will tell them." He looked at Lee. "What will I tell George Pickett? They were his men, not mine."

"You will tell him what you must."

Is this, Poe wondered, how Lee had got such a reputation for wisdom? Repeating these simple things with such utter sincerity?

Lee stepped forward, took Poe's arm. "Come. I would like to speak with you apart."

Poe allowed himself to be led off into the darkness. "Grant will move again," Lee said, "as soon as he gets his wounded to the rear and his cavalry comes back from the Yellow Tavern raid. There will be another battle, perhaps more than one. But sooner or later there will be a pause."

"Yes, sir."

"I would take advantage of that pause, General Poe. I would like to send a division to the Valley on this railroad you have saved us, to defeat the invaders there and strike at Washington. I would like to say, sir, that I am considering you for the command."

An independent Shenandoah Valley command, thought Poe. A chance for glory. The same command had been the making of Stonewall.

"My division is destroyed," Poe said. "I can't commit them to battle."

"Your division," gently, "is General Pickett's. When he recovers his health, he will return to command it. I refer to a new division, assembled with an eye to the Valley adventure."

"I see." Poe walked in silence for a moment, and stopped suddenly as his boots thudded against a wooden surface. He looked at it and realized it was the Starker girl's coffin, lying alone in the rutted cornfield. Apparently it had been bounced out of the wagon during the retreat.

Glory, he thought.

The Cause was lost. He couldn't believe in it anymore. That afternoon he'd told Moses one should fight for something noble, even if its time was gone. Now he no longer believed it. None of this was worth it.

however many people they need to finish in a reasonable amount of time. And when you've found out where the reports are, tell me and I'll call them myself, sort of let them know Daddy cares."

She walked out of the office in a blaze of warm colors. Trilling thought about the FDA and their annoying insistence that he read hundreds of boring follow-ups, and then with an angry motion, he opened his drawer. With the blind petulance of the inanimate, it parted company from the desk and spilled the hundreds of little pills and capsules all over his carpet.

"Ooohh . . ." Trilling moaned softly. He got down on his knees and began methodically to put them back in their little plastic bottles. The red pills and the white pills and the blue pills, all the patriot colors . . . they could sort of look like a flag if he moved them around and put this red one here and the blue one over there . . .

It was *very* hard to stay optimistic under these conditions, he thought. No choice but to soldier on.

. . . and the black pills and the blue pills with the yellow stripes and the *other* yellow pills . . .

10

Replace the first paragraph in the ADVERSE REACTIONS section with the following:

The following adverse reactions have been reported since the drug was marketed. A probability has been shown to exist between Riderophan and these adverse reactions. The adverse reactions that have been observed encompass observations for 2,722 patients, including 381 observed for at least 52 weeks . . .

II

Dr. Winkelstein peered with frowning attention into Mrs.
Kane's private parts. "Oh Jesus, oh Jesus," Mrs. Kane
moaned. "Oh fuck, oh Jesus." She was thrashing around
considerably, and Winkelstein found it hard to concentrate.
Shut up, you silly woman, he thought, and jabbed her very
precisely with his curette. Mrs. Kane gave a sudden
strangled yelp.

"Try not to move so much, Mrs. Kane," he said. "You
might hurt yourself."

"Careful now," the nurse said automatically. She was
frowning at her nails. "It'll be over soon."

"Sonofabitch shit oh fuck," said Norma Kane. But she
stopped thrashing.

Winkelstein finished cutting his tissue sample from Mrs.
Kane's uterus and dropped the bloody tidbit of flesh into his
clear plastic specimen container that his nurse had labeled.
He put the cap on it, left the room, gave it to the lab
assistant, and then returned to Mrs. Kane.

"You're doing fine, Mrs. Kane," he said.

"Jesus God Almighty," she said. Her forehead was
spangled with sweat.

He removed the speculum, trying not to pay attention to
his patient's occasional groans. Norma Kane, he knew, was
a perfect subject for the Tynadette study. She was a
fifty-eight-year-old black woman with graying hair and
good health. Two grown children, one in the navy and the
other in school somewhere in Tennessee. Menopause confirmed for at least three years, but still subject to hot flashes
as well as vaginal atrophy: she was thus good for both the
Baum study and the Tempel group. She was a widow who
lived on a small pension and had a hard time meeting her
medical bills. It hadn't been hard to find her: he'd just had

the office staff look through his records and call anyone who was currently employing his prescription for hormones.

Winkelstein thought he'd give her the new pills right away; if anything contraindicative came up from the lab, he'd call her and tell her to cancel.

He straightened and took off his gloves. "There," he said. "That wasn't so hard, was it?"

"That sin of Eve must have been some sin," breathed Mrs. Kane as she sat up.

"Some people think so," Winkelstein answered remotely. His mind was already on his next patient, Mae Nare. She was white, poor, married to a husband who was in prison for theft, had four teenaged kids, and lived on welfare. Another perfect subject for his study.

12

Well, thought Jeanie McGovern. So this is how some people live.

It was National Secretaries' Week, which meant that all the secretaries received nice bowls of flowers for their desks and got a free lunch from Tempel in the Executive Club that occupied the top floor of the Tempel International Building in Manhattan. The booths were padded with tooled red leather, and the glass-and-chrome tables gleamed with white tablecloths. Quite a change from the employees' cafeteria on the second floor. It was nice of Trilling—or more likely Natalia—to see that she was included.

Free food, Jeanie thought, has no calories. She ordered lobster and a margarita.

"And coffee," she said. "With lots of cream."

Trilling ordered mineral water and a cottage cheese salad. He had taken Dicryptomine and Paradol for the combined effects of lunch table wit and a sunny personality, but unfortunately, Paradol had as its major side effect the suppression of appetite. "They have a gym on the floor below," he said. "I have an appointment with Dr. Kaplan to work out and then play squash every night after work. That gives time for the rush hour to end before I head back home."

"Where's that?" Jeanie said.

"Hempstead. It's a long commute," he said.

"Your wife must never see you."

"We play tennis on weekends," Trilling said. The waiter came with Jeanie's coffee.

"Just leave the pot," she said. He lowered it expressionlessly to the table.

"Your margarita will be right up, miss," he said.

"You drink a lot of coffee, don't you?" Trilling said.

"I have to keep alive somehow. Margaritas help, too."

"I like white wine sometimes," Trilling said. "I don't drink much alcohol."

"You," said Jeanie, "don't need to."

Trilling pondered the implications of this remark for a moment. The margarita made its appearance: Jeanie smiled gratefully and drank about a third of it at a gulp.

Temporaries were so *different* from regular employees, Trilling thought. They were outside the structure of the corporate authority, and as a result were free of the usual office games. Sometimes it made them interesting. The rest of the time they were simply annoying.

Jeanie sat back in the padded booth and smiled. She had a broad mouth and a lot of white teeth. "I'm a dancer," she said. "That's why I'm working temp. My company folded, since we were new, and after the cutbacks all the art money is going to the rich, established groups—you know, the ones who already have money. I still take class every night."

"You're doing a very good job here," said Trilling. "You've picked up Tempel's way of doing things remarkably well." He wondered how long a thirty-year-old dancer had left.

"Thank you. I try."

"Where do you live?"

"Downtown. Lower East Side," said Jeanie. She gulped some more margarita.

"Oh. Isn't that dangerous?" Trilling's views of the Lower East Side came mainly from the eleven o'clock news, lots of dying people lying in alleys, all in the hard, lurid colors of night video.

Jeanie shrugged. "It's kind of like range war," she said. "There are a lot of rich people moving in now, taking over from the ethnics and the junkies and winos and artists. I'm kind of hoping the winos hang on—it's the only part of Manhattan where I can afford to live." She gave a low laugh. "I can protect myself, though," she said.

With a sudden grin, she unbuttoned the blue jacket she was wearing and showed him the gleaming butt of an automatic pistol tucked snugly in her armpit. The leather holster seemed to be approximately the size of the state of Colorado, and it was polished with use. Dr. Trilling felt sudden terror bleating shrilly in the hollows of his chest.

"Please put that away," he said. She closed her jacket, finished her margarita, and looked for the waiter.

"Don't worry. I got a permit after my apartment was broken into for the fifth time," Jeanie said. She never understood why New Yorkers, who were so often tough-minded people, felt so terrified of guns. Damned if she was going to be one of those herd animals, always bleating about their problems to an authority that never cared. By the time a Montana girl got out of high school, she knew how to take care of herself.

"Isn't that thing a little big for you?" Trilling asked. Maybe he'd order a margarita himself.

"No. The only problem is learning how to correct your aim after the recoil. It's my daddy's .45, and it jumps like crazy unless you know how to control it. He added a custom grip and competition sights, and when I can afford the ammunition I go down to the gun club and practice my quick draw." She patted the thing under her armpit. "I keep my jacket unbuttoned all the time when I'm outside in the weather. You never know."

You sure as hell don't, thought Trilling. If he had know this, he would have taken Shacocacine.

My God, he thought, how can people live like this?

13

Bennie Lovett hawked and spat into the sink, his phlegm having that lovely speedball aftertaste that promised cool excitement in his brain. He turned to look at the skulls sitting in the acid bath in his tub and grinned. More money tomorrow. This little sideline was turning out all right.

The acid was making a mess out of the chipped porcelain of the bathtub, not to mention the iron underneath it, but Bennie didn't much care. The tub was propped up on two-by-fours to keep it from crashing through the floor into the apartment below—the building was rent-controlled, and the landlord never bothered to maintain it. If he had to replace the bathtub, serve him right. Bennie hadn't taken a bath in weeks anyway.

14

Write "See Supplement B" alongside the product heading.

　　　Warning: Serious and fatal blood dyscrasias are known to occur after the administration of Moxalinophene. These include thrombocytopenia and aplastic anemia. Blood dyscrasias have been known to occur after both short-term and prolonged use of the drug.

15

Angel Hernandez stepped into his kitchen, patted Filomena affectionately on her behind, and put five-sixths of his Rolling Rock in the shaky refrigerator. He opened the other sixth and took a swallow. Filomena was listening to the radio—it had to be one of the college stations since it was playing Latin music—and dancing as she moved about the kitchen. He grinned.

"You feel better?" he asked.

"I don't feel that arthritis in my hips," she said. "Not since Mass on Sunday."

Angel put his arms around her. "*Mi señora,* you're looking better, too." He began to dance with her to the salsa coming from WKCR.

She *was* looking better. The darkness under her eyes was fading, and her skin seemed much fresher. Her ass wasn't so soft, either.

"It's having you around the house," she said, "and you being so good to me."

He felt a short throb of sadness at the reminder of his unemployed status, and he kissed her carefully on her forehead. "Hey," he said in wonder, running his hand through her hair. "Your hair's coming in black again."

16

Static was joining the Vidiots in her left ear. Kimberlee Winkelstein tapped the earpiece of her Walkman, bone conduction producing a strange sound. The static continued. She looked up, frowning, through the reception room window at the motley group of patients in the Health Group waiting area, and then returned to her typewriter. She was losing interest in the Vidiots anyway—who could retain respect for a band that played the Bottom Line and whose lead was becoming a movie star? They were getting old . . .

She was spending the summer doing the paperwork for her father's programs in Experimental Drugs. It had sounded interesting at first, but the whole experience had turned out to be awful. The job was in Brooklyn, for God's sake, not even in the city. And since she'd started working, she hadn't seen anything but sick people. Several pairs of eyes looked dully back at her. How could people live like that?

Oh, well. She would be working only until they went to Maine on vacation in August.

Patient failed 5-1-83, she typed carefully. *Physician attending reported there was no connection between patient's failure and Simulene.*

She detached the defective phones from her ears and looked up at Martha, the middle-aged black woman who ran the clerical staff of the Health Group. "What does it mean when it says that the patient failed?" she asked.

"It means they dead," said Martha.

"Oh. Thanks." *Everything* here was depressing. Maybe tomorrow she'd bring some of her father's vodka in her pocketbook and try to make things better.

17

Dr. Trilling's relaxed voice sounded in Jeanie's ear as she typed. "Make sure you stamp CONFIDENTIAL on this," he said for the second time. She took her foot off the Dictaphone pedal, adjusted her earphones, took a sip of coffee, and wondered for a moment why Dr. Trilling always seemed so anxious about things. Then she lit a cigarette and went back to her work.

"Recently," Trilling said, "I have received several inquiries about bleeding associated with use of the fourth-generation cephalosporins. Until now we've assumed that all bleeding that did occur was related to hypoprothrombinemia secondary to depletion of vitamin K. This seems to be in error."

Jeanie's fingers followed Trilling's words nimbly over the keyboard. "Recent reports, however, demonstrate bleeding due to alteration of prothrombin time. These reports usually involve elderly or debilitated profiles with deficient stores of vitamin K. Marked reversal of hypoprothrombinemia is demonstrated by prompt administration of vitamin K."

Jeanie had heard of vitamin K—dancers know a lot about vitamins—but hypoprothrombinemia was new. She decided to look it up in the medical encyclopedia when she got time, after she typed a new version of her résumé. There was nothing like a new job to increase one's knowledge.

18

Norma Kane balanced her bags of groceries carefully against the wall, took her keys out of her pocketbook, and unlocked the three locks on her door. She maneuvered herself and her bags inside, closed the door with a nudge of her foot, and put the bags on the sideboard.

She dusted her hands and turned back to the door to lock it. A few months ago, she would have been out of breath after that three-flight climb. She seemed to be feeling better lately, and the friends she met for regular games of bid whist were complimenting her on her looks. Her hair was even coming in black again.

There was a bid whist party again tonight at Serene's apartment, and Norma began washing potatoes so that she could bring some potato salad. Even the wrinkles around her knuckles were smoothing out. "You have the hands of a babychild, Norma," old Carey had said the other night. The odd thing was, she didn't used to have.

She put the potatoes on to boil and walked to the toilet. "Oh, lord," she said softly, discovering that the source of the slight feeling of abdominal pressure wasn't from her bladder.

Damned if it wasn't the Curse of Eve. It was the first time in almost two years, and she'd thought she'd long been done with it. She sighed and began to wonder if she had any sanitary napkins left.

Strange, though, that it had come so easy. A few years ago, the cramps would have driven her half-crazy. Well. Another strange miracle.

She heard the potatoes boiling in the kitchen. It was time to turn the gas down so they wouldn't boil over. She began to wonder seriously about the sanitary napkin supply.

19

"I'm sorry, Mrs. Nare," Winkelstein said. "It turns out you're right."

"God damn it, I knew it," said Mae Nare. She was a thin and perpetually angry woman of fifty-five, and when Winkelstein had first enrolled her in the Tempel and Baum Company studies, she had worn a ton of makeup and a blond wig. Now the cosmetic layer was thinner, revealing a smoother complexion, and the hair was short but genuinely blond and abundant. Heavy copper earrings brushed her shoulders when she turned her head. As she looked at Winkelstein, her thin lips became thinner.

"Look," she said. "You've got to do something about it. When my husband gets out of prison, he'll kill me."

"We'll arrange an abortion," Winkelstein said. This sometimes happened with the birth control studies; it was an unfortunate but necessary expense. "At no cost to you. The program will pay for it."

"It damn well better," said Mrs. Nare. She gave a short

bark of a laugh. "Hey," she said. "I ain't even had my *period* for a year. Who'd of thought this would happen?"

"We'll switch your medication," Winkelstein said. "I'll write you a new prescription."

Abortions, he thought. Arranging them seemed to be half his life. It occurred to him that once upon a time, when he was young and in medical school, he hadn't even believed in them, had supported the laws that made them criminal. He remembered making a speech to a friend about the value of continence and self-discipline. He had, of course, been a virgin then.

20

A disc jockey made a joke in stereo about a sweet strawberry-flavored drink spiked with vodka, and Kimberlee wondered if he'd been paid to mention the stuff and remembered it was okay, sort of like a watery milkshake that got you high, but she preferred her vodka straight.

Patient gravida, she wrote, *left study 7-8-83.*

She wondered briefly what "gravida" meant. She seemed to be writing that word a lot lately.

21

Write "See Supplement B" alongside product heading. Delete the first paragraph of the WARNINGS section and replace with the following:

Warning: The prolonged administration of Simulene often leads to the development of a positive antinuclear antibody (ANA) test. If a positive ANA titer develops, the benefit/risk ratio related to continued Simulene therapy should be assessed.

22

There was a liquid sadness in Angel Hernandez's eyes. Filomena looked down at her little feet with their bright red toenails. She was withdrawn again. Recently, during her monthly examinations, she had been livelier, more conversational, and Winkelstein had noticed she'd been losing weight steadily and picking up body and skin tone as if she were exercising regularly.

"I'm afraid I've bad news," Winkelstein said. He spoke to the husband; he was the only one who seemed to be taking an interest. "Mrs. Hernandez is pregnant. Five, six weeks."

"Doc," he said. "How can that happen?"

The usual way, of course, Winkelstein thought, but didn't say it. Things were going sadly awry with the Tynadette patients and The Baum Company study groups. Of the eighteen women who overlapped in the two studies, Mrs. Hernandez was the seventh to have become pregnant. In each case, menopause had been well advanced, and pregnancy was not to be suspected.

Which of the drugs was causing it? Winkelstein wondered. Now he didn't have his twenty-five usable case studies for *either* drug. He was seriously considering cutting his losses and withdrawing from both programs.

"Any treatment Mrs. Hernandez requires will continue to be without charge, Mr. Hernandez," Winkelstein said. "I think it would be best if we can arrange an abortion sometime soon."

"Dr. Winkelstein, we're *Catholics*," said Filomena Hernandez. It was the first time she'd spoken; the hoarse wail was forced up from deep inside her. Winkelstein steepled his fingertips and spoke quickly.

"Mrs. Hernandez is over fifty," he said. "She's overweight, and her last pregnancies had complications. I think it could be dangerous for her to bring a pregnancy to term, and in the case of danger to the mother, the church will sanction the termination of the pregnancy. I can give you the name of a priest who will speak to you about it, if you like. I don't think the church will give us any objections."

As long, Winkelstein thought, as she talks to a priest from *my* neighborhood. Bigoted old priests who got stuck in poor parishes might well be another matter. In these things, as in everything else, much depended on whom you knew.

There was no hope in Angel Hernandez's solemn eyes; he had clearly resigned himself to Winkelstein, the church, and fate. "Do what you can, Doc," he said.

23

Jeanie McGovern pulled on her cigarette and frowned at the collection of Form 1639 Drug Experimental Reports filed by Dr. Winkelstein. They were badly typed and featured a lot of correction fluid, but their impact was clear. Of the thirty women in the Tynadette study, all of whom had confirmed menopause, seven had become pregnant. There was something strange going on here; she'd been working on and off for Trilling for some time now, and there'd never been a case like this before. There was something about it she couldn't put her finger on.

She picked up the telephone and buzzed Trilling's number. He was a long time picking up.

"I've been reviewing the Tynadette file," she said. "I think I've found something strange." His pause before acknowledging was a long one, and she used the time to stub out her cigarette.

"Yes," he said finally. There was a halfhearted question in his tone.

"Seven women out of thirty have become pregnant," Jeanie said. "After using a drug supposed to relieve vaginal atrophy following menopause."

There was another thoughtful pause. "I suppose I'd better see the profiles," he said.

She gathered the forms from her desk, put them back in the folder, and entered his office. Trilling was staring with an uninterested expression at the office building opposite his window. Outside, the forty-story glass cube across the street was reflecting the frantic lights of a blocked fire engine. There was no sound: high in the Tempel Building, they were insulated from the siren.

"Do you suppose," Jeanie said, "that Tynadette could be used as a fertility drug?"

Trilling pursed his lip, his eyes never wavering from the window. "Tempel has fertility drugs already," he said. The red reflection slowly flashed away, the traffic flow suddenly unclogged. "I don't understand this. I suppose I should call Winkelstein and see if he had them on any other kind of medication. Maybe he misinterpreted the profile."

"I should think," Jeanie said, "that Tempel would want to discover the cause of this. Something that makes menopausal women fertile could be useful. This might help a new line of research."

Trilling gave her an irritated glance. "What this *is* is a pain," he said suddenly. He straightened in his chair and reached for the telephone. "What it *is* is a messed-up study and letters from the FDA and great big WARNING boxes in the PDR." And having unpleasant conversations that interfere with a man's optimism, he almost added.

"Let me know what you find out," Jeanie said. "I'm interested."

Trilling gave a savage nod, and she knew she was dismissed. She wanted to ask him to discover how many of the other women in the study were suddenly fertile, but he gave her another annoyed look as he began flipping through his Rolodex. He had put on a doctor-knows-best face, and she knew it wasn't the time.

Later, she thought. It would give her time to think about it, and the papers would cross her desk anyway.

24

Should it become necessary to terminate the
project prior to completion, the following finan-
cial arrangement is hereby agreed upon: *Investi-
gator receives payment prorated according to
completed case reports:*
        $1,200 for each completed evaluable case.
        $300 for each completed nonevaluable.

25

Jeanie had taken class, and the whirlpool and sauna at a
health club afterward—one of her friends had given her a
guest pass—had left her with a pleasant, warm feeling
oozing over her limbs. She hadn't met any hustlers or crazy
people on the way home, and that was cause for celebration,
too. She thought it would be nice to crawl into bed and
drink a few margaritas while reading the new Crumley; but
she couldn't afford margarita fixings and so decided to settle
for killing half the bottle of California red that was sitting in
the refrigerator.

    She unlocked her apartment building street door and saw,
slumped in the doorway, the present girlfriend of Joe Voss,
the Vidiot who lived upstairs. Her name, Jeanie thought,
was Angela. She looked up at Jeanie. "The club where I
dance fired me 'cause I got all skinned up in a fight. And
now *he's* thrown me out." She pointed with her bruised chin
upstairs. "He's taking back his wife 'cause she got her old
job back. Well, maybe she'll get beat up again and *I* can
come back."

    Well. One pleasant, dreamy mood smashed to hell.
Jeanie made some consoling remarks about men in general

and then climbed the two flights of stairs to get to her apartment. She opened the three locks on her door, pushed it open, and saw a ruin.

Part of the ceiling had caved in, and something vast and white had fallen onto her bathtub and broken the welds that held it together, shattering it. There was foul-smelling water all over the place, and her belongings, including a lot of books she had piled up on the floor, were slowly soaking the stuff up.

Anger blew through her like Krakatau saying hello to the record books. She leaped across her small kitchen to the refrigerator, behind which she'd hidden her gun, and reached back to seize the weapon. She didn't wear the holster in the summertime, or to class ever; and she had been afraid the gun would have been stolen. It was her only remaining valuable possession.

Then, still shaking with fury, she surveyed the damage. The damned rotten ceiling had collapsed, dropping the bathtub that belonged to the junkie upstairs onto her own. Fortunately the bathtub, like hers, was not directly connected to any plumbing except the drain, which had torn out, dripping some awful slime down her walls. No heavy water damage, anyway.

Rotten floors made rotten ceilings, and it all made for a rotten life. The hell with this city, anyway. But what was making that awful smell? She moved closer to the bathtub and peered inside it. Three skulls, still dripping flesh and hair, grinned back at her.

There was the sound of a footstep behind her, and she turned and fired.

The skinny junkie from upstairs had just come out of her bathroom, where he'd evidently been washing another skull. He looked dazed, hardly able to keep his eyes open. He carried the dripping skull in his hand.

Screaming, Jeanie unzipped him with four neatly spaced shots between larynx and sternum. In the sudden silence broken only by the sound of her brass rolling on the floor, Jeanie thought with surprising clarity. She'd tell the police that he had stolen her gun, that he'd threatened her with it and grabbed for her, and she'd wrestled the gun away from him and fired. He sure as hell would have grabbed her sooner or later, anyway.

She went to the phone, dialed 911, and told the cops to come. There were a dozen neighbors clustered in her doorway, including Joe Voss and his once and future lover, both staring at the mess with dull junkie eyes. Jeanie tried and failed to chase them away. That was a comforting thing about poor neighborhoods, she thought: everything was everyone else's business. In a newly gentrified neighborhood, her fellow tenants would probably have made sure their doors were locked and then put pillows over their ears.

She went into her bedroom alcove and lay down, drawing up her booted feet on the bed, and waited. She wondered what a ranch girl from Montana was doing in this crazy place anyway, and she thought hard about the long valleys filled with sagebrush scrub and the timbered highlands that gave a view of the wine-dark Rockies all far away. Tears stung her eyes. Damn, she thought, how could people live like this?

The first cop stepped into the apartment, treading cautiously as if walking on ice. She looked up from her pillow and answered her own question. "Gotta dance," she said. The policeman gave no indication he thought her remark was odd.

26

It took a couple of days for Trilling to get accustomed to the idea of a killer working in his office. He'd seen Bennie toes-up on the eleven o'clock news, with a bloody sheet over him, all in mute hideous color, and a morbid closeup of a cardboard box full of skulls. The tabloids had been featuring vast headlines, all screaming adjectives, about the East Side Addict Grave Robber, and Trilling had been forced to stare at them as they were upheld by other passengers on the long commute to Hempstead. It was all nightmarish.

Jeanie had been out for several days following the incident, though, and by the time she got back, Trilling had got used to the idea. He took some Pandrocene for a kind of calm gravity and ordered an extravagant bouquet of flowers for her desk. He wanted to be on hand when she arrived. She seemed a little pale, and he gave her a paternal hug.

"I'd rather not talk about it," she said.

He nodded. "Of course you don't," he said. He began fumbling in his pocket for one of his pill bottles. Perhaps she'd like a capsule or two.

Jeanie looked at her desk and saw the flowers. "Oh," she said. "They're pretty, aren't they?"

Trilling nodded and tried to smile in an encouraging way. "Thank you," said Jeanie, and sat down at her desk.

Well, Trilling thought. Things back to normal so quickly. Repressing the impulse to dust off his hands, he gave everyone in the office a sunny smile and returned to his desk.

Jeanie went straight to work, trying to ignore the solemn, inadvertent stares of her fellow workers as they walked past her alcove. She really didn't want to talk about it. It seemed that talk was all she'd done for days.

She'd spent the first night in jail, until her phone calls had got through to a lawyer she had once worked for. He'd come down and got her out, but that wasn't the end of it.

There was a very good chance she'd end up charged with murder. She had listened in amazement as her lawyer explained the facts.

"You were supposed to find out his intentions, Jeanie," he'd said. "You were supposed to ask him what he was doing in your apartment. If he was there to rob you, you should have let him. If he was there to rape you, you were justified in holding him at gunpoint or subduing him, but never shooting to kill. Only if he had expressed his intention to murder you were you justified in killing him. And even then the precedents aren't unanimous."

"But he had a *gun*," Jeanie had told him. "And a *skull*."

"Doesn't make any difference," the attorney said. "You've been watching too many Charles Bronson movies. Bronson never gets booked for murder, but that's just Hollywood. Here in reality, things are different."

And so the police investigation was continuing. Her friends and the personnel at the gun club were being interviewed by detectives. Even if no charges were eventually laid—and that was up to the district attorney, not the cops—there would be depositions to be given and appearances to be made, and for all of that she'd need a lawyer who was charging her five hundred an hour. Reporters from the tabloids were staking out her apartment in hopes she'd let something slip, and on top of everything, someone had broken into her apartment when she was in jail and cleaned everything out.

Even if she wanted to leave the city, she couldn't: the police had told her to stay in their jurisdiction, and besides, she couldn't afford to move. She'd had to return to Tempel, if only to pay her bills.

How can people live this way? she thought.

Late the next day, Jeanie was on the Dictaphone and realized that the letter she was typing canceled the Tynadette study. She took her foot off the pedal, pulled off her earphones, and lit a cigarette, trying to understand what was gnawing at her mind. Whatever it was, it wouldn't come.

Hell, she decided. I've got my own problems.

She put her foot down on the pedal and began to type.

27

Kimberlee Winkelstein typed her father's name and office address across the Tempel Request for Check form. *Program terminated*, she typed, *9-12-84*. She had to go to the correction fluid and retype the correct year. She'd had a little too much vodka during the break.

It was the second program termination in a week. The first had been the Baum Company study. Her father had been upset about it, but he'd now received approval to test new medications for both companies, different medications that were supposed to do the same thing without the side effects that had snarled up the programs. So he'd get his money anyway.

She'd forgotten her Walkman today, and glanced up in annoyance at the sounds of the children jumping up and down on the waiting room seats. Old people and young mothers and children, all sick with something. She wished she could cover up the noise with her bootleg cassette of the Headlickers. There were beginning to replace the Vidiots in her affections.

28

PARANOID DISORDERS (Definitions for basis of treatment):
1. Paranoia
2. Shared paranoia (folie à deux)
3. Acute paranoid disorder
4. Atypical paranoid disorder

29

Angel Hernandez sipped on his fourth beer of the afternoon and watched the television without interest as it showed an Argentine soap opera. Filomena moved slowly about the living room, picking up the children's toys. Since the abortion she'd been a lot less lively, and in the past few days, she'd been complaining that her arthritis was coming back. She came to the sports section of yesterday's *Post* and held it up mutely.

"I picked my horses," he said. "You can throw it away. How about a kiss?"

She gave a faint smile and bent over him for a peck. She seemed out of breath with the exertion, and in the instant before she straightened, he noticed sadly that her hair was coming in white again.

WITNESS

Author's Note: *"Witness" is a contribution to the Wild
Cards shared-world series, but it stands largely on its own.
In order to understand its premise, only a few things need
to be explained. An alien, known on Earth as Dr. Tachyon,
developed the gene-warping wild card virus, which killed
most of its victims horribly, which mutilated most of the
survivors, and which, to a lucky few, granted genuine
superpowers. In an alternate 1946, Jetboy, a famous World
War II ace, died in an unsuccessful attempt to prevent
terrorists from detonating a wild card bomb over Manhattan. The story begins only a few minutes after Jetboy's
death, as viral spores begin to rain on the city.*

*The part of the story I didn't make up consists of the
HUAC persecutions of the late '40s and '50s. A depressing
feature of this story was hearing from young (and a few
not-so-young) readers who assume that I invented the
McCarthy Period for the purposes of this alternate-worlds
story. I can only hope that this disbelief is a measure of how
far we've come since the days of HUAC, that it really can't*

happen again, rather than an indication of the political naïveté that allowed it all to occur in the first place.

—W. J. W.

When Jetboy died I was watching a matinee of *The Jolson Story*. I wanted to see Larry Parks's performance, which everyone said was so remarkable. I studied it carefully and made mental notes.

Young actors do things like that.

The picture ended, but I was feeling comfortable and had no plans for the next few hours, and I wanted to see Larry Parks again. I watched the movie a second time. Halfway through, I fell asleep, and when I woke the titles were scrolling up. I was alone in the theater.

When I stepped into the lobby the usherettes were gone and the doors were locked. They'd run for it and forgotten to tell the projectionist. I let myself out into a bright, pleasant autumn afternoon and saw that Second Avenue was empty.

Second Avenue is never empty.

The newsstands were closed. The few cars I could see were parked. The theater marquee had been turned off. I could hear angry auto horns some distance off, and over it the rumble of high-powered airplane engines. There was a bad smell from somewhere.

New York had the eerie feeling that towns sometimes got during an air raid, deserted and waiting and nervous. I'd been in air raids during the war, usually on the receiving end, and I didn't like the feeling at all. I began walking for my apartment, just a block and a half away.

In the first hundred feet I saw what had been making the bad smell. It came from a reddish-pink puddle that looked like several gallons of oddly colored ice cream melting on the sidewalk and oozing down the gutter.

I looked closer. There were a few bones inside the puddle. A human jawbone, part of a tibia, an eye socket. They were dissolving into a light pink froth.

There were clothes beneath the puddle. An usherette's

uniform. Her flashlight had rolled into the gutter and the metal parts of it were dissolving along with her bones.

My stomach turned over as adrenaline slammed into my system. I started to run.

By the time I got to my apartment I figured there had to be some kind of emergency going on, and I turned on the radio to get information. While I was waiting for the Philco to warm up I went to check the canned food in the cupboard—a couple cans of Campbell's was all I could find. My hands were shaking so much I knocked one of the cans out of the cupboard, and it rolled off the sideboard behind the icebox. I pushed against the side of the icebox to get at the can, and suddenly it seemed like there was a shift in the light and the icebox flew halfway across the room and damn near went through the wall. The pan I had underneath to catch the ice-melt slopped over onto the floor.

I got the can of soup. My hands were still trembling. I moved the icebox back, and it was light as a feather. The light kept doing weird shifts. I could pick up the box with one hand.

The radio warmed finally and I learned about the virus. People who felt sick were to report to emergency tent hospitals set up by the National Guard all over the city. There was one in Washington Square Park, near where I was living.

I didn't feel sick, but on the other hand I could juggle the icebox, which was not exactly normal behavior. I walked to Washington Square Park. There were casualties everywhere—some were just lying in the street. I couldn't look at a lot of it. It was worse than anything I'd seen in the war. I knew that as long as I was healthy and mobile the doctors would put me low on the list for treatment, and it would be days before I'd get any help, so I walked up to someone in charge, told him I used to be in the Army, and asked what I could do to help. I figured if I started to die I'd at least be near the hospital.

The doctors asked me to help set up a kitchen. People were screaming and dying and changing before the doctors' eyes, and the medics couldn't do anything about it. Feeding the casualties was all they could think to do.

I went to a National Guard deuce-and-a-half and started picking up crates of food. Each weighed about fifty pounds, and I stacked six of them on top of each other and carried them off the truck in one arm. My perception of the light kept changing in odd ways. I emptied the truck in about two minutes. Another truck had gotten bogged down in mud when it tried to cross the park, so I picked up the whole truck and carried it to where it was supposed to be, and then I unloaded it and asked the doctors if they needed me for anything else.

I had this strange glow around me. People told me that when I did one of my stunts I glowed, that a bright golden aura surrounded my body. My looking at the world through my own radiance made the light appear to change.

I didn't think much about it. The scene around me was overwhelming, and it went on for days. People were drawing the black queen or the joker, turning into monsters, dying, transforming. Martial law had slammed down on the city—it was just like wartime. After the first riots on the bridges there were no disturbances. The city had lived with blackouts and curfews and patrols for four years, and the people just slipped back into wartime patterns. The rumors were insane—a Martian attack, accidental release of poison gas, bacteria released by Nazis or by Stalin. To top it all off, several thousand people swore they saw Jetboy's ghost flying, without his plane, over the streets of Manhattan. I went on working at the hospital, moving heavy loads. That's where I met Tachyon.

He came by to deliver some experimental serum he was hoping might be able to relieve some symptoms, and at first I thought, Oh, Christ, here's some fruitbar got past the guards with a potion his Aunt Nelly gave him. He was a weedy guy with long metallic red hair past his shoulders, and I knew it couldn't be a natural color. He dressed as if he got his clothes from a Salvation Army in the theater district, wearing a bright orange jacket like a bandleader might wear, a red Harvard sweater, a Robin Hood hat with a feather, plus-fours with argyle socks, and two-tone shoes that would have looked out of place on a pimp. He was moving from bed to bed with a tray full of hypos, observing each patient and sticking the needles in people's arms. I put down the X-ray machine I was carrying and ran to stop him before he could do any harm.

And then I noticed that the people following him included a three-star general, the National Guard bird colonel who ran the hospital, and Mr. Archibald Holmes, who was one of F.D.R.'s old crowd at Agriculture, and who I recognized right away. He'd been in charge of a big relief agency in Europe following the war, but Truman had sent him to New York as soon as the plague hit. I sidled up behind one of the nurses and asked her what was going on.

"That's a new kind of treatment," she said. "That Dr. Tack-something brought it."

"It's *his* treatment?" I asked.

"Yeah." She looked at him with a frown. "He's from another planet."

I looked at the plus-fours and Robin Hood hat. "No kidding," I said.

"No. Really. He is."

Closer up, you could see the dark circles under his weird purple eyes, the strain that showed on his face. He'd been pushing himself hard since the catastrophe, like all the doctors here—like everyone except me. I felt full of energy in spite of only getting a few hours' sleep each night.

The bird colonel from the National Guard looked at me. "Here's another case," he said. "This is Jack Braun."

Tachyon looked up at me. "Your symptoms?" he asked. He had a deep voice, a vaguely mid-European accent.

"I'm strong. I can pick up trucks. I glow gold when I do it."

He seemed excited. "A biological force field. Interesting. I'd like to examine you later. After the"—an expression of distaste crossed his face—"present crisis is over."

"Sure, Doc. Whatever you like."

He moved on to the next bed. Mr. Holmes, the relief man, didn't follow. He just stayed and watched me, fiddling with his cigarette holder.

I stuck my thumbs in my belt and tried to look useful. "Can I help you with something, Mr. Holmes?" I asked.

He seemed mildly surprised. "You know my name?" he said.

"I remember you coming to Fayette, North Dakota, back in '33," I said. "Just after the New Deal came in. You were at Agriculture then."

"A long time ago. What are you doing in New York, Mr. Braun?"

"I was an actor till the theaters shut down."

"Ah." He nodded. "We'll have the theaters running again soon. Dr. Tachyon tells us the virus isn't contagious."

"That'll ease some minds."

He glanced at the entrance to the tent. "Let's go outside and have a smoke."

"Suits me." After I followed him out I dusted off my hands and accepted a custom-blended cigarette from his silver case. He lit our cigarettes and looked at me over the match.

"After the emergency's over, I'd like to run some more tests with you," he said. "Just see what it is that you can do."

I shrugged. "Sure, Mr. Holmes," I said. "Any particular reason?"

"Maybe I can give you a job," he said. "On the world stage."

Something passed between me and the sun. I looked up, and a cold finger touched my neck.

The ghost of Jetboy was flying black against the sky, his white pilot's scarf fluttering in the wind.

I'd grown up in North Dakota. I was born in 1924, into hard times. There was trouble with the banks, trouble with the farm surpluses that were keeping prices down. When the Depression hit, things went from bad to worse. Grain prices were so low that some farmers literally had to pay people to haul the stuff away. Farm auctions were held almost every week at the courthouse—farms worth fifty thousand dollars were selling for a few hundred. Half Main Street was boarded up.

Those were the days of the Farm Holidays, the farmers withholding grain to make the prices rise. I'd get up in the middle of the night to bring coffee and food to my father and cousins, who were patrolling the roads to make sure nobody sold grain behind their backs. If someone came by with grain, they'd seize the truck and dump it; if a cattle truck came by, they'd shoot the cattle and toss them on the roadside to rot. Some of the local bigwigs who were making a fortune buying underpriced wheat sent the American Legion to break the farm strike, carrying axe handles and wearing their little hats—and the whole district rose, gave the legionnaires the beating of their lives, and sent them scampering back to the city.

Suddenly a bunch of conservative German farmers were talking and acting like radicals. F.D.R. was the first Democrat my family ever voted for.

I was eleven years old when I first saw Archibald Holmes. He was working as a troubleshooter for Mr. Henry Wallace in the Department of Agriculture, and he came to Fayette to consult with the farmers about something or other—price control or production control, probably, or conservation, the New Deal agenda that kept our farm off the auction block. He gave a little speech on the courthouse steps on his arrival, and for some reason I didn't forget it.

He was an impressive man even then. Well-dressed, gray-haired even though he wasn't yet forty, smoked a cigarette in a holder like F.D.R. He had a Tidewater way of talking, which sounded strange to my ear, as if there was something slightly vulgar about pronouncing one's *R*'s. Soon after his visit, things started getting better.

Years later, after I got to know him well, he was always Mr. Holmes. I never could see myself calling him by his first name.

Maybe I can trace my wanderlust to Mr. Holmes's visit. I felt there had to be something outside Fayette, something outside the North Dakota way of looking at things. The way my family saw it, I was going to get my own farm, marry a local girl, produce lots of kids, and spend my Sundays listening to the parson talk about Hell and my weekdays working in the fields for the benefit of the bank.

I resented the notion that this was all there was. I knew, perhaps only by instinct, that there was another kind of existence out there, and I wanted to get my share of it.

I grew up tall and broad-shouldered and blond, with big hands that were comfortable around a football and what my publicity agent later called "rugged good looks." I played football and played it well, dozed through school, and during the long dark winters I played in community theater and pageants. There was quite a circuit for amateur theater in both English and German, and I did both. I played mainly Victorian melodramas and historical spectaculars, and I got good notices, too.

Girls liked me. I was good-looking and a regular guy and they all thought I'd be just the farmer for them. I was careful never to have anyone special. I carried rubbers in my watch pocket and tried to keep at least three or four girls in the air at once. I wasn't falling into the trap that all my elders seemed to have planned for me.

We all grew up patriotic. It was a natural thing in that part of the world: there is a strong love of country that comes with punishing climates. It wasn't anything to make a fuss over, patriotism was just there, part of everything else.

The local football team did well, and I began to see a way out of North Dakota. At the end of my senior season, I was offered a scholarship to the University of Minnesota.

I never made it. Instead, the day after graduation in May of 1942, I marched to the recruiter and volunteered for the infantry.

No big deal. Every boy in my class marched with me.

I ended up with the 5th Division in Italy, and had an awful infantryman's war. It rained all the time, there was never proper shelter, every move we made was in full view of invisible Germans sitting on the next hill with Zeiss binoculars glued to their eyes, to be followed inevitably by that horrific zooming sound of an 88 coming down . . . I was scared all the time, and I was a hero some of the time, but most of the time I was hiding with my mouth in the dirt while the shells came whizzing down, and after a few months of it I knew I wasn't coming back in one piece, and chances were I wasn't coming back at all. There were no tours, like in Vietnam; a rifleman just stayed on the line until the war was over, or until he died, or until he was so shot up he couldn't go back. I accepted these facts and went on with what I had to do. I got promoted to master sergeant and eventually got a Bronze Star and three Purple Hearts, but medals and promotions never meant as much to me as where the next pair of dry socks was coming from.

One of my buddies was a man named Martin Kozokowski, whose father was a minor theatrical producer in New York. One evening we were sharing a bottle of awful red wine and a cigarette— smoking was something else the Army taught me—and I mentioned my acting career back in North Dakota, and in a gush of inebriated goodwill he said, "Hell, come to New York after the war, and me and my dad will put you on the stage." It was a pointless fantasy, since at that point none of us really thought we were coming back, but it stuck, and we talked about it afterward, and by and by, as some dreams have a way of doing, it came true.

After V-E Day I went to New York and Kozokowski the elder got me a few parts while I worked an assortment of part time jobs, all of which were easy compared to farming and the war. Theater circles were full of intense, intellectual girls who didn't wear lipstick—not wearing lipstick was supposed to be sort of daring—and they would take you home with them if you listened to them talk about Anouilh or Pirandello or their psychoanalysis, and the best thing about them was that they didn't want to get married and make little farmers. Peacetime reflexes began to come back. North Dakota started to fade away, and after a while I began to wonder if maybe the war didn't have its consolations after all.

An illusion, of course. Because some nights I'd still wake up with the 88s whistling in my ears, terror squirming in my guts, the old wound in my calf throbbing, and I'd remember lying on my back in a shellhole with mud creeping down my neck, waiting for the morphine to hit while I looked up into the sky to see a flight of silver Thunderbolts with the sun gleaming off their stubby wings, the planes hopping the mountains with more ease than I could hop out of a jeep. And I'd remember what it was like to lie there furious with jealousy that the fighter jocks were in their untroubled sky while I bled into my field dressing and waited for morphine and plasma, and I'd think, If I ever catch one of those bastards on the ground, I'm going to make him pay for this . . .

When Mr. Holmes started his tests he proved exactly how strong I was, which was stronger than anyone had ever seen, or even imagined. Provided I was braced well enough, I could lift up to forty tons. Machine-gun slugs would flatten themselves on my chest. Armor-piercing 20mm cannon shells would knock me down with their transferred energy, but I'd jump back up undamaged.

They were scared to try anything bigger than a 20mm on their tests. So was I. If I were hit with a *real* cannon, instead of just a big machine gun, I'd probably be oatmeal.

I had my limits. After a few hours of it I'd begin to get tired. I would weaken. Bullets began to hurt. I'd have to go off and rest.

Tachyon had guessed right when he talked about a biological force field. When I was in action it surrounded me like a golden halo. I didn't exactly control it—if someone shot a bullet into my back by surprise, the force field would turn on all by itself. When I started to get tired the glow would begin to fade.

I never got tired enough for it to fade entirely, not when I wanted it on. I was scared of what would happen then, and

I always took care to make sure I got my rest when I needed it.

When the test results came in, Mr. Holmes called me in to his apartment on Park Avenue South. It was a big place, the entire fifth floor, but a lot of the rooms had that unused smell to them. His wife had died of pancreatic cancer back in '40, and since then he'd given up most of his social life. His daughter was off at school.

Mr. Holmes gave me a drink and a cigarette and asked me what I thought about fascism, and what I thought I could do about it. I remembered all those stiff-necked SS officers and Luftwaffe paratroops and considered what I could do about them now that I was the strongest thing on the planet.

"I imagine that now I'd make a pretty good soldier," I said.

He gave me a thin smile. "Would you *like* to be a soldier again, Mr. Braun?"

I saw right away what he was driving at. There was an emergency going on. Evil lived in the world. It was possible I could do something about it. And here was a man who had sat at the right hand of Franklin Delano Roosevelt, who in turn sat at the right hand of God, as far as I was concerned, and he was *asking* me to do something about it.

Of *course* I volunteered. It probably took me all of three seconds.

Mr. Holmes shook my hand. Then he asked me another question. "How do you feel about working with a colored man?"

I shrugged.

He smiled. "Good," he said. "In that case, I'll have to introduce you to Jetboy's ghost."

I must have stared. His smile broadened. "Actually, his name is Earl Sanderson. He's quite a fellow."

Oddly enough, I knew the name. "The Sanderson who used to play ball for Rutgers? Hell of an athlete."

Mr. Holmes seemed startled. Maybe he didn't follow sports. "Oh," he said. "I think you'll find he's a little more than that."

* * *

Earl Sanderson, Jr., was born into a life far different from mine, in Harlem, New York City. He was eleven years older than I, and maybe I never caught up to him.

Earl, Sr., was a railway car porter, a smart man, self-educated, an admirer of Frederick Douglass and Du Bois. He was a charter member of the Niagara Movement—which became the NAACP—and later of the Brotherhood of Sleeping Car Porters. A tough, smart man, thoroughly at home in the combustive Harlem of the time.

Earl, Jr., was a brilliant youth, and his father urged him not to waste it. In high school he was outstanding as a scholar and athlete, and when he followed Paul Robeson's footsteps to Rutgers in 1930 he had his choice of scholarships.

Two years into college, he joined the Communist party. When I knew him later, he made it sound like the only reasonable choice.

"The Depression was only getting worse," he told me. "The cops were shooting union organizers all over the country, and white people were finding out what it was like to be as poor as the colored. All we got out of Russia at the time were pictures of factories working at full capacity, and here in the States the factories were closed and the workers were starving. I thought it was only a matter of time before the revolution. The CP were the only people working for the unions who were also working for equality. They had a slogan, 'Black and white, unite and fight,' and that sounded right to me. They didn't give a damn about the color bar—they'd look you in the eye and call you 'comrade.' Which was more than I ever got from anyone else."

He had all the good reasons in the world for joining the CP in 1931. Later all those good reasons would rise up and wreck us all.

I'm not sure why Earl Sanderson married Lillian, but I understand well enough why Lillian chased Earl for all those years. "Jack," she told me, "he just *glowed*."

Lillian Abbott met Earl when he was a junior in high

school. After that first meeting, she spent every spare minute with him. Bought his newspapers, paid his way into the theaters with her pocket change, attended radical meetings. Cheered him at sporting events. She joined the CP a month after he did. And a few weeks after he left Rutgers, summa cum laude, she married him.

"I didn't give Earl any choice," she said. "The only way he'd ever get me to be quiet about it was to marry me."

Neither of them knew what they were getting into, of course. Earl was wrapped up in issues that were larger than himself, in the revolution he thought was coming, and maybe he thought Lillian deserved a little happiness in this time of bitterness. It didn't cost him anything to say yes.

It cost Lillian just about everything.

Two months after his marriage Earl was on a boat to the Soviet Union, to study at Lenin University for a year, learning to be a proper agent of the Comintern. Lillian stayed at home, working in her mother's shop, attending party meetings that seemed a little lackluster without Earl. Learning, without any great enthusiasm for the task, how to be a revolutionary's wife.

After the year in Russia, Earl went to Columbia for his law degree. Lillian supported him until he graduated and went to work as counsel for A. Philip Randolph and the Brotherhood of Sleeping Car Porters, one of the most radical unions in America. Earl, Sr., must have been proud.

As the Depression eased, Earl's commitment to the CP waned—maybe the revolution wasn't coming, after all. The GM strike was solved in favor of the CIO when Earl was learning to be a revolutionary in Russia. The Brotherhood won its recognition from the Pullman Company in 1938, and Randolph finally started drawing a salary—he'd worked all those years for free. The union and Randolph were taking up a lot of Earl's time, and his attendance at party meetings began to slide.

When the Nazi-Soviet pact was signed, Earl resigned from the CP in anger. Accommodation with the fascists was not his style.

Earl told me that after Pearl Harbor, the Depression ended for white people when the hiring at defense plants started, but few blacks were given jobs. Randolph and his people finally had enough. Randolph threatened a railway strike—right in the middle of wartime—that was to be combined with a march on Washington. F.D.R. sent his troubleshooter, Archibald Holmes, to work out a settlement. It resulted in Executive Order 8802, in which government contractors were forbidden to discriminate on account of race. It was one of the landmark pieces of legislation in the history of civil rights, and one of the greatest successes in Earl's career. Earl always spoke of it as one of his proudest accomplishments.

The week after Order 8802, Earl's draft classification was changed to 1–A. His work with the rail union wasn't going to protect him. The government was taking its revenge.

Earl decided to volunteer for the Air Corps. He'd always wanted to fly.

Earl was old for a pilot, but he was still an athlete and his conditioning got him past the physical. His record was labeled PAF, meaning Premature Anti-Fascist, which was the official designation for anyone who was unreliable enough not to like Hitler prior to 1941.

He was assigned to the 332nd Fighter Group, an all-black unit. The screening process for the black fliers was so severe that the unit ended up full of professors, ministers, doctors, lawyers—and all these bright people demonstrated first-rate pilots' reflexes as well. Because none of the air groups overseas wanted black pilots, the group remained at Tuskegee for months and months of training. Eventually they received three times as much training as the average group, and when they were finally moved, to bases in Italy, the group known as "the Lonely Eagles" exploded over the European Theater.

They flew their Thunderbolts over Germany and the Balkan countries, including the toughest targets. They flew over fifteen thousand sorties and, during that time, *not a single escorted bomber* was lost to the Luftwaffe. After word got out, bomber groups began asking specifically for the 332nd to escort their planes.

One of their top fliers was Earl Sanderson, who ended the war with fifty-three "unconfirmed" kills. The kills were unconfirmed because records were not kept for the black squadrons—the military was afraid the black pilots might get larger totals than the whites. Their fear was justified— that number put Earl above every American pilot but Jetboy, who was another powerful exception to a lot of rules.

On the day Jetboy died, Earl had come home from work with what he thought was a bad case of the flu, and the next day he woke up a black ace.

He could fly, apparently by an act of will, up to five hundred miles per hour. Tachyon called it "projection telekinesis."

Earl was pretty tough, too, though not as tough as I was—like me, bullets bounced off him. But cannon rounds could hurt him, and I know he dreaded the possibility of midair collision with a plane.

And he could project a wall of force in front of him, a kind of traveling shock wave that could sweep anything out of his path. Men, vehicles, walls. A sound like a clap of thunder and they'd be thrown a hundred feet.

Earl spent a couple weeks testing his talents before letting the world know about them, flying over the city in his pilot's helmet, black leather flying jacket, and boots. When he finally let people know, Mr. Holmes was one of the first to call.

I met Earl the day after I'd signed on with Mr. Holmes. By then I'd moved into one of Mr. Holmes's spare rooms and had been given a key to the apartment. I was moving up in the world.

I recognized him right away. "Earl Sanderson," I said, before Mr. Holmes could introduce us. I shook his hand. "I remember reading about you when you played for Rutgers."

Earl took that in stride. "You have a good memory," he said.

We sat down, and Mr. Holmes explained formally what he wanted with us, and with others he hoped to recruit later. Earl felt strongly about the term "ace," meaning someone with useful abilities, as opposed to "joker," meaning someone who was badly disfigured by the virus—Earl felt the terms imposed a class system on those who got the wild card, and didn't want to set us at the top of some kind of social pyramid. Mr. Holmes officially named our team the Exotics for Democracy. We were to become visible symbols of American postwar ideals, to lend credit to the American attempt to rebuild Europe and Asia, to continue the fight against fascism and intolerance.

The U.S. was going to create a postwar Golden Age, and was going to share it with the rest of the world. We were going to be its symbol.

It sounded great. I wanted in.

With Earl the decision came a little harder. Holmes had talked to him before and had asked him to make the same kind of deal that Branch Rickey later asked of Jackie Robinson: Earl had to stay out of domestic politics. He had to announce that he'd broken with Stalin and Marxism, that he was committed to peaceful change. He was asked to keep his temper under control, to absorb the inevitable anger, racism, and condescension, and to do it without retaliation.

Earl told me later how he struggled with himself. He knew his powers by then, and he knew he could change things simply by being present where important things were going on. Southern cops wouldn't be able to smash up integration meetings if someone present could flatten whole companies of state troopers. Strikebreakers would go flying before his wave of force. If he decided to integrate somebody's restaurant, the entire Marine Corps couldn't throw him out—not without destroying the building, anyway.

But Mr. Holmes had pointed out that if he used his powers in that way, it wouldn't be Earl Sanderson who would pay the penalty. If Earl Sanderson were seen reacting violently to provocation, innocent blacks would be strung from oak limbs throughout the country.

Earl gave Mr. Holmes the assurance he wanted. Starting the very next day, the two of us went on to make a lot of history.

The EFD was never a part of the U.S. government. Mr. Holmes consulted with the State Department, but he paid Earl and me out of his own pocket and I lived in his apartment.

The first thing was to deal with Perón. He'd gotten himself elected President of Argentina in a rigged election, and was in the process of turning himself into a South American version of Mussolini and Argentina into a refuge for fascists and war criminals. The Exotics for Democracy flew south to see what we could do about it.

Looking back on things, I'm amazed at our assumptions. We were bent on overthrowing the constitutional government of a large foreign nation, and we didn't think anything about it . . . Even Earl went along without a second thought. We'd just spent years fighting fascists in Europe, and we didn't see anything remarkably different in moving south and smashing them up there.

When we left, we had another man with us. David Harstein just seemed to talk himself aboard the plane. Here he was, a Jewish chess hustler from Brooklyn, one of those fast-talking curly-haired young guys that you saw all over New York selling flood insurance or used auto tires or custom suits made of some new miracle fiber that was just as good as cashmere, and suddenly he was a member of EFD and calling a lot of the shots. You couldn't help but like him. You couldn't help but agree with him.

He was an exotic, all right. He exuded pheromones that made you feel friendly with him and with the world, that created an atmosphere of bonhomie and suggestibility. He could talk an Albanian Stalinist into standing on his head and singing "The Star-Spangled Banner"—at least, as long as he and his pheromones were in the room. Afterward, when our Albanian Stalinist returned to his senses, he'd promptly denounce himself and have himself shot.

We decided to keep David's powers a secret. We spread a story that he was some kind of sneaky superman, like The Shadow on radio, and that he was our scout. Actually he'd just get into conferences with people and make them agree with us. It worked pretty well.

Perón hadn't consolidated his power yet, having only been in office four months. It took us two weeks to organize the coup that got rid of him. Harstein and Mr. Holmes would go into meetings with army officers, and before they were done the colonels would be swearing to have Perón's head on a plate, and even after they began to think better of things, their sense of honor wouldn't let them back down on their promises.

On the morning before the coup, I found out some of my limitations. I'd read the comics when I was in the Army, and I'd seen how, when the bad guys were trying to speed away in their cars, Superman would jump in front of the car, and the car would bounce off him.

I tried that in Argentina. There was a Perónist major who had to be kept from getting to his command post, and I jumped in front of his Mercedes and got knocked two hundred feet into a statue of Juan P. himself.

The problem was, I wasn't heavier than the car. When things collide, it's the object with the least momentum that gives way, and weight is a component of momentum. It doesn't matter how *strong* the lighter object is.

I got smarter after that. I knocked the statue of Perón off its perch and threw it at the car. That took care of things.

There are a few other things about the ace business that you can't learn from reading comic books. I remember comic aces grabbing the barrels of tank guns and turning them into pretzels.

It is in fact possible to do that, but you have to have the leverage to do it. You've got to plant your feet on something solid in order to have something to push against. It was far easier for me to dive under the tank and knock it off its treads. Then I'd run around to the other side and put my arms around the gun barrel, with my shoulder under the barrel, and then yank down. I'd use my shoulder as the fulcrum of a lever and bend the barrel around myself.

That's what I'd do if I was in a hurry. If I had time, I'd punch my way through the bottom of the tank and rip it apart from the inside.

But I digress. Back to Perón.

There were a couple critical things that had to be done. Some loyal Perónists couldn't be gotten to, and one of them was the head of an armored battalion quartered in a walled compound on the outskirts of Buenos Aires. On the night of the coup, I picked up one of the tanks and dropped it on its side in front of the gate, and then I just braced my shoulder against it and held it in place while the other tanks battered themselves into junk trying to move it.

Earl immobilized Perón's air force. He just flew behind the planes on the runway and tore off the stabilizers.

Democracy was victorious. Perón and his blond hooker took off for Portugal.

I gave myself a few hours off. While triumphant middle-class mobs poured into the street to celebrate, I was in a hotel room with the daughter of the French ambassador. Listening to the chanting mob through the window, the taste of champagne and Nicolette on my tongue, I concluded this was better than flying.

Our image got fashioned in that campaign. I was wearing old Army fatigues most of the time, and that's the view of me most people remember. Earl was wearing tan Air Force officer's fatigues with the insignia taken off, boots, helmet, goggles, scarf, and his old leather flying jacket with the 332nd patch on the shoulder. When he wasn't flying he'd take the helmet off and put on an old black beret he kept in his hip pocket. Often, when we were asked to make personal appearances, Earl and I were asked to dress in our fatigues so everyone would know us. The public never seemed to realize that most of the time we wore suits and ties, just like everyone else.

When Earl and I were together, it was often in a combat situation, and for that reason we became best friends . . . people in combat become close very quickly. I talked about my life, my war, about women. He was a little more guarded—maybe he wasn't sure how I'd take hearing his exploits with white girls—but eventually, one night when we were in northern Italy looking for Bormann, I heard all about Orlena Goldoni.

"I used to have to paint her stockings on in the morning," Earl said. "I'd have to make up her legs, so it would look like she had silk stockings. And I'd have to paint the seam down the back in eyeliner." He smiled. "That was a paint job I always enjoyed doing."

"Why didn't you just give her some stockings?" I asked. They were easy enough to come by. GIs wrote to their friends and relatives in the States to send them.

"I gave her lots of pairs," Earl shrugged, "but Lena'd give 'em away to the comrades."

Earl hadn't kept a photo of Lena, not where Lillian could find it, but I saw her in the pictures later, when she was billed as Europe's answer to Veronica Lake. Tousled blond hair, broad shoulders, a husky voice. Lake's screen persona was cool, but Goldoni's was hot. The silk stockings were real in the pictures, but so were the legs under them, and the picture celebrated Lena's legs as often as the director thought he could get away with it. I remember thinking how much fun Earl must have had painting her.

She was a cabaret singer in Naples when they met, in one of the few clubs where black soldiers were allowed. She was eighteen and a black marketeer and a former courier for the Italian Communists. Earl took one look at her and threw caution to the winds. It was maybe the one time in his entire life that he indulged himself. He started taking chances. Slipping off the field at night, dodging MP patrols to be with her, sneaking back early in the morning and

being on the flight line ready to take off for Bucharest or
Ploeşti . . .

"We knew it wasn't forever," Earl said. "We knew the
war would end sooner or later." There was a kind of
distance in his eyes, the memory of a hurt, and I could see
how much leaving Lena had cost him. "We were grownups
about it." A long sigh. "So we said goodbye. I got
discharged and went back to work for the union. And we
haven't seen each other since." He shook his head. "Now
she's in the pictures. I haven't seen any of them.".

The next day, we got Bormann. I held him by his monk's
cowl and shook him till his teeth rattled. We turned him
over to the representative of the Allied War Crimes Tribunal
and gave ourselves a few days' leave.

Earl seemed more nervous than I'd ever seen him. He
kept disappearing to make phone calls. The press always
followed us around, and Earl jumped every time a camera
bulb went off. The first night, he disappeared from our hotel
room, and I didn't see him for three days.

Usually I was the one exhibiting this kind of behavior,
always sneaking off to spend some time with a woman.
Earl's doing it caught me by surprise.

He'd spent the weekend with Lena, in a little hotel north
of Rome. I saw their pictures together in the Italian papers
on Monday morning—somehow the press found out about
it. I wondered whether Lillian had heard, what she was
thinking. Earl showed up, scowling, around noon on
Monday, just in time for his flight to India: he was going to
Calcutta to see Gandhi. Earl wound up stepping between the
Mahatma and the bullets that some fanatic fired at him on
the steps of the temple—and all of a sudden the papers were
full of India, with what had just happened in Italy forgotten.
I don't know how Earl explained it to Lillian.

Whatever it was he said, I suppose Lillian believed him.
She always did.

Glory years, these. With the fascist escape route to South
America cut, the Nazis were forced to stay in Europe where

it was easier to find them. After Earl and I dug Bormann out of his monastery, we plucked Mengele from a farm attic in Bavaria and we got so close to Eichmann in Austria that he panicked and ran out into the arms of a Soviet patrol, and the Russians shot him out of hand. David Harstein walked into the Escorial on a diplomatic passport and talked Franco into making a live radio address in which he resigned and called for elections, and then David stayed with him on the plane all the way to Switzerland. Portugal called for elections right afterward, and Perón had to find a new home in Nanking, where he became a military adviser to the generalissimo. Nazis were bailing out of Iberia by the dozen, and the Nazi hunters caught a lot of them.

I was making a lot of money. Mr. Holmes wasn't paying me much in the way of wages, but I got a lot for making the Chesterfield endorsement and for selling my story to *Life*, and I had a lot of paid speaking engagements—Mr. Holmes hired me a speechwriter. My half of the Park Avenue apartment was free, and I never had to pay for a meal if I didn't want to. I got large sums for articles that were written over my name, things like "Why I Believe in Tolerance" and "What America Means to Me," and "Why We Need the U.N." Hollywood scouts were making incredible offers for long-term contracts, but I wasn't interested just yet. I was seeing the world.

So many girls were visiting me in my room that the tenants' association talked about installing a revolving door.

The papers started calling Earl "the Black Eagle," from the 332nd's nickname, "the Lonely Eagles." He didn't like the name much. David Harstein, by those few who knew of his talent, was "the Envoy." I was "Golden Boy," of course. I didn't mind.

EFD got another member in Blythe Stanhope van Rens-saeler, who the papers started calling "Brain Trust." She was a petite, proper upper-crust Boston lady, high-strung as a thoroughbred, married to a scumbag New York congressman by whom she'd had three kids. She had the kind of beauty that took a while for you to notice, and then you wondered why you hadn't seen it before. I don't think she ever knew how lovely she really was.

She could absorb minds. Memories, abilities, everything.

Blythe was older than me by about ten years, but that didn't bother me, and before long I started flirting with her. I had plenty of other female companionship, and everyone knew that, so if she knew anything about me at all—and maybe she didn't, because my mind wasn't important enough to absorb—she didn't take me seriously.

Eventually her awful husband, Henry, threw her out, and she came by our apartment to look for a place to stay. Mr. Holmes was gone, and I was feeling no pain after a few shots of his twenty-year-old brandy, and I offered a bed to stay in—mine, in fact. She blew up at me, which I deserved, and stormed out.

Hell, I hadn't intended her to take the offer as a permanent one. She should have known better.

So, for that matter, should I. Back in '47, most people would rather marry than burn. I was an exception. And Blythe was too high-strung to fool with—she was on the edge of nervous collapse half the time, with all the knowledge in her head, and one thing she didn't need was a Dakota farm boy pawing at her on the night her marriage ended.

Soon Blythe and Tachyon were together. It didn't do my self-esteem any good to be turned down for a being from another planet, but I'd gotten to know Tachyon fairly well, and I'd decided he was okay in spite of his liking for brocade and satin. If he made Blythe happy, that was fine with me. I figured he had to have something right with him to persuade a bluestocking like Blythe to actually live in sin.

The term "ace" caught on just after Blythe joined the EFD, so suddenly we were the Four Aces. Mr. Holmes was Democracy's Ace in the Hole, or the Fifth Ace. We were good guys, and everyone knew it.

It was amazing, the amount of adulation we received. The public simply wouldn't *allow* us to do anything wrong. Even die-hard bigots referred to Earl Sanderson as "our colored flyboy." When he spoke out on segregation, or Mr. Holmes on populism, people listened.

Earl was consciously manipulating his image, I think. He was smart, and he knew how the machinery of the press worked. The promise he'd given with such struggle to Mr. Holmes was fully justified by events. He was consciously molding himself into a black hero, an untarnished figure of aspiration. Athlete, scholar, union leader, war hero, faithful husband, ace. He was the first black man on the cover of *Time*, the first on *Life*. He had replaced Robeson as the foremost black ideal, as Robeson wryly acknowledged when he said, "I can't fly, but then Earl Sanderson can't sing."

Robeson was wrong, by the way.

Earl was flying higher than he ever had. He hadn't realized what happens to idols when people find out about their feet of clay.

The Four Aces' failures came the next year, in '48. When the Communists were on the verge of taking over in Czechoslovakia we flew to Germany in a big rush, and then the whole thing was called off. Someone at the State Department had decided the situation was too complicated for us to fix, and he'd asked Mr. Holmes not to intervene. I heard a rumor later that the government had been recruiting some ace talents of their own for covert work, and that they'd been sent in and made a bungle of it. I don't know if that's true or not.

Then, two months after the Czechoslovakian fiasco, we were sent into China to save a billion-odd people for democracy.

It was not apparent at the time, but our side had already lost. On paper, things seemed retrievable—the generalissimo's Kuomintang still held all the major cities, their armies were well equipped, compared to Mao and his forces, and it was well known that the generalissimo was a genius. If he weren't, why had Mr. Luce made him *Time*'s Man of the Year twice?

On the other hand, the Communists were marching south at a steady rate of twenty-three point five miles per day, rain or shine, summer or winter, redistributing land as they went. Nothing could stop them—certainly not the generalissimo.

By the time we were called in, the generalissimo had resigned—he did that from time to time, just to prove to everyone that he was indispensable. So the Four Aces met with the new KMT president, a man named Chen who was always looking over his shoulder lest he be replaced once the Great Man decided to make another dramatic entrance to save the country.

The U.S. position, by then, was prepared to concede north China and Manchuria, which the KMT had already lost barring the big cities. The idea was to save the south for the generalissimo by partitioning the country. The Kuomintang would get a chance to establish itself in the south while they organized for an eventual reconquest, and the Communists would get the northern cities without having to fight for them.

We were all there, the Four Aces and Holmes—Blythe was included as a scientific adviser and ended up giving little speeches about sanitation, irrigation, and inoculation. Mao was there, and Zhou En-lai, and President Chen. The generalissimo was off in Canton sulking in his tent, and the People's Liberation Army was laying siege to Mukden in Manchuria and otherwise marching steadily south, twenty-three point five miles per day, under Lin Biao.

Earl and I didn't have much to do. We were observers, and mostly what we observed were the delegates. The KMT people were astonishingly polite, they dressed well, they had uniformed servants who scuttled about on their errands. Their interaction with one another looked like a minuet.

The PLA people looked like soldiers. They were smart, proud, military in the way that real soldiers are military, without all the white-glove prissy formality of the KMT. The PLA had been to war, and they weren't used to losing. I could tell that at a glance.

It was a shock. All I knew about China was what I'd read in Pearl Buck. That, and the certified genius of the generalissimo.

"*These* guys are fighting *those* guys?" I asked Earl.

"*Those* guys"—Earl was indicating the KMT crowd—"aren't fighting anyone. They're ducking for cover and running away. That's part of the problem."

"I don't like the looks of this," I said.

Earl seemed a little sad. "I don't, either," he said. He spat. "The KMT officials have been stealing land from the peasants. The Communists are giving the land back, and that means they've got popular support. But once they've won the war they'll take it back, just like Stalin did."

Earl knew his history. Me, I just read the papers.

Over a period of two weeks Mr. Holmes worked out a basis for negotiation, and then David Harstein came into the room and soon Chen and Mao were grinning at each other like old school buddies at a reunion, and in a marathon negotiating session China was formally partitioned. The KMT and the PLA were ordered to be friends and lay down their arms.

It all fell apart within days. The generalissimo, who had no doubt been told of our perfidy by ex-Colonel Perón, denounced the agreement and returned to save China. Lin Biao never stopped marching south. And after a series of colossal battles, the certified genius of the generalissimo ended up on an island guarded by the U.S. fleet—along with Juan Perón and his blond hooker, who had to move again.

Mr. Holmes told me that when he flew back across the Pacific with the partition in his pocket, while the agreement unraveled behind him and the cheering crowds in Hong Kong and Manila and Oahu and San Francisco grew even smaller, he kept remembering Neville Chamberlain and his little piece of paper, and how Chamberlain's "peace in Europe" turned into conflagration, and Chamberlain into history's dupe, the sad example of a man who meant well but who had too much hope, and trusted too much in men more experienced in treachery than he.

Mr. Holmes was no different. He didn't realize that while he'd gone on living and working for the same ideals, for democracy and liberalism and fairness and integration, the world was changing around him, and that because he didn't change with the world, the world was going to hammer him into the dust.

At this point the public were still inclined to forgive us, but they remembered that we'd disappointed them Their enthusiasm was a little lessened.

And maybe the time for the Four Aces had passed. The big war criminals had been caught, fascism was on the run, and we had discovered our limitations in Czechoslovakia and China

When Stalin blockaded Berlin, Earl and I flew in. I was in my combat fatigues again, Earl in his leather jacket. He flew patrols over the Russian wire, and the Army gave me a jeep and a driver to play with. Eventually Stalin backed down.

But our activities were shifting toward the personal. Blythe was going off to scientific conferences all over the world, and spent most of the rest of her time with Tachyon. Earl was marching in civil rights demonstrations and speaking all over the country. Mr. Holmes and David Harstein went to work, in that election year, for the candidacy of Henry Wallace.

I spoke alongside Earl at Urban League meetings, and to help out Mr. Holmes I said a few nice things for Mr Wallace, and I got paid a lot of money for driving the latest-model Chrysler and for talking about Americanism.

After the election I went to Hollywood to work for Louis Mayer. The money was more incredible than anything I'd ever dreamed, and I was getting bored with kicking around Mr. Holmes's apartment. I left most of my stuff in the apartment, figuring it wouldn't be long before I'd be back.

I was pulling down ten thousand per week, and I'd acquired an agent and an accountant and a secretary to answer the phone and someone to handle my publicity; all I had to do at this point was take acting and dance lessons. I didn't actually have to work yet, because they were having script problems with my picture. They'd never had to write a screenplay around a blond superman before.

The script they eventually came up with was based loosely on our adventures in Argentina, and it was called *Golden Boy*. They paid Clifford Odets a lot of money to use that title, and considering what happened to Odets and me later, that linking had a certain irony.

When they gave the script to me, I didn't care for it. I was the hero, which was just fine with me. They actually called me "John Brown." But the Harstein character had been turned into a minister's son from Montana, and the Archibald Holmes character, instead of being a politician from Virginia, had become an FBI agent. The worst part was the Earl Sanderson character—he'd become a cipher, a black flunky who was only in a few scenes, and then only to take orders from John Brown and reply with a crisp, "Yes, sir," and a salute. I called up the studio to talk about this.

"We can't put him in too many scenes," I was told. "Otherwise we can't cut him out for the Southern version."

I asked my executive producer what he was talking about.

"If we release a picture in the South, we can't have colored people in it, or the exhibitors won't show it. We write the scenes so that we can release a Southern version by cutting out all the scenes with niggers."

I was astonished. I never knew they did things like that. "Look," I said. "I've made speeches in front of the NAACP and Urban League. I was in *Newsweek* with Mary McLeod Bethune. I can't be seen to be a party to this."

The voice coming over the phone turned nasty. "Look at your contract, Mr. Braun. You don't have script approval."

"I don't want to approve the script. I just want a script that recognizes certain facts about my life. If I do this script, my credibility will be gone. You're fucking with my *image*, here!"

After that it turned unpleasant. I made certain threats and the executive producer made certain threats. I got a call from my accountant telling me what would happen if the ten grand per week stopped coming, and my agent told me I had no legal right to object to any of this.

Finally I called Earl and told him what was going on. "*What* did you say they were paying you?" he asked.

I told him again.

"Look," he said. "What you do in Hollywood is your business. But you're new there, and you're an unknown commodity to them. You want to stand up for the right, that's good. But if you walk, you won't do me or the Urban League any good. Stay in the business and get some clout, then use it. And if you feel guilty, the NAACP can always use some of that ten grand per week."

So there it was. My agent patched up an understanding with the studio to the effect that I was to be consulted on script changes. I succeeded in getting the FBI dropped from the script, leaving the Holmes character without any set governmental affiliation, and I tried to make the Sanderson character a little more interesting.

I watched the rushes, and they were good. I liked my acting—it was relaxed, anyway, and I even got to step in front of a speeding Mercedes and watch it bounce off my chest. It was done with special effects.

The picture went into the can, and I went from a three-martini lunch into the wrap party without stopping to sober up. Three days later I woke up in Tijuana with a splitting headache and a suspicion that I'd just done something foolish. The pretty little blonde sharing the pillow told me what it was. We'd just got married. When she was in the bath I had to look at the marriage license to find out her name was Kim Wolfe. She was a minor starlet from Georgia who'd been scuffling around Hollywood for six years.

After some aspirin and a few belts of tequila, marriage didn't seem like a half-bad idea. Maybe it was time, with my new career and all, that I settled down.

I bought Ronald Colman's old pseudo-English country house on Summit Drive in Beverly Hills, and I moved in with Kim, and our two secretaries, Kim's hairdresser, our two chauffeurs, our two live-in maids . . . suddenly I had all these people on salary, and I wasn't quite sure where they came from.

The next picture was *The Rickenbacker Story*. Victor Fleming was going to direct, with Fredric March as Pershing and June Allyson as the nurse I was supposed to fall in love with. Dewey Martin, of all people, was to play Richthofen, whose Teutonic breast I was going to shoot full of American lead—never mind that the real Richthofen was shot down by someone else. The picture was going to be filmed in Ireland, with an enormous budget and hundreds of extras. I insisted on learning how to fly, so I could do some of the stunts myself. I called Earl long-distance about that.

"Hey," I said. "I finally learned how to fly."

"Some farm boys," he said, "just take a while."

"Victor Fleming's gonna make me an ace."

"Jack." His voice was amused. "You're *already* an ace."

Which stopped me up short, because somehow in all the activity I'd forgotten that it wasn't MGM who made me a star. "You've got a point, there," I said.

"You should come to New York a little more often," Earl said. "Figure out what's happening in the real world."

"Yeah. I'll do that. We'll talk about flying."

"We'll do that."

I stopped by New York for three days on my way to Ireland. Kim wasn't with me—she'd gotten work, thanks to me, and had been loaned to Warner Brothers for a picture. She was very Southern anyway, and the one time she'd been with Earl she'd been very uncomfortable, and so I didn't mind she wasn't there.

I was in Ireland for seven months—the weather was so bad the shooting took forever. I met Kim in London twice, for a week each time, but the rest of the time I was on my own. I was faithful, after my fashion, which meant that I didn't sleep with any one girl more than twice in a row. I became a good enough pilot so that the stunt pilots actually complimented me a few times.

When I got back to California, I spent two weeks at Palm Springs with Kim. *Golden Boy* was going to premiere in two months. On my last day at the Springs, I'd just climbed out of the swimming pool when a congressional aide, sweating in a suit and tie, walked up to me and handed me a pink slip.

It was a subpoena. I was to appear before the House Committee on Un-American Activities bright and early on Tuesday. The very next day.

I was more annoyed than anything. I figured they obviously had the wrong Jack Braun. I called up Metro and talked to someone in the legal department. He surprised me by saying, "Oh, we thought you'd get the subpoena sometime soon."

"Wait a minute. How'd you know?"

There was a second's uncomfortable silence. "Our policy is to cooperate with the FBI. Look, we'll have one of our attorneys meet you in Washington. Just tell the committee what you know and you can be back in California next week."

"Hey," I said. "What's the FBI got to do with it? And why didn't you tell me this was coming? And what the hell does the committee think I know, anyway?"

"Something about China," the man said. "That was what the investigators were asking us about, anyway."

I slammed the phone down and called Mr Holmes. Ho and Earl and David had gotten their subpoenas earlier in the day and had been trying to reach me ever since, but couldn't get ahold of me in Palm Springs.

"They're going to try to break the Aces, farm boy," Earl said. "You'd better get the first flight east. We've got to talk."

I made arrangements, and then Kim walked in, dressed in her tennis whites, just back from her lesson. She looked better in sweat than any woman I'd ever known.

"What's wrong?" she said. I just pointed at the pink slip.

Kim's reaction was fast, and it surprised me. "Don't do what the Ten did," she said quickly. "They consulted with each other and took a hard-line defense, and none of them have worked since." She reached for the phone. "Let me call the studio. We've got to get you a lawyer."

I watched her as she picked up the phone and began to dial. A chill hand touched the back of my neck.

"I wish I knew what was going on," I said.

But I knew. I knew even then, and my knowledge had a precision and a clarity that was terrifying. All I could think about was how I wished I couldn't see the choices quite so clearly.

To me, the Fear had come late. HUAC first went after Hollywood in '47, with the Hollywood Ten. Supposedly the committee was investigating Communist infiltration of the film industry—a ridiculous notion on the face of it, since no Communists were going to get any propaganda in the pictures without the express knowledge and permission of people like Mr. Mayer and the Brothers Warner. The Ten were all current or former Communists, and they and their lawyers agreed on a defense based on the First Amendment rights of free speech and association.

The committee rode over them like a herd of buffalo over a bed of daisies. The Ten were given contempt-of-Congress citations for their refusal to cooperate, and after their appeals ran out years later, they ended up in prison.

The Ten had figured the First Amendment would protect them, that the contempt citations would be thrown out of court within a few weeks at the most. Instead the appeals went on for years, and the Ten went to the slammer, and during that time none of them could find a job.

The blacklist came into existence. My old friends, the American Legion, who had learned somewhat more subtle tactics since going after the Holiday Association with axe handles, published a list of known or suspected Communists so that no one employer had any excuse for hiring anyone on the list. If he hired someone, he became suspect himself, and his name could be added to the list.

None of those called before HUAC had ever committed a crime, as defined by law, nor were they ever accused of crimes. They were not being investigated for criminal activity, but for associations. HUAC had no constitutional mandate to investigate these people, the blacklist was illegal, the evidence introduced at the committee sessions was largely hearsay and inadmissible in a court of law . . . none of it mattered. It happened anyway.

HUAC had been silent for a while, partly because their chairman, Parnell, had gotten tossed into the slammer for padding his payroll, partly because the Hollywood Ten appeals were still going through the court. But they'd gotten hungry for all that great publicity they'd gotten when they went after Hollywood, and the public had been whipped into a frenzy with the Rosenberg trials and the Alger Hiss case, so they concluded that the time was right for another splashy investigation.

HUAC's new chairman, John S. Wood of Georgia, decided to go after the biggest game on the planet.

Us.

My MGM attorney met me at the Washington airport. "I'd advise you not to talk with Mr. Holmes or Mr. Sanderson," he said.

"Don't be ridiculous."

"They're going to try to get you to take a First or Fifth Amendment defense," the lawyer said. "The First Amendment defense won't work—it's been turned down on every appeal. The Fifth is a defense against self-incrimination, and unless you've actually done something illegal, you can't use it unless you want to *appear* guilty."

"And you won't work, Jack," Kim said. "Metro won't even release your pictures. The American Legion would picket them all over the country."

"How do I know that I'll work if I talk?" I said. "All you

have to do to get on the blacklist is be *called*, for chrissake."

"I've been authorized to tell you from Mr. Mayer," the lawyer said, "that you will remain in his employ if you cooperate with the committee."

I shook my head. "I'm talking with Mr. Holmes tonight." I grinned at them. "We're the Aces, for heaven's sake. If we can't beat some hick congressman from Georgia, we don't *deserve* to work."

So I met Mr. Holmes, Earl, and David at the Statler. Kim said I was being unreasonable and stayed away.

There was a disagreement right from the start. Earl said that the committee had no right to call us in the first place, and that we should simply refuse to cooperate. Mr. Holmes said that we couldn't just concede the fight then and there, that we should defend ourselves in front of the committee— that we had nothing to hide. Earl told him that a kangaroo court was no place to conduct a reasoned defense. David just wanted to give his pheromones a crack at the committee. "The hell with it," I said. "I'll take the First. Free speech and association is something every American understands."

Which I didn't believe for a second, by the way. I just felt that I had to say something optimistic.

I wasn't called that first day—I loitered with David and Earl in the lobby, pacing and gnawing my knuckles, while Mr. Holmes and his attorney played Canute and tried to keep the acid, evil tide from eating the flesh from their bones. David kept trying to talk his way past the guards, but he didn't have any luck—the guards outside were willing to let him come in, but the ones inside the committee room weren't exposed to his pheromones and kept shutting him out.

The media were allowed in, of course. HUAC liked to parade its virtue before the newsreel cameras, and the newsreels gave the circus full play.

I didn't know what was going on inside until Mr. Holmes came out. He walked like a man who'd had a stroke, one foot carefully in front of the other. He was gray. His hands trembled, and he leaned on the arm of his attorney. He looked as if he'd aged twenty years in just a few hours. Earl and David ran up to him, but all I could do was stare in terror as the others helped him down the corridor.

The Fear had me by the neck.

Earl and Blythe put Mr. Holmes in his car, and then Earl waited for my MGM limousine to drive up, and he got into the back with us. Kim looked pouty, squeezed into the corner so he wouldn't touch her, and refused even to say hello.

"Well, I was right," he said. "We shouldn't have cooperated with those bastards at all."

I was still stunned from what I'd seen in the corridor. "I can't figure out why the hell they're doing this."

He fixed me with an amused glance. "Farm boys," he said, a resigned comment on the universe, and then shook his head. "You've got to hit them over the head with a shovel to get them to pay attention."

Kim sniffed. Earl didn't give any indication he'd heard.

"They're power-hungry, farm boy," he said. "And they've been kept out of power by Roosevelt and Truman for a lot of years. They're going to get it back, and they're drumming up this hysteria to do it. Look at the Four Aces and what do you see? A Negro Communist, a Jewish liberal, an F.D.R. liberal, a woman living in sin. Add Tachyon and you've got an alien who's subverting not just the country but our chromosomes. There are probably others as powerful that nobody knows about. And they've all got unearthly powers, so who knows what they're up to? And they're not controlled by the government, they're following some kind of liberal political agenda, so that threatens the power base of most of the people on the committee right there.

"The way I figure it, the government has their own ace talents by now, people we haven't heard of. That means we can be done without—we're too independent and we're politically unsound. China and Czechoslovakia and the names of the other aces—that's an excuse. The point is that if they can break us right in public, they prove they can break anybody. It'll be a reign of terror that will last a generation. Not anyone, not even the President, will be immune."

I shook my head. I had heard the words, but my brain wouldn't accept them. "What can we do about it?" I asked.

Earl's gaze held my eyes. "Not a damn thing, farm boy."

I turned away.

My MGM attorney played a recording of the Holmes hearing for me that night. Mr. Holmes and his attorney, an old Virginia family friend named Cranmer, were used to the ways of Washington and the ways of law. They expected an orderly proceeding, the gentlemen of the committee asking polite questions of the gentlemen witnesses.

The plan had no relation to reality. The committee barely let Mr. Holmes talk—instead they screamed at him, rants full of vicious innuendo and hearsay, and he was never allowed to reply.

I was given a copy of the transcript. Part of it reads like this:

> Mr. RANKIN: When I look at this disgusting New Deal man who sits before the committee, with his smarty-pants manners and Bond Street clothes and his effete cigarette holder, everything that is American and Christian in me revolts at the sight. The New Deal man! That damned New Deal permeates him like a cancer, and I want to scream, "You're everything that's wrong with America. Get out and go back to Red China where you belong, you New Deal socialist! In China they'll welcome you and your treachery."
> CHAIRMAN: The honorable member's time has expired.
> Mr. RANKIN: Thank you, Mr. Chairman.
> CHAIRMAN: Mr. Nixon?

> Mr. NIXON: What were the names of those people in the State Department who you consulted with prior to your journey to China?
>
> WITNESS: May I remind the committee that those with whom I dealt were American public servants acting in good faith—
>
> Mr. NIXON: The committee is not interested in their records. Just their names.

The transcript goes on and on, eighty pages of it altogether. Mr. Holmes had, it appeared, stabbed the generalissimo in the back and lost China to the Reds. He was accused of being soft on communism, just like that parlorpink Henry Wallace, who he supported for the presidency. John Rankin of Mississippi—probably the weirdest voice on the committee—accused Mr. Holmes of being part of the Jewish-Red conspiracy that had crucified Our Savior. Richard Nixon of California kept asking after names—he wanted to know the people Mr. Holmes consulted with in the State Department so that he could do to them what he'd already done to Alger Hiss. Mr. Holmes didn't give any names and pleaded the First Amendment. That's when the committee really rose to its feet in righteous indignation: they mauled him for hours, and the next day they sent down an indictment for contempt of Congress. Mr. Holmes was on his way to the penitentiary.

He was going to prison, and he hadn't committed a single crime.

"Jesus Christ. I've got to talk to Earl and David."

"I've already advised you against that, Mr. Braun."

"The hell with that. We've got to make plans."

"Listen to him, honey."

"The hell with that." The sound of a bottle clinking against a glass. "There's got to be a way out of this."

When I got to Mr. Holmes's suite, he'd been given a sedative and put to bed. Earl told me that Blythe and

Tachyon had gotten their subpoenas and would arrive the next day. We couldn't understand why. Blythe never had any part in the political decisions, and Tachyon hadn't had anything to do with China or American politics at all.

David was called the next morning. He was grinning as he went in. He was going to get even for all of us.

> Mr. RANKIN: I would like to assure the Jewish gentle-
> man from New York that he will encounter no
> bias on account of his race. Any man who
> believes in the fundamental principles of Christi-
> anity and lives up to them, whether he is Catholic
> or Protestant, has my respect and confidence.
> WITNESS: May I say to the committee that I object to
> the characterization of "Jewish gentleman."
> Mr. RANKIN: Do you object to being called a Jew or
> being called a gentleman? What are you kicking
> about?

After that rocky start, David's pheromones began to infiltrate the room, and though he didn't quite have the committee dancing in a circle and singing "Hava Nagila," he did have them genially agreeing to cancel the subpoenas, call off the hearings, draft a resolution praising the Aces as patriots, send a letter to Mr. Holmes apologizing for their conduct, revoke the contempt of Congress citations for the Hollywood Ten, and in general make fools out of them- selves for several hours, right in front of the newsreel cameras. John Rankin called David "America's little Hebe friend," high praise from him. David waltzed out, we saw that ear-to-ear grin, and we pounded him on the back and headed back to the Statler for a celebration.

We had opened the third bottle of champagne when the hotel dick opened the door and congressional aides deliv- ered a new round of subpoenas. We turned on the radio and heard Chairman John Wood give a live address about how David had used "mind control of the type practiced in the

Pavlov Institute in Communist Russia," and that this deadly form of attack would be investigated in full.

I sat down on the bed and stared at the bubbles rising in my champagne glass.

The Fear had come again.

Blythe went in the next morning. Her hands were trembling. David was turned away by hall guards wearing gas masks.

There were trucks with chemical-warfare symbols out front. I found out later that if we tried to fight our way out, they were going to use phosgene on us.

They were constructing a glass booth in the hearing room. David would testify in isolation, through a micro phone. The control of the mike was in John Wood's hands.

Apparently HUAC were as shaken as we, because their questioning was a little disjointed. They asked her about China, and since she'd gone in a scientific capacity she didn't have any answers for them about the political decisions. Then they asked her about the nature of her power, how exactly she absorbed minds and what she did with them. It was all fairly polite. Henry van Renssaeler was still a congressman, after all, and professional courtesy dictated they not suggest his wife ran his mind for him.

They sent Blythe out and called in Tachyon. He was dressed in a peach-colored coat and Hessian boots with tassels. He'd been ignoring his attorney's advice all along— he went in with the attitude of an aristocrat whose reluctant duty was to correct the misapprehensions of the mob.

He outsmarted himself completely, and the committee ripped him to shreds. They nailed him for being an illegal alien, then stomped over him for being responsible for releasing the wild card virus, and to top it all off they demanded the names of the aces he'd treated, just in case some of then happened to be evil infiltrators influencing the minds of America at the behest of Uncle Joe Stalin. Tachyon refused.

They deported him.

* * *

Harstein went in the next day, accompanied by a file of Marines dressed for chemical warfare. Once they had him in the glass booth they tore into him just as they had Mr. Holmes. John Wood held the button on the mike and would never let him talk, not even to answer when Rankin called him a slimy kike, right there in public. When he finally got his chance to speak, David denounced the committee as a bunch of Nazis. That sounded to Mr. Wood like contempt of Congress.

By the end of the hearing, David was going to prison, too.

Congress adjourned for the weekend. Earl and I were going before the committee on Monday next.

We sat in Mr. Holmes's suite Friday night and listened to the radio, and it was all bad. The American Legion was organizing demonstrations in support of the committee all around the country. There were rounds of subpoenas going out to people over the country who were known to have ace abilities—no deformed jokers got called, because they'd look bad on camera. My agent had left a message telling me that Chrysler wanted their car back, and that the Chesterfield people had called and were worried.

I drank a bottle of scotch. Blythe and Tachyon were in hiding somewhere. David and Mr. Holmes were zombies, sitting in the corner, their eyes sunken, turned inward to their own personal agony. None of us had anything to say, except Earl. "I'll take the First Amendment, and damn them all," he said. "If they put me in prison, I'll fly to Switzerland."

I gazed into my drink. "I can't fly, Earl," I said.

"Sure you can, farm boy," he said. "You told me yourself."

"*I can't fly, dammit!* Leave me alone."

I couldn't stand it anymore, and took another bottle with me and went to bed. Kim wanted to talk and I just turned my back and pretended to be asleep.

* * *

"Yes, Mr. Mayer."

"Jack? This is terrible, Jack, just terrible."

"Yes, it is. These bastards, Mr. Mayer. They're going to wreck us."

"Just do what the lawyer says, Jack. You'll be fine. Do the brave thing."

"Brave?" Laughter. "*Brave?*"

"It's the right thing, Jack. You're a hero. They can't touch you. Just tell them what you know, and America will love you for it."

"You want me to be a rat."

"Jack, Jack. Don't use those kind of words. It's a patriotic thing I want you to do. The right thing. I want you to be a hero. And I want you to know there's always a place at Metro for a hero."

"How many people are gonna buy tickets to see a rat, Mr. Mayer? How many?"

"Give the phone to the lawyer, Jack. I want to talk to him. You be a good boy and do what he says."

"The hell I will."

"Jack. What can I do with you? Let me talk to the lawyer."

Earl was floating outside my window. Raindrops sparkled on the goggles perched atop his flying helmet. Kim glared at him and left the room. I got out of bed and went to the window and opened it. He flew in, dropped his boots onto the carpet, and lit a smoke.

"You don't look so good, Jack."

"I have a hangover, Earl."

He pulled a folded *Washington Star* out of his pocket. "I have something here that'll sober you up. Have you seen the paper?"

"No. I haven't seen a damn thing."

He opened it. The headline read: STALIN ANNOUNCES SUPPORT FOR ACES.

I sat on the bed and reached for the bottle. "Jesus."

Earl threw the paper down. "He wants us to go down. We kept him out of Berlin, for god's sake. He has no reason to love us. He's persecuting his own wild card talents over there."

"The bastard, the bastard." I closed my eyes. Colors throbbed on the backs of my lids. "Got a butt?" I asked. He gave me one, and a light from his wartime Zippo. I leaned back in bed and rubbed the bristles on my chin.

"The way I see it," Earl said, "we're going to have ten bad years. Maybe we'll even have to leave the country." He shook his head. "And then we'll be heroes again. It'll take at least that long."

"You sure know how to cheer a guy up."

He laughed. The cigarette tasted vile. I washed the taste away with scotch.

The smile left Earl's face, and he shook his head. "It's the people that are going to be called after us—those are the ones I'm sorry for. There's going to be a witch hunt in this country for years to come." He shook his head. "The NAACP is paying for my lawyer. I just might give him back. I don't want any organization associated with me. It'll just make it harder for them later."

"Mayer's been on the phone."

"Mayer." He grimaced. "If only those guys who run the studios had stood up when the Ten went before the committee. If they'd shown some guts none of this would ever have happened." He gave me a look. "You'd better get a new lawyer. Unless you take the Fifth." He frowned. "The Fifth is quicker. They just ask you your name, you say you won't answer, then it's over."

"What difference does the lawyer make, then?"

"You've got a point there." He gave me a ragged grin. "It really *isn't* going to make any difference, is it? Whatever we say or do. The committee will do what they want, either way."

"Yeah. It's over."

His grin turned, as he looked at me, to a soft smile. For a moment, I saw the glow that Lillian had said surrounded

him. Here he was, on the verge of losing everything he'd
worked for, about to be used as a weapon that would cudgel
the civil rights movement and antifascism and antiimperi-
alism and labor and everything else that mattered to him,
knowing that his name would be anathema, that anyone
he'd ever associated with would soon be facing the same
treatment . . . and he'd accepted it all somehow, sad-
dened of course, but still solid within himself. The Fear
hadn't even come close to touching him. He wasn't afraid of
the committee, of disgrace, of the loss of his position and
standing. He didn't regret an instant of his life, a moment's
dedication to his beliefs.

"It's over?" he said. There was a fire in his eyes. "Hell,
Jack," he laughed, "it's not over. One committee hearing
ain't the war. We're aces. They can't take that away.
Right?"

"Yeah. I guess."

"I better leave you to fix your hangover." He went to the
window. "Time for my morning constitutional, anyway."

"See you later."

He gave me the thumbs-up sign as he threw a leg over the
sill. "Take care, farm boy."

"You too."

I got out of bed to close the window just as the drizzle
turned to downpour. I looked outside into the street. People
were running for cover.

"Earl *really was a Communist*, Jack. He belonged to the
party for years, he went to Moscow to study. Listen,
darling"—imploring now— "*you can't help him*. He's going
to get crucified no matter what you do."

"I can show him he ain't alone on the cross."

"Swell. Just swell. I'm married to a martyr. Just tell me,
how are you helping your friends by taking the Fifth?
Holmes isn't coming back to public life. David's hustled
himself right into prison. Tachyon's being deported. And
Earl's doomed, sure as anything. You can't even carry their
cross for them."

"Now who's being sarcastic?"

Screaming now. *Will you put down that bottle and listen to me? This is something your country wants you to do! It's the right thing!*"

I couldn't stand it anymore, so I went for a walk in the cold February afternoon. I hadn't eaten all day and I had a bottle of whiskey in me, and the traffic kept hissing past as I walked, the rain drizzling in my face, soaking through my light California jacket, and I didn't notice any of it. I just thought of those faces, Wood and Rankin and Francis Case, the faces and the hateful eyes and the parade of constant insinuations, and then I started running for the Capitol. I was going to find the committee and smash them, bang heads together, make them run gabbling in fear. I'd brought democracy to Argentina, for chrissake, and I could bring it to Washington the same way.

The Capitol windows were dark. Cold rain gleamed on the marble. No one was there. I prowled around looking for an open door, and then finally I bashed through a side entrance and headed straight for the committee room. I yanked the door open and stepped inside.

It was empty, of course. I don't know why I was so surprised. There were only a few spotlights on. David's glass booth gleamed in the soft light like a piece of fine crystal. Camera and radio equipment sat in its place. The chairman's gavel glowed with brass and polish. Somehow, as I stood like an imbecile in the hushed silence of the room, the anger went out of me.

I sat down in one of the chairs and tried to remember what I was doing here. It was clear the Four Aces were doomed. We were bound by the law and by decency, and the committee was not. The only way we could fight them was to break the law, to rise up in their smug faces and smash the committee room to bits, laughing as the congressmen dived for cover beneath their desks. And if we did that we'd become what we fought, an extralegal force for terror and violence. We'd become what the committee claimed we were. And that would only make things worse.

The Aces were going down, and nothing could stop it.

As I came down the Capitol steps, I felt perfectly sober. No matter how much I'd had to drink, the booze couldn't stop me from knowing what I knew, from seeing the situation in all its appalling, overwhelming clarity.

I knew, I'd known all along, and I couldn't pretend that I didn't.

I walked into the lobby next morning with Kim on one side and the lawyer on the other. Earl was in the lobby, with Lillian standing there clutching her purse.

I couldn't look at them. I walked past them, and the Marines in their gas masks opened the door, and I walked into the hearing room and announced my intention to testify before the committee as a friendly witness.

Later, the committee developed a procedure for friendly witnesses. There would be a closed session first, just the witness and the committee, a sort of dress rehearsal so that everyone would know what they were going to talk about and what information was going to be developed, so things would go smoothly in public session. That procedure hadn't been worked out when I testified, so everything went a little roughly.

I sweated under the spotlights, so terrified I could barely speak—all I could see were those nine sets of evil little eyes staring at me from across the room, and all I could hear were their voices, booming at me from the loudspeakers like the voice of God.

Wood started off, asking me the opening questions: who I was, where I lived, what I did for a living. Then he started going into my associations, starting with Earl. His time ran out and he turned me over to Kearney.

"Are you aware that Mr. Sanderson was once a member of the Communist party?"

I didn't even hear the question. Kearney had to repeat it.

"Huh? Oh. He told me, yes."

"Do you know if he is currently a member?"

"I believe he split with the party after the Nazi-Soviet thing."

"In 1939."

"If that's what, when, the Nazi-Soviet thing happened. 'Thirty-nine. I guess." I'd forgotten every piece of stage-craft I'd never known. I was fumbling with my tie, mumbling into the mike, sweating. Trying not to look into those nine sets of eyes.

"Are you aware of any Communist affiliations main-tained by Mr. Sanderson subsequent to the Nazi-Soviet pact?"

"No."

Then it came. "He has mentioned to you no names belonging to Communist or Communist-affiliated groups?"

I said the first thing that came into my head. Not even thinking. "There was some girl, I think, in Italy. That he knew during the war. I think her name was Lena Goldoni. She's an actress now."

Those sets of eyes didn't even blink. But I could see little smiles on their faces. And I could see the reporters out of the corner of my eye, bending suddenly over their notepads.

"Could you spell the name, please?"

So there was the spike in Earl's coffin. Whatever could have been said about Earl up to then, it would have at least revealed himself true to his principles. The betrayal of Lillian implied other betrayals, perhaps of his country. I'd destroyed him with just a few words, and at the time I didn't even know what it was I was doing.

I babbled on. In a sweat to get it over, I said anything that came into my head. I talked about loving America, and about how I just said those nice things about Henry Wallace to please Mr. Holmes, and I'm sure it was a foolish thing to have done. I didn't want to change the Southern way of life, the Southern way of life was a fine way of life. I saw *Gone With the Wind* twice, a great picture. Mrs. Bethune was just a friend of Earl's I got photographed with. Velde took over the questioning.

"Are you aware of the names of any so-called aces who may be living in this country today?"

"No. None, I mean, besides those who have already been given subpoenas by the committee."

"Do you know if Earl Sanderson knows any such names?"

"No."

"He has not confided to you in any way?"

I took a drink of water. How many times could they repeat this? "If he knows the names of any aces, he has not mentioned them in my presence."

"Do you know if Mr. Harstein knows of any such names?"

On and on. "No."

"Do you believe that Dr. Tachyon knows any such names?"

They'd already dealt with this. I was just confirming what they knew. "He's treated many people afflicted by the virus. I assume he knows their names. But he has never mentioned any names to me."

"Does Mrs. van Renssaeler know the existence of any other aces?"

I started to shake my head, then a thought hit me, and I stammered out, "No. Not in herself, no."

Velde plodded on. "Does Mr. Holmes—" he started, and then Nixon sensed something here, in the way I'd just answered the question, and he asked Velde's permission to interrupt. Nixon was the smart one, no doubt. His eager, young chipmunk face looked at me intently over his microphone.

"May I request the witness to clarify that statement?"

I was horrified. I took another drink of water and tried to think of a way out of this. I couldn't. I asked Nixon to repeat the question. He did. My answer came out before he finished.

"Mrs. van Renssaeler has absorbed the mind of Dr. Tachyon. She would know any names that he would know."

The strange thing was, they hadn't figured it out about

Blythe and Tachyon up till then. They had to have the big
jock from Dakota come in and put the pieces together for
them.

I should have just taken a gun and shot her. It would have
been quicker.

Chairman Wood thanked me at the end of my testimony.
When the chairman of HUAC said thank you, it meant you
were okay as far as they were concerned, and other people
could associate with you without fear of being branded a
pariah. It meant you could have a job in the United States of
America.

I walked out of the hearing room with my lawyer on one
side and Kim on the other. I didn't meet the eyes of my
friends. Within an hour I was on a plane back to California.

The house on Summit was full of congratulatory bou-
quets from friends I'd made in the picture business. There
were telegrams from all over the country about how brave
I'd been, about what a patriot I was. The American Legion
was strongly represented.

Back in Washington, Earl was taking the Fifth.

They didn't just listen to the Fifth and then let him go.
They asked him one insinuating question after another, and
made him take the Fifth to each. Are you a Communist?
Earl answered with the Fifth. Are you an agent of the Soviet
government? The Fifth. Do you associate with Soviet spies?
The Fifth. Do you know Lena Goldoni? The Fifth. Was
Lena Goldoni your mistress? The Fifth. Was Lena Goldoni
a Soviet agent? The Fifth.

Lillian was seated in a chair right behind. Sitting mute,
clutching her bag, as Lena's name came up again and again.

And finally Earl had had enough. He leaned forward, his
face taut with anger.

"I have better things to do than incriminate myself in
front of a bunch of fascists!" he barked, and they promptly
ruled he'd waived the Fifth by speaking out, and they asked
him the questions all over again. When, trembling with

rage, he announced that he'd simply paraphrased the Fifth and would continue to refuse any answer, they cited him for contempt.

He was going to join Mr. Holmes and David in prison.

People from the NAACP met with him that night. They told him to disassociate himself from the civil rights movement. He'd set the cause back fifty years. He was to stay clear in the future.

The idol had fallen. He'd molded his image into that of a superman, a hero without flaw, and once I'd mentioned Lena the populace suddenly realized that Earl Sanderson was human. They blamed him for it, for their own naïveté in believing in him and for their own sudden loss of faith, and in olden times they might have stoned him or hanged him from the nearest apple tree, but in the end what they did was worse.

They let him live.

Earl knew he was finished, was a walking dead man, that he'd given them a weapon that was used to crush him and everything he believed in, that had destroyed the heroic image he'd so carefully crafted, that he'd crushed the hopes of everyone who'd believed in him . . . He carried the knowledge with him to his dying day, and it paralyzed him. He was still young, but he was crippled, and he never flew as high again, or as far.

The next day HUAC called Blythe. She broke down on the stand, all the personalities in her head talking at once, and years later she died in an asylum. I don't even want to think about it.

Golden Boy opened two months after the hearings. I sat next to Kim at the premiere, and from the moment the film began I realized it had gone terribly wrong.

The Earl Sanderson character was gone, just sliced out of the film. The Archibald Holmes character wasn't FBI, but he wasn't independent either, he belonged to that new organization, the CIA. Someone had shot a lot of new footage. The fascist regime in South America had been changed to a Communist regime in Eastern Europe, all run by olive-skinned men with Spanish accents. Every time one of the characters said "Nazi," it was dubbed in "Commie," and the dubbing was loud and bad and unconvincing.

I wandered in a daze through the reception afterward. Everyone kept telling me what a great actor I was, what a great picture it was. The film poster said *Jack Braun—A Hero America Can Trust!* I wanted to vomit.

I left early and went to bed.

I went on collecting ten grand per week while the picture bombed at the box office. I was told the Rickenbacker picture was going to be a big hit, but right now they were having script problems with my next picture. The first two screenwriters had been called up before the committee and ended up on the blacklist because they wouldn't name names. It made me want to weep.

After the Hollywood Ten appeals ran out, the next actor they called was Larry Parks, the man I'd been watching when the virus hit New York. He named names, but he didn't name them willingly enough, and his career was over.

I couldn't seem to get away from the thing. Some people wouldn't talk to me at parties. Sometimes I'd overhear bits of conversation. "Judas Ace." "Golden Rat." "Friendly Witness," said like it was a name, or title.

I bought a Jaguar to make myself feel better.

In the meantime, the North Koreans charged across the 38th Parallel and the U.S. forces were getting crunched at Taejön. I wasn't doing anything other than taking acting lessons a couple times each week.

I called Washington direct. They gave me a lieutenant colonel's rank and flew me out on a special plane.

Metro thought it was a great publicity stunt.

I was given a special helicopter, one of those early Bells, with a pilot from the swamps of Louisiana who exhibited a decided death wish. There was a cartoon of me on the side panels, with one knee up and one arm up high, like I was Superman flying.

I'd get taken behind North Korean lines and then I'd kick ass. It was very simple.

I'd demolish entire tank columns. Any artillery that got spotted by our side were turned into pretzels. I made four North Korean generals prisoner and rescued General Dean from the Koreans that had captured him. I pushed entire supply convoys off the sides of mountains. I was grim and determined and angry, and I was saving American lives, and I was very good at it.

There is a picture of me that got on the cover of *Life*. It shows me with this tight Clint Eastwood smile, holding a T–34 over my head. There is a very surprised North Korean in the turret. I'm glowing like a meteor. The picture was titled *Superstar of Pusan*, "superstar" being a new word back then.

I was very proud of what I was doing.

Back in the States, *Rickenbacker* was a hit. Not as big a hit as everyone expected, but it was spectacular and it made quite a bit of money. Audiences seemed to be a bit ambivalent in their reactions to the star. Even with me on the cover of *Life*, there were some people who couldn't quite see me as a hero.

Metro re-released *Golden Boy*. It flopped again.

I didn't much care. I was holding the Pusan Perimeter. I was right there with the GIs, under fire half the time, sleeping in a tent, eating out of cans and looking like someone out of a Bill Mauldin cartoon. I think it was fairly unique behavior for a light colonel. The other officers hated it, but General Dean supported me—at one point he was shooting at tanks with a bazooka himself—and I was a hit with the soldiers.

They flew me to Wake Island so that Truman could give me the Medal of Honor, and MacArthur flew out on the same plane. He seemed preoccupied the whole time, didn't waste any time in conversation with me. He looked incredibly old, on his last legs. I don't think he liked me.

A week later, we broke out of Pusan and MacArthur landed X Corps at Inchon. The North Koreans ran for it.

Five days later, I was back in California. The Army told me, quite curtly, that my services were no longer necessary. I'm fairly certain it was MacArthur's doing. He wanted to be the superstar of Korea, and he didn't want to share any of the honors. And there were probably other aces—nice, quiet, anonymous aces—working for the U.S. by then.

I didn't want to leave. For a while, particularly after MacArthur got crushed by the Chinese, I kept phoning Washington with new ideas about how to be useful. I could raid the airfields in Manchuria that were giving us such trouble. Or I could be the point man for a breakthrough. The authorities were very polite, but it was clear they didn't want me.

I did hear from the CIA, though. After Dien Bien Phu, they wanted to send me into Indochina to get rid of Bao Dai. The plan seemed half-assed—they had no idea who or what they wanted to put in Bao Dai's place, for one thing; they just expected "native anticommunist liberal forces" to rise and take command—and the guy in charge of the operation kept using Madison Avenue jargon to disguise the fact he knew nothing about Vietnam or any of the people he was supposed to be dealing with.

I turned them down. After that, my sole involvement with the federal government was to pay my taxes every April.

While I was in Korea, the Hollywood Ten appeals ran out. David and Mr. Holmes went to prison. David served three years. Mr. Holmes served only six months and then was released on account of his health. Everyone knows what happened to Blythe.

Earl flew to Europe and appeared in Switzerland, where he renounced his U.S. citizenship and became a citizen of the world. A month later, he was living with Orlena Goldoni in her Paris apartment. She'd become a big star by then. I suppose he decided that since there was no point in concealing their relationship anymore, he'd flaunt it.

Lillian stayed in New York. Maybe Earl sent her money. I don't know.

Perón came back to Argentina in the mid-1950s, along with his peroxide chippie. The Fear moving south.

I made pictures, but somehow none of them was the success that was expected. Metro kept muttering about my image problem.

People couldn't believe I was a hero. I couldn't believe it either, and it affected my acting. In *Rickenbacker*, I'd had conviction. After that, nothing.

Kim had her career going by now. I didn't see her much. Eventually her detective got a picture of me in bed with the girl dermatologist who came over to apply her makeup every morning, and Kim got the house on Summit Drive, with the maids and gardener and chauffeurs and most of my money, and I ended up in a small beach house in Malibu with the Jaguar in the garage. Sometimes my parties would last weeks.

There were two marriages after that, and the longest lasted only eight months. They cost me the rest of the money I'd made. Metro let me go, and I worked for Warner. The pictures got worse and worse. I made the same western about six times over.

Eventually I bit the bullet. My picture career had died years ago and I was broke. I went to NBC with an idea for a television series.

Tarzan of the Apes ran for four years. I was executive producer, and on the screen I played second banana to a chimp. I was the first and only blond Tarzan. I had a lot of points and the series set me up for life.

After that I did what every ex-Hollywood actor does. I went into real estate. I sold actors' homes in California for a while, and then I put a company together and started building apartments and shopping centers. I always used other people's money—I wasn't taking a chance on going broke again. I put up shopping centers in half the small towns in the Midwest.

I made a fortune. Even after I didn't need the money anymore, I kept it up. I didn't have much else to do.

When Nixon got elected President I felt ill. I couldn't understand how people could believe that man.

After Mr. Holmes got out of prison he went to work as editor of the *New Republic*. He died in 1955, lung cancer. His daughter inherited the family money. I suppose my clothes were still in his closets.

Two weeks after Earl flew the country, Paul Robeson and W.E.B. Du Bois joined the CPUSA, receiving their party cards in a public ceremony in Herald Square. They announced they were joining in protest of Earl's treatment before HUAC.

HUAC called a lot of blacks into their committee room. Even Jackie Robinson was summoned and appeared as a friendly witness. Unlike the white witnesses, the blacks were never asked to name names. HUAC didn't want to create any more black martyrs. Instead the witnesses were asked to denounce the views of Sanderson, Robeson, and Du Bois. Most of them obliged.

Through the 1950s and most of the 1960s, it was difficult to get a grasp on what Earl was doing. He lived quietly with Lena Goldoni in Paris and Rome. She was a big star, active politically, but Earl wasn't seen much.

He wasn't hiding, I think. Just keeping out of sight. There's a difference.

There were rumors, though. That he was seen in Africa during various wars for independence. That he fought in Algeria against the French and the Secret Army. When asked, Earl refused to confirm or deny his activities. He was courted by left-wing individuals and causes, but rarely committed himself publicly. I think, like me, he didn't want to be used again. But I also think he was afraid that he'd do damage to a cause by associating himself with it.

Eventually the reign of terror ended, just as Earl said it would. While I was swinging on jungle vines as Tarzan, John and Robert Kennedy killed the blacklist by marching past an American Legion picket line to see *Spartacus*, a film written by one of the Hollywood Ten.

Aces began coming out of hiding, entering public life. But now they wore masks and used made-up names, just like the comics I'd read in the war and thought were so silly. It wasn't silly now. They were taking no chances. The Fear might one day return.

Books were written about us. I declined all interviews. Sometimes the question came up in public, and I'd just turn cold and say, "I decline to talk about that at this time." My own Fifth Amendment.

In the 1960s, when the civil rights movement began to heat up in this country, Earl came to Toronto and perched on the border. He met with black leaders and journalists, talked only about civil rights.

But Earl was, by that time, irrelevant. The new generation of black leaders invoked his memory and quoted his speeches, and the Panthers copied his leather jacket, boots, and beret, but the fact of his continuing existence, as a human being rather than a symbol, was a bit disturbing. The movement would have preferred a dead martyr, whose image could have been used for any purpose, rather than a live, passionate man who said his own opinions loud and clear.

Maybe he sensed this when he was asked to come south. The immigration people would probably have allowed it. But he hesitated too long, and then Nixon was President. Earl wouldn't enter a country run by a former member of HUAC.

By the 1970s, Earl settled permanently into Lena's apartment in Paris. Panther exiles like Cleaver tried to make common cause with him and failed.

Lena died in 1975 in a train crash. She left Earl her money.

He'd give interviews from time to time. I tracked them down and read them. According to one interviewer, one of the conditions of the interview was that he wouldn't be asked about me. Maybe he wanted certain memories to die a natural death. I wanted to thank him for that.

There's a story, a legend almost, spread by those who marched on Selma in '65 during the voting rights crusade . . . that when the cops charged in with their tear gas, clubs, and dogs, and the marchers began to fall before the wave of white troopers, some of the marchers swore that they looked skyward and saw a man flying there, a straight black figure in a flying jacket and helmet, but that the man just hovered there and then was gone, unable to act, unable to decide whether the use of his powers would have aided his cause or worked against it. The magic hadn't come back, not even at such a pivotal moment, and after that there was nothing in his life but the chair in the café, the pipe, the paper, and the cerebral hemorrhage that finally took him into whatever it is that waits in the sky.

Every so often, I begin to wonder if it's over, if people have really forgotten. But aces are a part of life now, a part of the background, and the whole world is raised on ace mythology, on the story of the Four Aces and their betrayer. Everyone knows the Judas Ace, and what he looks like.

During one of my periods of optimism I found myself in New York on business. I went to Aces High, the restaurant in the Empire State Building where the new breed of ace hangs out. I was met at the door by Hiram, the ace who used to call himself Fatman until word of his real identity got out, and I could tell right away that he recognized me and that I was making a big mistake.

He was polite enough, I'll give him that, but his smile cost him a certain amount of effort. He seated me in a dark corner, where people wouldn't see me. I ordered a drink and the salmon steak.

When the plate came, the steak was surrounded with a neat circle of dimes. I counted them. Thirty pieces of silver.

I got up and left. I could feel Hiram's eyes on me the whole time. I never came back.

I couldn't blame him at all.

* * *

When I was making *Tarzan*, people were calling me well preserved. After, when I was selling real estate and building developments, everyone told me how much the job must be agreeing with me. I looked so young.

If I look in the mirror now, I see the same young guy who was scuffling the New York streets going to auditions. Time hasn't added a line, hasn't changed me physically in any way. I'm fifty-five now, and I look twenty-two. Maybe I won't ever grow old.

I still feel like a rat. But I only did what my country told me.

Maybe I'll be the Judas Ace forever.

Sometimes I wonder about becoming an ace again, putting on a mask and costume so that no one will recognize me. Call myself Muscle Man or Beach Boy or Blond Giant or something. Go out and save the world, or at least a little piece of it.

But then I think, No. I had my time, and it's gone. And when I had the chance, I couldn't even save my own integrity. Or Earl. Or anybody.

I should have kept the dimes. I earned them, after all.

WOLF TIME

Speakers in the hospital ceiling chimed a series of low, whispery, synthesized tones, tones that were scientifically proven to be relaxing. Reese looked down at the boy in the hospital bed and felt her insides twist.

The boy was named Steward, and he'd just had a bullet removed that morning. In the last few days, mad with warrior zen and a suicidal concept of personal honor, he'd gone kamikaze and blown up the whole network. Griffith was dead, Jordan was dead, Spassky was dead, and nobody had stopped Steward until everything in L.A. had collapsed entirely. He hadn't talked yet to the heat, but he would. Reese reached for her gun. Her insides were still twisting.

Steward had been lied to and jacked over and manipulated without his knowing it. Mostly it had been his friend Reese who had done it to him. She couldn't blame him for exploding when he finally figured out what had happened.

And now this.

Reese turned off the IV monitor so it wouldn't bleep when he died, and then Steward opened his eyes. She could see the recognition in his look, the knowledge of what was about to happen. She might have known he wouldn't make it easy.

"Sorry," she said, and raised the gun. What the hell else could she say? *Maybe we can still be friends, after this is over?*

Steward was trying to say something. She felt herself wring out again.

She shot him three times with her silenced pistol and left. The police guards didn't look twice at her hospital coat and ID. Proper credentials had always been her specialty.

CYA. Reese headed for Japan under a backup identity. Credentials her strong suit, as always. On the shuttle she drank a star beast and plugged her seat's interface stud into the socket at the base of her skull. She closed her eyes and silently projected the latest scansheets onto the optical centers of her brain, and her lips twisted in anger as for the first time she found out what had really gone down, what she'd been a part of.

Alien pharmaceuticals, tonnes of them, shipped down under illegal cover. The network had been huge, bigger than Reese, from her limited perspective, had ever suspected, and now the L.A. heat had *everything*. Police and security people everywhere, even in the space habitats, were going berserk.

All along, she'd thought it was friends helping friends, but her friends had jacked her around the same way she'd jacked around Steward. The whole trip to L.A. had been pointless—they had been stupid to send her. Killing Steward couldn't stop what was happening, it was all too big. The only way Reese could stay clear was to hide.

She ordered another drink, needing it badly. The shuttle speakers moaned with the same tuneless synthesized chords as had the speakers in the hospital room. The memory of Steward lying in the bed floated in her mind, tangled in her insides.

She leaned back against the headrest and watched the shuttle's wings gather fire.

Her career as a kick boxer ended with a spin kick breaking her nose, and Reese said the fuck with it and went back to light sparring and kung fu. Beating the hell out of herself in training only to have the hell beaten out of her in the ring was not her idea of the good life. She was thirty-six now and she might as well admit there were sports she shouldn't indulge in, even if she had the threadware for them. The realization didn't improve her mood.

Through the window of her condeco apartment, Reese could see a cold wailing northeast wind drive flying white scud across the shallow Aral Sea, its shriek drowning the minarets' amplified call to prayer. Neither the wind nor the view had changed in months. Reese looked at the grey Uzbek spring, turned on her vid, and contemplated her sixth month of exile.

Her hair was black now, shorter than she'd worn it in a long time. Her fingerprints were altered, as was the bone structure of her face. The serial numbers on her artificial eyes had been changed. However bleak its weather, Uzbekistan was good at that sort of thing.

The last person she'd known who had lived here was Steward. Just before he came to L.A. and blew everything to smithereens.

A young man on the vid was putting himself into some kind of combat suit, stuffing weapons and ammunition into pockets. He picked up a shotgun. Suspenseful music hammered from the speakers. Reese turned up the sound and sat down in front of the vid.

She had considered getting back into the trade, but it was too early. The scansheets and broadcasts were still full of stories about aliens, alien ways, alien imports. About "restructuring" going on in the policorps who dealt with the Powers. It was strange seeing the news on the vid, with people ducking for cover, refusing statements, the news item followed by a slick ad for alien pharmaceuticals.

People were going to trial—at least those who survived were. A lot were cooperating. Things were still too hot.

Fortunately money wasn't a problem. She had enough to last a long time, possibly even forever.

Gunfire sounded from the vid. The young man was in a shootout with aliens, splattering Powers with his shotgun. Reese felt her nerves turn to ice.

The young man, she realized, was supposed to be Steward. She jumped forward and snapped off the vid. She felt sickened.

Steward had never shot an alien in his life. Reese ought to know.

Fucking assholes. Fucking media vermin.

She reached for her quilted Chinese jacket and headed for the door. The room was too damn small.

She swung the door open with a bang, and a dark-complected man jumped a foot at the sound. He turned and gave a nervous grin.

"You startled me."

He had an anonymous accent that conveyed no particular origin, just the abstract idea of foreignness. He looked about thirty. He was wearing suede pumps that had tabs of velcro on the bottoms and sides for holding onto surfaces in zero gee. His hands were jammed into a grey, unlined plastic jacket with a half-dozen pockets all sealed by velcro tabs. Reese suspected one of his hands of having a weapon in it. He was shivering from cold or nervousness. Reese figured he had just come down the gravity well—he was wearing too much velcro to have bought his clothes on Earth.

Some descendants of the Golden Horde, dressed in Flieger styles imported from Berlin, roared by on skateboards, the earpieces of their leather flying helmets flapping in the wind.

"Been in town long?" Reese asked.

He told her his name was Sardar Chandrasekhar Vivekenanda and that he was a revolutionary from Prince Station.

His friends called him Ken. Two nights after their first meeting, she met him in the Natural Life bar, a place on the top story of a large bank. It catered to exiles and featured a lot of mahogany imported at great cost from Central America.

Reese had checked on Ken—no sense in being foolish—and discovered he was who he claimed to be. The scansheets from Prince mentioned him frequently. Even his political allies were denouncing his actions.

"Ram was trying to blame the February Riots on us," Ken told her. "Cheney decided I should disappear—the riots would be blamed on me, and Cheney could go on working."

Reese sipped her mataglap star, feeling it burn its way down her throat as she glanced down through the glass wall, seeing the wind scour dust over the Uzbeks' metal roofs and receiver dishes. She grinned. "So Cheney arranged for you to take the fall instead of him," she said. "Sounds like a friend of humanity to me, all right."

Ken's voice was annoyed. "Cheney knows what he's doing."

"Sure he does. He's setting up his friends. The question is, do you know what *you're* doing?"

Ken's fine-boned hands made a dismissive gesture. "From here I can make propaganda. Cheney sends me an allowance. I've bought a very good communications system."

She turned to him. "You going to need any soldiers in this revolution of yours?"

He shook his head. His lashes were full and black. "I think not. Prince Station is a hundred years old—it's in orbit around Luna, with ready access to minerals, but it cannot compete effectively with the new equipment on other stations. Ram wants to hang on as long as possible—his policy is to loot the economy rather than rebuild. He's guaranteed the loyalty of the stockholders by paying large dividends, but the economy can't support the dividends anymore, and the riots showed he has lost control over the situation. It is a matter of time only. We do not expect the change will be violent—not a military sort of violence, anyway."

"Too bad. I could use a job in someone's foreign legion about now." She glanced up as a group of people entered the bar—she recognized a famous swindler from Ceres named da Vega, his hands and face covered with expensive, glowing implant jewelry that reminded her of fluorescent slime mold. He was with an all-female group of bodyguards who were supposed to stand between him and any Cerean snatch teams sent to bring him to justice. They were all tall and round-eyed—da Vega liked women that way. He'd tried to recruit Reese when they first met. The pay was generous, round-eyed women being rare here, but sexual favors were supposed to be included.

One of *those* jobs, Reese thought. She was tempted to feed him his socks, bodyguards or not, but in the end told him she was used to a better class of employer.

Da Vega turned to her and smiled. Uzbekistan was suddenly far too small a place.

Reese finished her mataglap star and stood. "Let's go for a walk," she said.

"An architecture of liberation," Ken said. "That's what we're after. You should read Cheney's thoughts on the subject."

The night street filled with a welling tide of wind. Its alloy surface reflected bright holograms that marched up and down dark storefronts, advertising wares invisible behind dead glass. The wind howled in the latticework of radio receivers pointed at the sky, through a spiky forest of antennae. A minaret outlined by flashing red strobes speared a sky that glowed with yellow sodium light.

"Liberation," Reese said. "Right."

"Too many closed systems," Ken said. He shrugged into the collar of his new down jacket. "That's the problem with space habitats in general—they *strive* for closed ecological systems, and then try to close as much of their economy as

possible. There's not enough *access*. I'm a macroeconomist—I work with a lot of models, try to figure out
how things are put together—and the most basic obstacle
always seems to be the lack of access to data. We've got a
solar system filled with corporate plutocracies, all compet-
ing with each other, none giving free access to anything
they're trying to do. And they've got colonies in other solar
systems, and *nothing* about those gets out that the policorps
don't want us to know. The whole situation is far too
unstable—it's impossible to predict what's going to happen
because the data simply isn't available. Everything's con-
structed along the lines of the old Orbital Soviet—not even
the people who *need* the information get the access they
require.

"Prince Station's main business is processing minerals—
that's okay and it's steady, but the prices fluctuate a lot as
new mineral sources are exploited in the Belt and elsewhere, and it requires heavy capital investment to keep the
equipment up to date. So for the sake of a stable station
economy, it would be nice for Prince to develop another,
steadier source of export. Biologicals, say, or custom-
configured databases. Optics. Wetware. Export genetics.
Anything. But it takes time and resources—five years'
worth, say—to set something like that up, and there are
other policorps who specialize in those areas. We could be
duplicating another group's work, and never know it until
suddenly a new product comes onto the market and wipes
out our five years' investment. All this secrecy is making
for unstable economies. Unstable economies make for
unstable political situations—that's why whole policorps
suddenly go belly-up."

"So you want the policorps to give away their trade
secrets."

"I want to do away with the whole *concept* of trade
secrets. Ideally, what I'd like to do is create a whole new
architecture of data storage and retrieval. Something that's
so good that everyone will have to use it to stay competi-

tive, but something that by its very nature prohibits restriction of access."

Reese laughed. The sound echoed from the cold metal street. "You're dreaming."

He gave her a faint smile. "You're right, of course. I'd have to go back two hundred years, right to the beginning of artificial intelligence, and redesign everything from the start. Then maybe I'd have a chance." He shrugged. "Cheney and I have more practical plans, fortunately."

She looked at him. "You remind me of someone I used to know. He wanted to know the truth, just like you. Wanted *access*."

"Yes?"

The cold wind seemed to cut her to the bone. "He died," she said. "Somebody shot him in a hospital." Somehow, caught in the warm rush of memory, she had forgot that ending.

"A funny place to get shot."

She remembered Steward's last comprehending look, the final words that never came. The northeaster touched her flesh, chilled her heart. The lonely street where they walked suddenly seemed endless, not just a street but the Street, an endless alloy thoroughfare where Reese walked in chill isolation, moving between walls of neon that advertised phantom, unreal comforts . . . She shivered and took his hand.

Ken's voice was soft, almost drowned by wind. "Were you close?"

"Yes. No." She tossed her head. "I wanted to be a friend, but it would have been bad for business."

"I see."

She tasted bile on her tongue, gazing down the endless gleaming Street again, the dark people on it who touched briefly and then parted. Sometimes, she thought, she just needed reminding. She wondered what Steward's last words might have been.

A bare yellow bulb marked the door to Ken's apartment building. They entered, the yellow light streaming through the door to reveal the worn furniture, the bright new communications equipment. "Hey," Reese said, "it's Agitprop Central." She was glad to be out of the wind.

The room blinked to the distant red pulse of the minaret's air-hazard lights. Reese stopped Ken's hand on the light switch, stopped his mouth, every time he tried to talk, with her tongue. She really didn't care if he had someone special back on Prince, preferred this to happen in a certain restrained, ethical silence. Her nerves were wired for combat and she snapped them on, speeding her perceptions and making everything seem in slow motion, the way his hands moved on her, the susurrus of her own breath, the endless red beat of the strobe that sketched the outlines of his face in the warm darkness . . . She could hear the bluster of the northeaster outside, the way it knocked at the panes, shrieked around corners, flooded down the long and empty Street outside. Kept securely outside, at least for this slow-moving, comforting moment of exile.

A day later a maintenance seal blew out on Prince Station and killed sixteen people. Ken was pleased.

"We can do a lot with this," he said. "Demonstrate how the administration's cronies can't even do simple jobs right."

Reese stood by the window, looking out toward the distant brown horizon, tired of Ken's torn wallpaper and sagging furniture. In the distance, foreigners on Bactrian camels pretended they were carrying silk to Tashkent.

"Sabotage, do you think?" she asked, then corrected herself. "Sorry. *Destabilization* is the proper term, right?"

He sat cross-legged on his chair, watching the screen with an intent, calculating frown. "It could have been us, yes. An effective little action, if it was."

"The people who got killed weren't volunteers, anyway. Not your people."

He grinned in a puzzled way. "No. Of course not."

Reese turned to look at him, folding her arms. "That's what scares me about you idealists. You shoot sixteen people into a vacuum, and it's all for human betterment and the triumph of the revolution, so everything's okay."

Ken squinted as he looked at her against the light. "I'm not sure it's different from what you do."

"I'm a soldier. You're an ideologue. The difference is that you decide who gets killed and where, and I'm the one that has to do it and face the consequences if you're wrong. If it weren't for people like you, I wouldn't be necessary."

"You think this difference somehow makes you less responsible?"

Reese shook her head. "No. But the people I fight—they're volunteers, same as me. Getting paid, same as me. It's clean, very direct. I take the money, do a job. I don't know what it's about often as not. I don't really *want* to know. If I asked, the people I work for would just lie anyway." She moved to the shabby plush chair and sat, curling one leg under her.

"I fought for humanity once, in the Artifact War. I was on Archangel with Far Jewel, making the planet safe for the Freconomicist cause. Making use of the alien technology we'd stumbled on by accident, all that biochemware the Powers are so good at. It sounded like a noble adventure, but what we were doing was looting alien ruins and stealing from the other policorps. The war blew up, and next I knew I was below the surface in those alien tunnels, and I was facing extermination cyberdrones and tailored bugs with nothing between death and my skin but a very inadequately armored environment suit. And then I got killed."

Ken looked at her with his head cocked to one side, puzzled. "You had clone insurance? This is a different body?"

Anger burned in Reese as she spoke, and she felt it tempering her muscles, turning them rigid. Remembered dark tunnels, bodies piled in heaps, the smell of fear that burned itself into the fibers of her combat suit, the scent that no amount of maintenance and cleaning would ever remove.

"No. Nothing like that. *I* did the killing—I killed myself, my personality. Because everything I was, everything I'd learned, was just contributing to help my employers, my officers, and the enemy in their effort to murder me. I had to streamline myself, get rid of everything that didn't contribute in a positive way toward my own physical survival. I became an animal, a tunnel rat. I saw how qualities like courage and loyalty were being used by our bosses to get us killed, and so I became a disloyal coward. My body was working against me—I'm too tall for tunnels—but I tried real hard to get short, and funny enough it seemed to work. Because in times like that, if you've got your head right, you can do what you have to."

She looked at Ken and grinned, baring her teeth. An adrenaline surge, triggered by the violent memory, prickled the down on her arms. "I'm still an animal. I'm still disloyal. I'm still a coward. Because that's the only way to keep alive."

"If you feel that way, you could get out of the business."

She shrugged. "It's what I do best. And if I did something else—got a job as a rigger, or some kind of tech—then I'd just be somebody else's animal, a cow maybe, being herded from one place to another and fed on grass. At least this way, I'm my own animal. I get my reward up front."

"And during?" Ken's dark eyes were intent.

Reese shifted in her seat, felt a certain discomfort. Nerves, she thought, jinking from the adrenaline. "I'm not sure what you mean."

"You like the work. I have that impression."

She laughed. No reason to be defensive about it. "I like being wired and hanging right on the edge. I like knowing that I have to do things right, that any mistake I make matters."

He shook his head. "I don't understand that. People like you."

"You haven't had to become an animal. You're a macroeconomist, and you're trained to take the long view. A few people blown out a hatch, that's just an acceptable sacrifice. I tend to take this kind of thing personally, is all.

See, I figure everyone who ever tried to get me killed was looking at the long view."

Ken's gaze was steady. "I'm not planning on getting you killed. That's not part of my view."

"Maybe someday I'll end up standing between you and your revolution. Then we'll see."

He didn't say anything. In the steadiness of his dark eyes, the absence of expression, Reese read her answer, and knew it was the one she'd expected.

"Reese."

It was the first time she'd heard her name in six months, and now it came from a complete stranger on a streetcorner in Uzbekistan. Her hardwired nerves were triggered and her combat thread was evaluating the man's stance, calculating possible dangers and responses, before she even finished her turn.

He was about forty, tanned, with receding brown hair and a widow's peak. His stance was open, his hands in plain sight: he wore a blue down vest over a plaid shirt, baggy grey wool pants, old brown square-toed boots. He smiled in a friendly way. His build was delicate, as if he'd been genetically altered. His face was turning ruddy in the wind.

"You talking to me?" Reese asked him. "My name's Waldman." Her wetwear was still evaluating him, analyzing every shift in posture, movement of his hands. Had Ken shopped her? she wondered. Had Cheney, after deciding she was a danger to Ken?

His smile broadened. "I understand your caution, but we know who you are. Don't worry about it. We want to hire you."

His voice was as American as hers. Her speeded-up reflexes gave her plenty of time to contemplate his words.

"You'd better call me Waldman if you want to talk to me at all."

He put up his hands. Her nerves crackled. She noticed he had a ragged earlobe, as if someone had torn off an earring in a fight. "Okay, Miss Waldman. My name's Berger. Can we talk?"

"The Natural Life, in an hour. Do you know where that is?"

"I can find out. See you there."

He turned and walked casually up the narrow street. She watched till he was gone and then went to the apartment she rented in a waterfront condecology. She looked for signs anyone had been there in her absence—there weren't any, but that didn't mean anything—and then, to calm her jittery nerves, she cleaned her pistol and took a long, hot bath with the gun sitting on the side of the steel tub. She stretched out as far as the tub would let her, feeling droplets of sweat beading on her scalp while she watched the little bathroom liquid-crystal vidscreen show a bouncy pop-music program from Malaya. She changed her clothes, put the pistol back in its holster—the security softwear at the Natural Life would shred her with poisoned darts if she tried to carry it in—and then headed back into town. The muezzins' song hung in the gusty air. Her mind sifted possibilities.

Berger was the heat. Berger was an assassin. Da Vega had shopped her out of pique. Cheney had sold her name. Ken had regretted telling her so much about his revolution and decided to have her iced before she sold his plans to Ram.

Life was just so full of alternatives.

Berger hadn't arrived at the bar when she came in. The bartender was at prayer and so she turned on the desktop comp and read the scansheets, looking for something that might give her an edge, help her to understand what it was about.

Nothing. The aliens hadn't generated any headlines today. But there was a note about a Cerean exile named da Vega who had been found dead, along with a couple of his bodyguards. Another bodyguard was missing.

Reese grinned. The Uzbeks, a people who usually endorsed the long view, had probably turned da Vega into fertilizer by now.

The amplified muezzins fell silent. The bartender returned and flipped on todo music broadcast by satellite from Japan. He took her order and then Berger walked in, dabbing at his nose with a tissue. He hadn't been ready, he explained, for this bitter a spring. He'd have to buy a warm jacket.

"Don't worry, Miss Waldman," he added. "I'm not here to crease you. If I wanted to do that, I could have done it on the street."

"I know. But you might be a cop trying to lure me out of Uzbekistan. So I hope to hell you can prove to me who you are."

He grinned, rubbed his forehead uncomfortably. "Well. To tell you the truth, I *am* a policeman, of a sort."

"Terrific. That really makes my day."

He showed her ID. She studied it while Berger went on. "I'm a captain in Brighter Suns' Pulsar Division. We'd like to hire you for a job up the well."

"Vesta?"

"No. Closer to Earth."

Reese frowned. Policorp Brighter Suns was one of the two policorps that had been set up to deal with the alien Powers. It was almost exclusively into Power imports, and its charter forbade it from owning territory outside of its home asteroid, Vesta. A lot of Brighter Suns execs were running for cover ever since Steward had blown Griffith's network in L.A., and the whole Vesta operation was being restructured.

"The Pulsar Division handles internal security on Vesta," Reese said. "Your outside intelligence division is called Group Seven. So why is Pulsar handling a matter so far away from home?"

"What we'd like you to handle *is* an internal security matter. Some of our people have gone rogue."

"You want me to bring them back?"

Something twitched the flesh by one of Berger's eyes. She knew what he was going to say before the words came out his mouth. She felt her nerves tingling, her muscles warming. It had been a long time.

"No. We want you to ice them."

"Don't tell me anything more," she said. "I'm going to check you out before I listen to another word."

"It's not even murder, I'd say," Berger said. He was eating spinach salad in an expensive restaurant called the Texas Beef, named after a vaguely pornographic and wildly popular vid show from Alice Springs. Dressing spattered the creamy tablecloth as Berger waved his fork. "We've got tissue samples and memory thread, like we do for all our top people—hell, we'll clone 'em."

"That doesn't mean I can't end up in prison for it."

"Who's gonna catch you? It's a goddam asteroid fifty zillion klicks from anywhere."

She had checked him out as far as she could. After telling him what she was going to do, she'd sent a message to Vesta asking for confirmation of the existence of one Captain Berger of the Pulsar Division, that and a photo. Both arrived within twelve hours. If this was a plot to arrest her, it had some unlikely elements.

Reese took a mouthful of lamb in mustard sauce. She worked out hard enough, she figured, and deserved her pleasures.

"The rock's about two kilometers in diameter. The official name is 2131YA, but it's also called Cuervo Gold."

"Funny names they're giving asteroids these days."

"They've run out of minor Greek gods, I guess. Cuervo's officially owned by a nonpolicorporate mining company called Exeter Associates, which in turn is owned by us. Gold's an Apollo asteroid, crossing Earth's orbit on a regular schedule, and that makes it convenient for purposes of resupply, and also makes it a lot more isolated than any of the rocks in the Belt. We've had a lab there for a while, using it to develop some technology that—" He grinned. "Well, that we wanted to keep far away from any competition. Security on Vesta is tight, but it's a port, people are always coming in and out. What we've got on the asteroid is pretty hot stuff, and we wanted to keep it away from the tourists."

"I don't really want to know," Reese said.

"I don't know myself, so I couldn't tell you," Berger said. "The work was in a fairly advanced stage when certain activities relating to your old friend Griffith became public. It became an urgent matter to shut down the project and transfer its members to other duties in central Africa, where I work. If the investigators found out about our owning that asteroid, and what's on it, Brighter Suns could be very embarrassed."

"The techs refused to move?" Reese asked.

"They protested. They said their work was entering a critical stage. A transport was sent from Earth to pick them up, but they refused to evacuate, and then we lost touch with the freighter. We think the crew have been killed or made prisoner."

"Your people could have defected to another policorp, using the transport."

"We don't think so. Their work would have been hard to take with them. And they couldn't have gone far without attracting attention—some of the lab personnel were Powers."

A coolness moved through Reese's bones. She sat up, regarding Berger carefully. Powers were forbidden off the two entry ports—the official reason was that there was too much danger of cross-contamination from alien life-forms. Plagues had already devastated the two Power legations, and the reverse was always a possibility. The discovery of Powers in Brighter Suns' employ outside of Vesta would ruin Brighter Suns' credit for good.

But after a while the heat on Brighter Suns would die down. Trade with the aliens was too profitable for people to interfere with it for long. In a year or two, the lab could be reopened with cloned personnel and some very mean security goons to make certain they followed orders.

"I understand your sense of urgency," Reese said. "But why me? Why not go yourself?"

"We don't have anyone with your talents on Earth," Berger said. "I'm not wired the way you are. And . . . well, we'd like to know you're gainfully employed by us rather than floating around Uzbekistan waiting to be captured by the heat. If we can find you, they probably can."

Reese sipped her club soda. "How did you find me, exactly?"

"Someone recognized you."

"Who might that have been?"

The skin by Berger's eye gave a leap. "It's already taken care of," he said. "We didn't want him giving your name to anyone else."

Da Vega. Well. At least it wasn't Ken.

But there was also a threat: Berger didn't want her in this refugees' paradise, where the number of desperate people was higher than average and where a policorporate kidnap team could find her. If they'd already iced one person, they could put the ice on another.

"Let's talk payment," Reese said. "Brighter Suns, I think, can afford to pay me what I'm worth."

Ram's cops had beaten some woman to death during interrogation. Ken was busy at his console, putting out fact and opinion pieces, making the most of another death for the revolution. Reese paced the room, picking at the tattered wallpaper, eating Mongolian barbecue from a waxed paper container. Below the window, some drunken descendant of the Golden Horde was singing a sad song to the moon. He kept forgetting the lyrics and starting over, and the burbling ballad was getting on Reese's nerves.

"I'd feel better," she said, "if Cheney was paying you a decent wage."

"He pays what he can afford." Ken's fingers sped over his keyboard. "The money has to be laundered, and he has to be careful how he does it."

"You don't even have a promise of a job after it's all over."

Ken shrugged. "Prince can always use another economist."

"And you don't have protection. Ram could order you iced."

"He needs a live scapegoat, not a dead martyr." He frowned as he typed. "This isn't a mysterious business, you know. Ram knows our strength and most of our moves, and we know his. There aren't very many hidden pieces on the board."

The Uzbek began his song again. Reese clenched her teeth. She put her hand on Ken's shoulder.

"I'm disappearing tomorrow," she said.

He tilted his head back, looking up in surprise. His fingers stopped moving on the keys.

"What's wrong?"

"Nothing. I got a job."

She saw a confirmation in his eyes. "Not one you can talk about," he said.

"No. But it's not for Ram. In case you were wondering."

He took her hand in one of his. "I'll miss you."

Reese put her food carton on top of his video display. Her chopsticks jabbed the air like rabbit-ear antennae.

"I've got another twelve hours before I take the plane to Beijing."

Ken turned off his console. "I can send the rest out tomorrow," he said.

Reese was surprised. "What about the revolution?"

He shrugged and kissed the inside of her wrist. "Sometimes I feel redundant. The revolution is inevitable, after all."

"It's nice to know," Reese said, "that the devil can quote ideology to his purpose."

Outside, the Uzbek continued his wail to the desolate stars.

The tug was called *Voidrunner*, and it was thirty years old at least, the padding on its bulkheads patched with silver tape, bundles of cable hanging out of access hatches. Reese had been in enough ships like it not to let the mess bother her—all it meant was that the tug didn't have to impress its passengers. The air inside tasted acrid, as if the place was crammed full of sweating men, but there were only four people on board.

Berger introduced the other three to Reese, then left, waving cheerily over his shoulder. About four minutes later, *Voidrunner* cast off from Charter Station and began its long acceleration to its destination.

Reese watched the departure from the copilot's chair in the armored docking cockpit. The captain performed the maneuvers with his eyes closed, not even looking out the bubble canopy at the silver-bright floodlit skin of Charter, reality projected into his head through his interface thread, his eyelids twitching as his eyes reflexively scanned mental indicators.

His name was Falkland. He was about fifty, an Artifact War veteran who, fifteen years before, had been doing his level best to kill Reese in the tunnels of Archangel. A chemical attack had left his motor reflexes damaged, and he wore a light silver alloy exoskeleton. Fortunately his brain and interface thread had survived the war intact. He wore a grey beard and his hair long over his collar.

"Prepare for acceleration," he said, his eyes still closed. "We'll be at two gees for the first six hours."

Reese looked out at Earth's dull grey moon, vast, taking up most of the sky. "Right," she said. "Got my piss bottle right here." Hard gees were tough on the bladder.

After the long burn *Voidrunner* settled into a constant one-gee acceleration. Falkland stayed strapped in, his eyelids still moving to some internal REM light show. Reese unbuckled her harness, stretched her relieved muscles while her spine and neck popped, and moved downship.

Falkland offered no comment.

The crew compartment smelled of fresh paint. Reese saw the tug's engineer, a tiny man named Chung, working on a bulkhead fire alarm. His head was bobbing to music he was

feeding to his aural nerves. Chung was so into the techno-
philic Destinarian movement he was turning himself slice
by slice into a machine. His eyes were clear implants that
showed the interior silver circuitry; his ears were replaced
by featureless black boxes, and there were other boxes of
obscure purpose jacked into his hairless scalp. His teeth
were metal, and liquid-crystal jewelry, powered by nerve
circuitry, shone in ever-changing patterns on his cheeks and
on the backs of his hands. He hadn't said anything when
Berger introduced him, just looked at Reese for a moment,
then turned back to his engines.

Now he said something. His voice was hoarse, as if he
wasn't used to using it. "He's downship. In Cargo B."

His back was to Reese, and she had been moving quietly.
His head still bobbed to inaudible music. He hadn't even
turned his head to speak. "Thanks," she said. "Nice
implants."

"The best. I built 'em myself."

"Aren't you supposed to be monitoring the burn?"

He pointed at one of his boxes. "I am."

"Nice."

She always found she had common ground with control
freaks.

Vickers was in Cargo B, as Chung had promised. He was
Reese's armorer, hired by Berger for the sole purpose of
maintaining the combat suit that Reese was to wear on
Cuervo. Vickers was young, about eighteen, and thin. His
dark hair was cut short; he had a stammer and severe acne.
He was dressed in oil-spattered coveralls. When Reese
walked in, Vickers was peeling the suit's components out of
their foam packing. She helped him lay the suit on the deck.
Vickers grinned.

"W-wolf 17," he said. His voice was American Southern. "My favorite. You're gonna kick some ass with this.
It's so good it can p-practically do the job by itself."

The suit was black, long-armed, anthropoid. The helmet,
horned by radio antennae, was fused seamlessly to the
shoulders. Inside, Reese's arms, legs, and body would fit

into a complex web that would hold her tightly: the suit would amplify and strengthen her every move. It wasn't entirely natural movement—she'd have to get used to having a lot more momentum in free fall than she normally did.

"F-fuckin' great machine," Vickers said. Reese didn't answer.

The Wolf's dark viewplate gleamed in the cool cabin light. There was a clean functionality to its design that made it even more fearful—nothing in its look gave the impression that it was anything but a tool for efficient murder. The white Wolf trademark shone on the matte-black body of the suit. Reese fought a memory charged with fear—Wolf made most of the cyberdrones she'd encountered on Archangel. The combat suit, free of its packing, had a smell she'd hoped she'd never scent again.

"I want to look at the manual," she said. "And the schematics." If her life was going to depend on this monster, she wanted to know everything there was to know about it.

He looked at her approvingly. "I've got them on thread in m-my cabin. The suit's standard, except for some o custom thread woven into the t-target-acquisition unit. Berger knows who you're going to b-be gunning for, and he put in some specific target-identification routines. You're gonna be h-hot."

"That's the plan," Reese said. The smell of the Wolf, oil and plastic webbing and cold laminate armor, rose in her nostrils. She repressed a shiver.

Vickers was still admiring the Wolf. "One wicked son of a bitch," he said. When talking to machines, he lost his stammer.

Reese and the Wolf moved as one in the void. Amber-colored target-acquisition data glowed on the interior of the black faceplate. Below them the asteroid glittered as flecks of mica and nickel reflected the relentless sun.

No way they're not gonna know you're coming, Berger

had told her. *Not with your ship's torch coming at them. We stabilized the rock's spin, so you can try landing on the blind side, but they're smart enough to have put detectors out there, so we can't count on surprise. What we're going to have to do is armor you so heavily that no matter what they try to do to you, they can't get through.*

Great, she thought. Now the rock's little techs, human and alien, were probably standing by the airlocks with whatever weapons they'd been able to assemble in the last weeks, just waiting for something to try booming in. All she could do was hope they weren't ready for the Wolf.

The hissing of her circulating air was very loud in the small space of the helmet. Reese could feel sweat gathering under the Wolf's padded harness. The rock's short horizon scrolled below her feet. Attitudinal jets made brief adjustments, keeping Reese close to the surface. The Wolf's suit monitors were projected, through her interface stud, in a complex multidimensional weave, bright columns glowing in the optical centers of her brain. She watched the little green indicators, paying little attention as long as they stayed green.

The target rolled over the near horizon in an instant—a silver-bright pattern of solar collectors, transmission aerials, dishes pointed at different parts of the sky . . . In the middle squatted the gleaming bulk of the freighter that had been sent to retrieve the base personnel, its docking tube still connected to the big cargo airlock.

Reese had a number of choices for gaining entry: there were two personnel airlocks, or she could go through one of the freighter locks and then through the docking tube. There were nine personnel on station, five humans and four Powers.

They can brew explosives with the stuff they've got on station, Berger had told her. *But they can't put anything too big around the airlock, or they'd decompress the whole habitat—and they don't have enough stored air to repressurize. They can't set off anything too big inside, or they'd wreck their work. It's too small a place for them to plan anything major. We figure they'll depend on small explosives, and maybe gas.*

The base rolled closer. Reese felt her limbs moving easily in the webbing, the hum of awareness in her nerves and blood. A concrete certainty of her capabilities. All the things she had been unable to live without.

Coolant flow had increased, the suit baking in the sun. The webbing around her body was chafing her. She thought of explosive, of gas, the way the poison clouds had drifted through the tunnels on Archangel, contaminating everything, forcing her to live inside her suit for days, not even able to take a shit without risking burns on her ass . . . at least this was going to be quick, however it went.

Reese decided to go in through one of the small personnel airlocks—the brains inside the rock might have decided the cargo ship was expendable and packed its joints with homemade explosive. She maneuvered the Wolf in a slow somersault and dropped feet-first onto the velcro strip by Airlock Two. Berger wanted her to get in without decompressing the place if she could—there was stuff inside he didn't want messed up. Reese bent and punched the emergency entrance button, and to her surprise she began to feel a faint humming through her feet and the hatch began to roll up . . . she'd planned to open the hatch manually.

How naïve were these people? she wondered. Or was there some surprise in the airlock, waiting for her?

You're gonna c-carry that stuff? Vickers had asked in surprise, as he noticed the pistol snugged under the armpit and the long knife strapped to her leg.

I don't want to depend entirely on the Wolf, she'd said. *If it gets immobilized somehow, I want to be able to surprise whoever did it.*

There'd been an amused grin on Vickers' face. *They immobilize the Wolf, they sure as hell can immobilize you.*

Adjust the webbing anyway, she'd said. Because battle machinery always went wrong sooner or later, because if the mission directive didn't give her backup, she'd just have to be her own. Because she just didn't *like* the Wolf, its

streamlined design, its purposeful intent. Because even to
someone accustomed to violence, the thing was obscene.

Reese knelt by the airlock, pulled a videocamera from her
belt, and held it over the airlock, scanning down . . . and
fought back a wave of bile surging into her throat, because
the lock was full of dead men.

Mental indicators shifted as, with a push of her mind, she
ordered her attitudinal jets to separate the Wolf from the
velcro parking strip, then drop into the lock. The dead
swam in slow motion as she dropped among them. Her
heart crashed in her chest.

The crew of the freighter, she thought. The rebels had put
them in here, not having anyplace else. Their skins were
grey, the tongues protruding and black. Some kind of
poison, she thought.

"Welcome to Cuervo Gold," she said, and laughed.
Nerves.

She hit the button to cycle the airlock, found it refused to
work. Incurious dead eyes gazed at her as she cranked the
outer door shut manually, then planted thermocharges on
the inner door locks. She drifted up to the top of the airlock
again, the Wolf's horns scratching the outer door. The dead
men rose with her, bumping gently against the Wolf's arms
and legs.

Reese curled her legs under her, protecting the Wolf's
more vulnerable head and back. Adrenaline was beating a
long tattoo in her pulse.

A vulture smile crossed her face. Her nerves sang a mad
little song. *Here's where I take it up the ass*, she thought,
and pulsed through her wetware the radio code to set off the
detonators.

The lock filled with scorching bright light, smoke,
molten blobs of bright metal. Air entered the lock with a
prolonged scream. Suddenly her olfactory sensors were
overwhelmed with the smell of scorched metal, burning
flesh. Her gorge rose. She pulsed a command to cut out the
smell, then moved down to the inner lock door, seized it,
rolled it up with the enhanced strength of the Wolf . . .

An explosion went off right in her face. Projectiles thudded into corpse flesh, cracked against the faceplate. She and the dead men went flying back, slamming against the outer hatch. Her pulse roared in her ears. She gave the Wolf a command to move down, and move down fast.

Her nerves were shrieking as she smashed into a wall of the airlock, corrected, flew down again, out the lock this time, cracked into another wall. Her teeth rattled. A homemade claymore, she thought, explosive packed in a tube with shrapnel, bits of jagged alloy, wire, junk. Command-detonated, most likely, so that meant someone was here watching the airlock door. Targeting displays flashed bright red on the interior of her faceplate. She turned and fired. Slammed into a wall again. Fired a second time.

The targets died. Fixed to each of the Wolf's upper forearms was a semiautomatic ten-gauge shotgun firing shells packed with poison flechettes. Reese had more deadly equipment available—a small grenade launcher on the left lower forearm, and a submachine gun on the right, gas projectors on her chest—but the op plan was to kill the targets without taking a chance on disturbing any of the valuable equipment or experiments.

Dollops of blood streamed into the near-weightlessness, turning into crimson spheres. A man and a woman, one holding some kind of homemade beam weapon she'd never got the chance to fire, were slowly flying backward toward the sprayed grey plastic walls, their hearts and lungs punctured by a dozen flechettes each. Their faces were frozen in slow-gathering horror at the sight of the Wolf. Reese tried to move, then hit the wall again. She realized the shrapnel had jammed one of her maneuvering jets full on. Her wetware wove routines to compensate, then she leaped past the dying pair and through an open doorway.

No one was in the next series of partitioned rooms, the crew quarters. These people were incredibly naïve, she thought, hiding out next to an airlock they knew was going to be blown and not even getting into vac suits. They should have put the claymore on the interior hatch door, not inside the station itself. Maybe they couldn't face going into where they'd put the crew they'd killed. These weren't professionals, they were a bunch of eggheads who hadn't known what they were getting into when they signed their declaration of independence from a policorp that could not even afford to acknowledge their existence.

They weren't soldiers, but they were still volunteers. They'd already killed people, quite coldly it seemed, in the name of whatever science they were doing here. She clenched her teeth and thought about how some people, no matter how smart they were, remained just too stupid to live.

There was a new bulkhead door welded to the exterior of the crew quarters. Reese blew it open the same way as the airlock, then jetted through. Shrieks sounded on her audio thread, the strange organ sounds Powers made through their upper set of nostrils. Even as her mind squalled at the unearthly sight of a fast-moving, centauroid pair of aliens, she fired. They died before they could fire their homemade weapons. Her mind flashed on the video, the actor-Steward eradicating aliens with his shotgun. An idiotic memory.

She went through a door marked with biohazard warnings. The door gave a soft hiss as she opened it.

The next room was brightly lit, humming with a powerful air conditioning unit, filled with computer consoles plugged into walls of bare metal, not plastic. Cable stretched to and from something that looked like a hundred-liter aquarium filled with what appeared to be living flesh. Weird, she thought. It looked as if the meat were divided by partitions, like honeycomb in a cultured hive. Silver-grey wires, apparently variable-lattice thread, were woven through the meat. Elsewhere an engine hummed as it pumped crimson fluid. Monitors drew jagged lines across screens, holographic digits floated in air.

Weird, she thought again. Alien biochemistry.

There were three other rooms identical to the last. No one was in the first two.

In the third was a single man, gaunt, silver-haired. He

was floating by the room's aquarium, a frown on his face. He was in a vac suit with the helmet in his hand, giving the impression he simply didn't want to bother to put it on.

He looked at Reese as she came in. There was no fear in his eyes, only sadness.

He spoke as he pushed off from the aquarium, floating to the empty alloy ceiling, where Reese's shot wouldn't hit his experiment by mistake.

"It's over," he said. "Not that it matters."

Reese thought of Steward in the hospital bed, dying for something else equally stupid, equally futile, and filled the man's face with poison darts.

Past the next seal two Powers tried to burn her with acid. The stuff smoked pointlessly on her ceramic armor while she killed them. One of the remaining humans tried to surrender, and the other tried to hide in a toilet. Neither tactic worked. She searched the place thoroughly, found no one else, and disarmed the traps at each of the airlocks.

There was a pain deep in her skull. The air in the suit had begun to taste bad, full of sour sweat, burnt adrenaline. Sadness drifted through her at the waste, the stupidity of it all. Twelve more dead, and all for nothing.

Reese left the bodies where they lay—nobody was paying her to clean the place up—and used the other personnel lock to return to *Voidrunner*. Once she was in sight of the ship she pointed one of her microwave antennae at the ship and gave the code signaling success: "Transmit the following to base. *Mandate. Liquid. Consolidation.*" A combination of words unlikely to be uttered by accident.

She cycled through the ship's central airlock. Pain hammered in her brain, her spine. Time to get out of this obscene contraption. The door opened.

Targeting displays flashed scarlet on the interior of her faceplate. Reese's nerves screamed as the Wolf's right arm, with her arm in it, rose. The ten-gauge exploded twice and the impact spun Vickers back against the opposite wall. He impacted and bounced lightly, already dead. *"No!"* Reese cried, and the Wolf moved forward, brushing the body aside. Reese's arms, trapped in the suit's webbing, rose to a combat stance. She tried to tug them free. Targeting displays were still flashing. Reese tried to take command of the suit through the interface stud. It wouldn't respond.

"Take cover!" Reese shouted. *"The Wolf's gone rogue!"* She didn't know whether the suit was still on transmit or whether anyone was listening. The Wolf had visible light and IR detectors, motion scanners, scent detectors, sensors that could detect the minute compression wave of a body moving through air. There was no way the Wolf would miss anyone in the ship, given enough time.

Reese's heart thundered in her chest. "Get into vac suits!" she ordered. "Abandon ship! Get onto the station. Try and hold out there."

Chung's voice snapped over the outside speakers. "Where the hell are you?" At least someone was listening.

"I'm moving upship toward the control room. Oh, fuck." The heads-up display indicated the Wolf had detected motion from the docking cockpit, which meant the armored bulkhead door was open.

The wolf caught Falkland as he was trying to fly out of the cockpit and get to an airlock. The flechettes failed to penetrate the exoskeleton, so the Wolf flew after him, caught him bodily. Reese felt her left hand curling around the back of Falkland's head, the right hand draw back to strike. She fought against it. Falkland was screaming, trying to struggle out of the Wolf's grip. *"I'm not doing this!"* Reese cried, wanting him to know that, and closed her eyes.

Her right arm punched out once, twice, three times. The Wolf began to move again. When Reese opened her eyes there was blood and bone spattering the faceplate.

"I'm still heading upship," Reese said. "I don't think the Wolf knows where you are."

Chung didn't answer. No point, Reese thought, in his sending a radio signal that might give away his position. The Wolf reached the forward control room, then began a systematic search of the ship, moving aft. Reese reported the suit's movements, hoping to hell he'd get away. The ship was small, and a search wouldn't take long.

Custom thread, Vickers had told her. *Woven into the target-acquisition unit*. Berger had done it, she knew, not only wanting to wipe out the station personnel but anyone who knew of Cuervo's existence. She was riding in an extermination cyberdrone now, trapped inside its obscene, purposeful body. *Mandate. Liquid. Consolidation*. The code had sent the Wolf on its rampage. The liquidation is mandated. Consolidate knowledge about Cuervo.

Displays flickered on the screen. The thing had scented Chung. Reese could do nothing but tell him it was coming.

Chung was by the aft airlock, halfway into the rad suit he'd need to flee through the airless engine space. His face was fixed in an expression of rage. "*Steward!*" Reese screamed. The ten-gauge barked twice, and then the Wolf froze. The displays were gone. The Wolf, still with considerable momentum, continued to drift toward the aft bulkhead. It struck and rebounded, moving slowly toward Chung.

Reese tried to move in the suit, but its joints were locked. Her crashing pulse was the loudest sound in the helmet. She licked sweat from her upper lip, felt it running down her brows. Chung's body slowly collapsed in the insignificant gravity of the asteroid. Drops of blood fell like slow-motion rubies. The gravity wasn't enough to break the surface tension, and the droplets rested on the deck like ball bearings, rolling in the circulating air . . .

Reese's heart stopped as she realized that the sound of the Wolf's air-circulation system had ceased. She had only the air in the suit, then nothing.

Her mind flailed in panic. Shouting, her cries loud in her ears, she tried to move against the locked joints of the Wolf. The Wolf only drifted slowly to the deck, its limbs immobile.

Like Archangel, she thought. Nothing to look forward to but dying in a suit, in a tunnel, in the smell of your own fear. Just like her officers had always wanted. She tasted bile and fought it down.

I'm using air, she thought, and clamped down, gulping twice, trying to control her jackhammer heart, her panicked breath.

Chung's furious eyes glared into hers at a distance of about three feet. She could see a reflection of the Wolf in his metal teeth. Reese began to move her arms and legs, testing the tension of the web.

There was a pistol under her left arm. If she could get to it with her right hand, she might be able to shoot her way out of the suit somehow.

Fat chance.

But still it was something to do, anyway. She began to move her right arm against the webbing, pulling it back. Blood rubies danced before her eyes. She managed to get her hand out of the glove, but there was a restraining strap against the back of her elbow that prevented further movement. She pushed forward, keeping her hand out of the glove, then drew back. Worked at it slowly, synchronizing the movement with her breath, exhaling to make herself smaller. Steward, she thought, would have been quoting Zen aphorisms to himself. Hers were more direct. *You can get smaller if you want to*, she thought, *you've done it before*.

She got free of the elbow strap, drew her arm back, felt her elbow encounter the wall of the suit. She was beginning to pant. *The air can't be gone this quickly*, she thought, and tried to control panic as she pulled back on her arm, as pain scraped along her nerves. Sweat was coating her body. She tried to think herself smaller. She could feel warm blood running down her arm. The Wolf was saturated with the scent of fear.

Reese screamed as her arm came free, part agony, part exultation. She reached across her chest, felt the butt of the pistol. It was cold in her hand, almost weightless.

Where to point it? She could try blowing out the faceplate, but she'd have the barrel within inches of her face, and the faceplate was damn near impervious anyway. The bullet would probably ricochet right into her head. The Wolf was too well armored.

Chung's angry glare was making it impossible for her to think. Reese closed her eyes and tried to think of the schematics she'd studied, the location of the variable-lattice thread that contained the suit's instructions.

Behind her, she thought. Pressed against her lower spine was the logic thread that operated the Wolf's massive limbs. If she could wreck the thread, the locked limbs might move.

She experimented with the pistol. There wasn't enough room to completely angle the gun around her body.

Sweat floated in salty globes around her as she thought it through, tried desperately to come up with another course of action. The air grew foul. Reese decided that shooting herself with the pistol would be quicker than dying of asphyxiation.

She tried to crowd as far over to the right as possible, curling the gun against her body, holding it reversed with her thumb on the trigger. The cool muzzle pressed into her side, just below the ribs. Line it up carefully, she thought. You don't want to have to do this more than once. She tried to remember anatomy and what was likely to get hit. A kidney? Adrenal glands?

Here's where I really take it up the ass, she thought. She screamed, building rage, and fired . . . and then screamed again from pain. Sweat bounced against the faceplate, spattering in the fierce momentum of the bullet's pressure wave.

The Wolf's limbs unlocked and the cyberdrone sagged to the deck. Reese gave a weak cheer, then shrieked again from the pain.

She had heard it wasn't supposed to hurt when you got hit, not right away. Another lie, she thought, invented by the officer class.

There was something wrong with the world, with the way it was manifesting itself. She realized she was deaf from the pistol blast.

Reese leaned back, took a deep breath of foul air. Now, she thought, comes the easy part.

Reese managed to put her right arm back into the sleeve, then use both arms—the armor, thankfully, was near weightless—to get herself out of the suit. She moved to the sick bay and jabbed endorphin-analogue into her thigh, then X-rayed herself on the portable machine. It looked as if she hadn't hit anything vital, but then she wasn't practiced at reading X-rays, either. She patched herself up, swallowed antibiotics, and then out of nowhere the pain slammed down, right through the endorphin. Every muscle in her body went into spasm. Reese curled into a ball, her body a flaming agony. She bounced gently off one wall, then another. Fought shuddering waves of nausea. Tears poured from her eyes. It hurt too much to scream.

It went on forever, for days. Loaded on endorphins, she looted the station, moving everything she could into the freighter, then pissed bright blood while howling in agony. Fevers raged in her body. She filled herself with antibiotics and went on working. Things—people, aliens, hallucinations—kept reaching at her, moving just outside her field of vision. Sometimes she could hear them talking to her in some strange, melodic tongue.

She grappled *Voidrunner* to the freighter's back, then lifted off Cuervo and triggered the charges. She laughed at the bright blossoms of flame in the locks, the gush of air that turned to white snow in the cold vacuum, and then into a bright rainbow as it was struck by the sun. Reese accelerated toward Earth for as long as she could stand it, then cut the engines.

There was a constant wailing in her ears, the cry of the fever in her blood. For the next several days—one of them was her birthday—Reese hung weightless in her rack, fought pain and an endless hot fever, and studied the data she'd stolen, trying to figure out why nine tame scientists were willing to commit murder over it.

The fever broke, finally, under the onslaught of antibiotics. Her urine had old black blood now, not bright new crimson. She thought she was beginning to figure out what the station crew had been up to.

It was time to decide where she was going to hide. The freighter and the tug were not registered to her, and her appearance with them was going to result in awkward questions. She thought about forging records of a sale—credentials, after all, were her specialty. Reese decided to tune in on the broadcasts from Earth and see if there were any new places for refugees to run to.

To her surprise she discovered that Ram's executive board on Prince Station had fallen three days before, and Cheney had been made the new chairman. She waited another two days, studying the data she'd stolen, the bottles of strange enzymes and tailored RNA she had moved to the freighter's cooler, and then beamed a call to Prince and asked for S. C. Vivekenanda. She was told the vice president of communications was busy. "I can wait," she said. "Tell him it's Waldman."

Ken's voice came on almost immediately. "Where are you?" he asked.

"I'm coming your way," Reese told him. "And I think I've got your architecture of liberation with me. But first, we've got to cut a deal."

What the lab's inhabitants had been up to wasn't quite what Ken had been talking about that gusty spring night in Uzbekistan, but it was close. The Brighter Suns biologists and artificial intelligence people had been working on a new way of storing data, a fast and efficient way, faster than variable-lattice thread. They had succeeded in storing information in human DNA.

It had been tried before. Genetically altered humanity had been present for a century, and the mysteries of the genetic mechanism had been thoroughly mapped. There had long been theories that genetic material, which succeeded in coding far more information on its tiny strand than any comparable thread-based technology, would provide the answer to the endless demand for faster and more efficient means of data storage.

The theories had always failed when put into practice. Just because specialists could insert desirable traits in a strand of human DNA didn't mean they had the capability of doing it at the speed of light, reading the genetic message the strand contained at similar speed, or altering the message at will. The interactions of ribosomes, transfer RNA, and enzymes were complex and interrelated to the point where the artificial intelligence/biologist types had despaired of trying to control them with current technology.

Alien genetics, it turned out, were simple compared to the human. Power DNA chains were much shorter, containing half the two hundred thousand genes in a human strand, without the thousands of repetitions and redundancies that filled human genes. Their means of reproducing DNA were similar, but similarly streamlined.

And the Power method of DNA reproduction was compatible with human genetics. The transfer and message RNA were faster, cleaner, more controllable. Information transfer had a theoretically astounding speed—a human DNA strand, undergoing replication, unwound at 8000 RPM. Power RNA combined with human DNA made data transfers on thread look like slow motion.

Once the control technology was developed, information could be targeted to specific areas of the DNA strand. The dominant genes could remain untouched; but the recessive genes could be altered to contain information. Nothing could be kept secret when any spy could code information in his own living genetic makeup. And no one could discover the spy unless they knew what code he was using and what they were looking for.

The architecture of liberation. Risk-free transfer of data.

It would be years before any of this was possible—Prince Station's newly hired biologists would have to reconstruct all the station's work and then develop it to the point where it was commercially viable. But Prince Station was going to have its new source of technology, and Reese a new source of income—she'd asked for a large down payment in advance of a small royalty that should nevertheless make her a billionaire in the next forty years. She'd asked for that, plus Prince's help in disposing of a few other problems.

Reese looked down at her double, lying on a bed in a room that smelled of death. Her twin's eyes were closed, her breasts rose and fell under a pale blue sheet. Bile rose in Reese's throat.

Reese was blond again, her nose a little straighter, her mouth a little wider. She had a new kidney, a new eardrum. New fingerprints, new blue irises. She liked the new look. The double looked good, too.

Two bodies, a man and a woman, were sprawled at the foot of the bed: assassins, sent by Berger to kill her. They had followed a carefully laid trail to her location here on Prince, and when they came into her apartment they'd been shot dead by Prince's security men firing from concealment in the wide bedroom closet. Reese had waited safely in the next room, her nerves burning with adrenaline fire while she clutched Ken's hand; her nerves alert for the sound of gunfire, she watched her double breathe under its sheet.

Then the security people came for the mannikin. They were going to kill it.

The double was Reese's clone. Her face had been restructured the same way Reese's had, and her artificial eyes were blue. Her muscles had been exercised via electrode until they were as firm as Reese's. There was even a metal pin in her ankle, a double of the one Reese carried. The clone was an idiot—her brain had never contained Reese's mind.

The idea was to make it appear that Reese and the assassins had killed each other. Reese looked down at her double and felt her mouth go dry. The security people were paddling around the room, trying to make appearances perfect. Hot anger blazed behind Reese's eyes. Fuck this, she thought.

She pried the pistol out of one of the assassins' hands and raised it.

She was a tunnel rat, she thought. An animal, a coward, disloyal. Sometimes she needed reminding.

"It's not murder," Ken said, trying to help.

"Yes it is," Reese said. She raised the killer's gun—an ideal assassin's weapon, a compressed-air fletcher—and fired a silent dart into the mannikin's thigh. Then she closed her eyes, not wanting to see the dying thing's last spasm. Instead she saw Steward, dying in his own silent bed, and felt a long grey wave of sadness. She opened her eyes and looked at Ken.

"It's also survival," she said.

"Yes. It is."

A cold tremor passed through Reese's body. "I wasn't talking about the clone."

While Ken's assistants made it look as if she and the assassins had killed each other, Reese stepped through the hidden door into the next apartment. Her bag was already packed, her identity and passport ready. Credentials, she thought, her specialty. That and killing helpless people. Group rates available.

She wanted to live by water again. New Zealand sounded right. It was getting to be spring there now.

"You'll come back?" Ken asked.

"Maybe. But in the meantime, you'll know where to send the royalties." There was pain in Ken's eyes, in Steward's eyes. Attachments were weakness, always a danger. Reese had a vision of the Street, people parting, meeting, dying, in silence, alone. She wouldn't be safe on Prince and couldn't be a part of Ken's revolution. She was afraid she knew what it was going to turn into, once it became the sole possessor of a radical new technology. And what that would turn Ken into.

Reese shouldered her bag. Her hands were still trembling. Sadness beat slowly in her veins. She was thirty-seven now, she thought. Maybe there were sports she shouldn't indulge in.

Maybe she should just leave.

"Enjoy your new architecture," she said, and took off.

She had been up here too long. This place—and every-place else she'd ever been—was too damn small. She wanted sea air, to live in a place with seasons, with wind.

She wanted to watch the world grow wide again.

THE BOB DYLAN SOLUTION

I

Pus-yellow smog drifts through the artificial canyons of Hollywood like windblown sand silting over the foundations of a Western ghost town. Anything moving below the smog curtain is invisible, certainly insignificant. Robertson takes a certain satisfaction in the thought.

"I've heard the songs Sorrel's recorded so far," says Brenner. "They're a mess, I agree with you. He's spending millions in studio time and the project isn't even near completion. A disaster."

"The computer projections aren't good, either." Robertson, staring down at the smog from his air-conditioned aerie, feels a reflex irritation at the back of his throat. Suddenly he's glad he gave up smoking. He clears his throat. "The whole middle-class rebellion thing is dying out. The declining economy won't support it. People are too interested in hanging on to their jobs to worry about ideology." He clears his throat again. "Sorrel's career peaked two albums ago. He's going to lose his audience in the next eighteen months. Something has to happen to make him recast his message. He needs to go affirmative."

"The psych profiles aren't encouraging, either." Hose-covered thighs sing against one another as Brenner crosses her legs. "He's losing his inspiration. Velda isn't helping. He needs something to shake him up, jump-start his creativity. Move him in a new direction."

Robertson nods. Sorrel had been his discovery, the means by which he ascended from among the smog-bound proles below to the highest penthouse atop the Lizard Records building. Talent like that comes once a decade. But what happens when the talent uses itself up?

"Velda," Brenner says, "could have an accident." Her voice is tentative.

"He'll find someone else just like her. Veldas aren't hard to find. Then we're in the same bind."

Robertson turns away from the transparent, bulletproof, evolved-aluminum window and steps toward his desk. He opens a drawer and takes out an atomizer of throat spray. He sprays his throat carefully, thrice. Brenner opens her compact and stares into the mirror.

"You know what to do," Robertson says.

Brenner, fluffing her hair, gives a single, precise nod.

2

Brenner's office is covered with diagrams of road accidents. Semi trucks, cars, motorcycles, all with little arrows, notations of velocity and direction. X-rays of broken skulls are stuck to the evolved-aluminum window with Scotch tape. Labels are affixed: Dean, Berry, Dylan, Clift, Allman. "The chief variable," Brenner says, "is Sorrel's speed. We can't control that. That's why I recommend Scenario Four. If we keep him boxed in, we can control his speed up until the moment he swings out to pass the truck."

"Good work," Robertson says.

Brenner purses her painted lips doubtfully. "There are risks."

Robertson opens his briefcase, removes some graphs. "This sequence displays posthumous earnings by major stars. James Dean's biggest movie was after he died. Hendrix, Elvis, Joplin, Holly, Croce . . . they all made more money for their estates than they ever did for themselves."

"Jan and Dean," Brenner reminds him.

"That was before we had modern PR techniques. Besides"—dropping the graphs on the desktop—"we insured the hell out of Sorrel before we let him into the studio."

Brenner looks at the graphs. "Looks like a go."

"I've already got Publicity working on the campaign for the posthumous album. Just in case things go wrong. We can get some studio hacks to fix up those uncompleted tapes. He'll sound more like himself than ever."

Brenner glances up. "The only problem," she says, "is who gives him the motorcycle?"

Robertson looks at her. "Why not Velda?"

Brenner thinks about it for a moment, then smiles. "Why not?"

3

Velda closes her lips on a Virginia Slims sticking out of the pack, draws the pack away with a clean, perfect motion of her hand. The cigarette dances in the corner of her mouth as she speaks. "I want to be executor," she says. Robertson's mouth is watering at the thought of the cigarette, old habits dying hard.

Brenner shakes her head. "Too much."

Velda lights the cigarette. Her twenty-eight-carat diamond engagement ring sparkles in the blue and amber spots of the corporate lounge. "I want to see where the money goes. You're already insured for the lost studio time. You won't lose money there."

Robertson looks from one to the other. "Co-executor," he says.

Velda blows twin curls of smoke from her chiseled ex-model nostrils. Her grey eyes gaze clearly into Robertson's. "Draw up the papers," she says. "I'll find them among Sorrel's effects if it's necessary."

4

Sorrel looks in baffled astonishment at the motorcycle standing in front of his door, a dark, ominous, retro-figured shape standing between clusters of frangipani. Here in the canyons behind L.A., the smog is only a memory and the blue sky reflects off the bike like a distant ocean horizon.

"Vincent Black Shadow," Velda says. "I thought you deserved it."

Sorrel gives an amazed grin. He steps out into the hot California sun and straddles the bike. His ropy arms reach for the handlebars.

"I gotta get some pictures," Sorrel says. "Me in a leather jacket."

Velda shakes her head. "Leather jackets are for wimps. You want denim."

Sorrel considers this. "Yeah."

"And a headband. Definitely a headband." Steering him away from the very idea of a helmet.

"Yeah!" There's a light in Sorrel's eyes.

Velda steps up to the bike, puts her arm around Sorrel's shoulders, kisses him. "Go crazy, man," she says.

The stunt drivers have been practicing in the canyon for five days.

"S-Day's tomorrow," Brenner says. The diagram of the accident—Scenario Four—lies open across her lap.

Robertson sprays his throat, coughs. "The PR team will be coming in early. We should have the word out in time for the noon broadcasts on the East Coast."

"I'll have an ambulance standing by. Along with a brain specialist and neurologist. The whole thing will look like a lucky coincidence."

"After I have breakfast with Samel I'll alert the drivers from my phone in the Maserati."

Brenner gives him a careful smile. She folds the plan carefully, puts it in a folder. "We make a good team."

"Yes. We do."

"I'm staying in a poolside room tonight," Brenner says. "Maybe we can have dinner sent to the room."

Robertson considers her for a moment: tousled fair hair, green eyes, painted smile. He decides against it. They know too much about one another to be involved on anything but a business level.

Once upon a time, maybe, the music business had been about joy. Then it became about money. Now it was about power, power over minds, over masses. The future.

"Perhaps some other time," he says. He rises from his chair, looks at the folder sitting next to Brenner on the couch. "Gather up all the papers and scenarios," he says. "I'll want to destroy them tomorrow."

"Good."

All the memos and diagrams have Brenner's name on them. Robertson won't destroy them; he'll keep them in a safe. One never knows when compromising documents might come in handy.

"Bye, then." He waves as he leaves, and closes the door on her smile.

6

"We're aware of your project." This three A.M. voice is somehow familiar.

"Ah," says Robertson. "What project was that?" His wife stirs uneasily on the bed beside him.

"Your project in regard to Mr. Sorrel. We wanted you to know that we approve."

"Thank you," says Robertson cautiously. "We hope the album will be a success." Where has he heard this voice before?

"During the harsh economic times to come, with their inevitable restructuring, voices such as Mr. Sorrel's can only cause discord and division. The nation requires unity, vigor, affirmation. We hope the people will hear that positive message."

The phrase *discord and division* jogs Robertson's memory; he's heard it before. He realizes the voice is that of the President.

"Thank you, sir."

"Bless you, Mr. Robertson." The President—or his voice—hangs up. For a moment Robertson listens to the distant whispers and clicks of the world's communication network, then puts the phone gently on its cradle.

Was that really the President? he wonders. Or was it someone—maybe someone in Lizard Records—with a simulacrum of the President's voice?

Or was the President himself a simulacrum?

Robertson decides it doesn't much matter.

He sleeps very well.

7

"Thanks for breakfast. I hope I wasn't imposing."

"Not at all, man." Sorrel is smiling as he shrugs into his denim vest. He reaches into a pocket and takes out a pair of Ray-Bans, puts them on his nose. Velda, dressed in tennis whites, follows them out the door, a racket dangling in her hand.

"It was delicious," Robertson says. "I haven't had a shrimp omelette in years."

"Velda's recipe."

Robertson opens the door of his Maserati. He looks from his car to the bike and back. "You're heading for the studio, right?"

"Yeah."

"So am I." He gives Sorrel a grin. "Think you can beat me?"

Sorrel laughs. "The way I can weave in traffic? You crazy?"

"A hundred bucks?"

Delight spreads across Sorrel's face. "Whatever you say, man. But I'll beat you by half an hour. I've been going down that canyon road every morning at a hundred twenty klicks."

Robertson reaches for his cellular phone. "Let me just make a call first. Let people know I'm coming."

Velda steps up to Sorrel, kisses him goodbye. "Be careful," she says. "You know how I worry."

"I can take care of myself," says Sorrel.

8

Brenner's voice comes cool into Robertson's ear. "The PR's going out. We're the top story on all the radio networks."

"Good."

"Any news from the doctors?"

"Looks like it's not fatal."

"I'll put that on the five o'clock bulletin. That'll get us on the early evening TV news broadcasts."

"Good." Robertson clears his throat and wishes he had his atomizer. "Make sure to have that package on my desk, okay?"

"It's already there."

"Thanks. You have no idea how relieved I am at how this turned out."

9

"I hope and trust that Sorrel will be back in the studio in a matter of weeks." Robertson gives the vidcams a hesitant smile. "More than that I can't say. It's just too early."

He turns from the cameras and steps into the intensive care ward. Velda is there, sucking one of the smokeless cigarettes they sell in the hospital gift shop. Above her, familiar-looking X-ray negatives are displayed on a light board. Two doctors are pointing with their pencils and talking.

"The left cerebral cortex shows no sign of electrical activity," says one. "The right is damaged also, but to a lesser degree." His eyes gaze firmly into Velda's from behind steel-rimmed spectacles. His voice is cool, dispassionate. He might be talking about the weather in Fresno.

The other doctor sucks on his cheeks. "We can expect, at best, only a slight recovery from Mr. Sorrel's eyes. He will only be able to see dimly, if at all. When the shards from his sunglasses went in, they created massive damage. Both eyes may still have to be removed."

Velda toys with her cigarette. "Thank you, gentlemen." She nods.

"Be brave, Mrs. Sorrel." This from the second.

Velda nods. "I will."

After the doctors leave, Robertson takes Velda's arm and leads her away. Velda licks her lips. "They say the centers of personality and memory are gone," she says.

"He's a vegetable?"

"In the left hemisphere, anyway." Annoyance flickers across her perfect face. "He turned his head just before the impact, damn it. All the damage was on the left side."

"Couldn't be helped. That was one of the things that we couldn't control."

"That's why his neck snapped. He'll be a quadriplegic."

"And the right hemisphere?"

"Probably okay. Most of it, anyway."

Robertson thinks for a moment. "Miss Brenner has had some work done with regard to this contingency. The right hemisphere is the creative side. It's what we want, anyway."

Velda lets out a long breath. "It'll be okay, then?"

Robertson gives her an encouraging smile. "You'd be surprised what doctors can do nowadays."

10

Sorrel sits expressionlessly in his wheelchair. The right side of his face is curiously slack. Electrodes creep across his cheek, disappear beneath a bandage over his empty right eye socket. The other empty socket is covered by a black patch.

Dr. Sivitsky, round and bespectacled, crouches over his controls. "He may sound strange," he says. "He can do no more than whisper. There is no control over the right side or the right vocal cord."

Robertson's mouth waters as Velda's cigarette smoke drifts to his nostrils. He nods, starts his recorder. "Go ahead, Doctor."

Sivitsky touches a control, feeds minute stimulating

currents to Sorrel's speech centers. Sorrel's mouth drops open, begins working.

"Torrent of wind at nighttime," he says. His voice is hushed. "Catalog of the dead."

Robertson smiles, nods.

"Sun-dapples. Sheep. The drains are clogged."

"It's all chance, you see," Sivitsky says. "What remains of his mind is accessing partial memories at random."

"How the world spins. Arizona can be the site of the safari. Velda's smile is very special."

Velda scowls. "Gibberish."

Robertson looks at her and smiles. "Not gibberish. Lyrics."

Velda looks at him.

"Lyrics we can choose," Robertson says. "Lyrics we can control. Lyrics that can reflect any trend, mean anything we need them to mean."

A hesitant smile begins to move across Velda's face. "It's okay, then?"

The vegetable's mouth continues to move, his whisper continuing without cease. Robertson looks at Sorrel in utter satisfaction. He thinks about the words just rolling out forever, granting power to whoever could shape them. He wonders if words rolled out of the President in the same way.

"It's better than we could have hoped," he says.

He reaches for his cellular phone to tell Brenner to get the PR rolling. Sorrel, he says, is writing again.

II

How the World Spins ships platinum.

With a bullet.

DINOSAURS

The Shars seethed in the dim light of their ruddy sun. Pointed faces raised to the sky, they sniffed the faint wind for sign of the stranger and scented only hydrocarbons, far-off vegetation, damp fur, the sweat of excitement and fear. Weak eyes peered upward, glistened with hope, anxiety, apprehension, and saw only the faint pattern of stars. Short, excited barking sounds broke out here and there, but mostly the Shars crooned, a low ululation that told of sudden onslaught, destruction, war in distant reaches, and now the hope of peace.

The crowds surged left, then right. Individuals bounced high on their third legs, seeking a view, seeing only the wide sea of heads, the ears and muzzles pointed to the stars.

Suddenly, a screaming. High-pitched howls, a bright chorus of barks. The crowds surged again.

Something was crossing the field of stars.

The human ship was huge, vaster than anything they'd seen, a moonlet descending. Shars closed their eyes and shuddered in terror. The screaming turned to moans.

Individuals leaped high, baring their teeth, barking in defiance of their fear. The air smelled of terror, incipient panic, anger.

War! cried some. *Peace!* cried others.

The crooning went on. *We mourn, we mourn,* it said, *we mourn our dead billions.*

We fear, said others.

Soundlessly, the human ship neared them, casting its vast shadow. Shars spilled outward from the spot beneath, bounding high on their third legs.

The human ship came to a silent rest. Dully, it reflected the dim red sun.

The Shars crooned their fear, their sorrow. And waited for the humans to emerge.

These? Yes. These. Drill, the human ambassador, gazed through his video walls at the sea of Shars, the moaning, leaping thousands that surrounded him. Through the mass a group was moving with purpose, heading for the airlock as per his instructions. His new Memory crawled restlessly in the armored hollow atop his skull. *Stand by,* he broadcast.

His knees made painful crackling noises as he walked toward the airlock, the silver ball of his translator rolling along the ceiling ahead of him. The walls mutated as he passed, showing him violet sky, far-off polygonal buildings, cold distant green . . . and here, nearby, a vast, dim plain covered with a golden tissue of Shars.

He reached the airlock and it began to open. Drill snuffed wetly at the alien smells—heat, dust, the musky scent of the Shars themselves.

Drill's heart thumped in his chest. His dreams were coming true. He had waited all his life for this.

Mash, whimpered Lowbrain. Drill told it to be silent. Lowbrain protested vaguely, then obeyed.

Drill told Lowbrain to move. Cool, alien air brushed his skin. The Shars cried out sharply, moaned, fell back. They seemed a wild, sibilant ocean of pointed ears and dark, questing eyes. The group heading for the airlock vanished in the general retrograde movement, a stone washed by a pale tide. Beneath Drill's feet was soft vegetation. His translator floated in the air before him. His mind flamed with wonder, but Lowbrain kept him moving.

The Shars fell back, moaning.

Drill stood eighteen feet tall on his two pillarlike legs, each with a splayed foot that displayed a horny underside and vestigial nails. His skin was ebony and was draped in folds over his vast naked body. His pendulous maleness swung loosely as he walked. As he stepped across the open space he was conscious of the fact that he was the ultimate product of nine million years of human evolution, all leading to the expansion, diversification, and perfection that was now humanity's manifest existence.

He looked down at the little Shars, their white skin and golden fur, their strange, stiff tripod legs, the muzzles raised to him as if in awe. *If your species survives,* he thought benignly, *you can look like me in another few million years.*

The group of Shars that had been forging through the crowd were suddenly exposed when the crowd fell back from around them. On the perimeter were several Shars holding staffs—weapons, perhaps—in their clever little hands. In the center of these were a group of Shars wearing decorative ribbon to which metal plates had been attached. *Badges of rank,* Memory said. *Ignore.* The shadow of the translator bobbed toward them as Drill approached. Metallic geometries rose from the group and hovered over them.

Recorders, Memory said. *Artificial similarities to myself. Or possibly security devices. Disregard.*

Drill was getting closer to the party, speeding up his instructions to Lowbrain, eventually entering Zen Synch. It would make Lowbrain hungrier but lessen the chance of any accidents.

The Shars carrying the staffs fell back. A wailing went up from the crowd as one of the Shars stepped toward Drill. The ribbons draped over her sloping shoulders failed to

disguise four mammalian breasts. Clear plastic bubbles
covered her weak eyes. In Zen Synch with Memory and
Lowbrain, Drill ambled up to her and raised his hands in
friendly greeting. The Shar flinched at the expanse of the
gesture.

"I am Ambassador Drill," he said. "I am a human."

The Shar gazed up at him. Her nose wrinkled as she
listened to the booming voice of the translator. Her answer
was a succession of sharp sounds, made high in the throat,
somewhat unpleasant. Drill listened to the voice of his
translator.

"I am President Gram of the InterSharian Sociability of
Nations and Planets." That's how it came through in
translation, anyway. Memory began feeding Drill referents
for the word "nation."

"I welcome you to our planet, Ambassador Drill."

"Thank you, President Gram," Drill said. "Shall we
negotiate peace now?"

President Gram's ears pricked forward, then back. There
was a pause, and then from the vast circle of Shars came a
mad torrent of hooting noises. The awesome sound lapped
over Drill like the waves of a lunatic sea.

They approve your sentiment, said Memory.

I thought that's what it meant, Drill said. *Do you think
we'll get along?*

Memory didn't answer, but instead shifted to a more
comfortable position in the saddle of Drill's skull. Its job
was to provide facts, not draw conclusions.

"If you could come into my Ship," Drill said, "we could
get started."

"Will we then meet the other members of your delegation?"

Drill gazed down at the Shar. The fur on her shoulders
was rising in odd tufts. She seemed to be making a
concerted effort to calm it.

"There are no other members," Drill said. "Just myself."

His knees were paining him. He watched as the other
members of the Shar party cast quick glances at each other.

"No secretaries? No assistants?" the President was saying.

"No," Drill said. "Not at all. I'm the only conscious mind on Ship. Shall we get started?"

Eat! Eat! said Lowbrain. Drill ordered it to be silent. His stomach grumbled.

"Perhaps," said President Gram, gazing at the vastness of the human ship, "it would be best should we begin in a few hours. I should probably speak to the crowd. Would you care to listen?"

No need, Memory said. *I will monitor.*

"Thank you, no," Drill said. "I shall return to Ship for food and sex. Please signal me when you are ready. Please bring any furniture you may need for your comfort. I do not believe my furniture would fit you, although we might be able to clone some later."

The Shars' ears all pricked forward. Drill entered Zen Synch, turned his huge body, and began accelerating toward the airlock. The sound of the crowd behind him was like the murmuring of wind through a stand of trees.

Peace, he thought later, as he stood by the mash bins and fed his complaining stomach. *It's a simple thing. How long can it take to arrange?*

Long, said Memory. *Very long.*

The thought disturbed him. He thought the first meeting had gone well.

After his meal, when he had sex, it wasn't very good.

Memory had been monitoring the events outside Ship, and after Drill had completed sex, Memory showed him the outside events. *They have been broadcast to the entire population,* Memory said.

President Gram had moved to a local elevation and has spoken for some time. Drill found her speech interesting—it was rhythmic and incantorial, rising and falling in tone and volume, depending heavily on repetition and melody. The crowd participated, issuing forth with excited barks or low moans in response to her statements or questions, sometimes babbling in confusion when she posed them a conundrum. Memory only gave the highlights of the speech. "Unknown . . . attackers . . . billions dead . . . preparations advanced . . . ready to defend ourselves . . . offer of peace . . . hope in the darkness . . . unknown . . . willing to take the chance . . . peace . . . peace . . . hopeful smell . . . peace." At the end the other Shars were all singing "Peace! Peace!" in chorus while President Gram bounced up and down on her sturdy rear leg.

It sounds pretty, Drill thought. *But why does she go on like that?*

Memory's reply was swift.

Remember that the Shars are a generalized and social species, it said. *President Gram's power, and her ability to negotiate, derives from the degree of her popular support. In measures of this significance she must explain herself and her actions to the population in order to maintain their enthusiasm for her policies.*

Primitive, Drill thought.

That is correct.

Why don't they let her get on with her work? Drill asked. There was no reply.

After an exchange of signals the Shar party assembled at the airlock. Several Shars had been mobilized to carry tables and stools. Drill sent a Frog to escort the Shars from the airlock to where he waited. The Frog met them inside the airlock, turned, and hopped on ahead through Ship's airy, winding corridors. It had been trained to repeat "Follow me, follow me" in the Shars' own language.

Drill waited in a semireclined position on a Slab. The Slab was an organic subspecies used as furniture, with an idiot brain capable of responding to human commands. The Shars entered cautiously, their weak eyes twitching in the bright light. "Welcome, Honorable President," Drill said. "Up, Slab." Slab began to adjust itself to place Drill on his feet. The Shars were moving tables and stools into the vast room.

Frog was hopping in circles, making a wet noise at each landing. "Follow me, follow me," it said.

The members of the Shar delegation who bore badges of rank stood in a body while the furniture-carriers bustled around them. Drill noticed, as Slab put him on his feet, that they were wrinkling their noses. He wondered what it meant.

His knees crackled as he came fully upright. "Please make yourselves comfortable," he said. "Frog will show your laborers to the airlock."

"Does your Excellency object to a mechanical recording of the proceedings?" President Gram asked. She was shading her eyes with her hand.

"Not at all." As a number of devices rose into the air above the party, Drill wondered if it were possible to give the Shars detachable Memories. Perhaps human bioengineers could adapt the Memories to the Shar physiology. He asked Memory to make a note of the question so that he could bring it up later.

"Follow me, follow me," Frog said. The workers who had carried the furniture began to follow the hopping Frog out of the room.

"Your Excellency," President Gram said, "may I have the honor of presenting to you the other members of my delegation?"

There were six in all, with titles like Secretary for Syncopated Speech and Special Executive for External Coherence. There was also a Minister for the Dissemination of Convincing Lies, whose title Drill suspected was somehow mistranslated, and an Opposite Minister-General for the Genocidal Eradication of Alien Aggressors, at whom Drill looked with more than a little interest. The Opposite Minister-General was named Vang, and was small even for a Shar. He seemed to wrinkle his nose more than the others. The Special Executive for External Coherence, whose name was Cup, seemed a bit piebald, patches of white skin showing through the golden fur covering his shoulders, arms, and head.

He is elderly, said Memory.

That's what I thought.

"Down, Slab," Drill said. He leaned back against the creature and began to move to a more relaxed position.

He looked at the Shars and smiled. Fur ruffled on shoulders and necks. "Shall we make peace now?" he asked.

"We would like to clarify something you said earlier," President Gram said. "You said that you were the only, ah, conscious entity on the ship. That you were the only member of the human delegation. Was that translated correctly?"

"Why, yes," Drill said. "Why would more than one diplomat be necessary?"

The Shars looked at each other. The Special Executive for External Coherence spoke cautiously.

"You will not be needing to consult with your superiors? You have full authority from your government?"

Drill beamed at them. "We humans do not have a government, of course," he said. "But I am a diplomat with the appropriate Memory and training. There is no problem that I can foresee."

"Please let me understand, your Excellency," Cup said. He was leaning forward, his small eyes watering. "I am elderly and may be slow in comprehending the situation. But if you have no government, who accredited you with this mission?"

"I am a diplomat. It is my specialty. No accreditation is necessary. The human race will accept my judgment on any matter of negotiation, as they would accept the judgment of any specialist in his area of expertise."

"But why *you.* As an individual?"

Drill shrugged massively. "I was part of the nearest diplomatic enclave, and the individual without any other tasks at the moment." He looked at each of the delegation in turn. "I am incredibly happy to have this chance, .

honorable delegates," he said. "The vast majority of human diplomats never have the chance to speak to another species. Usually we mediate only in conflicts of interest between the various groups of human specialties."

"But the human species will abide by your decisions?"

"Of course." Drill was surprised at the Shar's persistence. "Why wouldn't they?"

Cup settled back in his chair. His ears were down. There was a short silence.

"We have an opening statement prepared," President Gram said. "I would like to enter it into our record, if I may. Or would your Excellency prefer to go first?"

"I have no opening statement," Drill said. "Please go ahead."

Cup and the President exchanged glances. President Gram took a deep breath and began.

Long, Memory said. Very long.

The opening statement seemed very much like the address President Gram had been delivering to the crowd, the same hypnotic rhythms, more or less the same content. The rest of the delegation made muted responses. Drill drowsed through it, enjoying it as music.

"Thank you, Honorable President," he said afterward. "That was very nice."

"We would like to propose an agenda for the conference," Gram said. "First, to resolve the matter of the cease-fire and its provisions for an ending to hostilities. Second, the establishment of a secure border between our two species, guaranteeing both species room for expansion. Third, the establishment of trade and visitation agreements. Fourth, the matter of reparations, payments, and return of lost territory."

Drill nodded. "I believe," he said, "that resolution of the second through fourth points will come about as a result of an understanding reached on the first. That is, once the cease-fire is settled, that resolution will imply a settlement of the rest of the situation."

"You accept the agenda?"

"If you like. It doesn't matter."

Ears pricked forward, then back. "So you accept that our initial discussions will consist of formalizing the disengagement of our forces?"

"Certainly. Of course I have no way of knowing what forces you have committed. We humans have committed none."

The Shars were still for a long time. "Your species attacked our planets, Ambassador. Without warning, without making yourselves known to us." Gram's tone was unusually flat. Perhaps, Drill thought, she was attempting to conceal great emotion.

"Yes," Drill said. "But those were not our military formations. Your species were contacted only by our terraforming Ships. They did not attack your people, as such—they were only peripherally aware of your existence. Their function was merely to seed the planets with lifeforms favorable to human existence. Unfortunately for your people, part of the function of these lifeforms is to destroy the native life of the planet."

The Shars conferred with one another. The Opposite Minister-General seemed particularly vehement. Then President Gram turned to Drill.

"We cannot accept your statement, your Excellency," she said. "Our people were attacked. They defended themselves, but were overcome."

"Our terraforming Ships are very good at what they do," Drill said. "They are specialists. Our Shrikes, our Shrews, our Sharks—each is a master of its element. But they lack intelligence. They are not conscious entities, such as ourselves. They weren't aware of your civilization at all. They only saw you as food."

"You're claiming that you *didn't notice us?*" demanded Minister-General Vang. *"They didn't notice us as they were killing us?"* He was shouting. President Gram's ears went back.

"Not as such, no," Drill said.

President Gram stood up. "I am afraid, your Excellency,

your explanations are insufficient," she said. "This conference must be postponed until we can reach a united conclusion concerning your remarkable attitude."

Drill was bewildered. "What did I say?" he asked.

The other Shars stood. President Gram turned and walked briskly on her three legs toward the exit. The others followed.

"Wait," Drill said. "Don't go. Let me send for Frog. Up, Slab, up!"

The Shars were gone by the time Slab had got Drill to his feet. The Ship told him they had found their own way to the airlock. Drill could think of nothing to do but order the airlock to let them out.

"Why would I lie?" he asked. "Why would I lie to them?" Things were so very simple, really.

He shifted his vast weight from one foot to the other and back again. Drill could not decide whether he had done anything wrong. He asked Memory what to do next, but Memory held no information to comfort him, only dry recitations of past negotiations. Annoyed at the lifeless monologue, Drill told Memory to be silent and began to walk restlessly through the corridors of his Ship. He could not decide where things had gone bad.

Sensing his agitation, Lowbrain began to echo his distress. *Mash,* Lowbrain thought weakly. *Food. Sex.*

Be silent, Drill commanded.

Sex, sex, Lowbrain thought.

Drill realized that Lowbrain was beginning to give him an erection. Acceding to the inevitable, he began moving toward Surrogate's quarters.

Surrogate lived in a dim, quiet room filled with the murmuring sound of its own heartbeat. It was a human subspecies, about the intelligence of Lowbrain, designed to comfort voyagers on long journeys through space, when carnal access to their own subspecies might necessarily be limited. Surrogate had a variety of sexual equipment designed for the accommodation of the various human subspecies and their sexes. It also had large mammaries that gave nutritious milk, and a rudimentary head capable of voicing simple thoughts.

Tiny Mice, that kept Surrogate and the ship clean, scattered as Drill entered the room. Surrogate's little head turned to him.

"It's good to see you again," Surrogate said.

"I am Drill."

"It's good to see you again, Drill," said Surrogate. "It's good to see you again."

Drill began to nuzzle its breasts. One of Surrogate's male parts began to erect. "I'm confused, Surrogate," he said. "I don't know what to do."

"Why are you confused, Drill?" asked Surrogate. It raised one of its arms and began to stroke Drill's head. It wasn't really having a conversation: Surrogate had only been programmed to make simple statements, or to analyze its partners' speech and ask questions.

"Things are going wrong," Drill said. He began to suckle. The warm milk flowed down his throat. Surrogate's male part had an orgasm. Mice jumped from hiding to clean up the mess.

"Why are things going wrong?" asked Surrogate. "I'm sure everything will be all right."

Lowbrain had an orgasm, perceived by Drill as scattered, faraway bits of pleasure. Drill continued to suckle, feeling a heavy comfort beginning to radiate from Surrogate, from the gentle sound of its heartbeat, its huge, wholesome, brainless body.

Everything will be all right, Drill decided.

"Nice to see you again, Drill," Surrogate said. "Drill, it's *nice* to see you again."

The vast crowds of Shars did not leave when night fell. Instead they stood beneath floating globes dispersing a cold reddish light that reflected eerily from pointed ears and muzzles. Some of them donned capes or skirts to help them keep warm. Drill, watching them on the video walls of the command center, was reminded of crowds standing in awe before some vast cataclysm.

The Shars were not quiet. They stood in murmuring groups, but sometimes they began the crooning chants they had raised earlier, or suddenly broke out in a series of shrill yipping cries.

President Gram spoke to them after she had left Ship. "The human has admitted his species' attacks," she said, "but has disclaimed responsibility. We shall urge him to adopt a more realistic position."

"Adopt a position," Drill repeated, not understanding. "It is not a position. It is the truth. Why don't they understand?"

Opposite Minister General Vang was more vehement. "We now have a far more complete idea of the humans' attitude," he said. "It is opposed to ours in every way. We shall not allow the murderous atrocities which the humans have committed upon five of our planets to be forgotten, or understood to be the result of some inexplicable lack of attention on the part of our species' enemies."

"That one is obviously deranged," thought Drill.

He went to his sleeping quarters and ordered the Slab there to sing him to sleep. Even with Slab's murmurs and comforting hums, it took Drill some time before his agitation subsided.

Diplomacy, he thought as slumber overtook him, was certainly a strange business.

In the morning the Shars were still there, chanting and crying, moving in their strange crowded patterns. Drill watched them on his video walls as he ate breakfast at the mash bins. "There is a communication from President Gram," Memory announced. "She wishes to speak with you by radio."

"Certainly."

"Ambassador Drill." She was using the flat tones again. A pity she was subject to such stress.

"Good morning, President Gram," Drill said. "I hope you spent a pleasant night."

"I must give you the results of our decision. We regret that we can see no way to continue the negotiations unless you, as a representative of your species, agree to admit responsibility for your people's attacks on our planets."

"Admit responsibility?" Drill said. "Of course. Why wouldn't I?"

Drill heard some odd, indistinct barking sounds that his translator declined to interpret for him. It sounded as if someone other than President Gram were on the other end of the radio link.

"You admit responsibility?" President Gram's amazement was clear even in translation.

"Certainly. Does it make a difference?"

President Gram declined to answer that question. Instead she proposed another meeting for that afternoon.

"I will be ready at any time."

Memory recorded President Gram's speech to her people, and Drill studied it before meeting the Shar party at the airlock. She made a great deal out of the fact that Drill had admitted humanity's responsibility for the war. Her people leaped, yipped, chanted their responses as if possessed. Drill wondered why they were so excited.

Drill met the party at the airlock this time, linked with Memory and Lowbrain in Zen Synch so as not to accidentally step on the President or one of her party. He smiled and greeted each by name and led them toward the conference room.

"I believe," said Cup, "we may avoid future misunderstandings, if your Excellency would consent to inform us about your species. We have suffered some confusion in regard to your distinction between 'conscious' and 'unconscious' entities. Could you please explain the difference, as you understand it?"

"A pleasure, your Excellency," Drill said. "Our species, unlike yours, is highly specialized. Once, eight million years ago, we were like you—a small, nonspecialized species type is very useful at a certain stage of evolution. But once a species reaches a certain complexity in its social and technological evolution, the need for specialists becomes too acute. Through both deliberate genetic manipulation and natural evolution, humanity turned away from a generalist species, toward highly specialized forms adapted to particular functions and environments. We understand this to be a natural function of species evolution.

"In the course of our explorations into manipulating our species, we discovered that the most efficient way of coding large amounts of information was in our own cell structure—our DNA. For tasks requiring both large and small amounts of data, we arranged that, as much as possible, these would be performed by organic entities, human subspecies. Since many of these tasks were boring and repetitive, we reasoned that advanced consciousness, such as that which we both share, was not necessary. You have met several unconscious entities. Frog, for example, and the Slab on which I lie. Many parts of my Ship are also alive, though not conscious."

"That would explain the *smell*," one of the delegation murmured.

"The terraforming Ships," Drill went on, "which attacked your planets—these were also designed so as not to require a conscious operator."

The Shars squinted up at Drill with their little eyes. "But why?" Cup asked.

"Terraforming is a dull process. It takes many years. No conscious mind could possibly enjoy it."

"But your species would find itself at war without knowing it. If your explanation for the cause of this war is correct, you already have."

Drill shrugged massively. "This happens from time to time. Sometimes other species which have reached our stage of development have attacked us in the same way. When it does, we arrange a peace."

"You consider these attacks normal?" Opposite Minister-General Vang was the one who spoke.

"These occasional encounters seem to be a natural result of species evolution," Drill said.

Vang turned to one of the Shars near him and spoke in several sharp barks. Drill heard a few words: "Billions lost . . . five planets . . . atrocities . . . *natural result!*"

"I believe," said President Gram, "that we are straying from the agenda."

Vang looked at her. "Yes, honorable President. Please forgive me."

"The matter of withdrawal," said President Gram, "to recognized truce lines."

Species at this stage of their development tend to be territorial, Memory reminded Drill. *Their political mentality is based around the concept of borders. The idea of a borderless community of species may be perceived as a threat.*

I'll try and go easy on them, Drill said.

"The Memories on our terraforming Ships will be adjusted to account for your species," Drill said. "After the adjustment, your people will no longer be in danger."

"In our case, it will take the disengage order several months to reach all our forces," President Gram said. "How long will the order take to reach your own Ships?"

"A century or so." The Shars stared. "Memories at our exploration basis in this area will be adjusted first, of course, and these will adjust the Memories of terraforming Ships as they come in for maintenance and supplies."

"We'll be subject to attack for *another hundred years?*" Vang's tone mixed incredulity and scorn.

"Our terraforming Ships move more or less at random, and only come into base when they run out of supplies. We don't know where they've been till they report back. Though they're bound to encounter a few more of your planets, your species will still survive, enough to continue your species evolution. And during that time you'll be searching for and occupying new planets on your own. You'll probably come out of this with a net gain."

"Have you no respect for life?" Vang demanded. Drill considered his answer.

"All individuals die, Opposite Minister-General," he said. "That is a fact of nature which no species has been able to alter. Only *species* can survive. Individuals are easily replaceable. Though you will lose some planets and a large number of individuals, your species as a whole will survive and may even prosper. What more could a species or its delegated representatives desire?"

Opposite Minister-General Vang was glaring at Drill, his ears pricked forward, lips drawn back from his teeth. He said nothing.

"We desire a cease-fire that is a true cease-fire," President Gram said. Her hands were clasping and unclasping rhythmically on the edge of her chair. "Not a slow, authorized extermination of our species. Your position has an unwholesome smell. I am afraid we must end these discussions until you alter it."

"Position? This is not a position, honorable President. It is truth."

"We have nothing further to say."

Unhappily, Drill followed the Shar delegation to the airlock. "I do not lie, honorable President," he said, but Gram only turned away and silently left the human Ship. The Shars in their pale thousands received her.

The Shar broadcasts were not heartening. Opposite Minister-General Vang was particularly vehement. Drill collected the highlights of the speeches as he speeded through Memory's detailed remembrance. "Callous disregard . . . no common ground for communication . . . casual attitude toward atrocity . . . displays of obvious savagery . . . no respect for the individual . . . defend ourselves . . . *this stinks in the nose.*"

The Shars leaped and barked in response. There were strange bubbling high-pitched laughing sounds that Drill found unsettling.

"We hope to find a formula for peace," President Gram

said. "We will confer with all the ministers in session."
That was all.

That night, the Shars surrounding Ship moaned, moving
slowly in a giant circle, their arms linked. The laughing
sounds that followed Vang's speech did not cease entirely.
He did not understand why they did not all go home and
sleep.

Long, long, Memory said. No comfort there.

Early in the morning, before dawn, there was a communication from President Gram. "I would like to meet with
you privately. Away from the recorders, the coalition
partners."

"I would like nothing better," Drill said. He felt a small
current of optimism begin to trickle into him.

"Can I use an airlock other than the one we've been using
up till now?"

Drill gave President Gram instructions and met her in the
other airlock. She was wearing a night cape with a hood.
The Shars, circling and moaning, had paid her no attention.

"Thank you for seeing me under these conditions," she
said, peering up at him from beneath the hood. Drill smiled.
She shuddered.

"I am pleased to be able to cooperate," he said.

Mash! Lowbrain demanded. It had been silent until Drill
entered Zen Synch. Drill told it to be silent with a snarling
vehemence that silenced it for the present.

"This way, honorable President," Drill said. He took her
to his sleeping chamber—a small room, only fifty feet
square. "Shall I send a Frog for one of your chairs?" he
asked.

"I will stand. Three legs seem to be more comfortable
than two for standing."

"Yes."

"Is it possible, Ambassador Drill, that you could lower
the intensity of the light here? I find it oppressive."

Drill felt foolish, knowing he should have thought of this
himself. "I'm sorry," he said. "I will give the orders at

once. I wish you had told me earlier." He smiled nervously as he dimmed the lights and arranged himself on his Slab.

"Honorable ambassador." President Gram's words seemed hesitant. "I wonder if it is possible . . . can you tell me the meaning of that facial gesture of yours, showing me your teeth?"

"It is called a smile. It is intended as a gesture of benevolent reassurance."

"Showing of the teeth is considered a threat here, honorable Ambassador. Some of us have considered this a sign that you wish to eat us."

Drill was astonished. "My goodness!" he said. "I don't even eat meat! Just a kind of vegetable mash."

"I pointed out that your teeth seemed unsuitable for eating meat, but still it makes us uneasy. I was wondering . . ."

"I will try to suppress the smile, yes. Eating meat! What an idea. Some of our military specialists, yes, and of course the Sharks and Shrikes and so on . . ." He told his Memory to enforce a strict ban against smiling in the presence of a Shar.

Gram leaned back on her sturdy rear leg. Her cape parted, revealing her ribbons and badges of office, her four furry dugs. "I wanted to inform you of certain difficulties here, Ambassador Drill," she said. "I am having difficulty holding together my coalition. Minister-General Vang's faction is gaining strength. He is attempting to create a perception in the minds of Shars that you are untrustworthy and violent. Whether he believes this, or whether he is using this notion as a means of destabilizing the coalition, is hardly relevant—considering your species' unprovoked attacks, it is not a difficult perception to reinforce. He is also trying to tell our people that the military is capable of dealing with your species."

Drill's brain swam with Memory's information on concepts such as "faction" and "coalition." The meaning of the last sentence, however, was clear.

"That is a foolish perception, honorable President," he said.

"His assurances on that score lack conviction." Gram's eyes were shiny. Her tone grew earnest. "You must give me something, Ambassador. Something I can use to soothe the public mind. A way out of this dilemma. I tell you that it is impossible to expect us to sit idly by and accept the loss of an undefined number of planets over the next hundred years. I plead with you, Ambassador. Give me something. Some way we can avoid attack. Otherwise . . ." She left the sentence incomplete.

Mash, Lowbrain wailed. Drill ignored it. He moved into Zen Synch with Memory, racing through possible solutions. Sweat gathered on his forehead, pouring down his vast shoulders.

"Yes," he said. "Yes, there is a possibility. If you could provide us with the location of all your occupied planets, we could dispatch a Ship to each with the appropriate Memories as cargo. If any of our terraforming Ships arrived, the Memories could be transferred at once, and your planets would be safe."

President Gram considered this. "Memories," she said. "You've been using the term, but I'm not sure I understand."

"Stored information is vast, and even though human bodies are large we cannot always have all the information we need to function efficiently even in our specialized tasks," Drill said. "Our human brains have been separated as to function. I have a Lowbrain, which is on my spinal cord above my pelvis. Lowbrain handles motor control of my lower body, routine monitoring of my body's condition, eating, excretion, and sex. My perceptual centers, short-term memory, personality, and reasoning functions are handled by the brain in my skull—the classical brain, if you like. Long-term and specialized memory is the function of the large knob you see moving on my head, my Memory. My Memory records all that happens in great detail, and can recapitulate it at any point. It has also been supplied with information concerning the human species' contacts with other nonhuman groups. It attaches itself easily to my nervous system and draws nourishment from my body. Specific memories can be communicated from one living Memory to another, or if it proves necessary I can simply give my Memory to another human, a complete transfer. I have another Memory aboard that I'm not using at the moment, a pilot Memory that can navigate and handle Ship, and I wore this Memory while in transit. I also have spare Memories in case my primary Memories fall ill. So you see, our specialization does not rule out adaptability—any piece of information needed by any of us can easily be transferred, and in far greater detail than by any mechanical medium."

"So you could return to your base and send out pilot Memories to our planets," Gram said. "Memories that could halt your terraforming ships."

"That is correct." Just in time, Memory managed to stop the twitch in Drill's cheeks from becoming a smile. Happiness bubbled up in him. He was going to arrange this peace after all!

"I am afraid that would not be acceptable, your Excellency," President Gram said. Drill's hopes fell.

"Whyever not?"

"I'm afraid the Minister-General would consider it a naïve attempt of yours to find out the location of our populated planets. So that your species could attack them, Ambassador."

"I'm trying very hard, President Gram," Drill said.

"I'm sure you are."

Drill frowned and went into Zen Synch again, ignoring Lowbrain's plantive cries for mash and sex, sex and mash. Concepts crackled through his mind. He began to develop an erection, but Memory was drawing off most of the available blood and the erection failed. The smell of Drill's sweat filled the room. President Gram wrinkled her nose and leaned back far onto her rear leg.

"Ah," Drill said. "A solution. Yes. I can have my pilot

Memory provide the locations to an equivalent number of our own planets. We will have one another's planets as hostage."

"Bravo, Ambassador," President Gram said quietly. "I think we may have a solution. But—forgive me—it may be said that we cannot trust your information. We will have to send ships to verify the location of your planets."

"If your ships go to my planet first," Drill said, "I can provide your people with one of my spare Memories that will inform my species what your people are doing, and instruct the humans to cooperate. We will have to construct some kind of link between your radio and my Memory . . . maybe I can have my Ship grow one."

President Gram came forward off her third leg and began to pace forward, moving in her strange, fast, hobbling way. "I can present it to the council this way, yes," she said. "There is hope here." She stopped her movement, peering up at Drill with her ears pricked forward. "Is it possible that you could allow me to present this to the council as my own idea?" she asked. "It may meet with less suspicion that way."

"Whatever way is best," said Drill. President Gram gazed into the darkened recesses of the room.

"This smells good," she said. Drill succeeded in suppressing his smile.

"It's nice to see you again."

"I am Drill."

"It's nice to see you again, Drill."

"I think we can make the peace work."

"Everything will be all right, Drill. Drill, I'm sure everything will be all right."

"I'm so glad I had this chance. This is the chance of a lifetime."

"Drill, it's *nice* to see you again."

The next day President Gram called and asked to present a new plan. Drill said he would be pleased to hear it. He met the party at the airlock, having already dimmed the lights. He was very rigid in his attempts not to smile.

They sat in the dimmed room while President Gram presented the plan. Drill pretended to think it over, then acceded. Details were worked out. First the location of one human planet would be given and verified—this planet, the Shar capital, would count as the first revealed Shar planet. After verification, each side would reveal the location of two planets, verify those, then reveal four, and so on. Even counting the months it would take to verify the location of planets, the treaty should be completed within less than five years.

That night the Shars went mad. At President Gram's urging, they built fires, danced, screamed, sung. Drill watched on his Ship's video walls. Their rhythms beat at his head.

He smiled. For hours.

The Ship obligingly grew a communicator and coupled it to one of Drill's spare Memories. The two were put aboard a Shar ship and sent in the direction of Drill's home. Drill remained in his ship, watching entertainment videos Ship received from the Shars' channels. He didn't understand the dramas very well, but the comedies were delightful. The Shars could do the most intricate, clever things with their flexible bodies and odd tripod legs—it was delightful to watch them.

Maybe I could take some home with me, he thought. *They can be very entertaining.*

The thousands of Shars waiting outside Ship began to drift away. Within a month only a few hundred were left. Their singing was quiet, triumphant, assured. Sometimes Drill had it piped into his sleeping chamber. It helped him relax.

President Gram visited informally every ten days or so. Drill showed her around Ship, showing her the pilot Memory, the Frog quarters, the giant stardrive engines with their human subspecies' implanted connections, Surrogate in its shadowed, pleasant room. The sight of Surrogate seemed to agitate the President.

"You do not use sex for procreation?" she asked. "As an expression of affection?"

"Indeed we do. I have scads of offspring. There are never enough diplomats, so we have a great many couplings among our subspecies. As for affection . . . I think I can say that I have enjoyed the company of each of my partners."

She looked up at him with solemn eyes. "You travel to the stars, Drill," she said. "Your species expands randomly in all directions, encountering other species, sometimes annihilating them. Do you have a reason for any of this?"

"A reason?" Drill mused. "It is natural to us. Natural to all intelligent species, so far as we know."

"I meant a conscious reason. Is it anything other than what you do in an automatic way?"

"I can't think of why we would need any such reasons."

"So you have no philosophy of constant expansion? No ideology?"

"I do not know what those words mean," Drill said.

Gram closed her eyes and lowered her head. "I am sorry," she said.

"No need. We have no conflicts in our ideas about ourselves, about our lives. We are happy with what we are."

"Yes. You couldn't be unhappy if you tried, could you?"

"No," Drill said cheerfully. "I see that you understand."

"Yes," Gram said. "I scent that I do."

"In a few million years," Drill said, "these things will become clear to you."

The first Shar ship returned from Drill's home, reporting a transfer of the Memory. The field around Ship filled again with thousands of Shars, crying their happiness to the skies. Other Memories were now taking instructions to all terraforming bases. The locations of two new planets were released. Ships carrying spare Memories leaped into the skies.

It's working, Drill told Memory.

Long, Memory said. *Very long.*

But Memory could not lower Drill's joy. This was what he had lived his life for, and he knew he was good at it. Memories of the future would take this solution as a model for negotiations with other species. Things were working out.

One night the Shars outside Ship altered their behavior. Their singing became once again a moaning, mixed with cries. Drill was disturbed.

A communication came from the President. "Cup is dead," she said.

"I understand," Drill said. "Who is his replacement?"

Drill could not read Gram's expression. "That is not yet known. Cup was a strong person, and did not like other strong people around him. Already the successors are fighting for the leadership, but they may not be able to hold his faction together." Her ears flickered. "I may be weakened by this."

"I regret things tend that way."

"Yes," she said. "So do I."

The second set of ships returned. More Memories embarked on their journeys. The treaty was holding.

There was a meeting aboard Ship to formalize the agreement. Cup's successor was Brook, a tall, elderly Shar whose golden fur was darkened by age. A compromise candidate, President Gram said, his election determined after weeks of fighting for the successorship. He was not respected. Already pieces of Cup's old faction were breaking away.

"I wonder, your Excellency," Brook said, after the formal business was over, "if you could arrange for our people to learn your language. You must have powerful translation modules aboard your ship in order to learn our language so quickly. You were broadcasting your message of peace within a few hours of entering real space."

"I have no such equipment aboard Ship," Drill said. "Our knowledge of your language was acquired from Shar prisoners."

"Prisoners?" Shar ears pricked forward. "We were not aware of this," Brook said.

"After our base Memories recognized discrepancies," Drill said, "we sent some Ships out searching for you. We seized one of your ships and took it to my home world. The prisoners were asked about their language and the location of your capital planet. Otherwise it would have taken me months to find your world here, and learn to communicate with you."

"May we ask to arrange for the return of the prisoners?"

"Oh," Drill said. "That won't be possible. After we learned what we needed to know, we terminated their lives. They were being kept in an area reserved for a garden. The landscapers wanted to get to work." Drill bobbed his head reassuringly. "I am pleased to inform you that they proved excellent fertilizer for the gardens. The result was quite lovely."

"I think," said President Gram carefully, "that it would be best that this information not go beyond those of us in this room. I think it would disturb the process."

Minister-General Vang's ears went back. So did others'. But they acceded.

"I think we should take our leave," said President Gram.

"Have a pleasant afternoon," said Drill.

"It's important." It was not yet dawn. Ship had awakened Drill for a call from the President. "One of your ships has attacked another of our planets."

Alarm drove the sleep from Drill's brain. "Please come to the airlock," he said.

"The information will reach the population within the hour."

"Come quickly," said Drill.

The President arrived with a pair of assistants, who stayed inside the airlock. They carried staves. "My people will be upset," Gram said. "Things may not be entirely safe."

"Which planet was it?" Drill asked.

Gram rubbed her ears. "It was one of those whose location went out on the last peace shuttle."

"The new Memory must not have arrived in time."

"That is what we will tell the people. That it couldn't have been prevented. I will try to speed up the process by which the planets receive new Memories. Double the quota."

"That is a good idea."

"I will have to dismiss Drook. Opposite Minister-General Vang will have to take his job. If I can give Vang more power, he may remain in the coalition and not cause a split."

"As you think best."

President Gram looked up at Drill, her head rising reluctantly, as if held back by a great weight. "My son," she said. "He was on the planet when it happened."

"You have other offspring," Drill said.

Gram looked at him, the pain burning deep in her eyes. "Yes," she said. "I do."

The fields around Ship filled once again. Cries and howls rent the air, and dirges pulsed against Ship's uncaring walls. The Shar broadcasts in the next weeks seemed confused to Drill. Coalitions split and fragmented. Vang spoke frequently of readiness. President Gram succeeded in doubling the quota of planets. The decision was a near one.

Then, days later, another message. "One of our commanders," said President Gram, "was based on the vicinity of the attacked planet. He is one of Vang's creatures. On his own initiative he ordered our military forces to engage. Your terraforming Ship was attacked."

"Was it destroyed?" Drill asked. His tone was urgent. There is still hope, he reminded himself.

"Don't be anxious for your fellow humans," Gram said. "The Ship was damaged, but escaped."

"The loss of a few hundred billion unconscious organisms is no cause for anxiety," Drill said. "An escaped terraforming Ship is. The Ship will alert our military forces. It will be a real war."

President Gram licked her lips. "What does that mean?"

"You know of our Shrikes and so on. Our military people are worse. They are fully conscious and highly specialized in different modes of warfare. They are destructive, carnivorous, capable of taking enormous damage without impairing function. Their minds concentrate only on tactics, on destruction. Normally they are kept on planetoids away from the rest of humanity. Even other humans find their proximity too . . . disturbing." Drill put all the urgency in his speech that he could. "Honorable President, you must give me the locations of the remaining planets. If I can get Memories to each of them with news of the peace, we may yet save them."

"I will try. But the coalition . . ." She turned away from the transmitter. "Vang will claim a victory."

"It is the worst possible catastrophe," Drill said.

Gram's tone was grave. "I believe you," she said.

Drill listened to the broadcasts with growing anxiety. The Shars who spoke on the broadcasts were making angry comments about the execution of prisoners, about flower gardens and values Drill didn't understand. Someone had let the secret loose. President Gram went from group to group outside Ship, talking of the necessity of her plan. The Shars' responses were muted. Drill sensed they were waiting. It was announced that Vang had left the coalition. A chorus of triumphant yips rose from scattered members of the crowd. Others only moaned.

Vang, now simply General Vang, arrived at the field. His followers danced intoxicated circles around him as he spoke, howling their responses to his words. "Triumph! United will!" they cried. "The humans can be beaten!

Treachery avenged! Dictate the peace from a position of strength! We smell the location of their planets!"

The Shars' weird cackling laughter followed him from point to point. The laughing and crying went on well into the night. In the morning the announcement came that the coalition had fallen. Vang was now President-General.

In his sleeping chamber, surrounded by his video walls, Drill began to weep.

"I have been asked to bear Vang's message to you," Gram said. She seemed smaller than before, standing unsteadily even on her tripod legs. "It is his . . . humor."

"What is the message?" Drill said. His whole body seemed in pain. Even Lowbrain was silent, wrapped in misery.

"I had hoped," Gram said, "that he was using this simply as an issue on which to gain power. That once he had the Presidency, he would continue the diplomatic effort. It appears he really means what he's been saying. Perhaps he's no longer in control of his own people."

"It is war," Drill said.

"Yes."

You have failed, said Memory. Drill winced in pain.

"You will lose," he said.

"Vang says we are cleverer than you are."

"That may be the case. But cleverness cannot compete with experience. Humans have fought hundreds of these little wars, and never failed to wipe out the enemy. Our Memories of these conflicts are intact. Your people can't fight millions of years of specialized evolution."

"Vang's message doesn't end there. You have till nightfall to remove your Ship from the planet. Six days to get out of real space."

"I am to be allowed to live?" Drill was surprised.

"Yes. It is our . . . our custom."

Drill scratched himself. "I regret our efforts did not succeed."

"No more than I." She was silent for a while. "Is there any way we can stop this?"

"If Vang attacks any human planets after the Memories of the peace arrangement have arrived," Drill said, "the military will be unleashed to wipe you out. There is no stopping them after that point."

"How long," she asked, "do you think we have?"

"A few years. Ten at the most."

"Our species will be dead."

"Yes. Our military are very good at their jobs."

"You will have killed us," Gram said, "destroyed the culture that we have built for thousands of years, and you won't even give it any thought. Your species doesn't think about what it does anymore. It just acts, like a single-celled animal, engulfing everything it can reach. You say that you are a conscious species, but that isn't true. Your every action is . . . instinct. Or reflex."

"I don't understand," said Drill.

Gram's body trembled. "That is the tragedy of it," she said.

An hour later Ship rose from the field. Shars laughed their defiance from below, dancing in crazed abandon.

I have failed, Drill told Memory.

You knew the odds were long, Memory said. *You knew that in negotiations with species this backward there have only been a handful of successes, and hundreds of failures.*

Yes, Drill acknowledged. *It's a shame, though. To have spent all these months away from home.*

Eat! Eat! said Lowbrain.

Far away, in their forty-mile-long Ships, the human soldiers were already on their way.

THE BEST IN SCIENCE FICTION

THE BEST IN FANTASY